Eden's Green
Book One

Come Morning Light

CHARLOTTE DAE

Come Morning Light
Eden's Green Book One

Copyright © 2023 by Charlotte Dae

Cover Design: Cat (TRC Designs)
Interior Design & Formatting: Quirky Circe Book Design
Editing & Proofreading: Beth Lawton (VB Edits)

FIRST EDITION

ISBN 979-8-9879428-0-2 (paperback)
ISBN 979-8-9879428-1-9 (ebook)

www.charlottedae.com

Author's Note

This book is a dark contemporary romance, meaning it contains sexually explicit scenes, graphic violence, and other mature situations. I understand that these themes may be triggering, so please feel free to email me at **charlottedaeauthor@gmail.com** or visit my website at **www.charlottedae.com** for a full list of content warnings.

Warning: the epilogue of *Come Morning Light* ends on a cliffhanger. If you would like to enjoy this novel as a standalone, please skip the epilogue, and relish in the happily ever after that awaits you. However, if you would like to continue James's and Evelyn's journey, please revisit the epilogue, and continue through to the sequel novel that releases November 2024.

The full story concludes in the upcoming sequel, *Come the First Snowfall*.

*To my incredible husband, who pushed me to sit down, shut up, and write a book like I've always talked about doing, but never did.
Until now.
And for allowing me to use him as a test subject for the Adam's apple scene...
He didn't mind one bit.*

*This book also goes out to all the "Pretty in Pink" fans who thought Andie should have chosen Duckie instead of Blane at the end of the movie.
That ending goes to show that you should always go with your gut instinct and stick with your original ending. I mean, seriously, John Hughes, what the fuck?
Nerds need love too.*

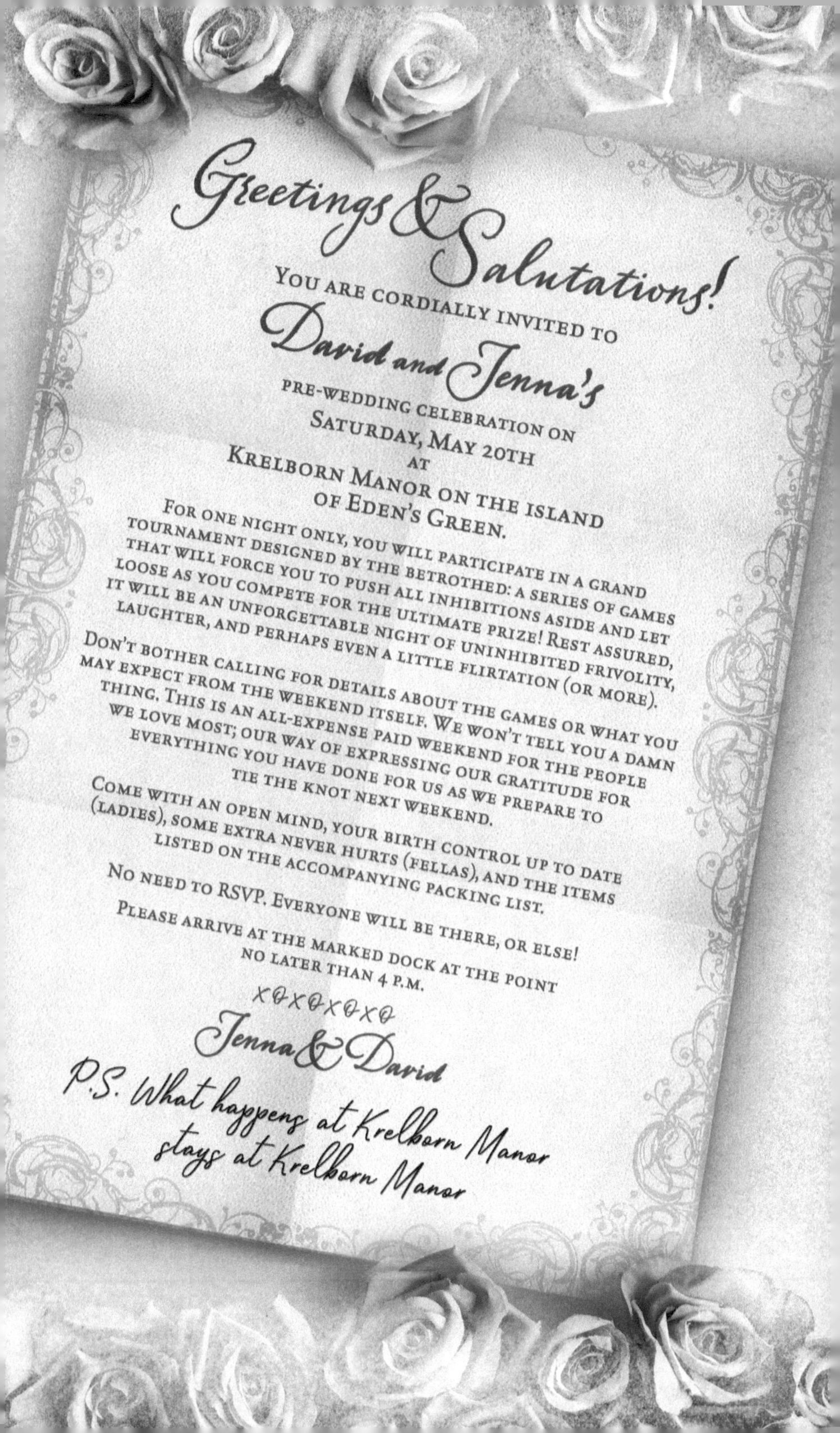

Greetings & Salutations!

YOU ARE CORDIALLY INVITED TO

David and Jenna's

PRE-WEDDING CELEBRATION ON
SATURDAY, MAY 20TH
AT
KRELBORN MANOR ON THE ISLAND
OF EDEN'S GREEN.

FOR ONE NIGHT ONLY, YOU WILL PARTICIPATE IN A GRAND
TOURNAMENT DESIGNED BY THE BETROTHED: A SERIES OF GAMES
THAT WILL FORCE YOU TO PUSH ALL INHIBITIONS ASIDE AND LET
LOOSE AS YOU COMPETE FOR THE ULTIMATE PRIZE! REST ASSURED,
IT WILL BE AN UNFORGETTABLE NIGHT OF UNINHIBITED FRIVOLITY,
LAUGHTER, AND PERHAPS EVEN A LITTLE FLIRTATION (OR MORE).

DON'T BOTHER CALLING FOR DETAILS ABOUT THE GAMES OR WHAT YOU
MAY EXPECT FROM THE WEEKEND ITSELF. WE WON'T TELL YOU A DAMN
THING. THIS IS AN ALL-EXPENSE PAID WEEKEND FOR THE PEOPLE
WE LOVE MOST; OUR WAY OF EXPRESSING OUR GRATITUDE FOR
EVERYTHING YOU HAVE DONE FOR US AS WE PREPARE TO
TIE THE KNOT NEXT WEEKEND.

COME WITH AN OPEN MIND, YOUR BIRTH CONTROL UP TO DATE
(LADIES), SOME EXTRA NEVER HURTS (FELLAS), AND THE ITEMS
LISTED ON THE ACCOMPANYING PACKING LIST.

NO NEED TO RSVP. EVERYONE WILL BE THERE, OR ELSE!
PLEASE ARRIVE AT THE MARKED DOCK AT THE POINT
NO LATER THAN 4 P.M.

XOXOXOXO

Jenna & David

P.S. What happens at Krelborn Manor
stays at Krelborn Manor

Chapter 1
Evie

It's only been ten minutes since the ferry left the dock, and I'm already a mess. *Shit.* Champagne coats the deck in a lazy spray as I shake the stickiness from my hands, the remnants dripping down my wrist and fingertips and onto my stilettos.

"What happened?" Jenna exclaims, her eyes wide at my compromised state.

"Nothing, I just...lost my balance or something. I bumped the railing and tried to catch my drink before it fell." I release a labored sigh. "I don't know."

"Come on, let's get you cleaned up." She hooks her arm in mine and guides me to the cramped one-person head in the belly of the boat.

"You need to find your sea legs, girl," she jokes before flipping the sink faucet on and pulling my hands under the warm water.

"I shouldn't be too surprised." I sigh. "I haven't been on a boat since my dad took me fishing when I was little."

We find each other in the mirror for a fleeting moment before she averts her gaze, her sudden discomfort tangible. I can't help but wonder if it's her overprotectiveness creeping back in. Although unnecessary, it feels incredible knowing someone cares so strongly about my happiness and well-being. Jenna might be the only person in this world who really gives a shit about me.

"There, good as new," she says, wiping my hands and arms with a bundle of paper towels. "Thank goodness you didn't get anything on this beautiful dress of yours. It's stunning. Where on earth did you get it?"

I roll my eyes. "Thanks, I got it from Closet à la Jenna. Such an amazing selection."

She lets loose an obnoxious laugh. "Oh, I know. I have great taste."

Her signature smile is endearing, full of heart. It could quite literally win over anyone. Perhaps that's how she got me to agree to come to this insane party off the coast of Cape Cod in the first place. I'm far from immune to her gift of persuasion. That talent got us into all kinds of shenanigans in college.

"If I don't get to pick my own outfit, you could have at least let me be involved in the planning of this shindig, Jen. It's your bachelorette party, after all. Maybe just once you could let someone else surprise you with something. That someone being me, you know, your maid of honor. At least I got to plan your bridal shower, your engagement party...Oh wait, never mind, you took over planning all of those too, you annoying little bitch."

She chuckles. "It's like you don't know me at all. I love planning this kind of shit."

"You're just using your professional party planner status to disguise your controlling tendencies," I tease.

"Oh, please."

Holding back a quip, I pull my cell phone from my purse, scroll back to a string of text messages from several months back, and hold it in front of her face.

ME

Hey, I've been thinking about your bachelorette party. I want to run some ideas by you because I know you'd kill me if I left you completely in the dark...

JEN

Eves, there's no need to plan anything! David and I already have something special in mind for both the bachelor and bachelorette parties. Call it a "pre-wedding party" if you will. All I need from you is a trip or two out here for last-minute dress alterations

ME

Wait, no bachelorette party? Or bachelor party? How did David agree to that???

JEN

We're still having them, we're just combining them into something, well, unique. Don't worry about it. I have it all taken care of. Just be here for the dress stuff, k?

Oh, and the cake tasting!

ME

Umm, I doubt very much you need my help telling your fiancé what flavor of cake you've already ordered behind his back. Lol

JEN

I haven't ordered the cake yet, smart-ass. I need you there because David likely wants red velvet, and you can't let him talk me into it!

ME

Since when has anyone been able to talk you into anything?

JEN

David is different. He has a way with words. I may have met my match. Lord help me.

ME

> So you're saying he has quite the talented tongue, then? ;)

JEN

> YES!!!

"If this conversation right here doesn't prove that you're controlling, I don't know what does." I hand her the phone.

She scrolls through the conversation with smugness stretched across her face. "I'm a woman who knows what she wants," she jests.

"Planning your own surprise parties, deciding what your friends should wear, who they should date...?"

"Now you're getting it."

I exhale the most sardonic sigh I can muster. "One more week..." I trail off, cocking my eyebrow and taking my phone back.

She mimics my expression, baiting me to continue.

"One more week, and you're finally *David's* pain in the ass and not mine."

"Oh, Evie, I will never stop being a pain in your ass." She doubles over and laughs, releasing a snort that sends me into my own laughing fit. We bump against one another inside the cramped space, and with one sharp sway of the boat, I land practically in her arms.

"You promise?" I ask, my tone turning serious as the laughter ebbs and I regain my footing.

"I promise." She runs a gentle hand through my hair, tucking a bit behind my ear. Red splotches caused by her laughing fit form across her fair skin. At least I hope that's all it is. A whole gamut of emotions will pronounce her redness, her neck often bearing the brunt. By the way she holds my gaze, though, I can't be sure.

She heads for the door, her long, fiery-red hair dancing across her back as she gives me a glance over her shoulder. "See you out there."

I oblige with a grin as she leaves me to gather my things.

After a quick check of the time—almost four thirty—I toss my phone into my purse. It lands with a *plunk* on top of the party invitation I tossed in at the last minute. I reach in to readjust it so as not to crinkle it under the weight of my phone, my fingers brushing against the parchment that accompanied the invitation. Already knowing its contents verbatim, I unfold it to read it for my own amusement for the umpteenth time.

I scan Jenna's beautiful penmanship:

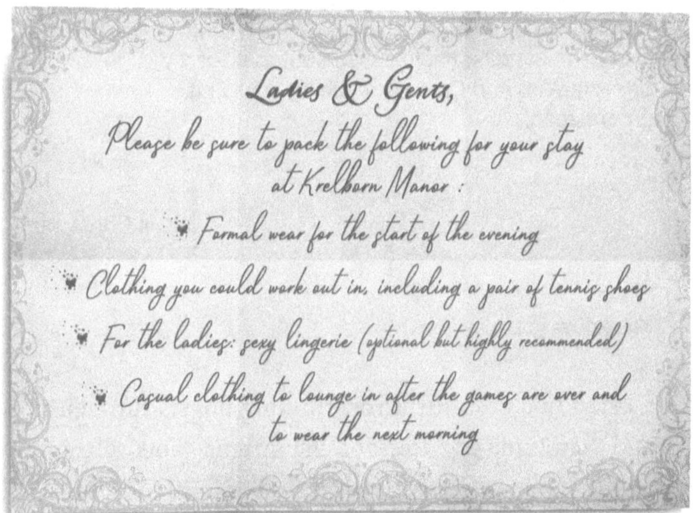

Returning the list to my purse, I reach for the invitation and skim it over as well. The words at the bottom of the invitation, still etched into my brain all these months later, call out to me. Their ambiguity, their playfulness, their *mystery* taunt me. My stomach churns with excitement and apprehension at what awaits me when I set foot on solid ground again:

P.S. What happens at Krelborn Manor stays at Krelborn Manor

It's enough to tie me up in knots.

Ugh, and that line about making sure my birth control is up to date...Seriously, Jen, *what the fuck*? She's pushing me out of my comfort zone; that much is as clear as that princess-cut diamond on her finger. But nothing—and I mean *nothing*—tops the text message she sent days after the invitation arrived:

JEN

> Hey girl, I need everyone to have a "clean bill of health" (including an STD screening) before the tournament on May 20th. Not saying you aren't clean. I'm sending this message out to all of my bridesmaids. And David is reaching out to his groomsmen.

ME

> Jesus Christ, Jen

JEN

> You know you love me ;)

As I stand before the mirror, running fingers through my dark locks and examining my dress for champagne spots, a laugh ripples through me. This entire weekend getaway is ingenious. Making it all about her wedding is honestly the perfect way to coerce me into anything she has planned. I'm her maid of honor, for Christ's sake. She knows I could never—and *would* never—refuse attendance or participation in wedding-related activities.

She assured me she hadn't "invited me to an orgy," and that I was to "shut up, trust me, and be there." And she ended that particular conversation with a comment about having never steered me wrong before. And I couldn't deny it.

She knows I don't easily oblige on the whims of phrases like "trust me." In fact, the thought of that conversation makes my father's panicked voice—his desperate pleas and his countless assurances to *trust* him—pull like a ghost tethered to my flesh, even all these years later. The memory of my father echoes through me like a child hollering her name into an old abandoned well: deep, dissipating over time, but never truly gone.

A sigh of contention compromises my balance as I read her invitation for the thousandth time.

Don't worry, I'm all in on this one.

A sense of calm replaces the knots in my stomach, and the boat's swaying motion fades as I concede to the evening's events. For a moment, I forget I'm not on land.

A tenuous horn from above brings me back into the present. I twist to examine my reflection, taking in my dress from all angles. It looks great despite the low light. Not a single champagne drop as far as I can see.

After returning the invitation to my purse, I reach for the disk of pills buried beneath my phone. I pop a single pink pill into my mouth and swallow it dry.

You're lucky I'm already taking these, Jen.

Steadying myself against the sway beneath my feet, I make my way back up to the bow.

The late spring sun is slowly dipping toward the horizon, casting beautiful streaks of ruby and ochre across the evening sky. Specks of sea water catch the boat as the wind kicks across the Atlantic waters, the island up ahead approaching.

"All right, let's try this again," Jenna announces to the gathered group of bridesmaids, handing me a fresh flute of champagne. She raises her glass, and the rest of us follow suit, holding our billowing dresses against our thighs in the unforgiving breeze. "Thank you all so much for joining me on this crazy little adventure David and I cooked up. It means the world to me to see all my dearest friends put so much trust and faith in me. I know the instructions were vague—maybe even a touch weird—but I'm confident you'll all have a great time this weekend. I mean, our wedding party is made up of five single women and five single men. How could we possibly go wrong?" Her voice is borderline salacious, and the smirk doesn't leave her face throughout her entire speech.

A few hoots and hollers resound among the group. "I'm always down for a good time, lovely," Jenna's cousin Lacey cries out from the circle, raising her glass. Her yellow dress reveals a bit of ass cheek as the skirt whips in the breeze.

"Oh trust me, we know," Jenna replies with a wink. The girls all feign shock, then erupt in laughter. "And in case you all need a reminder—in exactly one week, I will be a married...*freaking*...woman." Jenna squeals with erratic delight. There are several distinct "Ow, ows" from the group—myself included—followed by surges of praise that saunter off into the ocean wind. "Cheers, bitches."

We clink our glasses and drink to Jenna, the woman of the hour.

Three gulps. That's all it takes to down my glass of champagne. It takes the edge off, but my apprehension creeps back in with each passing second as the celebration fades. Jenna refuses to tell me who David's groomsmen are, but there is a good chance I know at least one. We haven't seen them yet. She insisted they come on a separate ferry, departing from a different dock. Why? Who knows. But I try to take comfort in the thought that some of David's friends Jenna has tried to nudge in my direction may be there. Even though I was uninterested at the time, sick of the ridiculous games so many men play—feigning interest but then pricked bloody by that elusive phone call that never comes—at least the faces would be familiar.

Sick of the ridiculous games.

Here I am, an obstinate woman insisting to her matchmaker best friend that she only wants straightforward relationships, embarking on a night filled with uncertainty, game-playing, and zero commitment.

The irony is not lost on me.

A snicker lodges itself deep in my throat, and I smother it with my empty champagne flute.

I never said I was perfect.

"To the future Mrs. Denardo," Lacey exclaims before taking another sip of champagne.

"Oh, that's right. Have you decided whether you're going to take his last name?" asks Heather, Jen's business partner.

The woman next to her crinkles her nose.

"Hmm..." Jenna runs a finger along the rim of her glass. "Jenna Denardo doesn't quite have the same ring to it, does it? It's weird hearing a last name other than Murphy."

"Do it. You love him," says Steph, her blond hair blowing as erratically as her light pink dress. "It's romantic."

Jenna meets my gaze. "What do you think, Eves? Do you think I look like a Denardo?" She strikes an exaggerated Vogue pose.

"Are you asking me if a fair-skinned redhead can pull off an Italian last name?" I tease.

Her smile turns sly, and she raises her brows with a quick flick.

"If anyone can pull it off, you can." I raise my empty glass to her in a playful toast.

The ferry's horn blares as we approach the dock. The deafening sound cuts into our conversation, forcing our attention to the oncoming shore.

I pull up on the sweetheart neckline of my sleeveless dress, making sure I'm not showing too much. It's a real *tit-flattering dress*, as Jenna called it when she pulled it from her closet and handed it to me. And she was right. My girls have never looked better. But Jenna is a bit shorter than me, and her dress makes it blatantly obvious. It's supposed to hit above the knee. But not on my tall frame. This dress will never reach my knees no matter how badly I beg. Ordinarily, I would be fighting the urge to yank it up and pull it down at the same time.

But I'm trying to surrender to the whims of my friend tonight, and the light green color really makes my eyes pop. What can I say, I look incredible in it, so fuck it.

We file down the gangplank, and I sigh in relief at the feel of solid ground beneath my feet.

A long black limousine awaits us beyond the dock, and after a moment of gawking, we race to pile inside. In less than a minute, the cork of a champagne bottle pops, and I'm handed another glass. Our unknown destination, however, has me far too distracted to indulge in yet another round of drinks.

The island is vacant of other houses as far as I can tell, and there are few roads. It only serves to enhance the beauty, the isolation, and the overgrown nature of Eden's Green. Countless trees tower over us on one side of the limousine, and a sparkling azure ocean spans the other. It's breathtaking in all directions.

"Is this a private island?" Lacey asks, her nose practically smooshed against the limousine window.

"Not exactly," Jenna replies. "There are a couple other estates on the island. Krelborn Manor encompasses the south part. And there's a small fishing village at the north end. Just a handful of houses, I believe."

You'd never know it. We don't pass any cars or pedestrians the entire way there. A sailboat catches my eye off in the distance, silhouetted against the fading light at the horizon.

Less than fifteen minutes of chatter among the girls later, Jenna announces, "We have arrived."

The limousine slows to a crawl as it passes through a pair of looming iron gates. Adorned with a large *KM* at the top, they split apart to accommodate our ride. Every one of us is plastered to the windows, admiring the estate's grounds.

The property has no visible end or beginning, surely encompassing many square acres of the island. A dramatic row of trees guides our limousine up the drive, which comes to an end at a prim cobblestone circle. The estate is old, certainly, with vines creeping up the brick palatial edifice, framing the windows in a timeless elegance.

Its charm is truly captivating.

Jenna laughs at our agape mouths, her hair bouncing over one shoulder. "I'm so glad you all love it."

Several staff members stand in formation along the circle drive, waiting to greet us and carry in our bags. After we shake their hands and gush over how beautiful Krelborn Manor is, we're ushered inside.

The rich wooden doors open into a foyer, with an ornate round table in the center topped with a bouquet of flowers. Spilling out into the space is a grand mahogany staircase that narrows upward to the second floor, beyond my line of sight.

Pieces of framed artwork line both sides of the long entryway, embossed in gold leaf and bearing paintings that span across centuries. Many I recognize, but never have I seen them in such decorated splendor. The manor even puts the art museum where I work to shame.

Jenna waves her hands, signaling us to gather around.

"We beat the boys here, so you have first dibs on the rooms upstairs." She points over her shoulder toward the staircase as the echo of her voice fades. "Once you've picked a room, let me know your room number, and the staff can sort your belongings. So, go ahead, pick a room, get settled, and meet me down here in fifteen." She waves a hand at the stairs. "Oh, and leave your cell phones in your rooms, please. They aren't allowed during the games." She surveys us with anticipation, but no one moves. We're all still admiring the place, necks craned in all directions.

Jenna slaps her hands together with a loud *clap*, the sharp noise echoing around us and knocking me back to reality with a jolt.

"Move your asses, ladies. You want first pick, don't you? *Move, move, move.*" She claps her hands again, and we all bolt for the stairs, trying our best not to spill champagne as we fumble among each other. Jenna's unmistakable laughter trails behind us and disappears.

At the top of the stairs, we're greeted by a wide hallway of crimson carpet lined by more framed pieces of artwork, broken up by mahogany doors.

I don't care which room I end up with. I'm too fascinated by the paintings to make haste toward any of the doors. The manor is very Victorian era in its decor, and the art is no exception.

As the ladies scatter, doors opening and closing around me while they call dibs, I ease my way farther down the hallway in admiration.

The framed displays don't seem to be arranged in any discernible way. The time periods are all over the place, the style from one painting to the next inconsistent.

But the one to my left gives me pause. It's one of my favorites: *Proserpine* by Dante Gabriel Rossetti. It stands floor to ceiling, immersing me in the goddess Proserpine's imprisoned world. The pomegranate she holds in her hand is so simplistic in form, yet so enticing, its juices not so unlike those of an aroused woman in the hands of her lover. It's the fruit that tethered her to the underworld —and Hades—forever. I take in the way the forbidden fruit's beautiful hue intentionally matches the color of her luscious lips.

The lips we can *see.* And perhaps even the ones we can't.

If mythology is anything to go by, men find women bearing delectable fruit irresistible. It's arousing in ways I could only dream of.

"Miss," a kind but stern voice calls out behind me.

"Yes?" I ask, forced back to reality yet again.

"My apologies." The woman flushes. "Which room did you select?"

"Oh, I'm so sorry. I haven't made it that far yet. I was admiring the artwork. It's beautiful."

"Yes." She resembles a server in a fancy restaurant in her white dress shirt, white bow tie, and black slacks. Her graying hair is tied back in a neat, low bun. Her posture is relaxed, unhurried, but she doesn't break eye contact as she waits for me to move along.

"I'll pick my room now. Do you know which ones are still available?"

She points down the hall. "Rooms one through four are spoken for. Anything beyond that is free for your choosing."

"Wonderful, thank you."

She returns my smile with a slight nod before turning toward the staircase.

Giving the goddess a touch more of my much-deserved attention, I glance back at *Proserpine* one last time, then turn my back on her as most of the world has and make my way farther down the hall.

I pass by rooms five and six, at which point the hallway splits into a T-junction. Both directions are lined with paintings, and the fiery sconces cast shadows that bring each of them to life. The manor may be understandably creepy to some, but I find it exotic, historic.

Perfect.

I bank left at the junction and open the door to room seven.

It's even more beautiful than the main foyer. A large fireplace of white marble graces nearly an entire wall. Above the mantel is a painting of Frank Dicksee's *Chivalry,* a classic representation of a damsel in distress, brought to life with delicate strokes of a paintbrush more than a century ago. From the setting sun in the background to the woman's beautiful, disheveled gown and luminous skin, it is certainly a striking image.

Across from the fireplace is an oversized four-poster canopy bed.

Each mahogany poster is carved with spirals that wind their way up to the delicate linens draped over the top and sides of the bed frame.

The crimson bedspread with gold embroidery is soft under my languid touch. The statement piece, however, is the gaudy headboard, adorned with intricate carvings and standing nearly as high as the posters at each of the bed corners.

On one of the nightstands is a gift bag. Courtesy of Jenna and David, I imagine. I'll have to dive into it later.

Crossing the room, I make my way toward the French doors and step out onto the balcony. Despite the breathtaking view, I manage to suck in a deep, satisfying breath as I admire the grounds. It overlooks the rear courtyard and its stunning display of hedges, with pebble paths of white-washed stone weaving their way through the endless clusters of flower gardens.

Renting this place must have cost Jenna and David a fortune.

But Jenna never spares any expense. And she's probably showing off a bit.

At least I hope that's all it is.

The gardens in the near distance fade to blue as the sun sinks below the horizon. The trees sing, rustling in the mild breeze, causing small strands of hair to tickle my forehead and exposed back.

At the knock on my door, I call, "Come in."

"Apologies, miss." It's the same woman as before. "We have your bags. And Ms. Jenna has requested that all guests make their way downstairs as soon as possible."

"Oh, of course."

Rushing into the bathroom, I cross the black and white marble floor, past the claw-foot tub, and stop in front of the mirror. Relieved to see everything still in its place, I hurry from my room.

The banister's smoothness sends an erotic tingle through my fingers as I rush down the steps. But it's short-lived and instantly replaced with a tight knot in my stomach when the foyer and everyone—including the guys—comes into view.

And they're all watching me.

"Good, Evie, you're here," Jenna calls out, a little too loudly. "We were afraid you got lost."

"I'm sorry." I race down the steps, trailing my hand along the banister in search of that tingle once again. "I got carried away. There's a lot to admire in this place."

As I round out the final steps, someone among the sea of faces catches my attention, a crooked grin stretched across his lips and his eyes fixed on me, snapping fire. He stands a bit taller than the rest of the crowd, his face gentle and seemingly wise beyond his years. His lavender dress shirt—the sleeves rolled up to the elbow—does little to disguise the way the muscles of his arms press against the fabric. To describe him as gorgeous would be an understatement, and my heart tweets like an early morning bird at the sight of him.

Through my perusal, those eyes continue burrowing straight through me.

Jenna rushes over to me as I cross the foyer and hands me a flute of champagne.

Good Lord, the night's only beginning, Jen.

"All right, everyone, gather round," she begins. David joins her by her side. "It really means the world to David and me that you're here. We wanted to create a special night for you all as a way of saying thank you for being part of our big day; for helping us prepare, for being a shoulder for me to bitch and cry on during these stressful times"—she motions toward me with her glass—"I'm looking at you, Evie."

A rumble of laughter fills the foyer, and I raise my drink back in her direction.

"So I want to toast each and every one of you." She raises her glass, and we all follow suit.

"Cheers to you," she and David say together, addressing the crowd.

"Cheers to you," we repeat in unison and clink glasses with each other. I tap glasses with Lacey, then turn to my left and repeat the gesture with a woman with jet-black hair who, as I recall, is a friend of Jenna's from high school.

When I turn to my right, I am greeted by, well, a neck. *His* neck. And one hell of an Adam's apple. Glancing upward beyond the chiseled contours of his jaw, I eye his chestnut hair, which is styled back and away from his face in a controlled fashion. The first few buttons of his shirt are unbuttoned, enough to tease but not torment. And his forearms show themselves off as he raises his glass to meet mine.

"Cheers," he says, studying me.

"Cheers," I reply, returning the attention for a bit too long.

We sip from our respective flutes, our eyes still locked.

He breaks the silence that follows the toast. "How do you know the—"

"All right, everyone," David addresses the room, "time to move to the study where we can mingle and get to know one another before dinner. Have more drinks if you're so inclined..." He waves and turns his back to the group. "Follow me."

We're ushered toward a towering door off to the right, the sounds of our heels and dress shoes clacking against the wood floor in an erratic pattern.

Floor-to-ceiling bookshelves without a single gap catch my eye as we file inside. The group naturally disperses, some of the guests moving toward the emerald Chesterfield sofas positioned around a stone fireplace, champagne flutes still in hand. I plant myself next to the massive shelving on the opposite side of the room.

A ping of disappointment singes my insides when, rather than following me to continue the conversation he initiated in the foyer, the man in lavender leans against the mantel and braces himself with an outstretched arm.

Nonetheless, he watches me as I slink to the back of the room, seeking comfort in the wall of publications and away from the gathering of strangers.

Heat rushes up my neck and across my face, my heart racing from his piercing gaze. My attempts to evade it become downright awkward as my eyes dart everywhere in the room except to him. Before long, I turn to face the shelves, avoiding the room entirely and focusing on one of my guaranteed sources of comfort: books.

With my hand encircling my narrow glass, the chill in my champagne dissipates. I've barely touched it beyond the few sips necessary for the toasts. But it soon becomes an afterthought once Jenna pops up behind me.

"Drink this instead." She holds out a tumbler filled with ice and an apple-red liquid. "I think you'll like it. I made it especially for you."

I nod to my champagne glass. "Still working on this one."

She snatches it from my hand and replaces it with the tumbler, insistent.

"Geez, Jenna, you didn't drug this one, did you?" I tease, not at all surprised by her need to ply me with the drink of the hour.

"Would it keep you from drinking it if I did?"

"Considering I have no idea what you have in store for me tonight... no, it wouldn't." I swirl the liquid, the ice clinking against the glass.

"Enjoy," she remarks with a twitch of her lips, then turns and rushes off to mingle.

I raise the tumbler to my lips for a sip, but a tall man with broad shoulders—dressed to the nines in a navy button-up shirt and gray slacks—approaches me. He sticks his hand out for me to shake it. His hair is long enough to remain tucked behind his ears, and a single dimple forms on his right cheek when he smiles.

"Hey, I'm Ashton."

I shake his hand. "It's a pleasure."

"Yes, it is." He gives me a lascivious once-over, grin firmly in place, making no qualms about undressing me with his eyes. My stomach knots in discomfort when his focus lands full-stop on my breasts.

He inches closer, and I take a subtle step back to match.

When he finally drags his attention up to my face, he says, "I'm a friend of David's. From the office." The gap between us shrinks with each step he takes.

"From the office?" I crinkle my brow and take another baby step back. My flesh is on fire, and not in a desirable way. His presence is assertive, sure, which ordinarily I don't mind. But it's unsettling. In an instant, I'm skimming the room for Jenna...

"That's right, I—"

"Oh, Ashton, there's someone I'm dying for you to meet." Jenna miraculously appears at his side and grabs him by the arm.

Thank Christ.

"But I was talking to this stunning lady here," he protests, gesturing in my direction.

"Don't worry, Ash, this one's pretty too." She guides him away, looking over her shoulder and giving me a reassuring glance.

A deep breath calms the nerves that are firing on all cylinders. With hesitation but also immense relief, I turn to admire the vast selection, running my free hand along their leather spines. I know more people between the covers of the novels in front of me than I do at the party behind me. With the exception of Jenna's cousin Lacey, the other guests are complete strangers. And Lacey is three drinks in already with some guy's lips grazing her ear.

The conversations floating throughout the room create a soothing din. In a matter of moments, I forget about Ashton entirely.

As I run my fingers across the spine of an old copy of *The Picture of Dorian Gray*, a deep, masculine voice sounds behind me.

"You a fan of the classics?"

I spin around.

My heart thumps with a new sense of purpose when I immediately see lavender and that incredible Adam's apple. "I am, as a matter of fact." I turn my attention back to the countless works to avoid his smoldering gaze and any inappropriate behavior it may bring out of me.

He moves to my side, skimming the volumes alongside me and forcing the energy to shift throughout the room. The din disappears and the study transforms into an empty space in which only he and I exist.

"It's certainly a passion of mine," I say. "What about you?"

"Absolutely. They're a fail-safe. You can never go wrong with the classics." He ripples a finger across multiple spines. "For two reasons: one, they're guaranteed conversation starters, as is evident right here and now." He looks at me with a side-eye and a crooked grin. "And because talking about even a few tends to make you sound smarter than you really are." He removes a copy of M. P. Shiel's *The Purple Cloud* from the shelf and flips it over. "But to be perfectly honest, I didn't come over here to impress you with a bunch of books I haven't actually read." His grin is infectious. "Like this one here." He holds the book out to me. "I've never read it."

"To be fair, even if you told me you'd read that, it wouldn't have impressed me as much as you think."

"Oh, is that so?" he asks with a twitch of his brow.

I nod.

He angles closer, his voice lowering. "And why is that?"

I mimic his movement and lean in, his scent sending me into an unprecedented state of euphoria, and whisper, "Because I haven't read it either."

He responds with a Cheshire smile.

God, that smile.

"What's your name?" he asks.

"Evelyn Foster, the maid of honor." I extend my hand, which he accepts.

"It's very nice to meet you, Evelyn. I'm James Pierce. The best man." His shake is firm, purposeful.

"It's a pleasure to meet you." He releases my hand, and the void between my legs twitches in frustration. "Best man? You and David must be close then."

"He and I met in college, but I quit school temporarily to join the military."

"Oh?"

"Yeah. I was able to go back and finish, though, after my last deployment. By then, David was in graduate school, so we still, you know, did the college thing together."

"Oh, wait, yes." I snap my fingers in realization, and he jerks in surprise. "You're David's friend from the Air Force. Of course. I swear Jenna brings you up in conversation every time we're together anymore. It's so nice to finally meet you." I beam.

"Likewise." He chuckles and clinks his glass against mine. "I hope it was all good things."

"I don't know David well, but I will say that, whenever you come up in conversation, he always speaks very highly of you. I'm shocked our paths didn't cross sooner. You live in Boston, right?"

"Not anymore, actually. I was transferred to the NASA branch office in New York a few years back. That's probably why we've never run into each other."

"Hold on. You work for NASA?" I can't help but smile. "What do you do there?"

"I'm an aerospace engineer."

"So you're, like, a rocket scientist?" I gush, but my stomach knots at how ridiculous the words sound when spoken aloud.

He laughs, but I duck my head and fix my attention on my feet, raising a hand—thankfully cold and damp and soothing from the condensation on my glass—to my forehead in an attempt to hide my blushing face. "Sorry. I'm such a dork. You probably hear that all the time."

"I have heard that a lot," he replies with a wink. "But it's cute when you say it."

My stomach performs a series of flips like a goddamn Olympic gymnast.

"I, um." Words escape me. Thoughts escape me. My tongue is all twisted up.

Get it together, Evie.

"What do you do, Evelyn?" he asks, ignoring the sudden stagger in my speech.

"Oh, you can call me Evie. Everyone does."

"What do you do, Evie?" His voice is a velvety rumble that rattles my core.

My knees quiver under the weight of his gaze, but I swallow hard and manage to find my voice. "I'm a restorative artist at an art museum in Providence. I was working as an associate professor of English literature at Brown during graduate school, but it was an adjunct position, and I couldn't turn down the opportunity at the museum."

"Hmm, that explains the love of the classics." He tips his head toward the bookshelves.

"Yeah, I may be what some people call a book nerd," I reply, biting my lower lip.

"Well, then, I have to ask...what's your desert island book?"

"Desert island book?"

"Yeah, the one book you'd take with you if you were stranded on a desert island."

I pause for a moment. How on earth does one choose a favorite work in general, let alone what would be the *only* one available for the foreseeable future?

"Honestly, I don't know if I could decide. What's yours?" I reply.

"Nah, I asked you first," he teases, tipping his head back, exposing the length of his neck and finishing the last of his champagne.

I can't help but fixate on the way his Adam's apple bobs as he drinks, but I give a slight shake of my head and clear my throat so I can respond. "I suppose this is the part where I pick something heady and highbrow because I taught English lit, right? Not something like, I don't know, *The Princess Bride* by William Goldman?"

"Is that your answer?"

"You know, I think it might be. If nothing else, it would make me laugh despite my dire situation."

He raises an eyebrow at me. "Touché."

"*And* what's yours?" I nudge my head in his direction.

"To be honest, it's been forever since I've read anything other than manuals, blueprints, and work-related texts. But I'm a sucker for *Hitchhiker's Guide to the Galaxy*. And I did love *The Martian*, by Andy Wier. I would read that one over and over again if I had to. Hell, it may even help me science my way out of being stranded on that island."

"Now that's a great choice. I loved that book. You have excellent taste."

His eyes square with mine, consuming me with the heat that lies behind them. "Yeah, I'm thinking I really do." His smile says more in this moment than the words of a thousand classics. An invisible force all but yanks the ground right out from under me. I'm weightless, breathless under his regard.

"What's your poison?" he asks, motioning toward the drink in my hand. I blink past the fog of desire and peer down at my hand. The ice is nearly melted, the perspiring glass disguising my sweaty palms.

"Oh, it's something Jenna handed me. I haven't tasted it yet, so I'm not sure what it is, to be honest."

I bring the tumbler to my lips and take a sip.

Delicious.

"Pomegranate. One of my favorites. And something else. Rum maybe?" His attention is fixed on the moisture on my lips, and my stomach tumbles. For the first time in ages, I feel little control over my body. I love it, but I desperately hope he can't see it.

"Would you like to try it?" I ask.

"Sure." He takes the drink as I pass it to him, then sips from the spot where my lips had pressed.

"You're right about the pomegranate. It's good. But I also detect a hint of something else. Strawberry?"

Oh my God.

"Oh, that's just, um. That's"—I touch my lips—"my lip gloss. It's strawberry flavored."

His face lights with a flirtatious grin. "You're a fan of the forbidden fruit, I see." First the pomegranate and now the strawberries?"

"You know your art. Few notice the numerous depictions of forbidden fruit throughout history or within the different mythos."

"It's never actually stated that the forbidden fruit was an apple. I personally like the idea that it was a strawberry. They're sinfully sweet, and the shape is rather erotic, don't you think?"

Holy mother of God, this man is going to be the death of me.

My mouth falls agape, and I beg my mind to respond with something, *anything.*

Fortunately, he's the first to speak. "I couldn't help but admire your ring." He points to the middle finger of my right hand. The piece of jewelry in question consists of a single snowflake made of white gold with a small blue gem in the center. I hold my hand out to look at it.

"Oh, thanks." I reply, caught slightly off guard by the sudden change in topic. "It was my mother's."

"Was?" A softness consumes him, and for the first time since we met, I notice the subtlest of wrinkles at the far corners of his eyes. They age him a bit, sure, but I don't mind. In fact, they're downright sexy.

I don't want to talk about my mother. A conversation about her would be a short one, indeed. I've spent my entire life wondering if the pain of knowing her but still losing her would be as horrible as never knowing her to begin with. In the former, I'd at least have the memory of her face. But I don't even have that much. No photos, no old diaries, no home videos. Only a ring. A single snowflake that hung around my neck as a child and now adorns my finger. It's an answer I'll never obtain, and it has haunted me my entire life.

"Well, she—"

Cling-cling-cling-cling

A bell resounds from high up in the corner of the study, startling us both and diverting our attention away from each other.

The conversations throughout the room stall in confusion.

"Dinner is ready. Let's move to the dining room," Jenna exclaims, hooking her arm in David's and leading the way for the rest of us.

Inside the dining room, the expansive table is truly a sight to behold, stretching nearly the room's entire length. There are twelve of us tonight, but the table could easily fit twice as many.

The settings are already in place, a decorative display of charger plates, fine polished silverware, and crystal glasses. The centerpieces that span the length of the table atop a white lace runner consist of an assortment of lavender and powder blue flowers with white embellishments: Jenna and David's wedding colors. The table is arranged with five settings on either side, with two settings side-by-side at the head of the table, no doubt meant for the betrothed.

Dozens of framed pieces of art arranged on the nearby wall. I would expect nothing less.

"There are name cards next to each plate. Find yours and have a seat," Jenna instructs.

My assigned seat is located next to the head of the table, beside Jenna. Before I reach for my chair, I scan the room for James, anxious to see where he has been seated. But my search is fruitless.

"Allow me." His voice sounds behind me.

On instinct, I spin to face him and watch as he pulls my chair away from the table.

My stomach flips at the gesture.

I nod in thanks, gather my dress under me, then sit as he pushes my seat toward the table. By then, every wedding party member is seated but him. He makes his way to the only remaining vacant seat.

Directly across from me.

He regards me with a subtle nod, causing my heart to thump with abandon, and a blazing heat colors my neck and cheeks all over again.

His lavender shirt matches the flowers perfectly, and I wonder if it was intentional.

Jenna and David stand before the group, holding their glasses high. "Thank you all for joining us tonight. I know I sound like a broken record, but it really does mean the world to me that you're here." She skims the group. "And I know you're all wondering what I have in store for you. Well, I'm here to tell you that the suspense... ends...now."

She's toying with us.

"We brought you here to participate in a series of games. Five, to be exact. You'll be divided into teams of two, and each team will be awarded a set of points at the end of each game. The pair with the most points at the end of all five games will win the grand prize. Sounds simple, right?"

The wedding party exchanges glances. I can't help but settle my gaze on James, remaining there beyond the point of casualness.

"The person sitting across from you will be your partner," David explains.

A rush of relief pours over me like an avalanche in a winter storm. Our eyes remain locked as he mouths *we got this* and gives me a little smirk. Those sexy-as-hell creases at the far corners of his eyes are more prominent than ever.

"You may not switch partners. We have personally selected each pairing based on how well we think you will work together as a team," he continues. "Remember, we left all inhibitions at the door tonight, so we're asking you to proceed with open minds as we make our way through the games."

My stomach twists again as my mouth turns to cotton. I hope I'm brave enough to see the games through. But Jenna would never hurt or endanger us. This is meant to be a night of fun. I imagine there will be some rowdiness in our future, and now that I know James is my partner, I'm more elated than apprehensive.

"Take this time to get to know your partners. The better you know each other, the greater the advantage you'll have throughout the games."

Jenna raises her glass alongside David. "May the best couple win," she says. "Cheers."

We raise our glasses in response.

"What's the prize?" a bridesmaid asks, her shimmery silver dress damn near blinding me as it reflects beneath the chandelier.

Everyone pauses from their indulgence in the beautiful canapés, eager to learn more.

"That will be revealed in time. But for now, we eat," she replies, taking a seat.

The dining room doors part and a train of wait staff enters, carrying trays full of various starters.

In time, conversations erupt around me, and I turn my attention back toward James and our friends. "David," I begin, "I finally have the pleasure of meeting your military buddy."

David gives James a friendly punch on the arm.

"Since he's my partner for the night, is there anything I should know about him? Strengths? Weaknesses? Fears that might make us lose this thing?"

James drops his fork, crosses his arms, and smirks at me.

"Ooh." David rubs his hands together. "What to tell, what to tell...?" He looks back and forth between us.

I rest my chin on two pointed fingers, looking straight at James, accepting his unspoken challenge.

"I wish I had juicy dirt on the guy to embarrass the hell out of him. But honestly, he has a pretty squeaky-clean past, at least as far as I know. The only mistake of his I recall is wasting too much time on the wrong girl..."

James turns red in the face and averts his gaze to his plate of food. He's a stranger in every sense of the word, our knowledge of each other less than an hour old. But learning of his heartache makes my own heart sting like an angered wasp nest; a protectiveness I was not expecting.

"He's nerdy as all get out. While the rest of us were off playing beer pong and staying out all night, he was studying for physics tests and shit like that. Every professor's wet dream. Always blowing the grading curves for the rest of us idiots."

"*David*," he tuts, his eyes wide in a playful warning.

"Just own it, man. You were captain of the chess club in high school, right? You let that one slip years ago and I don't plan on letting you live it down." David throws his head back in laughter.

He buries his face in his hands, his embarrassment adorable beyond words.

"But, in all honesty, this guy right here," David puts a hand on his shoulder, easing into a more serious tone, "was there for me at a time when no one else was. I was lost. Drinking, fights, misdemeanor arrests, you name it. I damn near gave up on myself, thinking there was no way I could ever turn my life around. But this guy—"

he slaps James' back—"never gave up on me."

"You aren't giving yourself enough credit," James replies. "You got into Harvard business school because of your hard work and dedication. I just nudged your silly ass in the right direction."

They share a laugh, and David punches him lightly on the arm once more.

The wait staff clear our starters and replace them with cloche-adorned plates, which they remove with panache.

"What about you?" James asks. "How did you and Jenna end up such good friends?"

She and I exchange glances, and her infectious smile makes me light up like Christmas morning.

"She and I also met in college. We were roommates freshman year," I begin.

"Yeah, she was shy and reclusive, and I did everything I could to pull her out of her shell." Jenna beams. "I was in the drama club and convinced her to join. I figured if that didn't do it, nothing would."

"You were in the drama club?" David asks Jenna, his head tilted in a quizzical fashion. "How did I not know this?"

She laughs. "You never asked. I was really good at it too. And it worked. Evie became more assertive over the years, to the point that *she* was the one dragging *me* to shit even I didn't want to do."

"Ooh, like what?" James asks, propping his elbows on the table and leaning closer.

"Spill it and die," I warn my best friend, fighting the smirk playing on my lips.

She drags her index finger and her thumb across her closed lips and flicks away the imaginary key.

"Aw, c'mon," James begs.

"Yeah, what the hell? You can't leave it like that," David whines.

"We can, and we will." Jenna presses her lips against his in a quick peck.

"How on earth did Jenna convince you to join a drama club?" James asks me.

I huff a laugh. "You've met her, right? She could sell underwear to a nudist." I turn to my friend, chin resting in my palm. "You know, you really should have been a lawyer, Jen."

She raises her glass to me with a smirk.

"Honestly," I continue. "I've always wanted to be an artist, and I do paint for pleasure when I have time. I thought the challenge of improvisation would help me learn to shape my visual thoughts. It's a bit of a stretch, I know."

I sip my champagne then turn to my friend and give her a soft smile. "But Jenna is one of the most fearless people I've ever met. It seemed like there was nothing she was afraid of. And I suppose I wanted a bit of that for myself. Plus, she helped me through a difficult time..." I trail off.

My heart skips a beat at the sudden and unmistakable shift in the air. I regret not cutting myself off sooner.

Jesus, it's quiet in here.

Avoiding the looks from what feels like all sides, I trace my fingers through the condensation that trickles down the outside of my water glass. Jenna rubs my back, like a mother would a child who has awoken from a nightmare. James notices and, rather than shy away from it and change the subject, regards me, his expression tender, and presses, "May I ask what happened?"

"It was, um...my father. He and I were close. He was my whole world, you could say." A painful yet all-too-familiar tightness forms in my throat.

"Anyway, he passed away when I was eleven. I never knew my mother, so he was all I had. As I got older, I learned to cope, but every once in a while, things, *memories* I guess you could say, would creep in at the most inopportune times. Jenna, unfortunately, had to bear witness to some of the more difficult moments. But she was there for me, no judgments, no questions. It meant the world to me." She and I exchange looks of endearment.

"My God, Evie. I'm so sorry," he says, his tone low and sincere.

"It's okay, really. It was a long time ago." I wave my hand in the air, brushing the negativity away.

Desperate to change the subject, I pick up my champagne with a quick smile. smile. "So tell me, James, do you have any brothers or sisters?"

His stare is blank for a moment, as if taken aback by the sudden shift in energy once again. And perhaps from curiosity. But I can't talk about it. Not here. Not with him. We just met, after all. I've already said too much, and my burning face is paying the price.

"I have a younger sister, Sara. She's a teacher upstate. She's married, and my niece, Maya, just turned six. Super cute but a total handful. And she looks so much like her mom." His face is aglow. It's probably the sweetest thing I've ever seen.

"What about you?" he returns the question.

"I'm an only child."

"Same," David chimes in, giving me a long, unwavering look.

His gaze lingers a bit too long, and a sense of unease ripples down my spine.

"Well, actually, that's not entirely true." He runs a hand over his shadow of a beard, his attention still on me. But despite my urge to look away, I'm captivated. In a strange, inexplicable way, I want him to continue.

Jenna shoots him a horrified look. "David, you don't have to—"

"No, no, no, Jen, it's okay. Evelyn is your best friend, and I've hardly had the chance to get to know her." He leans back and props an outstretched arm across the back of her chair. "That's part of why we decided to throw this shindig in the first place, right? So I could get to know your best friend better? Besides, she's lost someone too. Maybe we have a lot more in common than we know."

The pulling desire in my gut to look away is stronger than ever. Yet my eyes never leave his.

"I don't think this is the time or the place—" Jenna inserts.

"She's right," James agrees.

"It was my baby sister," he remarks, ignoring them. "We lost her when she was three."

My stomach sinks, forcing me to choke on my own words as I whisper, "I'm so sorry. How old were you?" It seems inappropriate to engage the conversation further, but David's tumultuous regard piques my interest. His expression is plagued with a need for normalcy, desperate for someone—*anyone*—to relate to. We recognize a commonality in each other; tacit yet undeniable. Strong enough to potentially create a bond thicker than blood if cultivated.

"Twelve," David answers.

"Jesus, I'm so sorry," I repeat with the utmost sincerity. I'm at a loss for words. The introvert inside me creeps toward the surface, absolving me of my ability to initiate words of endearment or condolences, despite my desire to do so.

So I speak the only words that enter my mind, breaking the silence. "What was her name?"

He hesitates for a moment, staring at me. "Brina."

"And what was your father's name?" James asks me.

My heart skips at the shift to my father once more. "Eugene."

He raises his glass. "To Brina and Eugene."

We follow suit and toast those we have lost, my father's panicked voice—*"don't make a sound, baby bird"*—rattling around in my head and forsaking me to the endless echoing of that abandoned memory well.

CHAPTER 2
JAMES

From the moment I saw her on the stairs, I was intrigued. At first glance, she was stunning; that light green dress hugged her in all the right places, yet flowed around her hips, leaving something to the imagination.

It wasn't until she was clinking my glass during the toast in the foyer that I knew she was the one Jenna picked for me. She had to be.

Prior to the tournament, Jenna had gone on and on about this friend of hers. *"She's spunky and fun, smart as hell and beautiful. She's a little self-conscious about her height, but she'll parade around in heels with the best of us when the mood strikes. And she has a tender heart, James. Truly. I think you'll really hit it off. So please don't scoop up some last-minute date to my wedding. At least wait until after you meet her at the party."*

I conceded easily. Jenna is nothing if not persuasive. She had come up occasionally in conversations when having drinks or shooting pool with David. *"Jenna stayed home to chat on the phone all night with Evie,"* he would say. But that's as far as it went. David never talked about her. Likely because he barely knew her himself, and more so because we all knew Jenna was the one to meddle in people's love lives, not David.

Overall, the woman was a complete mystery to me.

When she turned to me for the first time, it was as if the world had fallen away, and we were all that remained in that vast space and time.

Those piercing eyes, Jesus; much like her dress, such a light shade of green, like a blanket of seafoam riding the ocean waves on a cloudless summer day. Bold and beautiful. Daring to imprison me without mercy or regret.

When I watched her in the study with Jenna, I knew I had to make my move. But my mind was devoid of ideas as to what to say or how to time my approach.

As Ashton introduced himself to her, I damn near suffocated on the bile that rose in my throat.

I'm not a jealous guy, but I've certainly been accused of being protective. Mainly by my sister, who told me once when we were teenagers that I reminded her of the Greek god, Soter. *"He's the god of preservation and safety,"* she once told me—during her Greek mythology phase in high school. *"You seek out storm clouds in the eyes of the people you care about. Just like Soter, you're protective and will stop at nothing until you have expelled that person's sadness."*

In that moment, I looked at her like she was insane and brushed off her ridiculous babble. But I'll never forget the seriousness in her voice when she described it as my superpower. I had never heard of Soter until then. Believe it or not, she was an even bigger nerd than I was when we were kids, not that she would ever admit it. The conversation petered out when I told her she was full of it. She told me to suck a nut and left me to my own ignorance.

Goddamn if she didn't turn out to be right, though.

Twice in my life, I've experienced that unshakable urge to chase away the storm clouds in the eyes of someone I care about. Once as I watched David slowly come apart at the seams back in college. He was wasting away in drink and sorrow, chasing after a father figure we both knew he would never catch.

And four years ago, when that fucking prick laid a hand on my sister. I wanted to kill him. I may have if she hadn't stopped me. I had never seen red before. Never. But when she opened the door to her house after she'd called me, frantic, and I saw her tear-stricken face and the discolored swelling under her eye, all my hard work, everything I owned, each of my life's accomplishments, were tossed to the wind in an instant. I would sacrifice it all, even my life, to injure the man who hurt her.

By the time I was done with him, my hand was broken in two places, his nose was fractured, and his jaw was dislocated. Sara's cries shook me out of my rage, my senses leaving me in a haze of confusion. I still remember the sound of her screams as she pleaded for me to stop. She loved him; I had no doubt. But I like to think she was screaming more out of concern for me.

I never asked.

And I never will.

I scooped up my niece, and we gathered their things while he writhed like an injured dog on the floor, groaning in agony and cursing my name. She never spoke to him again; I made damn sure of it. Worse than the bruises on her face was the look in her eyes. The *cloudiness*, as she once put it. Sadness, betrayal. Desperation for answers she'd never receive from the man she loved and trusted implicitly. The father of her child. The man to whom she'd surrendered her heart, her hopes, her fears.

The look in her eyes was the worst thing I had ever seen. The sense of helplessness wrenched my gut and ate at me like a cancer. To say my protectiveness of her grew exponentially after that day would be an understatement. But I never saw that look in her eyes again. In anyone's, for that matter.

Until tonight.

I saw it in Evie at dinner. A sadness, a need for understanding, clarity, *answers*. She didn't explain how her father died, and I wouldn't have assumed that his death left her with so many unanswered questions if it wasn't for that horribly familiar look in her eyes. The *cloudiness* lurked behind that mesmerizing seafoam, screaming for protection and closure.

Even David was fortunate enough to have answers regarding his sister's death. A tragic accident, sure, but an accident all the same. His father misplaced his blame on David, his sister having died on his watch. For far too many nights, David sought solace at the bottom of a bottle. I bore witness to his rock bottom and that tropical storm that raged in his eyes. Fortunately, he found strength in self-forgiveness and allowed me to help him get his shit together.

As euphoric as it was to see that beautiful woman show such vulnerability, especially after only knowing me for a brief time, I ached to know more.

When we toasted her father and David's sister, she brought her glass to her strawberry-coated lips and locked her eyes on mine, unwavering and captivating in their seductiveness.

Champagne never tasted so sweet.

So *sinful.*

I knew right then and there, without a sliver of doubt, she would open herself up to me completely before the night was through.

Emotionally. Physically.

Any way I wanted.

***

Jenna and David stand to address the room as servers clear the dessert plates and set a piece of paper and a pen in front of each of us.

"On the sheet of paper in front of you, write one thing that your heart desires." Jenna scans the room, meeting each of our confused yet intrigued gazes as we stir in our seats. "It should be something that can be obtained by reasonable means. A trip you've always wanted. Or a launch party for your new product line...I'm looking at you, Ami." She points to a woman in a gorgeous red satin dress. Her jet-black hair is tied back into a bun, with a long decorative hairpin stuck through the center. "Or even a new car..." she teases. A humming elation reverberates throughout the dining room.

Yet, despite the excitement around me, my mind draws a blank.

Evie and I exchange glances, and she gives me a shrug of her shoulders. She has no idea what to write either, which is comforting.

"Please be sure to include your name at the top of the paper," Jenna explains. "When you're done, fold it up and place it in the slot on the lock box that will be passed around the room."

Confusion stays my hand. Is this the grand prize? There's no way I'll ask my closest friend for a new car or a trip to Paris or anything of the sort. Jenna and David both come from wealthy families, sure, and neither would make promises they couldn't deliver, but it's too much.

Evie drags her pen across the paper, writing something down. In only a few moments, she's folding it up and placing it inside the box.

My body hums with an uncontrollable urge to snatch it, break it open, and devour her every word. It's the not knowing that causes my heart to thump in my chest with an insuppressible passion. What is it that her heart desires? The answer is right there, so close I can almost taste it. Will I only find out if we win tonight? Will every desire be revealed regardless of who wins?

Her curiosity seems piqued as she remains transfixed on my blank sheet.

But with a flick of her lashes, her eyes find mine.

What is one thing my heart desires?

It's such an oddly ambiguous question.

Yet my answer is suddenly crystal clear.

I drag my pen across the paper, sheltering it with my water and wine glasses to keep wandering eyes away. With a swiftness that damn near gives me a papercut and attracts attention from several people at the table, I fold the paper and stuff it into the box before I can change my mind.

Evie smiles, her face riddled with amusement.

"It looks like everyone has submitted their answers. So let's take this party into the billiard room where the fun can really begin." David's lips upturn into a devilish grin.

We stand from our seats, except Evie, who I motion to stay put. I hurry around to her side of the table and pull her chair out for her.

"Thanks, partner," she says.

I laugh. "Yes, I guess you're stuck with me tonight."

"That's incredibly unfortunate," she teases with a warm smile.

My hand finds the small of her back as I escort her toward the billiard room with the rest of the group. In the foyer, she moves in close and whispers in my ear, "Is it just me, or does the term 'billiard room' make you think we're in the game Clue?"

"I was thinking the same thing," I reply with a chuckle. "A billiard table *is* just a pool table, right?"

"If I remember correctly, billiard tables don't have pockets, but I've honestly never seen one. Besides, you have to admit, 'billiard room' sounds way fancier than 'pool table room.'"

I stop mid-stride and she pauses beside me, confusion creasing her brow. The rest of the group continues on, disappearing into the billiard room and leaving me alone with my new partner.

"How much do you want to bet it's just your run-of-the-mill pool table in there?" I ask.

"Ooh I'll take that bet. What's your wager?"

"Hmm...I think I'll leave that up to you," I reply with a crooked smile.

"How about, once we're off this island, the loser buys the winner a drink?" Her eyes bounce back and forth between mine.

With a hand extended, I accept the terms of her wager. "It's a deal."

I find the small of her back again, and a subtle redness creeps onto the apple of her cheeks.

Inside the billiard room, a large pool table stands off to one side with a red cloth top and cream-colored bumpers. The balls are arranged in a triangle, ready to be broken, and a dozen sticks hang in a display case on the closest wall.

The table has pockets. *Ha.*

Leaning in, I whisper, "Looks like you owe me a drink."

She peers over her shoulder with an innocent little smile. Goose bumps form across the exposed flesh of her shoulders and neck, and I salivate with the urge to run my tongue over each and every one of them.

"A deal's a deal," she flirts.

My stomach rolls with the anticipation of that drink and the possibility of what may come after.

Across from the pool table are five upholstered chairs with scrolled feet, arranged in a circle in front of another ornate fireplace. Off in the corner is a stocked bar.

"Teams, pick a seat. But don't sit yet," Jenna instructs.

Evie and I select a chair at random and stand behind it, same as everyone else.

The engaged couple stand in the center, rotating as they address the room. "We'll start with an icebreaker round to get everyone loosened up. So who's ready?" David asks with a little too much enthusiasm.

We holler and clap, ready to get the party started.

Jenna chimes in, "This is merely a warm-up. But the winner will be awarded ten bonus points, which will be added to that person's team total once all five games are complete. So let's get started." She walks over to a large Bluetooth speaker in the corner opposite the bar, hits a few buttons, and the song "I'm Sexy and I Know It" by LMFAO booms from the surround system, vibrating the floor beneath us.

"That's right. It's time for a good ol' fashioned *striptease*." Jenna shakes her chest and raises her glass in the air. An eruption of chatter fills the room, bouncing against the walls at a volume even louder than the music's bass. The lights in the room dim dramatically, and I squint, struggling to adjust to the change. Colorful strobe lights power on from somewhere and transform the room into a makeshift nightclub.

Despite the low lighting, I find a deep blush spreading from Evie's chest to her cheeks.

"But not you, ladies. No way. Guys, *you* are going to strip," Jenna hollers above the music.

Cheers from the women ignite the room, and Evie points a finger at me and laughs.

"All right, smart-ass, have a seat," I order, and she promptly drops into the chair like a good girl.

I tilt forward, grip the arms of the chair on either side of her, caging her in, and press my forehead against hers.

"And enjoy the show."

Her wicked smile is enough to make me want to capture it between my teeth and make it behave.

Jenna announces, "David and I will tap you out if your striptease is not up to snuff. The last remaining couple wins the bonus points. Let's begin, gentlemen."

A powerful bass punches straight through me like a battering ram as she cranks the volume up higher. The floor shakes beneath my feet, invigorating me with the courage I need to strip in front of my gorgeous partner. The room swells with the sound of women swooning as we remove articles of clothing and toss them aside.

I stand with my back to Evie, unbuttoning my shirt, bumping

my body to the beat. Peals of laughter ripple through the music behind me as I pull each sleeve off my shoulders in slow motion, teasing her.

Around the room, men's clothing articles are flung, asses twerk in faces, butts are slapped, and women grope anything within reach. We're all letting loose tonight.

Once my shirt is off, I turn and face her. Mouthing the lyrics to the song I know better than I care to admit, I move in to straddle her, jerking my hips to the beat. I'm dying to see that beautiful skin blush again, and I'll do whatever it takes to make it happen.

And it works.

I thrust my bare chest in her face, and when she reaches up to stifle her giggles, I grab her hands and place them on my abs instead. Small beads of sweat gather in the crevices of my stomach, and I make sure to rub her hands across every contour. Based on her ear-to-ear grin, she doesn't mind.

I scoop my shirt off the floor. Grabbing it by the sleeves, I fling it around her shoulders and pull her toward me. Leaning even closer, our faces nearly touching, I grind my groin against the folds of her dress. My cock is standing at full attention, straining against my pants. There's no way she can't feel it against her lap. Her legs part at the invasion, and my mind rushes with curiosity, desperate to know if it was intentional.

We're transfixed on each other, eyes locked as I move above her and her chest heaves with each breath. Her mouth falls open, as if begging for either a passionate kiss or the thrust of my cock deep in her throat. When she tilts her head toward the ceiling and mouths the words *"don't stop,"* I almost come undone. I drop my shirt, dip closer, and graze my lips over her exposed neck, not thinking beyond the moment. I don't know how she'll respond, but to my relief, she releases a moan loud enough to be heard over the music. My cock flexes against her, and another desperate sound escapes her lips, her grip on my chest tightening.

Women squeal all around me, and the pounding bass sends vibrations straight to my core, but it all fades in Evie's presence. I grab her hand and place it on my belt, enticing her to remove it herself. Which she does—such a good girl. Without a moment's hesitation, she works the buckle with slender fingers and whips it out of the loops with one quick pull. I can't wipe the grin from my face. Every movement she makes floods me with desire. She drops it to the ground and returns her palms to my chest, touching me everywhere, as if trying to memorize every line, every curve.

Still rocking my hips to the song's beat—now "You Shook Me All Night Long" by AC/DC—I move to climb off her lap, but she sits upright and grabs me by my waist, holding me in place.

She shakes her head, silently instructing me to stay right where I am.

I oblige.

Her attention is locked on my face as she slides her hand up my torso and grips my throat, stifling my breath with her aggressive touch. I gulp intentionally, and my Adam's apple bobs beneath her thumb. It's erotic in a way I've never experienced. I arch my neck, pushing deeper into her hold and closing my eyes to the unforgiving sensation. The strobe lights pulsate against my lids, mimicking the thumbing bass' beat and sending me into a state of euphoric mayhem.

As she brushes her thumb over me again, a guttural groan escapes from deep within my chest. At the sound, she tangles the fingers of her other hand in my hair and pulls my face close to hers. My stomach flips in anticipation of a kiss.

Instead, she brings her lips to my ear, and whispers, "My turn."

She shifts her weight beneath me, and I climb off her in compliance. The song changes to "Milkshake" by Kelis as I land on my feet again. My cock is fully erect in my unfastened pants as she pushes me down onto the chair, parts her legs, and straddles me. From this new perspective, I see three teams have been tapped out. We're now competing with only one other team.

And everyone is watching us.

Those seafoam eyes bore into me, and she gyrates her hips against my lap with a yearning that vibrates between our bodies. My cock aches with each teasing sway of her hips, throbbing along with the music. She reaches behind herself and unzips the top half of her dress, freeing her chest from the garment and exposing her strapless lace bra to the room. To me. Grabbing the back of my neck and arching herself backward, she juts her chest toward the ceiling and rocks her hips in time with the music.

Cries of elation erupt around us. Men and women alike clap and cheer my girl on as she heightens my arousal and enslaves me to her every whim. I grip her arched neck, ripe for the taking, and wrap my other arm around her waist, grinding her sex on mine. Her wetness soaks into the front of my slacks. If I keep going, I may make her come right here. And with that thought, my cock springs a leak and precum seeps into my boxer briefs.

With a seductive pout on her face and heavy-lidded eyes, she whips her head in circles, her hair fanning out. She then pitches forward and wraps both arms around my neck, nestling her nose against my ear.

I trace a hand up her thigh, under her dress, to the edge of her panties, exploring the edges with my fingers. Her gaze lances mine, tempting me to shove the fabric aside and ram my fingers straight into her wet pussy in front of the crowd.

As if reading my thoughts, a smile graces her lips, and the world disappears around me all over again. The music and the cheers go mute, and the room grows dark around us. She settles in on my lap, claiming it. The feeling is more than comfortable. It's right.

But the music comes to an abrupt halt, and our moment is cut short by the sounds of delighted screeches and clapping. No one expected my girl to take over the guys' lap dancing session, but she killed it.

Jenna moves in, grabbing her by the arm and, much to my dismay, pulling her off me.

I don't even bother to cover my boner.

Thank God it's so dark in here.

The bride-to-be throws one of Evie's arms in the air. "We have a winner," she cries.

The wedding party breaks out into laughter and cheers all over again.

"Ten bonus points to Evie and James."

Evie races back to me and plops down into my lap. "We won," she gushes. "Can you believe it? I've never done anything like that before." Her face is flushed and her breathing is heavy. She slaps me double high-fives, then moves to pull her dress back up over her breasts.

"Me neither," I reply, brushing her hair over her shoulder so I can zip her dress.

I slip my shirt back on, and she works to fasten the buttons, leaving a few at the top unbuttoned as I originally had it. Placing her hand against the exposed part of my chest, she says, "There. Good as new." She shifts in my lap, teasing my cock, and leans in close. "There's no way that was your first striptease."

I nod. "Actually, it was."

She cocks a doubtful brow.

The look makes me want to bend her over my knee and spank her red. "It's true, sweet girl. You bring it out of me, I guess." My arms are still wrapped around her hips, keeping her in place. I make a mental note of how the corners of her mouth twitched when I called her "sweet girl."

David hollers something about heading to the ballroom to start the first game, and everyone shuffles toward the door.

"After you," I say, patting her thigh.

Her eyes sparkle as she climbs off and holds a hand out for me, her absence leaving me exposed and vulnerable. I fight the urge to yank her back down onto me to keep her there for good.

Instead, I let her help me up, then scoop my belt off the floor, drape an arm around her shoulders, and walk with her toward the ballroom to find out what the crazy bride- and groom-to-be have in store for us next.

CHAPTER 3
EVIE

The expansive ballroom is empty save for a statement piece grand piano in the far corner alongside a white and gold marble fireplace. The parquet flooring is perfectly polished, revealing hints of our reflections as we gather inside. On the opposite wall is a bank of floor-to-ceiling windows covered with thick burgundy curtains.

In front of the windows stands a round wooden table containing three large, clear bowls. One holds miscellaneous objects. The other two are full of folded pieces of paper: red paper in one bowl, and blue paper in the other. Next to the bowls are ten blindfolds: five red and five blue, and a dial timer.

"Everyone, please come to the front of the room." Jenna waves an arm, motioning us closer to the table. "It's time for the first game. Something simple but still along the lines of an icebreaker."

"Ooh another striptease? But this time the ladies? I am *so* down," Mark insists. Errant strands of sandy-blonde hair that matches his scruff of a beard have escaped his low ponytail during the striptease, and now casually brush the sides of his face. His partner Ami nudges him with her shoulder, laughing.

"Not quite," Jenna replies. "But you may enjoy this one just as much."

"Line up into two rows. Ladies in one row. Gentlemen in the other. Once you're in line, face your partners," David instructs.

I shift until I'm standing opposite James at the far end of the line.

"The rules are simple. The ladies will go first, each one drawing a random object from this bowl." David holds up the bowl of miscellaneous items. "The object you draw will be hidden somewhere on your person. Jenna will then draw a piece of paper from the red bowl, which will state where on the body the item must be hidden. You must hide it in that spot. The gentlemen will be blindfolded, and they will have sixty seconds to find it using touch alone. Gentlemen, when you find the object, hold it up and announce it so we know you have it. The person who finds the piece first will be awarded five points, the next one to finish will be awarded four points, and so on. You must find the object before the timer runs out, or you will not receive any points. The ladies will do the hiding for two rounds, then they'll be blindfolded, and the guys will take over the task for two rounds. Four rounds total, one cumulative score."

David gathers up the blue blindfolds and passes them out to the guys.

"And keep in mind," Jenna says, "we're still getting to know each other, so at no point in time should you have to actually feel someone's junk to find the item. But you may have to get a little *frisky*—"

Ashton lets out a catcall, and a couple others follow suit.

"Would anyone like a drink before we begin?" David asks.

Reese runs a hand through his brown wavy hair. "This calls for shots."

David presses a button on the side of the marble fireplace. Seconds later, a staff member enters and takes orders for drinks.

"Let's start the first round while we wait." Jenna walks the line of women, each one removing an object from the bowl. I'm the last to draw. I swish my hand around before removing a red plastic button the size of a quarter. Despite its simplicity, it's unusual in that its four buttonholes are shaped like hearts.

I show it to James.

"Guys, put on your blindfolds. Ladies, feel free to check the other guys' to make sure they're nice and secure."

Mark is still sweaty from the icebreaker round as I tug on the band of his blindfold. It's nice and tight. I then move over to Reese and catch Ami checking James's blindfold out of the corner of my eye. When it's secure, she gives me a smile and a thumbs-up before making her way back to her spot next to me.

Once we're back in our places, Jenna draws a folded sheet of paper from the red bowl—the ladies' bowl—and reveals the first location.

ON YOUR TONGUE

She holds the piece of paper out and walks down the aisle, showing it to each of us.

The smooth plastic is oddly soothing to suck on. I let mine dance on my tongue as Jenna continues. "Ladies, step forward until you're in reach of your partner."

My heels click against the floor as I close the gap between James and me. A subtle yet distinct inhale grazes his lips as I approach. I remain silent despite my desire to whisper something salacious under my breath. But if the button clicks against my teeth, it's certain to give its hiding spot away.

"I'll start the timer in three...two...one. *Go.*"

No sooner does my mind register the ticking of a timer, than James reaches for me. He fumbles, not knowing where to search first, which quickly becomes part of the fun. He starts high, brushing against my neck, and I release a sharp exhale at the sensation of his warm, rough hands on my skin.

Finding his bearings with my anatomy, he touches me with much more purpose despite the blindfold. He glides his hands to the edge of my sweetheart top, his fingers slinking below the fabric.

He pats me down along my breasts and cups his hands under them to feel for the elusive object. When his search yields no button, he sinks to his knees and runs his hands down my body. Seeing him blindfolded, on his knees before me, forces a deep, tingling heat to settle between my legs.

When he reaches my feet, he grabs my other leg and works his way up toward my hemline. An overwhelming desperation bites into me. In that moment, I want him to break the rules, reach under my dress, and search the more secluded parts of my anatomy. As he caresses up my thigh and under the wavy folds of my dress, my pussy clenches tight with anticipation, aching for him to venture closer.

He traces along the edge of my panties, running a finger between the material and my burning flesh, across my pelvis and along my upper thigh, but never exploring beyond the lace material's edges.

The insufferable void between my legs throbs in protest.

When he doesn't find what he's looking for, he works his way back up, grazing my breasts on the outside of my dress and gripping my bare shoulders.

He brings his hands up to my face...

That's it. *Warmer...*

He teases my hair, running his fingers behind my ears. Like a blind man trying to *see* me for the first time, he begins tracing the features of my face. My mouth is still agape with the pleasure of his closeness. His natural scent floods my senses—something new, musky, and delicious—and I tremble as he inches closer.

Several men have hollered "found it" over the last few seconds, but I don't care. I could do this with him all night.

He finds my lips with his thumb and brushes across them, wiping away some of my lip gloss.

You're *so* warm. So close. So very close...

He sucks my strawberry flavor from his thumb, the quiet suckle sending a new wave of ecstasy piercing through me, soaking my panties with sexual vitality. He brings his moistened thumb back to my lips, and I want to suck on it and never free it from its oral cage. But this button, this goddamn button in my mouth, prevents me from taking what I want.

It doesn't matter, because before I can anticipate his next move, he forces my lips apart, and my breath catches in my throat. My wrist is captured by his free hand as I drag my tongue across his imprisoned thumb—suck on it even—and the button brushes against his intrusive digit.

"Found it," he whispers into my ear, his breath hot against my flesh. I stick my tongue out for him, and he removes it, holding it up and announcing it to the room.

Within seconds, the timer goes off. An audible gasp escapes my lungs at the sound, my nerves frayed amid my lustful panting. I'd forgotten about the timer, the game, the others in the room. For those sixty seconds, it was only James and me.

He releases my wrist and steps back toward his line.

"Awesome job, everyone. You all found your object before the time ran out. And here are the scores for the first round..." Jenna rattles off the placement of each pair. James and I finish last, accruing one point. But I don't care. That it took him so long to find that erotic button is a win in my book.

"One more round for the ladies. Guys, keep your blindfolds off while they draw the next item." She brings the bowl back around to each of us. This time, I withdraw a single Starburst candy still in its wrapper. A pink one. *Yes.*

The guys replace their blindfolds as instructed, and Jenna turns to the red bowl and withdraws a folded sheet of paper.

TUCKED AROUND YOUR BREASTS

This should be a quick round. The guys probably have a propensity to *start* there. Maybe we'll make up some points this time. I tuck the candy into my bra toward the front clasp, up against my left breast. The edges of it are subtle but still detectable as I run a hand over the outside of my dress.

I can't help but laugh at the rules of the game. It's quite an anomaly, really. If the object is hidden in an obvious way, we finish quickly and win more points. But the longer it takes for him to find, the more fun it is for the both of us. Maybe I don't want him to find it at all. Maybe I should toss it onto the floor and let him spend the whole sixty seconds searching my body.

Good God, that thought is arousing as hell.

Jenna cuts into my thoughts. "Time will start in three...two...one...*Go.*"

With a gentle touch, James grabs my face, as if picking up where we left off. He traces his thumb along my lips again, then shoves it into my mouth. He can't possibly think we would be instructed to hide the objects in the same spot twice. It isn't about winning for him, that's clear. It's about sixty seconds to unabashedly touch me however and wherever he wants.

I suck on his thumb, and his breathing morphs into low pants. With his face nearly touching mine, his breath is hot against my neck as I savor the taste of him. He lets out a deep moan, then removes his thumb with a sharp *pop*. He traces it down my neck, across my decolletage, and to the valley between my breasts. I pray he doesn't find the candy. I don't want this to end so soon. My pussy aches, reacting to every bit of his skin against mine.

He cups my breasts, gliding over each one. I can't help but drop my head to the side as my staggered breathing increases, my eyes closing at the sensation.

You're getting hotter. So hot. *Scorching.*

In mere seconds, he reaches into my bra, fingering my breast as he removes the wrapped candy, then holds it up.

"Found it."

Goddammit.

I should have dropped it on the floor.

Three more couples are still in the game, I note, as I survey our surroundings, their partners apparently lazy in their search for the hidden tokens, enjoying the flesh of their partners far too much. Lips skim across collarbones and hands explore underneath skirts. The vibe in the room is moving from pre-wedding celebration to sex party.

James removes his blindfold and regards me with hooded eyes.

"Nicely done," I tell him. "I think we got second place that round." It takes everything in my power to disguise my disappointment, though I'm likely doing a lousy job of it.

He unwraps the Starburst and slides it between my parted lips. The sweetness is divine, and I close my eyes against the flavor as it rolls around my tongue.

"The night is only beginning," he whispers in my ear.

I don't hear the scores announced. I'm immersed in James and the way those wrinkles at the corners of his eyes bring a warmth to his entire face.

The shots Reese requested were delivered sometime during the last round, and David passes them around to each player. "They're ice cold; who wants one?"

James and I exchange pensive glances.

"Maybe we should let everyone else get piss drunk. It'll make winning the tournament a cakewalk," he suggests.

"You read my mind."

We wave off David's offer, watching as our companions slam them back and hand them off to the waiting staff.

Jenna passes out the red blindfolds as David collects the blue ones from the guys. The sensual, satin material slips between my fingers, and without thought, I caress it against my cheek.

When it's his turn, James reaches into the bowl of objects and withdraws a golf tee.

Jenna instructs us to adorn our blindfolds as David reaches into the bowl with blue paper, each bearing a bodily location. I give James one last piquant glance.

"Good luck," he says with a shy smile.

I shrug. "Who knows? I may not need it." I return the look then place the blindfold around my eyes, instantly consumed by darkness. I remain still, no longer trusting my own sense of direction or wherewithal. Fortunately, a sliver of light is visible at the bottom of the blindfold, and the overlapping sounds of voices and shuffling feet help keep me in the present.

And not the past.

Hands grip the back of my blindfold—likely not James. We aren't supposed to check our own partners' blindfolds.

As thoughts of James's touch send phantom shivers racing through every inch of my body, my dress shifts across my buttocks.

My breath hitches with shock as the person behind me begins caressing my bare skin. I recoil from the cold, foreign touch. But as I push at the offender, he pinches my ass cheek. *Hard.* I release a sharp gasp and lift my blindfold, spinning as I do.

Ashton.

He surveys me but doesn't say a word. Instead, he smirks and steps back to his partner, Heather, who is oblivious due to her own blindfold. I should slap him, demand an apology. But I don't want to make a scene. I scan the room for James, who is at the other end of the row fastening Steph's blindfold—the girl in the light pink dress. He's oblivious. Like everyone else.

A bottomless pit begins swallowing me whole.

Perhaps it's for the best? James and I barely know each other, after all.

Would he even step in and speak up at this point? I mean, we only just met.

I hesitate before reaffixing the blindfold, fearing the darkness that follows. But with a deep exhale, I adorn it with mind-numbing apprehension.

As I await the start of the next round, my bottom aches where Ashton pinched me, his unwanted touch lingering as the tantalizing sensations from James soon disappear.

I listen to the sounds of approaching footsteps, peering down at the floor in anticipation through my sliver of light and freedom, waiting for James to return.

James.

What if he did see what happened but didn't step in? What then?

Do I have the right to expect him to? Do I have the right to expect *anything* from him? The thought makes me dizzy, and it's at this very moment that I realize how much I care about him. The desire to know whether he feels the same is damn near unbearable.

James.

My partner.

Practically a stranger.

CHAPTER 4
JAMES

Blindfold in hand, Evie runs the satin material between her fingers. Thoughts of using that very blindfold in private quarters consume me; obscuring her vision while her parted lips gasp for air and she bucks her hips with feral lust against me.

It takes several deep breaths to calm myself. The last thing I want is for my dick to be fully erect while she's running her hands all over me. Or maybe it's the *first* thing I want? Those hands searching around my hard-on? It sounds good to me. Amazing, in fact.

David brings the bowl around to each of us. Next to me, Mark removes a wrapped stick of gum and gives a wide, eager grin to his partner. I withdraw a golf tee, which Evie regards before fastening her blindfold. The girl next to her in the red dress has fastened hers nice and tight. There's no need for me to adjust it. I move over to Heather and check hers too. Last, I check Steph's, and she giggles under my touch.

I catch sight of Evie, who hasn't moved an inch since I left her. Despite the blindfold, her head is bent low, and her shoulders are rigid. Something is off. She looks shaken, perhaps even afraid, and an unexpected rush of concern crashes over me. A blistering heat attacks my body, starting in my gut and radiating outward to my fingertips, my toes. Hell, even my ears burn.

I hurry over and reach for her. She jumps, jerking from my gentle touch, and my concern escalates. "Hey, are you all right?" I murmur, despite my hammering heart.

She only nods and wraps her arms around herself.

"You're not. Something's wrong." The words catch in my throat.

She holds her hands up as if to stop me, but instead, I reach for them and hold them in mine.

"You know, you can tell me if..."

"Guys, step away from your partners so you can hide your items," David calls out. A frustrated sigh makes my lungs collapse. Reluctantly, I release Evie's hands and take a step away from her and back into my row.

"But first, let's see where we're putting them..." David unfolds the withdrawn piece of paper and presents it to us.

PALM OF YOUR HAND

"And round three starts in three...two...one...*Go*." The timer's ticking resumes.

She reaches for me as I close the gap between us, and her hands land square on my chest. The trepidation in her touch all but vanishes as she runs her fingers down the placket of my shirt. Lower and lower, she roams my torso, feeling along the contours of my abdomen, a soft sigh escaping her lips.

A sense of relief soothes the tension in my back and shoulders. Her frightened look from moments earlier is long gone.

She runs her hands back up my chest, to my neck and over my Adam's apple, giving it a gentle squeeze.

Fuck.

It's impossible to disguise the moan that pours from the recesses of my chest as she works her magic. My jaw clicks under her touch as she traces her fingers along my chin, stopping at my mouth and stunting my groans. She parts my lips with eager fingers and shoves her index finger between them. I encircle it with my tongue, sucking it to the hilt. She sucks in a breath at the sensation, and my cock twitches with each pass I make.

Freeing her imprisoned finger, she drags it down to my waistband, feeling around the top hem of my pants. She presses her tall frame against my cock where it stands erect, waiting for her attention, as she inches her hands around to my buttocks. She dives deep into my rear pockets, searching—*groping*—with intent. My breaths evolve into pants and my boner fills to the max. I tense under her touch, and she presses herself harder against me, teasing me, then raises her face toward mine and bites her lower lip in approval.

My rear pockets are empty, and she knows it, but her hands linger there as I hoped, slowly caressing the curvature of my ass.

What began as a single flicker erupts into a ball of blistering flame; an uncontrollable desire to force her onto all fours and fuck her until her knees give out and her screams bring the world crashing down around us. Those fucking pouty, strawberry-flavored lips. I want to bite on the bottom one and claim it. Before the night is through, they'll be grazing across every square inch of my body, choking on my cock and humming against my flesh.

But above all else, my need to ask—no, *demand*—that she tell me what she wrote on that slip of paper at dinner, and what shook her mere moments ago, consumes me with a rage that sends a shiver straight up my spine.

I have to know. There's no way around it.

If she doesn't comply, I may be forced to bend her over my knee and punish her firm ass with the palm of my hand until she spills all her secrets.

My thoughts are my best and worst enemy when Evie is near, unconquerable as she holds me in her grasp. She drags her focus to the front pockets of my slacks and pushes both hands to the very bottom of each one. A single finger grazes the shaft of my cock, a little tease from my blindfolded angel, and I flex it under her touch. She chuckles, the fairness of her delicate complexion flushing to perfection.

Falling to her knees—*oh dear God*—she runs her hands down my pant legs, patting them down one at a time. But she finds nothing.

She's precisely where I want her, the red satin blindfold making her oblivious to how close my erection is to her parted lips. I force myself to look away, the decision torturous but necessary, lest I make a complete mess of myself right here, right now.

The object hidden on my body is eluding her. But it doesn't stop her from standing and bringing her face close to mine once more. I reach out and tuck a rogue piece of her hair behind her ear.

The timer sounds with an obnoxious *buzz*.

We jump at the sound and laugh together.

She raises her blindfold, and I hold the golf tee out to her in the palm of my hand.

"Well, shit, it's always the last place you look," she says, feigning defeat.

"I mean, if you find what you're searching for, why would you keep looking? Of course it's in the *last* place you look."

Her lips twitch in a hint of a smile. "Touché."

"But for future reference, if you're unsure, sweet girl, the answer is *always...*" I hold my open hand out to her once more. "Here."

She presses her palm flush with mine, intertwining our fingers.

"I'll keep that in mind," she replies, her smile fading, but her eyes still vibrant and full of sass.

I run my thumb over her cheek, studying her face. This would have been the perfect moment to kiss her. Heaven knows I want to. It's clear she wants it too if the striptease and all our explorations are any indication. But I won't start such an intimate moment knowing we can't finish it, and at any second now, we're bound to be interrup—

"And now for the fourth and final round," David announces.

See?

"Ashton and Heather are in the lead, by the way, with twelve points."

"There's no way for us to win. Even if we get all five points this round, we'll only come out with ten for this game." She gnaws on her lower lip.

Grabbing her by the chin and bringing her gaze square with mine, I reply, "There's no reason to rush through it then, is there?"

She frees her lip from the prison of her teeth and cocks a brow. "You make an excellent point."

"Blindfolds back on, ladies," David instructs after I remove my final item—a guitar pick. The piece of paper he draws from the blue bowl reveals one simple word.

WAISTBAND

I tuck it into the band of my boxer briefs above my ass.

"Final round in three...two...one...*Go.*"

She finds my shoulders first, gripping them with steadied breaths, then teasing down my arms with a featherlight touch. As her fingers trace my forearms, exposed beyond my rolled-up sleeves, tantalizing goose bumps cascade across my body. Her flirtatious laugh tells me she's well aware of how my body is surrendering to her touch.

Her fingers land on my palms, which are both empty.

"Just checking," she coos.

Fingertips lingering on mine, she works a caress down each digit to my palms and back again. I grab her hands then and enclose them in mine, interlocking our fingers and ceasing her ability to explore my body further.

She concedes to the forfeit as I angle closer and press my forehead to hers, her blindfold brushing lightly against my lashes. Her lips are so close to mine I can already taste the sweetness that lingers there. We exchange the same air with each staggered breath, and my heart flutters like a hummingbird ready for its morning feed as I wrap my arms around her in a protective embrace.

In what feels like only a modicum of time, the buzzer rings, and I'm forced back to reality once again.

Her breath hitches at the alarm, and I pull her blindfold off.

I remove the guitar pick from my waistband and show it to her.

A wistful sigh escapes her lips. "I'm *really* terrible at this game. We lost for sure."

"We're doing just fine." I throw my arms back around her, knowing somehow that it's exactly what she needs right now.

As I hold her in my arms, daring to keep her there forever, I realize it's exactly what I need too.

CHAPTER 5

EVIE

The break between games is the first opportunity the guys have to select their rooms, and I can't help but wonder which one James ended up in. If, for no other reason, than to know how far—or close—he may be at this very moment.

Four more games with him.

My anticipation is mind-numbing.

I remove my dress and change into a white, form-fitting crew neck T-shirt that bears nothing except for a set of lips from *The Rocky Horror Picture Show* on the front. The outfit is rounded out with a pair of distressed jean shorts and good ol' fashioned bare feet, per Jenna's suggestion. The heels have already caused enough discomfort for one night. After sweeping my hair up into a ponytail and fixing my eye makeup, I'm on my way.

Eager to not be the last one this time, I race to the foyer. Pausing at the top of the stairs, I spy James down below, talking to Keith.

Much to my relief, we're waiting on a few others.

"Whoa, are you ready to do the Time Warp, or what?" James asks, pointing at my shirt as I approach.

I laugh. "Are you a *Rocky Horror* fan?"

"Of course, who isn't?"

"Anyone who doesn't know the meaning of a good time?" I reply with a smirk.

"Right? Tim Curry in drag is the very definition of a good time."

"Exactly."

"And may I say, I'm also a huge fan of your shoes?" he jokes, glancing at my bare feet.

I huff. "You try wearing heels all day, then tell me that going foot-commando afterward isn't borderline orgasmic."

"Well, shit, in that case, I should go foot-commando too."

He's dressed as simply as me, wearing a navy-blue Air Force shirt with a small, white outline of a fighter jet on the front; the words *Aim High* stretch across the back. His outfit is complete with a pair of shorts and tennis shoes.

"Nah, I'm kind of digging your footwear of choice right now," I reply out of playful spite.

The rest of the wedding party files into the room, and Jenna claps her hands, garnering our attention. "We're all set to begin game number two," she announces, holding a clipboard against her torso.

We gather around in anticipation.

"How many of you have done an escape room?" she asks.

A thrum of excitement spreads throughout the room like a brush fire.

"Each team will be placed in a preselected room that has been converted into your very own custom-made escape room. You and your partner will have exactly one hour to solve the clues, discover the five-digit code to unlock your door, and escape. Then you'll make your way back here," she gestures to the table beside her, "and ring this call bell."

She studies her clipboard. "Heather and Ashton, you'll be in the library; Mark and Ami, you'll be in the study; Evie and James, you'll be in the dining room; Lacey and Reese, you'll be in the lounge; and Steph and Keith, you'll be in the billiard room."

The group is alive with an animated buzz.

"The team that rings the bell first will be awarded fifty points. The next team forty, and so on. If you do not escape before the time runs out, you'll receive no points."

David interjects, "And so you're all aware, there are cameras in each escape room. This will ensure everyone's safety and may also be an integral part of escaping certain rooms. If a clue requires an action, the next one will be revealed by a gamemaster. It's also an insurance policy in case something is broken. So please be careful. If it doesn't open easily, it's not meant to be opened."

"Once every door is closed, they will lock simultaneously. The lock will buzz, which is your cue to begin. Now, make you way to your designated room, and we'll start game two." Jenna beams.

James grabs my hand and leads me toward the dining room, then shuts the door behind us with a heavy *clang*.

The first thing I notice is that the dining table has been set with all twelve place settings, to include the charger plates, glasses, silverware, folded napkins, and name cards back in their original places. The only obvious difference is that the centerpieces have been removed.

The plethora of artwork along the wall next to the table is even more apparent now that the room is vacant.

After we've moved only a few paces inside the room, the lock buzzes as it clicks into place. The sound lances me with panic as beads of sweat bud along my hairline. I place a hand over my chest to calm my beating heart and push out unwanted memories.

"Whoa, hey, are you okay?" James asks, rushing over to me. "You look pale."

"I'm okay, it's just..." Where do I begin? What would I even tell him? I already said too much about my father at dinner. "I just have this fear, I guess, of being locked inside of places."

Keep it vague, *Eves. Short and simple.*

"Feeling trapped," I continue. "Especially dark places." I pause, avoiding his gaze, terrified of the judgment that may lie there. "Just the sound of the lock, it…" I sigh, frustrated with myself.

Move on, Eves…

"But this room isn't too dark…" I trail off, shifting to a more blasé tone.

"Evie, it's okay. No one likes feeling trapped. But hey…" he reaches for me and holds my face in his hands. "You're with me. I won't let anything happen to you. And in one hour, that door will open whether we solve this room or not, and we'll both be free."

His smile is warm, and a sense of calm washes over me as he steps away. He's right. And in the meantime, there are plenty of things to keep my mind occupied.

"Have you ever done one of these things before?" I ask, examining the open room.

"Once with a few buddies. It was a Sherlock Holmes-themed room."

"Did you solve it in time?"

"Barely."

"It's better than my experience with these things, then, which is *none*. I love puzzles and riddles, but I would never voluntarily set foot in an escape room if I had the choice. Because…well…" I gesture toward the locked door.

To my relief, he doesn't inquire further. "Not that I don't want to be here, now, with you." I smile, embarrassed.

"Oh, you don't have to convince me of that."

"Oh really?" I tease. "And why is that?"

"Because this," he runs a thumb over my wrist, my pulse thundering beyond my control, "tells me everything I need to know."

As my heart hammers against my ribcage, I brush his hand away with a playful laugh, and ask, "Well, *Sherlock*, where do we start, then?" My smile is coy and deliberate as I take several steps away to absorb the room's contents.

"Well, *Dr. Watson*, I guess we look for something out of the ordinary that may point us to our first clue," he returns with a subtle wink.

"You know, you should probably be Dr. Watson, seeing as how you're the one with the military background."

"Yeah, but you're shorter than me."

My breath trips in my throat. "Wow, it's not often that I hear that."

Slinking toward me with his hands in his pockets, he says, "Let me guess, you towered over all of your friends growing up, had to stand in the back of class photos, have spent your life being asked if you played basketball."

"Yes, exactly. How on earth did you know?" A laugh ripples through my belly.

His pace slows, teasing at the small space that separates us until he's practically on me. "Because it's not often I meet a woman who even comes close to meeting me eye to eye."

My heart damn near bursts in my chest.

"And it's not every day I come across a woman with legs like yours. It's been damn near impossible to take my eyes off them all evening..."

With the words nearly catching, I reply, "Damn, I hope your puzzle-solving skills are as good as your flirting. Then we'll win this thing for sure."

He's the one to blush this time, an unapologetic grin consuming his face as he turns away from me to look for clues.

I make my way to the dining table while he heads to a large wooden hutch against the opposite wall.

"Was Sherlock, in fact, taller than Watson, though?" I ask, peering over at him in jest.

"He was in the BBC series," he responds, pointing in my direction.

"Oh, that settles it then. Good ol' Benedict Cumberbatch."

"You mean Benedict Cabbage Patch?"

"Nah, I meant Benedict Candy Snatch..."

We exchange glances and laugh, a gentle heat consuming my cheeks. As I settle from the euphoria of my present company, something about the dining table catches my attention.

Something odd.

"The table setting looks different from before, doesn't it?" I ask. "And not just because the centerpieces are gone."

"It does now that you mention it."

In a few strides, he's by my side.

"Wait, look." I point at the center of the table. "The runner is also missing."

"Yeah, you're right. And do you see those circles? Etched in the wood?"

Where the centerpieces had once been placed, two circles are etched into the table. The circles, identical in size, are spaced a few feet apart. James and I press on the two circles simultaneously, thinking they may be some sort of button or hidden compartment.

Nothing happens.

"There's a hinge point here," he says, canting forward and tracing his fingers around one of the circle's edges. "It isn't etched into the wood; it's cut through it."

"Is something supposed to press down on top of it? Like, should we climb onto the table and push on them harder?"

"Wouldn't hurt to try," he says. We clamor onto the polished surface and scoot ourselves to the center. His eyes meet mine, reminding me how there are far more interesting things I would rather be doing on this table right now.

"On the count of three, we push together, ready?" he asks, cutting into my thoughts.

I nod, regaining focus.

"One...two...*three*." We press on each circle at the same time, harder than the puzzle warrants, I'm sure. But nothing happens. No *click*, nothing.

Dead end.

James releases a moan, my new favorite sound. "Huh. Maybe it requires equal weight. We need two objects of the same size and weight, with round bases."

Squinting as I scan the dim room, an unlit candelabra sitting on top of a credenza near the door catches my attention. It's made of polished brass and has five candles at tiered heights.

And a round base.

I scoot off the table and rush over to it. It's solid and heavy, forcing me to find my balance as I lift it. When I bring it over to James, he places it over one of the circles.

A perfect fit.

"Yes," he exclaims, looking around for a second one.

"There." I point behind him. He hops down and heads over to an end table tucked away in the far corner. A second candelabra, identical to the first, sits atop it. He snatches up the fixture and places it over the other circle.

Standing back, ripe with anticipation, we watch as both candelabras sink several inches into the table. A loud *click* echoes through the room as a small drawer pops out from under the tabletop toward the art-bearing wall.

I reach it first.

Inside is a small scroll tied with a red ribbon. James shifts in my periphery as I slide the ribbon off, reaching into his pocket and removing a pair of glasses. He adorns them and skims the scroll while I work it open.

His glasses, however—sexy in their own right and framing his handsome face perfectly—distract me from the task at hand.

"You're staring." His broken laugh breaks through my haze of desire. "Are they really that bad?" He moves to remove them from his face, but I stop him, placing a gentle hand on his arm in protest.

"Don't. They look great." It takes everything in my power not to beg. "I just didn't know you wore glasses."

"Only for reading. You know, like an old man." Those wrinkles around his eyes crease deeper as he smiles. "I forgot them in my suitcase earlier. Thankfully, I didn't need them during the first game."

"Leave them on," I request.

His brow cocks upward with intrigue.

"I-I...they suit you. You look very handsome with them on. Even more so than before, I'd say."

His gaze is long and impenetrable, and it sets my core ablaze.

Relieving me of the anguish that accompanies the sudden silence, he asks, "They aren't too nerdy?" He adjusts them, pushing them farther up the bridge of his nose.

The innocence of his question is almost too much. The thought of him being self-conscious about such a simple, dismissible thing as eyewear has me fighting back a smile. But I'd squash those feelings for good if I could. He's gorgeous. And I want to see those glasses exactly where they truly belong: perched between my splayed legs.

"They're perfect." I pop up onto my toes and plant a single kiss on the arm over one of his temples, grazing his ear with my lips in the process.

"Well," he begins, his voice catching, "you drive a hard bargain, but I think you've convinced me to keep them on."

"*Perfect*," I purr in his ear.

He turns to square his frame with mine, cupping my face in one hand and pressing a gentle kiss to my cheek. As I blush beneath his touch, he holds his kiss for what feels like an eternity and a single instant all at once, time melding together—senseless, immeasurable, completely irrelevant.

Shit.

The grandfather clock's ticking arm slaps me back to reality. I pull away from him, craning my neck to eye the antique timepiece against the wall behind me.

"We'll never solve this room if you keep distracting me like this," he jests, one arm around my waist.

"Yeah, well, you're the one who donned the glasses. It's all your fault, you know."

"*Ha.* Now that I know the effect they have on you, they're never coming off." His grin is infectious.

"Promise?"

"I promise, Watson."

As much as it pains me, I turn my attention to the scroll in my hand.

Our first clue.

In beautiful penmanship that I would recognize anywhere—*Jenna's*—are three simple words:

Her first love

We look at each other, confused. By *her*, does it mean me? And what do they mean by *first love*? I pace the room.

James observes me with a curious tilt of his head. The clue is obviously directed at me, after all. "It looks like we're about to get personal," he teases.

"You mean *more* personal." I'm desperate to avoid talking about my *first love* for as long as possible.

"Different kind of personal, I suppose." He moves in closer, a motion that would be uncomfortable with virtually anyone else. But the move—because it's him—makes my pulse quicken and my vision narrow like an abandoned tunnel in the night, with only James at the far end.

In the light.

With our bodies nearly touching, he says, "I'm ready. Let's hear about this first love of yours."

I sigh. *Dammit, Jen.*

"I don't really know what to say, to be perfectly honest. I don't know what the clue is asking. His name was Connor Matthews. We dated for almost three years, and we broke up last summer."

My stomach hitches at the memory of him.

Of his betrayal.

"Maybe the clue has something to do with his name?"

"Perhaps." I release a deep exhale. "But, if Jenna and David designed these games specifically for us, I don't see her dredging up my ex-boyfriend all for the sake of a clue. She always encouraged me to move on and put it behind me. The clue must mean something else…"

Ducking his head, he examines the clue one more time.

I turn away, meandering around the room, looking for some-thing—*anything*—that might reveal the answer.

The large wooden hutch against the opposite wall catches my eye. I make my way over to it and pull on its knobs.

Locked.

James's reflection appears in the glass panes of the hutch behind me. I'm not startled by it. In fact, I welcome his closeness.

With a rough and determined grip on my arm, he spins me to face him. Leaning in, he secures his hands around my waist and captures my lips in a passionate kiss. It's eager yet unhurried, and my ragged breaths catch in my throat as my body awakens under his touch. Every cell, every pore ignites in a flame of desire.

When I part my lips, his tongue dances against mine with unspeakable need. Remnants of my strawberry taste are still detectable on his lips, causing a wistful sigh to sing between us. Heat pulsates between my legs, a torrent of excitement tearing through me.

When he pulls away, his eyes are molten with arousal and concern. "I…I'm sorry," he stammers, "I-I…just wanted…"

I reply by pressing my lips against his again, tasting him, consuming him, as I tremble under his touch.

After several moments of irrevocable pleasure, he pulls away again. Peering into my eyes with an almost carnal need, he asks, "It's over between you two, right?" His voice is commanding. Worried even.

It makes my stomach hitch, not from fear, but from an overwhelming desire to tease it out of him again.

"I-I have to know..." he demands.

The flames in his eyes catch me by surprise, an unmistakable hint of jealousy rooted within their blazing heat.

Before I can reply, snuff out the flickering embers of his brazen tone, he says, "I mean, you...you don't have to tell me..." The light in his eyes transforms from one of concern to an almost youthful innocence that makes me want to wrap him in my arms and never let go.

"Yes, absolutely, James. I swear."

Without another word, he stoops low and hitches my legs around his waist, and I hold on to the back of his neck to steady myself. He sets me on the edge of the dining table and traces his lips against the contours of my jaw.

In seconds, his hands are under my shirt, groping at my bra. It's the same one I had on during the striptease icebreaker: lace, strapless. He yanks it down, releases one of my breasts, and palms it roughly, squeezing with a primal urge that sends bolts of electricity racing outward from my core. Arching my back, I press myself farther into his grip, exposing my neck, ripe for the taking.

And he takes it without hesitation.

He buries his face in the crook and suckles hard along my collarbone. My clit hums, begging to be rubbed raw.

Through my closed eyelids, flickering lights garner my attention. James pauses his ravaging to turn his attention to the display. It's coming from the crystal chandelier over the dining table; the illuminations bounce off the walls, the floor, our bodies, like fireflies in the brush on a still summer evening.

It's breathtaking.

"What could it mean?" he asks, entranced.

"Maybe that we're running low on time?"

"Or that we should focus and get back to solving the room?"

"Oh, shit. I forgot we're being watched." A lump of embarrassment forms at the back of my throat.

But when James laughs, I can't help but join in.

We readjust our clothing and run a quick set of fingers through each other's hair. I straighten his glasses, fix my ponytail, and we get back to business.

Unfortunately, not the business I'd like to attend to.

It takes everything in my power not to acknowledge the obvious erection that pitches against his shorts.

"Maybe we missed something early on," he says, ignoring his predicament and making his way over to the compartment under the table.

"Wouldn't hurt to reassess." I follow his lead.

Peering into the hidden compartment, he reaches in and runs a hand along the inside edges.

"Look." He stops short along the front edge to grab my hand and guide it along the same spot.

A button.

"You feel that?" he asks, a cocky grin on his face. "That, my dear Watson, is what we like to call a clue." He presses it, and loud popping noises resound throughout the room. I jump as each piece of framed artwork on the main wall lights up, one at a time in quick succession—*pop, pop, pop*. In seconds, each painting is lit from within the frame itself.

The garish lights bring the room to life, igniting the dim space and drawing me in like a moth to a flame.

"The clue is clearly leading us to these paintings. So, what do you think? Now what?" I ask.

"The clue says 'her first love.' So, your first love must be somewhere in one of these paintings. It has to be."

We skim over the multitude of artwork. How on earth will I find the answer within them when I don't know what *"first love"* is referring to?

I sigh and force myself to focus on the contents of each painting. Many of them I recognize, discernible by their notoriety. There are only a handful I've never seen before, which I give special attention. Some are simple, depicting bowls of fruit, a bouquet of flowers, or a sunset. Those are easy to eliminate. Some consist of tasteful female nudes, others of sailboats, and there are a shockingly large number of works depicting cherubs.

"Was your first love art?" James asks. "You work at an art museum; you minored in Art History..." He touches one of the pieces, Edvard Munch's *The Scream*, and a loud buzzer rings. The image turns red, and a large X appears across it.

Below the X, "Strike 1" flashes.

"Holy shit, that was weird," he mutters, stepping back in amazement. "Wait, no way." His jaw falls slack as he moves in close and examines one of the framed pieces alongside *The Scream*. "These aren't real," he exclaims. "They're holograms. They aren't canvas; they're *screens*."

"Really? But they look so real. Are they all holograms?"

"I have no idea." He moves to my side and runs a slow hand over his jaw, a kernel of amazement still detectable in his voice.

"It says 'Strike 1.' I'm going to assume we only get three guesses before the whole thing locks up and we can't solve the clue," I say.

"And I just wasted one of our attempts. Shit, I'm sorry, Wats." The casual use of my new nickname makes a tingle shimmer in my stomach.

"It may have helped us. At least now we know how to guess. We press on the painting. The question is, which one?"

I've already eliminated more than half that couldn't possibly relate to my *first love*.

As I move farther down the wall, a particular work catches my eye. It's of a little boy fishing off the edge of a dock into a lake surrounded by dense woods.

It triggers one of my favorite memories: fishing with my father while camping at the lake. I could barely hold the rod on my own, yet he would string the line, bait the hook, and turn it over to me, trusting me to hold on tight and not drop it. And I never did.

Although the image is reminiscent of a simple yet beautiful memory for me, I'm failing to connect it to the clue: *My first love*.

Is the answer my father? Possibly.

As much as I enjoy fishing, I would never consider it my first love. And the painting is of a little boy sitting at the dock's edge, alone. It doesn't add up.

But nothing else stands out to me the way this image does.

So I press it.

A red X covers the painting, along with "Strike 2," that unmistakable alarm indicating a wrong answer.

"Well, shit," I mutter.

James examines the second red X from the other end of the wall.

"It's okay. We have one more guess. But talk to me. Tell me about the things you loved growing up. I'm feeling kind of useless during this leg of the game."

Where do I even begin?

"It's just so vague." I shake my head in confusion and continue down the row of paintings toward the far corner. "When I was a kid, I guess I was a fan of—"

And then I see it. It's smaller than the others, but it catches my attention all the same. The piece depicts a young woman in a cascading ivory dress, sitting in a chair with a cello propped between her thighs.

"Of course," I whisper. "*My first love.*"

James hurries over. "What is it?"

"The cello," I explain, gesturing toward the image. "I've played it for most of my life. I begged my father for lessons when I was little, but he always said we couldn't afford it. But when I was seven, he conceded, and I was able to take lessons with a cello he rented from a local vendor. I'll never forget the Christmas when he told me he bought the cello outright and it was mine to keep. It was the best gift I ever received."

A beat of pensive silence passes between us before he asks, "Do you still play?"

"I do. Any chance I get."

"Would you be willing to play for me sometime?" He turns away from the painting and studies me. My heart welters, and not only from his words. The implication of time spent together past tonight sends my mind soaring.

"You'll have the opportunity at the wedding. I agreed to play at the reception."

Another beat of silence thrums between us. "I can't wait," he replies in a soft, velvety tone.

Nervousness forces my hesitation. This is our last guess before it's game over.

I press the screen.

The entirety of it goes green. A giant check mark covers the image, and a loud bell echoes throughout the room. The hologram painting clicks open and swivels away from its mounted frame, revealing a secret compartment.

Inside is another scroll, tied with a crimson ribbon like the first.

With James by my side, I open it. The parchment is longer and narrower than the previous piece. A series of typed letters stretches down the paper's length, seemingly random and scattered about.

"This is weird," I say, biting my lower lip.

"Ooh we may be in luck," he hails. "I had a clue like this in the other escape room. We need something long and thin, like a walking stick or"—he scans the room, then hurries toward the hutch—"a cane." He picks a long black cane out of an antique umbrella stand on the floor.

I hand him the piece of paper, and with quick hands, he wraps the parchment around the item. Words appear vertically down its length:

THE GREATEST LOVE SONG, WITH AN APT TITLE

"I'm sensing a pattern," I joke. "Jenna wasn't kidding when she said the rooms were personalized."

"Let's end the suspense. What's your favorite love song?" he asks.

"'In Your Eyes' by Peter Gabriel."

"Wow, you answered that fast."

"I've loved it forever." I shrug.

"So you're a *Say Anything* fan then? That scene with the boombox and the Peter Gabriel song is classic."

"To be honest, I loved that song long before I saw the movie. But I am a big John Hughes fan."

He snaps his fingers. "Quick, which one is your favorite?"

I cock my eyebrow at him. "Come on, that's an impossible question."

"Just go with the first one that comes to mind."

"All right all right." I pause, but only for a moment. "If you're pushing me to pick one, I'd go with *Sixteen Candles*. There, happy?"

"Very. But I would have pegged you as more of a *Pretty in Pink* fan."

"Really?" I recoil and feign shock. "I do love that movie, don't get me wrong. But she chose wrong at the end."

His wide-eyed look of pleasant surprise is pure gold. "You think so? You think she should have picked Duckie?"

"Doesn't everyone? Blane wasn't good for her. And besides..." I slide alongside him, lean in close, and whisper, "I have a thing for *nerds*, remember?" With my fingers on his chin, I turn his head until he's facing me. In one fluid motion, I dot a single kiss on the frame of his glasses where it rests on the bridge of his nose.

His breath hitches against my neck like a flick of warm satin.

"I was always Team Duckie," I whisper, meeting his gaze. "I suppose I have a soft spot in my heart for movies where the nerd gets the girl."

Redness pools in his cheeks. "Can't say that happens too often."

"Sure, it does. In *Clueless*, she ends up with her nerdy step-brother, in *Romy and Michelle's High School Reunion*, Michelle ends up with that nerd who pined over her all through high school. Heck, in *10 Things I Hate About You*, there are *two* nerdish charac-ters who get the girl in the end. They may not be a nerd in the tradi-tional sense, but it's certainly the trope they're playing. Those are some of my favorites for that very reason."

A softness consumes his features as a smile graces his lips. For the first time this evening, I think I've made him speechless.

"Now it's your turn to name your favorite John Hughes flick," I say, breaking the silence.

Still shaken, he replies, "Psh, I could never pick a favorite. Are you kidding?"

"Why, you little—" I squeal, giving him a playful shove.

With a hearty laugh, he captures my arms and pins them against his chest. Locking his eyes on mine, he holds me there, and the butterflies in my stomach stir beyond my control. I'm under his command—*captured*—and I melt under his forceful grasp.

He angles in close, so close that the warmth of his breath tickles against my impatient mouth. Without hesitation, he claims me in an eager kiss. I part my lips to welcome him, and he slides his tongue in with ease, sucking my breath from my lungs.

With one hand, he grips my wrists, still pinning them against him, then reaches around to my backside with his other hand and gropes my bottom. His grip is firm, sinful, and my breath stutters with each deliberate squeeze. He traces his fingers along my back pocket and up under my shirt. They're so warm, providing a sense of comfort I didn't realize I was lacking. With slow movements, he runs his hands along my ribcage and tickles my stomach, eliciting goose bumps on my flesh and a moan from his lips.

He releases me and runs his hands down to my palms, fixing his eyes on mine.

"But I don't think that's the answer," I whisper.

"Why's that? You answered with such certainty."

"Because it says *the greatest love song*. It may be referring to Jenna. This room may not only be testing how well they know us, but also how well we know them."

We pull away from each other, his fingers still tinkering along my palm.

"One Friday night after midterms," I explain, "she and I got drunk off homemade cocktails. We grew sappy as the drinks flowed, regaling each other with what we thought were the most romantic movies and songs of all time. She told me that she thought the song 'Only You' by Yazoo was the greatest song because it was *so* romantic. It certainly makes sense, considering her obsession with eighties pop music. She played it for me, and I was hooked. We spent the rest of the night listening to it on repeat and tossing back lukewarm margaritas..." My voice trails off at the memory.

"You two sound like quite the party animals," he teases, his smile matching mine. "Do you think the answer is in the title? Or a lyric? I've heard the song before, but I don't know it well."

"Let's look for clues that relate to the title and artist.

Although..." I snap my fingers as an idea comes to light. "There's a line in the song about thinking of someone's name and it being only a game. This is *all* a game, right? So maybe that's it."

"You think the answer is a name? Whose?"

A sigh flees from my lips. "I have no clue."

"Yours?"

"Could be. But the clue says *with an apt title*. Maybe we should focus our attention there."

"We have enough to start with, at least. Let's see what we can find."

I make my way over to the curio cabinet in the corner next to the covered windows. James ducks toward the credenza, falling away from my periphery. The hutch is locked, so there aren't many other places to search.

The curio cabinet is full of knick-knacks similar to those behind the hutch's glass panes. Small porcelain figurines decorate an entire shelf: rabbits, elephants, Hummels, and other weathered creatures. The other three shelves hold a variety of eclectic items: decorative lanterns, snow globes, patinaed collectible spoons, hunks of amethyst and other stones, miniature gnomes, empty vases, small candlesticks.

I look under each figurine, each stone, each lantern, but come up with nothing. Moving onto the snow globes, I examine each one. Some are as small as an airport souvenir, while others are so large, I can only imagine their heft. For the most part, their themes are apparent. Several contain cottages or mountainscapes or cityscapes, each waiting to be transformed into a winter wonderland. I push them aside one by one.

Wait.

A globe in the back catches my eye. Not because it contains a log cabin or a cute animal or a skyscraper. But because it contains nothing at all. Aside from the snow itself, it's empty.

"James, come over here for a sec."

Shuffling feet hurry toward me.

"Have you ever seen a snow globe like this?" I hold it out to him. "One with nothing inside, just snow?"

"No, never." He takes it from me and gives it a good shake. Snowflakes dance around the dome, coming to a slow and silent rest at the bottom.

"The snowflakes look weird, don't they?" he inquires.

"What do you mean?"

"Look closely." He shakes it again, and I lean in, watching the flakes drift and dance.

"They don't look like snowflakes," I note. As they gather into a pile at the bottom, their odd shape becomes apparent.

"That's because they're letters. Look."

I angle even closer.

"I only see the letter *U*."

A moment passes, and we exchange looks, the answer dawning on us all at once.

"Only You," we say aloud, together.

"Only *U—s*," James repeats, a wide grin stretching across his face. "This," he motions with the globe in his hand, "is the answer to the clue. Nice job, Wats." He flips it over. Sure enough, on the underside is a compartment held closed by a small metal latch.

My pulse quickens as he opens it.

Inside is another scroll.

Except this one is lumpy. As he unrolls it, a small key falls out and into his hand.

In the same penmanship as before, the scroll reads:

His first love

"Ooh, looks like you're in the hot seat now," I tease. But my stomach drops at the notion that the answer may be a *whom* and not a *what.* I brace myself for the answer that will soon spill from his lips; the lips of my partner, a devilishly handsome nerd of a man, who has patiently listened to me divulge some of my most personal shit.

For which I'm bathing in adoration.

However, now that it's my turn to simply shut up and listen —*his first love*—I'm not so sure I can return the favor.

And it scares me to death.

CHAPTER 6

EVIE

"James, I—"

Cutting into my furtive thoughts, he holds the key out to me. "I don't think there are many places this can go."

Releasing a labored sigh to quell my apprehension, I join him as he moves to the hutch. He inserts the key in the lock, and with a quick twist, we each swing a door open wide.

Inside the giant oak cabinet is a variety of items, similar to the curio. China plates on easels, tattered hardback books, Viking drinking horns, and classic model cars stare back at us. It's like an antique shop threw up inside.

"Your first love is in there somewhere," I say. "Better head on in and rescue her."

A crease forms between his eyebrows as he forces and exaggerated squint. "Such as smart-ass, Watson." He grips my cheek and places his thumb over my lips to silence me. I open my mouth and take it in, sucking it down to the hilt.

"Holy fuck," he groans as I bob my head back and forth with each suck.

I release it from my mouth with a *pop* and nuzzle against his palm. He runs his free hand over his crotch to muzzle his own desires.

"Tell me about your first love, and I'll help you find her," I flirt.

"It's no woman, I can assure you," he teases.

To say I'm relieved would be an egregious understatement.

"It's aviation," he says, turning back to the implements spread out in front of us.

"Yeah? You loved airplanes even as a child?"

"My first toy was a plastic fighter jet, my favorite superhero was Superman, and the rest is history."

We rummage through the assortment of items together. I flip through books, setting them aside as they lead us to more dead ends; I examine all the model cars; I look inside each Viking horn. James rustles through papers, jostles what sounds like a bag of marbles, feels along the cabinet's edges for secret buttons or trap compartments.

Nothing.

The six China plates are lined up on easels, and each is adorned with intricate floral scroll work in gold along the perimeter. On one of the plates, integrated among the design, are the outlines of small golden airplanes. I lift it from its stand, and he leans in close to admire it. Nothing stands out on the front. Only the scrollwork.

He takes the plate from me and flips it over.

On the back are the words:

What's in a name?

"I don't get it," I admit. "Other than it's a quote from—"

"Romeo and Juliet," we say at the same time.

"*What's in a name?* That's as ambiguous as the last clue." He huffs and drops his shoulders.

"Maybe something that has to do with roses?"

"Roses?"

"Yeah, the next line is: 'That which we call a rose by any other name would smell as sweet...'"

There are flowers and roses all over the room, of course, particularly in many of the paintings on the walls.

After giving the space a scan, he crosses the room and pauses to peer at the table settings.

"Hold up," he says.

He grabs a name card off the easel placed at Lacey's seat. Her name is written on the front, no different from earlier.

When a small chuckle escapes him after he flips it over, I know he's found the next clue. On the back are the words:

And therefore

I snatch up the name card next to it, bearing Ami's name, and examine the back.

with the eyes

We gather all ten name cards and lay them out across the table. As we flip each card over, they read:

And therefore
with the eyes
blind
looks not
is winged
painted
the mind
Cupid
Love
but with

"It's another poem," I exclaim, recognizing it the moment James flipped over the cards that bore the words "Blind" and "Cupid." I rearrange them in their proper order:

Love looks not with the eyes, but with the mind,
And therefore is winged Cupid painted blind.

"How do you know this?" he asks.

"English Lit professor, remember? Jenna knows me well. Plus, it's more Shakespeare. It's a quote from *A Midsummer Night's Dream*."

"The one with the fairies?"

Now it's my turn to be pleasantly surprised.

"That's right," I reply with a beaming smile.

"Don't look so surprised. I've read my fair share of Shake-speare." His lips upturn in a wide grin as he pokes my side. I release a spirited cry as the jolt shoots through my torso. In an instinctive attempt to prevent future jabs, I cover the area with my arm.

"My guess is that it has something to do with Cupid," he says, bringing us back to the task at hand. "There are tons of paintings of angels and cherubs on that wall alone."

"Were any of them actually Cupid, though? Holding a bow and arrow?"

We move closer, examining each work.

"Would he have to hold a bow and arrow? This one is full of chubby-cheeked cherubs." He points to *The Annunciation of Our Lord*.

"Not necessarily. Earlier art depicts Cupid without his imple-ments, but the typical image is with a bow and arrow."

James disappears from my side.

There are at least a dozen pieces of art throughout the dining room that depict the ethereal creatures. From what I see, none bear a bow and arrow and are simply cherubs.

"Oh, hey," James calls out from near the door. He's on his knees, leafing through the cabinet he went through earlier, which is full of tattered, hard-cover books. The one he removes is entitled "Seventeenth-Century Italian Art."

"An art book." I state the obvious.

"These caught my eye earlier, but I didn't get a chance to search through them. The others in the cabinet are real art books, but this one feels far too light for a book this thick." He hefts it in his hands.

My mouth slacks in surprise when he opens it, revealing a hollow compartment containing nothing more than a wooden bow and arrow carved as a single unit. It's only a few inches in length and solid wood.

I crouch alongside him for a closer look. "This must go to something. But what?"

James flips it over in his hands several times and holds it close to his face before admitting defeat and handing it over to me.

"There must be a Cupid around here missing his arrow," I say.

We stand, the box sliding to the floor with a gentle *thud*.

"Let's check for a statue or painting or figurine or something that might fit with this."

We disperse, and I'm hovering at the art wall in seconds. The sound of James pushing knickknacks around behind me devolves into a subtle white noise as I scan the paintings one by one.

In minutes, a smaller one tucked away on an adjacent wall commands my attention. The painting itself consists of heavy shadows, easily lost against the burgundy wallpaper.

"The name of that book box thing. What century did it say it was?" I call out to him.

"Uh..." There's a brief pause as he shuffles back over to the box. "Seventeenth-Century Italian art. Why?"

"I think this is a Caravaggio," I reply with a point of my finger.

"And this might be his *Sleeping Cupid* painting." The dark tones are lost in the room's recessed corner in which is hangs, making the sleeping boy appear almost luminescent. "But I don't see a bow and arrow. This might just be a portrait of a boy. But the style is very Caravaggisti, which explains the book we found that in." I gesture toward the bow and arrow in his hand as he moves closer to me.

With a gentle touch, he places his fingers against the canvas, releasing a low snort of amusement. "This one isn't a hologram. But it isn't canvas either. I think it's etched wood."

"Wood?" I lean in for a closer look.

When he brushes across the boy's right hand, he lets out a sharp exhale of surprise. "There's something missing here. A void in the etching."

We exchange glances.

He brings the bow and arrow up to the void in the artwork and, rotating it, holds it against the sleeping boy's hand. After a few minor shifts, it finds its proper placement, fitting inside the etching like a missing puzzle piece.

A loud *clink* sounds somewhere overhead. I spin, looking for what has changed.

"I don't understand," I say, studying the ceiling, the floor, *every-thing*, and finding nothing out of the ordinary.

"The clue led us this far. But..."

"And therefore is winged Cupid painted blind." The clue's final line rolls off my tongue in a whisper. "Something with the eyes?" I inquire. "But in the carving, they're shut. Sleeping—"

"Painted *blind*," James reiterates, his inquisitive look giving me pause.

"He isn't blind in this painting; he's sleeping. Maybe the clue is referring to us. Perhaps we're the ones who are too blind to see what's right in front of us?"

"Are you saying that—"

Ignoring me, James moves to the light switches by the door and flips them off, enveloping us in darkness.

A ripple of panic threatens my faculties. "You trying to get me alone in the dark, Sherlock?" I feign lightheartedness, working to quell my nerves.

I have no time to plummet into the abyss of fear that teases my mind, because in an instant, a neon pink glow appears across the opposite wall near the head of the dining table.

It's a much-needed distraction.

"And what if I am?" The rough edge of his voice is pure lust.

The words on the wall are perfectly legible, painted across the wallpaper in all caps.

**I AM SILVER AND EXACT.
I HAVE NO PRECONCEPTIONS.**

**I AM NOT CRUEL, ONLY TRUTHFUL.
THE EYE OF A LITTLE GOD.**

"It's a riddle," he says. "I wonder if..." He trails off and shuffles away.

In a flash, the words disappear, along with their luminescence, and we're truly alone in the dark. Nerves coil in my belly all over again, opening a deep pit inside me.

A split-second passes, and the familiar *click* sounds again. The words appear on the wall once more, garish and bright.

"The bow and arrow snapping into place turns the letters on. There must be a blacklight illuminating the wall. Probably mounted in the chandelier." His vague pink silhouette shifts beside me as he points overhead.

The riddle is so familiar. I've heard it before but can't, for the life of me, recall where.

It's killing me.

"Do you know this one?" he asks. "Is it a poem?"

"It must be. I know I've heard it before, but I'm blanking big-time." With my hands on my hips, I rack my brain, growing irritated by the fruitless pull on my memory.

"Let's spread out and look for something silver. Maybe it will come to us." He flicks the lights back on, and the neon script disappears from the wall.

The room is filled with possibilities—the silverware at the place settings, the candelabra stands. Even the chandelier has a mount that could be silver.

"The eye of a little god," I repeat aloud. Goddamn, that is familiar.

"Something silver and truthful?" James asks, scrutinizing the objects in his proximity. "Aha," he exclaims, making me jump out of my freaking skin. "Sorry," he says on his way to the door.

He points to a mirror mounted on the half wall adjacent to the door.

"A mirror. Of course. Not cruel, only truthful," I say.

I move to his side and find his reflection in the mirror—*the eye of a little god*. An overwhelming sense of calm consumes me—a peace that is strangely foreign to me, as if forbidden.

Until now.

I HAVE NO PRECONCEPTIONS.

And neither do I.

Only hopes and fantasies and the incessant aching pulse between my legs as his eyes meet mine through the silver truth teller.

The gilded frame is etched with an intricate leaf-like scrollwork that swirls and twists in on itself. I run my hand along one side while James runs his hand along the other, looking for a button or lever.

As I run my hand along the bottom, my fingers graze a round seam about the size of a dime flush with the frame's edge.

The instant I press it, a touchscreen keypad—arranged like a small computer keyboard—appears at the bottom of the mirror's glass face.

We exchange curious glances.

I press the *H* button on the keyboard, and that same letter appears—larger—across the mirror in bright red. When I hit Enter, a buzzer noise sounds, and the single letter disappears.

"Maybe there are a limited number of guesses like there were with the paintings," James speculates.

"Maybe. But what's the clue? How do we know what to type?"

"It has to be in or on the mirror, right? This is where the neon words led us." He presses on the glass in several areas, feeling for seams or hidden buttons, but finds nothing.

My nose practically touches the mirror when I crouch low to examine the bottom right corner.

Hmm.

An *A* is carved into one of the swirls.

"There's a letter here," I announce, pointing to it.

He squats low to examine it for himself. "So the clue is carved into the frame?" There's an excited uptick in his voice. He pops back up and looks over the frame's top half while I search the bottom.

After looking so closely at the frame that I practically make it to second base with the thing, I make out six letters across the bottom.

In order, the letters are:

S-T-E-L-L-A

"Stella. The frame spells out stella."

"And nauta."

"Nauta?"

"Yeah, N-A-U-T-A are engraved across the top here," he points out.

"Nauta stella? What do you think it means?"

"It's Latin," he answers without skipping a beat. "Directly translated, it means star sailor."

"Star sailor?"

My confusion is eclipsed when a *tsk, tsk, tsk* emerges from his lips and cuts into the silence. A chortle follows.

"Nicely played, David," he whispers.

"What is it?"

"Star sailor is the direct translation, sure, but it's actually the Latin word for astronaut," he explains with a grin.

"Astronaut?" The game is coming together now, revealing itself layer by layer. "Which is the answer, though?"

"We could try both. What could it hurt?"

I type in the keypad the letters N-A-U-T-A-S-T-E-L-L-A, followed by the Enter key.

The buzzer sounds, loud and grating, and the letters promptly disappear. Clinging to the hope that still flickers in my chest, I type our next guess: A-S-T-R-O-N-A-U-T.

A *pop* bursts forth from the mirror. The reflective glass swings open and away from the frame, revealing a hidden compartment.

Side by side, we peer into the dark void, our faces nearly touching.

James reaches inside and removes a glass cylinder encircled by five parallel rows of letters.

"It's a cryptex," he says before I have the chance. "I saw this in a movie once."

"Same here. To open it, we need a five-letter word. We have to line up each row to spell the word, and then the top should pop open. But what's the five-letter word?"

"Look..." He reaches back into the mirror compartment and removes another scroll tied with a ribbon—red, of course. "*Another* scroll. Shocker." He boops my nose with the parchment, then slides the ribbon off.

He reads the clue aloud:

HIS FAVORITE SONG

It's printed in thick, bold letters. Around the paper's perimeter is a series of small hearts, creating a makeshift border around the clue.

"Looks like it's your turn to dish *your* favorite song," I jest. "Go on, fess up."

"That's a hard one to answer. How does one truly pick a favorite song? You did in half a second, but you're also a weirdo," he teases, that beautiful smile consuming his face.

I playfully poke him like he did to me earlier, but I'm interrupted by the sound of a bell off in the distance. One of the teams has completed their escape room and has rung the bell in the foyer.

I peek at the grandfather clock. We only have ten minutes left to escape.

"This room is designed *for us* by Jenna and David. What kind of music does David know you love?"

"Shit," he says on a heavy sigh. "All sorts of music."

"Can you narrow it down to a few? Maybe bands you both have a common affinity for?"

"I mean, he knows I'm a sucker for Elvis."

"No kidding?" I love that. Plain and simple. And I can't contain how smitten I am by it.

"Are you an Elvis fan?"

"Of course. My father played Elvis all the time when I was little. Who doesn't love him?"

"No one worth knowing," he replies with a laugh. "So the clue wants to know my favorite song, likely an Elvis song." He's pacing now, lost in thought as he rattles off a list of Elvis songs to himself.

"Maybe you have a shared memory of one song in particular?" I interject. "A drunken night at karaoke perhaps?"

His forehead creases and he stops pacing, his gaze distant as if pulled by a sudden memory.

"You know, now that you mention it..."

I urge him to continue with a quick nod.

"After I got back from my deployment, David and I drove up to New York and he took me out to celebrate at what I thought was just a regular old bar. But when we got there, it turned out it was Elvis night. Impersonators, one after the other, performed on the stage, on the bar, amongst the crowd. It was one of the best nights we've shared. At one point, we were completely hammered and he insisted that we each put in a request for a song. He requested 'Jail House Rock.'" His lips twitch into a crooked smirk at the memory. "Maybe that's the answer to the clue?"

"I don't think so," I reply, drumming my fingers on the side of my thigh.

"Why's that?"

I take the paper from him and point to the perimeter of hearts. "Do you see this here? The hearts along the edges?"

"Yeah."

"This one in the corner is bold. Filled in. It's the only one like that."

"You think it means something?"

"The clue itself is in bold. Maybe the heart is part of it? Maybe they want to know your favorite *love* song? At least that narrows it down a bit, especially if it's an Elvis song."

Pensiveness overtakes his beautiful face as he mulls it over. "But what if it means David's favorite love song and not mine? Like the other clue did for Jenna? I have no idea what David's favorite love song is."

"We'll start with you first. I think you may be on to something with Elvis night. What request did you put in that night?"

A deep sigh coalesces with his laughter. "Oh hell, David never let me live it down." He runs a hand through his hair. "All these classic, badass Elvis songs being performed left and right. And then my drunk ass brings the mood of the whole bar down from raucous to prom-night slow dance when I requested 'Can't Help Falling in Love.'"

My grin spreads so wide at his carefree honesty that it hurts.

"What can I say," he continues. "I have a soft spot for that song, I guess."

"It is a love song, so it fits the clue." The paper crinkles in my hand as I move in closer. "Besides, it's a great song to have a soft spot for. I absolutely love that one."

In one swift motion, he throws an arm around my waist, pulls me against him, and captures my mouth in a tender kiss. No tongue, just the warmth of his lips against mine and the caress of his hands on the small of my back. Chills shoot down my spine and plant themselves in my tailbone, causing my belly to go wild.

He pulls away. "Only a few more minutes until this round is over. I think we're very close to solving this room. What do you think?"

"I should hope so. I have a feeling the code we need to open the door is inside the cryptex."

"Hmm. A five-letter word based on the song 'Can't Help Falling in Love'..."

"We can start with the obvious." I grab the object from him and spell out the word E-L-V-I-S, then pull the metal tab at one end.

It doesn't open.

"What do we know about the song, or about Elvis, that's five letters?" I ask.

We stand in silence for several beats, pondering our options, the grandfather clock's subtle ticking more apparent than ever and grinding my nerves.

"He's the king of rock 'n' roll, right? He's known for his risqué dance moves. He died on the toilet..."

"Okay, let's try..." I move the rows of letters around and spell out the word C-R-O-W-N. What's a king without his crown?

But the cryptex remains locked.

James takes the contraption from me and spins the letters, then pulls the tab.

Nothing.

"What did you try?"

"D-A-N-C-E. Any other ideas?" he asks, defeat rooting itself in his tone, mirroring my own.

The clock ticks onward like a bomb about to explode.

"What album is that song featured on?" I inquire.

"It wasn't so much on an album. It was from his movie *Blue Hawaii*."

"Maybe the clue has something to do with that?"

James stares at the ceiling as he recounts moments from the film: the names of characters and places, the actors and locations.

Finally he stops, his shoulders slumped.

"Maybe we're thinking too deeply," I say. "The movie takes place in Hawaii. The clue is asking for my favorite love song. Do you know what the Hawaiian word for 'love' is?" His grin tells me he already knows the answer.

I do too.

"Aloha," we say together.

"And...it's five letters." He gives me a tricksy, crooked grin that sends a sharp twinge to my core. Good God, in the bedroom, that salacious look would no doubt have me begging for more. Hell, screw the bedroom. If it weren't for the cameras, I'd be on my knees right here, right now.

Trying my best to pull back from the fantasy tearing my horny mind in two, I take the cylinder and spell out the word A-L-O-H-A.

I pull on the tip.

It pops open.

The tension in my shoulders eases as adrenaline takes over and courses through my veins like a drug. Inside is yet another scroll. James removes it, unrolls it, and reads it aloud:

CONGRATULATIONS!
YOU HAVE SUCCESSFULLY OPENED THE CRYPTEX AND SOLVED THE ROOM! AND KUDOS FOR DOING SO WITHOUT THE USE OF YOUR **PHONES**!

YOU CAN NOW MAKE YOUR GRAND ESCAPE.
—ALOHA!

We exchange confused glances. We need a five-digit code to escape the room. The paper doesn't give us one.

"It's implying we completed all the clues, but we still don't have a five-digit code." My voice is pinched with frustration. What more is there to solve?

"If there's a pattern we've seen so far, it's that the *way* in which the clues are typed and worded is crucial." He studies the paper, even flipping it over. The back side is blank.

"You mean like how *Aloha* and *phones* are in bold when nothing else is?" I ask.

"Yes, exactly."

The bell rings outside. Another team is finished.

We look at the clock. Less than five minutes before the time runs out.

"Aloha has five letters. It's in bold. And we need a five-digit code," he says.

"Could the letters correspond with numbers? Like on a phone? The word *phone* is certainly on display in the clue."

"Excellent, my dear Watson." He gives me a wink.

"The letters on a phone's keypad are in groups of three, more or less, right? So wouldn't the code be 1-4-5-3-1?" I move for the pad above the door handle.

"Wait," he interjects, stopping me mid-reach. "The letters don't start on number 1, do they? They start on 2. We need to shift every-thing by one number." He punches 2-5-6-4-2 into the keypad.

The highly anticipated *click* echoes as the door unlocks, and a surge of adrenaline courses through me all over again.

James pushes the door open and grabs me by the hand.

"Go ahead," he says once we reach the table in the foyer. "Together."

We ring the hotel lobby bell as one, our fingers intertwined.

Two teams stand off to the side, waiting for the final minutes to tick downward as the last of the players work to escape.

James maneuvers himself behind me, wrapping his arms around my waist in a silent embrace, and nestles his face in the crook of my neck.

In less than two minutes, the second round will be over.

Which means I have two minutes to silently pant as this gorgeous man makes himself at home pressed against my body.

Or anywhere else he might like.

CHAPTER 7
JAMES

We gather inside the ballroom again for round three, where two rows of large pillows are arranged on the floor. Off to one side is a small banquet of bite-size delectables—fruit, truffles, bite-sized sandwiches.

It smells divine, not that I'm particularly hungry. My mind is still reeling from our time spent inside the escape room, where Evie and I shared our first kiss and then some. I'm addicted to making her laugh, not only because the sound sends my heart racing with a newfound sense of vitality, but because it's impossible for her to do so without trying to cover her face to hide her cherry-colored cheeks. The euphoria of her amusement consumes me, becoming even more apparent when, afterward, without fail, she meets my gaze and begs me to kiss her with a look. It's enough to drive me wild, and I inevitably find myself wanting, *needing*, to bring about her coquettish mannerisms.

And she lets me. That's the best part. She knows it will make her blush. But she never resists the laughter, despite the crimson hue of her face. In fact, I think she secretly yearns for it.

Jenna and David address the group, but honestly, I miss the first part of the instructions. It's probably a recap of scores from the last round. Evie and I came in third, accruing thirty points. I don't know what our score is at this point, and I'm not entirely sure I care. How can I when Evie keeps pushing her backside into me like that? The slow movements of her hips against my cock as she surrenders herself to my embrace are subtle yet unmistakable. The little minx is determined to give me a hard-on right here and now. In front of everyone. And fuck, she's close to succeeding.

She pushes her ass into my groin again, a slight movement that has a huge impact. My cock, in love with all the attention like the horny devil it is, obeys her body's commands and soon fills to the brim against her. I know she can feel it, because she pushes into it even more, positioning me between her cheeks, and releases an innocent little sigh. Using the arm I have wrapped around her waist, I pull her into me even harder.

Two can play this game, sweet girl.

She suppresses her giggles at the sudden intrusion, and I plant a soft kiss on the crook of her neck.

With my other hand, I pinch one of her butt cheeks, making her flinch and jump in my arms. She squeals into her hand, and I chuckle at our shared vulnerabilities. Evie's squirming catches Steph's attention nearby, and she shoots us a quick smirk before turning back to her partner, Keith.

I tune in long enough to hear Jenna encourage us to eat before we begin the next round, motioning toward the banquet table.

As the people around us disperse, Evie turns to face me and motions toward the table. "After you," she teases, knowing my boner is still raging.

"Oh no, no, no. I don't think so, Wats." I push her from behind, using her as a human shield.

We walk to the table together, joined at the hip.

"Are you going to stay back there forever?" she jests.

"I just might." I press my erection against her again with a quick jab that makes her squeal more loudly than before. It earns a few curious looks, including one from Ashton, who shoots me a glare from the opposite side of the banquet table.

Evie and I have very little interest in the food. We opt rather to continue teasing each other between small bites of items within reach.

"It's time for round three," Jenna announces after several minutes, ushering us to the pillows on the floor nearby. "This one is nice and simple. A fun and easy game at the halfway point, before we really get into the thick of things. Ladies, take a seat in this row." She motions to the row on her right. "Guys, sit opposite your partners."

Evie and I take seats near the middle on pillows positioned so close we can touch each other if we want to.

Once everyone is settled, Jenna hands out small dry erase boards and markers to the ladies, and David does the same for the guys. Jenna then hands out unrecognizable objects to each of us. They're red, bulky, and shrink-wrapped.

She instructs us to open them.

Ripping the wrapper open, I dump the contents out and suppress a chuckle at what falls into my hand. It's a set of red wax lips, exaggerated in their size; too large on purpose, almost like that of a cartoon or a caricature. On the back side of the lips is a wax protrusion.

"What the—" Mark mutters.

Subtle laughter fills the room.

Evie chuckles across from me.

God, I love that laugh.

"Jenna, oh my God, I haven't seen these since I was a kid. Where did you find them?"

"At an old-fashioned candy shop in Boston. Aren't they hilarious? I remember goofing off with these when I was little. It's impossible to wear them and not laugh at yourself."

Heather leans over to Evie and asks, "Are they flavored? Like, can you eat them?" She turns the thing over, confused.

"I wouldn't. It's just wax. No flavoring. It would be like eating a candle," Evie replies.

Heather scrunches her face in disgust.

"This round is simple. We'll ask ten questions. The first five will be general get-to-know-you questions about your partner, and the last five will be a bit more, shall I say, *risqué*?" Jenna explains.

"We'll start with the men this time. Guys, we'll ask you the first five questions, and you'll write your answer. Then the ladies will write down their guesses. Girls, you want your answer to match his. So it doesn't have to be an honest answer so long as you write what you think his answer will be. Then we'll switch. Every match gets one point, so the max score for this round of games is twenty points. Does everyone understand?"

There's a rumbling of yeses and a wave of nodding heads.

"But what are the wax lips for?" Keith asks, holding his in front of him.

"Oh, yes." Jenna claps her hands. "My favorite part. You'll hold yours in your mouth for the duration of this game. This way you can't mouth your answer to your partner."

"Like so," David chimes in, donning his own set of wax lips.

Laughter erupts throughout the ballroom at how ridiculous he looks.

"Ooh, I'm having a flashback to freshman year," I tease, pointing at David. "Hey, Denardo, remember when you fell asleep in Hank's dorm room, and we used his girlfriend's lipstick to—"

"Yeah, yeah," he interjects after popping the lips out. "Just can it, smart-ass." He then gives me the finger before resuming his instructions. "I hope you all have been using this time to get to know each other, because now is when it will really come in handy."

"Everyone ready?" Jenna asks. "Lips on. No cheating."

We affix the fake lips, the enthusiastic warble among the group palpable. Evie looks as ridiculous as I'm sure I do, but goddamn, does she also look cute. And her cheeks are about as red as the adornment.

Jenna raises her clipboard and reads off the first question.

"Boys, the first five questions are for you to answer and for her to guess. You'll have thirty seconds for each question.

"First question:

"Where is your partner originally from?"

Evie furrows her brow in contemplation. I never told her that I'm from San Antonio, Texas. She only knows that I currently live in New York. With hesitation, she drags her marker across the dry erase board. I write *New York City* on mine to score the point. The timer ticks down to a sharp, obnoxious *buzz*.

"All right, show your answers," Jenna instructs.

Evie flips her board around, and the letters *NYC* are written out in her red marker.

My same answer is written in blue.

She smiles at me through her goofy wax lips, her eyes sparkling beneath the chandelier light.

One point.

We erase our answers.

"Okay, question two:

"How many siblings does your partner have?"

Ugh, too easy.

I jot down a quick answer on my board, then watch with adoration as she does the same.

"And flip," Jenna hollers.

I spin my board, revealing my answer: *1*, and she mirrors the movement, revealing a match.

"Question three:

"How old is your partner?"

Ah shit.

To be honest, I don't know her age, and a sense of dread overwhelms my insides. When guessing a woman's age, there's no right answer. If the guess is too high, I'm an ass. If guessed correctly, it implies that she looks exactly her age, which women hate. And too low signals a lie.

I write down my own age, amused when I peek up at her and see deep contemplation creased across her face. She doesn't know my age either, and I stifle a laugh. She's likely brain-fucking her answer as much as I will be when it's my turn to guess.

Finally, she puts her guess in writing.

When the buzzer sounds, we flip our boards around.

Her answer for me: 35

My answer: 39

She laughs, lightly banging her forehead with her dry erase board in playful shame. The wink I give her only makes her blush more.

"The next question:

"*Where did your partner go to college?*"

We both quickly scrawl *Harvard*, earning ourselves another point.

"And the last question before we switch:

"*What is your partner's profession?*"

Shit, we so got this.

We spin our boards around to reveal the same words: *Aeronautical Engineer.*

She holds up four fingers for four points.

Not bad.

"And now, guys, it's your turn to guess. Same set of questions. Ready?"

We all nod in our wax-covered silence.

"First question:

"*Where is your partner originally from?*"

Providence is sloppy in my haste as I scribble the word. I have no idea if it's correct, but it's the only thing I have to go on.

My answer matches hers, earning us another point.

It's my turn to hold up fingers, five to be exact. She responds with a smile behind the waxy embellishment, her eyes igniting my core and sending embers of arousal through every square inch of my body.

"Next question:

"How many siblings does your partner have?"

I draw a giant goose egg on my board.

Another match.

"Third question:

"How old is your partner?"

Oh, dear God. The answer I've been dreading.

Okay, let me really put my Sherlock Holmes cap on and deduce this in thirty seconds. She said she once worked part time as an adjunct professor while in graduate school, so she's old enough to have a graduate-level degree. Fuck, why didn't I ask if it was a master's degree or a doctorate?

Wait. She met Jenna during undergrad and I know Jenna is thirty. But did they start college at the same age?

The timer ticks its way onward, the sound sending a mild irritation surging through me like I'm Captain Hook himself. Any second now, it will go off with a *buzz* like a horrible jack-in-the-box waiting to startle the piss out of me.

Oh well, here goes nothing.

I jot down Jenna's age on my dry erase board.

Evie flips her board around, and I'm met with a red *31*.

At least I guessed low, the better of the evils. And she's laughing, my new favorite sight.

She holds her hand out flat and rocks it in a *so-so* motion, likely telling me that she's *barely* thirty-one. It's fucking adorable.

Jenna cuts into our moment, announcing the next question.

"Where did your partner go to college?"

The word *Brown* takes mere seconds to write.

This game is too easy.

"Last question for this set:

"*What is your partner's profession?*"

I write *Restorative Artist* on my board, rather pleased with myself for knowing so much about her over such a short period. Certainly enough to mop the floor with the competition. Yet a shocking blow and hearty amusement hits me all at once when she flips her board around and reveals her answer in big red letters:

STRIPPER

I suck in a breath, and she doubles over laughing, her face as crimson as the wax lips that shoot straight from her mouth and land in her lap. I can't help but guffaw when she points at me. "I'm sorry. I threw that question just so I could see your face."

The teams around us are staring at her, but soon join her in raucous laughter. Even Jenna.

Popping the wax adornment out of my mouth, I whisper, "You are *so* going to pay for that one later."

She responds with a demure little smirk as she retrieves the wax lips from her lap and pops them back into her mouth.

"And now for the last set of questions," David announces. "We'll go back to the guys. Ladies, it's your turn to guess your partners' answers. Everyone ready?"

"There's no way I can keep this in my mouth," Keith calls out, holding up the offending accessory. "It tastes like I'm sucking on a candle." He tosses it over to his partner, Steph, who catches it with fumbling hands.

"Here, have another set of lips," he jokes. "What's one more, am I right?"

Her face and neck turn red at the innuendo.

"Yeah, I second that," Lacey replies, her blond ponytail bouncing as she shifts her weight on the pillow at the end of the row nearest to Jenna. "We won't cheat, Jen."

One by one we remove our wax lips, not waiting for permission.

Keith is right. After a while, they taste awful.

"All right, just no mouthing the answers to each other, capisce?" David warns with a cocked eyebrow.

"Yeah, yeah," Ashton huffs. "Ask your questions already. We have a game to win." He looks over at Heather. "'*Sup*, baby?"

She responds by blowing him an exaggerated air kiss.

"Okay, first question." Jenna ignores Ashton and his fratboy antics.

"How old was your partner when he lost his virginity?"

I give Evie a teasing look, amused by the absurdity of this game along with all the rest we've played so far. She tilts her head, searching my face, as if the answer may reveal itself in the creases and crevices if only she looks hard enough.

I write my honest answer on my board. A big, fat *17*.

"Seven seconds left," Jenna announces.

Evie drags her marker across her board.

The buzzer makes its presence known.

"Show your answers."

Evie flips her board around to reveal a red *18*.

So close.

She slumps her shoulders in lighthearted defeat.

"I was close," she says, shifting her weight on the pillow, ready to tackle what comes next.

"Moving on," Jenna says.

"What is your partner's favorite body part...of yours?"

"Ooh this just got interesting," I say, partially to Evie but mostly to myself. What would Evie say is her favorite body part of mine? I'd love to think she adores my lips, my butt. I'm sure every other guy here is going to write the word *cock* or some variation thereof. But I need to put some thought into this one. And I have only eighteen seconds left to do it. Some of our more intimate moments come racing into my mind, and as I welcome them wholeheartedly, I also curse the damn timer's ticking as it threatens to disrupt them.

There are so many moments to replay. This may be a shot in the dark. But then I remember one of our first intimate encounters—one I will certainly never forget: the moment she traced her fingers along my palms when she forfeited her search for the guitar pick. Afterward, she sank into my arms for the first time and let me just *hold* her.

I scribble my answer as the buzzer rings.

When I look up, I find her staring at me.

We flip our boards, and find our answers to be a perfect match: *Hands*

"Hmm you've been paying attention, Sherlock," she says, reaching into her back pocket and pulling out the guitar pick from the first game.

"I didn't realize you'd kept it." My pulse spikes with affection until I'm damn near shaking from it.

"For luck."

And there she is with that devilish grin again. What I wouldn't give to see those snarky lips wrapped around my cock.

Soon.

She tucks the pick back into her pocket, and I've never wished to be an inanimate object so badly in my life.

I don't hear the next question. Something about bedroom toys? Am I picking my favorite toy or hers? To use on me or her? Shit. My guess is random at best, barely scribbled down before the buzzer rings.

She shows me her board.

Mine says *Blindfold*.

Hers says *Strap On?* With a question mark and everything.

We cannot contain our laughter.

"Feeling rather adventurous, are we?" I ask.

"Oh no, no, Sherlock. It's for the nights *you're* feeling adventurous," she flirts.

I lean forward and raise my hand out to her, and she slaps me a high five.

"Two more questions for this round," Jenna chimes.

"Next question:

"Where is the craziest place your partner has had sex?

"And we're talking locations here, not body parts, okay?" She points at Ashton as a facetious warning.

"Bummer," he replies, brushing her off.

"Hmm. Is a bowling alley considered a crazy location?" Mark asks.

"Hey, no cheating," Jenna warns with a laugh. "Now you can't use that answer."

"Oh, don't worry. I have plenty of options."

"Good God, you make my sex life sound so vanilla," Reese complains, running the back of his hand over his bottom lip.

"Don't worry, I'm sure he's all talk," his partner Lacey replies.

"Mmm, I wouldn't say that," Mark retorts.

I study my dry erase board. Evie will never guess this. And I don't know what fake answer she might guess correctly. In a way, this question feels *too* personal. Do I care if she knows the craziest place I've ever had sex? I guess not. But do I want to know her answer when the time comes?

Absolutely not.

A strange jealousy creeps in, starting deep in my gut and radiating up into my chest and into my throat at the thought of her with someone else.

"Five seconds," Jenna hollers.

I write the first thing that comes to my mind, which, honestly, is not my craziest answer.

The buzzer goes off with a shrill ring that I'm becoming accustomed to.

My answer: *a pool table*

Her answer for me: *public bathroom?*

Her eyes widen when she gets a look at my board. Does she feel a twinge of jealousy too?

She presses her lips together, then asks, "You've had sex on a pool table? Like in *American Pie*?"

I let out a relieved chuckle. "You could say the movie gave me the idea."

"Nice," she replies.

"Never did have sex in a public bathroom, though," I say, nodding toward her guess.

"Safe guess." She shrugs. "I had no idea what to put." A flush creeps up her neck as she scrutinizes her board. Then she wipes away the silly answer, tips her chin up, and straightens her shoulders, ready to move on to the next question.

"Final question," Jenna announces.

"What is your partner's safe word?"

An energetic buzz surges through the room once again. People are loving these dirtier questions, and I'm no exception.

The question screams inside joke, but have we established any, yet? Hell, we already have nicknames for one another. I've touched almost every square inch of her body, felt her tongue caress mine, experienced the warmth of her skin as it sends chills cascading into my most intimate parts. We've shared drinks, escaped locked rooms together, stripped for each other, flirted like crazy...

Wait. Stripped...*Yes.* The song in which she stole the show earworms its way into my mind.

My hand nearly cramps as I race to scribble my answer.

"Okay everyone, time's up," David warns.

Written in beautiful red script—script that matches mine in the best possible way: *Milkshake*

"Hell yeah," I holler far too loudly. "That's my girl." I slap her a high five as adrenaline takes over, making me antsy as hell with this pillow under my ass.

She laughs at the inside joke that is now cemented between us. I want her. I *need* her. And when her eyes lock on mine, I'm overcome with the urge to scoop her up and kiss her until our lips are numb and our flesh is singing with desire.

"And now it's time for the guys to guess the ladies' answers," David starts. "Everyone ready?

"First question:

"*How old was your partner when she lost her virginity?*"

I have no fucking clue. But I have to guess something. I can't help but wonder if she guessed eighteen for me because that's how old she was when she lost hers. It makes sense that it would be the first number to come to her mind. It's as good of a guess as any, really.

When we flip our boards around, it's a match.

She holds up all her fingers for ten points. "Nicely done," she remarks as she erases her answer.

The next question is announced:

"*What is your partner's favorite body part...on you?*"

Yet another tricky one. I have so many, and the night is still so young. But I have to write what *her* guess will be. Does she think I like her lips the best? Her breasts? Ass? Any of those answers would be correct. Hell, she has legs for days too. May as well write that down as well.

But if I must choose only one, it would be those captivating eyes. It's cliché as hell, I know, but I have never seen irises that shade of green before. They pop against her dark hair and fair skin, alluring in every conceivable way, and they draw me in like a siren's call.

But if I use that as my answer, two things will likely happen. First, we'll lose the point. Women rarely see and appreciate their more subtle qualities, which are often our favorite attributes. Sure, we may say shit like we love a taut ass or large breasts. It's almost expected of us. But what often goes unspoken and understated is our love of the little things, like the way she runs a timid hand across her neck, the softness of her skin, or the way she tastes so fucking delicious. But we're supposed to say "big tits," so that's precisely the response we give.

Fuck it. My time is almost out, and I'm clueless as to what she might guess.

So I go with my most honest answer.

When we reveal our answers to each other, she has written *chest*.

She chuckles at my confession. "That's very sweet, but you *have* to say that," she states, proving my point entirely.

"Not always, Wats. In this case, it's the truth. But your answer is seriously on point."

A smile flickers across her lips as she averts her gaze.

David announces the next question, which I hear this time.

"*What is your partner's favorite toy to use in the bedroom?*"

Ooh, now *that's* a question I want to know her answer to.

If she answers handcuffs, I may come undone right here.

Please, dear God up above, let her answer be handcuffs.

The idea of restraining her, ravaging her body until it's raw and trembling as she lies powerless makes my cock twitch with abandon.

I wait until Evie isn't looking before I adjust myself with a quick brush of my hand. I then write *handcuffs* on my board, my pulse racing as I await her answer.

When she spins it around, her response makes my stomach twist into a series of knots.

Wrist restraints.

I throw my head back, jab my elbow downward, and growl "Yes."

"That's eleven points so far. Not bad," she tells me, ignoring my theatrics.

"*The craziest place you've ever had sex.*" David repeats the fourth question.

I have been dreading this one. Whatever her answer is, I'm not sure I want to know. But like it or not, in thirty seconds I'll learn this little "fun fact" about my dear Watson, so I may as well venture some sort of guess.

She guessed *public bathroom* for me. So with the same logic I used with the virginity question, I scribble *public bathroom?*, mirroring her earlier answer.

When the buzzer rings for the umpteenth time, we reveal our boards to each other. Much to my surprise, she has written *electrical closet*.

My jaw goes slack. "You've had sex in an electrical closet?" As soon as the words have left my lips, I regret asking. I don't want to know.

"Yeah, a long time ago, at Brown. Just once." Her face is flushed, but she shrugs it away.

I fight off the image of her fucking someone in a dark closet, suppressing the jealousy that threatens to creep high into my throat. She's being honest and playing the game, just as I have been. It's unfair to show signs of distress over her answer. So I simply reply, "That's definitely something I have *not* done."

She looks me square in the eyes. "*Yet*, you mean."

My anxiety is replaced by an erotic swirl in my groin. Swirl? Hell, forget that. It's a goddamn hurricane. Is she implying she wants to do such a thing with me? If her flirtatious gaze is anything to go by, she is.

"Last question, and then we'll tally up the points," David exclaims.

"*What is your partner's safe word?*"

This is the easiest one yet. Partners can have the same safe word, right?

I repeat her answer on my dry erase board and wait for the timer to run out.

When that cheeky little buzzer sounds off for the last time, we reveal our responses and sink deep into the laughter and chatter in the room.

Milkshake is once again displayed on her board in red ink.

Mine echoes it in blue.

"What can I say, it's a great safe word," she says.

"I couldn't agree more." A smitten heat rises up my neck and singes my ears. "How many points is that, Wats? I lost track."

"I believe that's twelve. Not too shabby, partner."

We slap each other a double high five. But after the slap, I snatch her wrists, catching her off guard based on the look of surprise that rattles her face. I pull her to me, sliding her and her pillow across the floor until she's against me. Leaning in, I kiss her on her cheek.

"Good game," I whisper in her ear.

A slight tremble shakes her.

"The night is young, Watson. Are you up for more?" I exhale against her ear.

She lets out a tiny sigh. It's so soft—barely audible, in fact—but it caresses me like warm satin against my skin.

"I'm up for anything," she replies against my neck, her forehead pressed against my chin. "As long as it's with you."

CHAPTER 8

EVIE

After a brief interlude in which we were instructed to change into activewear, we're ushered to the back of the manor grounds. In tandem with our partners, we follow a long, winding stone pathway through the gardens toward the property's north end. The scents of roses and gardenias permeate the night air like honey, and the spring field crickets chirp a hypnotic chorus as we leave the comforts of the house behind.

It's pitch dark, save for the full moon's radiance overhead, a lustrous pearl in a black sea illuminating our way. I haven't checked the time since we were in the escape room, but it must be close to midnight by now.

A subtle breeze lowers the temperature, making the spring night comfortable. The stars shine brighter here than I've seen in years, adorning their canvas without obscurity from city lights.

Several yards from either side of the path are thick tree lines with monstrous silhouettes. The midnight breeze sends their leaves quivering in surround sound, accompanied by the plodding of our feet.

The path's end dumps us out into an open space at the edge of the wood. Directly ahead is a sight I never expected to see in real life. We line up before the spectacle, in awe of its sheer size and magnitude as it towers over us.

A row of hedges looms overhead, perfectly pruned and kempt, nestled in its private corner of the island and hidden by the trees. Up ahead, they part in a wide gap, an iron archway standing between us and the entrance into the topiary labyrinth.

"Ladies and gents, what you see before you is a hedge maze," Jenna explains, unable to contain her excitement. "Spanning more than twelve acres, it is the largest private hedge maze in the world and is arguably the most secluded. This is what spawned the whole idea for tonight. And I'm so excited that you all get to experience it."

"This is a maze?" Ami asks, her mouth agape as she tips her head back in awe.

"Yes, and you'll all have the opportunity to solve it. But first, you need to select a color." She reaches into a canvas bag and removes five bandanas: blue, green, red, orange, and yellow.

"We are so going to win this one," I whisper to James.

He drags his attention from the maze to peer down at me. "You already know what the game is?"

"No, but I assume we'll have to work through the maze together. Maybe there are riddles or puzzles throughout?"

My competitive spirit is impossible to conceal anymore. This is so up my alley, and I can't wait to see what clues James and I must solve. And the maze's seclusion, he and I lost together, is certainly a bonus.

He wraps his arm around my waist and pulls me close, which I accept as an invitation to nestle my cheek against his shoulder.

Jenna and David hold up the bandanas. "Ladies, come on up and grab a bandana in the color of your choosing."

I move away from James, but his grip only tightens around my waist as he tips close and whispers, "Grab the red one."

"Why?"

"Because I want the color that'll match your ass after I'm done smacking the hell out of it later." My stomach tumbles, blood rushing straight to my neck and cheeks.

"Is that a threat?" I ask, meeting his salacious gaze.

"Not at all, dear Watson. It's a *promise*."

Holy shit.

I've never been spanked before. But I've always wanted it. The taboo nature of back-end play arouses me in ways that other kinks fall short. It's such an uncharted part of my body. In the past, I was always too bashful to ask, even worrying that I would be horribly judged for it.

And none of my previous partners ever brought it up.

Maybe because they were nervous too.

The way James flirts, so unabashed and forthcoming—I've never experienced such openness with a man. It makes me feel like I could open up in that way to him and not be judged for it. Goddamn, it's hot as hell. I know before the night is through, I'll hold him to his unsubtle promise.

Rushing to the front, I yank the red bandana from Jenna's hand, perhaps a bit too eagerly but not caring in the least.

When I hand it to James, he gives me that crooked smirk I adore and whispers, "That's my good girl."

I suck in a ragged breath.

Once we have our team colors, Jenna passes out two belts to each team: one bearing four flags of our corresponding color, and one bearing no flags at all.

She starts with Lacey, handing her a belt with blue flags and her partner, Reese, an empty one. Moving down the line, she passes out a belt to each person.

When she approaches James and me, she reaches into the bag and hands me a belt of four red flags—bandanas, actually—each hanging by a patch of Velcro sewn into one of the corners.

She then hands James a belt bearing five clips but no flags.

Once they've all been distributed, David begins, "All right, ladies and gentlemen, go ahead and fasten the belts around your waist."

I open mine, wrap it around my waist, and secure it with the snap in front. It hangs limply around my hips, resting along the waistband of my maroon leggings. I readjust the white tank top that's tied into a knot at the side of my stomach, revealing a sliver of midriff.

James reaches for my belt and tugs to "make sure it's secure." But when he runs his fingers along the sliver of exposed skin on my lower back, his ulterior motive is revealed. The contact sends goose bumps erupting across my body in one rapid wave of excitement.

"Does everyone have their belts secured?" Jenna asks.

We all nod.

"Good. Now ladies, take the flag that you used to select your team color and give it to your partner. Guys, take it and attach it to your belt."

I follow Jenna's instructions and hand it to James, who fastens it to one of the Velcro clips around his waist.

"Here's how game four of the tournament will go," she states. "Ladies, you'll run into the maze alone with two things in mind: One, solving the maze as quickly as you can by reaching the center. Two, protecting your flags from being taken by the guys.

"Guys, your task is simple: when we give you the okay, you'll run into the maze and try to capture one flag of each color. That means, you'll want to find each of the women and capture one flag from her. Excluding your partner, of course. You already have that flag, and you're working together on this. Please note that if you take more than one of the same color, points will be deducted."

My nerves fire on all cylinders as Jenna continues. "Ladies, if you make it to the center of the maze with some or all of your flags in tow, it's a safe zone and they cannot be stolen as long as you're there. Men, once you have collected all four colors from the other teams, you must locate your partner in the maze and make your way back here to the entrance, together."

"If you do not have your partner with you when you exit the maze, it will not count as a win, and you must go back in and find her. To put it bluntly, you must escape the maze as a team and with the guys bearing all five colors. The team that completes this task first will win one hundred points. Second place is only fifty, so you want to finish first on this one."

"Ladies, if you complete the maze with your partner and still have flags hanging, you will be awarded ten points for each, so time is of the essence. You have one hour in the maze. We'll send a rescue team to find anyone still inside after your time is up."

"And last," Jenna explains, "regarding the center of the maze... it's to your advantage to meet up with your partners there so you don't have to wander around and look for each other. However, once a team is reunited, it's no longer a safe zone, and the ladies' flags are fair game. Therefore, if your lady still has flags, guys, it's to your benefit to protect her in any way you can as you make your way out...within reason, that is." Her lip twitches into a smirk.

Slight panic creeps into the recesses of my mind at the idea of entering the maze alone. Aside from the broad strokes of moonlight and the two large spotlights positioned along the opposite edges of the outer perimeter, it seems incredibly dark in there.

My phobia of being trapped consumes my senses, an unwanted passenger I haven't fully encountered in ages. *Cleithrophobia*, the doctors call it. Not the fear of small spaces, or even the dark, but the fear of being locked inside a location or object, unable to escape.

Relax, I reassure myself, you can't be locked in a maze. The entrance and exit are open, you only have to find them. And regardless, in one hour, you will be free, like the escape room. You won't be trapped there forever. And you won't be alone. James will be there. Even if you can't see him...

James rubs his hands together, amped up and ready for the challenge. My trepidation ebbs at the thought of him searching for me. In fact, the thought is downright erotic.

But he won't be searching for me right away. He'll come looking if and only if he finds all the other ladies first and captures their flags. Like some cruel joke, my gorgeous partner will be hunting everyone else before me.

In an instant, the intensity of my desire to be hunted bears down on me like the looming hedges. A pulling sensation like I've never experienced. And I crave it more than anything.

Never before have my phobias danced so intimately with my desires. It's disconcerting yet thrilling, so I'll let it play out as the night unfurls its wicked games.

David instructs the ladies to line up in front of the entrance.

"On the count of three, you'll run into the maze. Try to find the center as quickly as possible. You'll have a sixty-second head start before we let the guys into the maze. Are you ready?"

He raises one arm above his head.

"Three...two...one. *Go.*"

We dart under the iron archway as a group and into the green unknown.

It's like stepping into an alternate world. It's quiet, *too* quiet, as all noises seem to absorb into the topiary. What remains are the sounds of our shoes pounding the gravel path and our ragged breaths expelling from our lungs.

I bank right at the first split, and Heather follows me, the other three continuing forward. We follow each other for many twists and turns, stopping short and turning back as we encounter one dead end after the other.

Soon, Heather turns right, wishing me good luck as we part ways.

I'm completely alone.

Stopping to gain my bearings, I crane my neck to listen for the sound of David's voice, hoping to hear him announcing the guys' turn to enter the maze. But I'm too deep inside to hear anything other than my heavy breathing and my pulse pounding against my eardrums.

The greenery takes on a life of its own, pitch black despite the full moon and cloudless sky. My imagination insists on torturing me as my eyes struggle to adjust. Desperate, I fight to suppress the fear that lurks beneath the surface of my chilled skin.

I creep deeper into the labyrinth, rounding a corner and noting how the large spotlights along the perimeter illuminate some areas, but cast wide, deep shadows across far too many others.

Another dead end.

Hopefully James finds me first. Then we can seek out the other women together to capture their flags; he can protect me, and we'll leave united before anyone else.

But my mind speaks too soon. Turning to leave the dead end behind me, I release a startled gasp when I find Keith blocking my way out.

"Hey, Evie," he says in a friendly tone, his breathing labored from the running.

His belt doesn't have any flags yet aside from his own.

"Hey, Keith." I smile, searching for possible escape routes around him as discreetly as possible. He takes several steps closer, and I instinctively reach to cover the flags at my hips.

"No flags yet, huh?" I ask with a shallow laugh.

"Nope. Not 'til now." Even in this darkness, I can detect his cocky grin.

"You're quite sure of yourself, aren't you?"

"You won't make it past me, Evie. May as well just hand it over." With a palm out, he moves closer. We watch each other, monitoring every move until he's only a few strides away.

I bounce on my tiptoes, ready to bolt.

He lunges, reaching for my belt. But I sidestep out of his reach, anticipating his move. I race past him as he fumbles for one of my flags, which billow around me as I dart away from the dead end and into the unknown belly of the maze.

Away from him.

An unintentional squeal fueled by excitement and adrenaline bursts from my chest as I put distance between us. Knowing he's not far behind, I run until all sounds of footsteps have disappeared. It's only then that I pause to catch my breath.

I've lost him.

Finally.

Looking around, I realize I've lost my bearings as well. Up until now, I had at least a general idea of where I was in the maze. But fleeing from Keith made me lose all sense of direction.

Soon, the sense of elapsed time fades along with my sense of direction, the shadows shifting and mocking me with each failed turn. The occasional nearby voice reminds me I'm not alone, but I encounter no one aside from Lacey, who I bump into with a startled cry before she disappears into the abyss.

The lack of people I meet is a bit of a relief, as I still have all my flags. But it's also cause for trepidation, as the twists and turns of each hedge line seem endless.

Where is James?

I make two right turns, then a left, then another right. It has been a full minute or more since I last hit a dead end. A good sign, I hope.

No sooner does the thought cross my mind than I round the corner and end up in Reese's path. He snatches a flag from Steph, and she releases a cry of defeat as he guffaws into the night, her yellow flag in tow. He takes off running and leaves her cursing in frustration.

I spin and head back the way I came, hoping he didn't see me. But his footsteps quicken against the gravel as he chases me down, hollering, "Ooh, two of 'em, back-to-back." His taunting laughter follows me at every turn as I try to outrun him.

As I round a tight corner, I come to an abrupt stop.

Dead end.

"Fuck," I mutter aloud.

I don't even have the chance to face him before a flag is tugged from my belt. Reese holds it up in front of me, rubbing his victory in my face. "Thanks, doll." He takes off again before I can call him a douche to his face.

My frustrated sighs meld with his dissipating footsteps.

Three flags left.

Although Reese has a fighting chance at winning the game at this point, the fat lady is far from belting out her a cappella solo piece.

Turning away from the dead end, I make a left where Reese went right, and slow my pace, choosing stealth over speed. I don't want to risk giving my position away again.

I creep up to each junction before rounding it, peering around every corner, happening upon no one.

Not even James.

The maze is quiet again. No footsteps, no cries of victory or defeat, no laughter between players. It's unbearable. With each passing minute, I grow more fearful of someone jumping out and scaring the shit out of me.

After another handful of corners and turns, I worry I'm circling the same areas over and over rather than penetrating deep enough to reach the center. It all looks the same; there are no markers along the ground, no clues or signs throughout. If only I had a trail of bread-crumbs I could leave as I went...

Crunch.

Slow, calculated footsteps crunch behind me, sending a bone-deep chill into the nape of my neck.

I spin and jump back, startled, as Keith once again stares me down. His face is mostly concealed by the shadow that envelops us both. He's on me in a flash—not waiting for me to calculate an escape route this time—and snatches a flag from my waist before I can even register what's happening. He chuckles, playfully smacks me on the shoulder, and takes off running without a word.

Goddammit.

Not long after Keith departs, a faint cry sounds in the distance —a female voice. Another stolen flag, I'm sure.

The nip in the air does nothing to cool the adrenaline-fueled heat coursing through my veins. The imposing hedges leave little breathing room for me and my imminent panic.

When a tingle takes root in the base of my spine, I attempt several deep breaths, a trick my therapist taught me for moments such as this. But my mind won't focus. Instead, my throat tightens until it aches.

Unable to decipher madness from logic, I no longer approach each corner with caution. Instead, I barrel through at full speed, desperate to find the center, a wider space in this stifling maze as panic bites me bloody.

I bank left and come to another dead end.

Not again.

Bending at the waist, I rest my hands on my knees, desperate for a fulfilling breath. I squeeze my eyes shut as I work to control my breathing.

In...

Out...

In...

Out...

With each deep inhale, my heartbeat sinks into a more maintainable rhythm and the tingle in my spine dissipates.

When the panic that threatens my mind and body eases to a manageable level, I stand straight and arch my back, stretching my arms over my head, and take in another euphoric deep breath.

There it is. I can see it now.

The North Star.

It's straight above me. Considering the limited visibility, its help is minimal, but it's something; a constant in this sea of twists, turns, and dead ends. My lips upturn in a smile, a silent act of gratuity to the night sky.

Turning toward the hedge junction, I continue the game with a newfound energy and confidence. Which, unfortunately, has infected me much too soon. Because I'm blocked in by someone who remains eerily still. Watching me.

Standing between me and my way out.

Ashton.

I'm not sure I want to know how long he's been standing there watching me. He could have easily grabbed one of my flags while my attention was pulled to the sky. But instead, he chose to stare.

The incident in the ballroom washes over me. His wandering, invasive hands touching me with blithe disregard.

I chastise myself for not anticipating this threat. And for not telling James, who likely wouldn't have let me out of his sight if he knew the truth. Even if it meant forfeiting, he wouldn't have risked leaving me on my own in such a place with Ashton on the loose.

I knew Ashton would seek me out at some point, and I foolishly entered without so much as a word to Jenna or James about what happened. Had I subconsciously convinced myself that it was nothing? That I would make it to the center of the maze— the safe zone —before he found me? Or that he would merely seek me out for a flag and nothing more?

Worse yet, maybe I believed the altercation in the ballroom was a drunken fluke and that he craved nothing beyond that unexpected, unwanted moment.

Regardless, none of it matters now.

He's here.

And I'm trapped.

He approaches with slow, intentional steps, like a lion stalking its prey.

"So, Evie, we meet again," he purrs. "I hoped we'd get some time alone tonight. I can't stop thinking about that taut little ass of yours." He bites his bottom lip, encroaching on the space between us, his hair reflecting the small beam of spotlight above. In only a few steps, he moves into the same shadow that has swallowed me whole, making it impossible to read his expression in the darkness.

I unclip a flag from my belt with a shaky hand and hold it out to him. "Here. Just take it." My tone is firm, a desperate attempt to disguise my trepidation.

He moves closer.

I ball the flag in my fist and throw it at him. He makes no move to catch it, and it lands near his feet.

With his eyes fixed on me, he walks over the flag, slinking closer. I step back to match until branches scrape against the back of my shirt and catch in my hair.

Ashton reaches me with a sudden lunge, grabbing my arms and pinning them to my sides, forcing a startled breath from my lungs. He grazes my cheek with his nose and lets out a low chuckle against my skin. The alcohol on his breath is rank and repulsively sweet.

I freeze. In an instant, I forget how to move, how to scream, how to fight. Surely this is all a sick joke. I squeeze my eyes shut, hoping to God that if it isn't a twisted prank, then it's a nightmare. I haven't prayed this hard to be somewhere—*anywhere*— else since I was a little girl.

My stomach curls up into painful knots, and I turn away from him, disgusted, as he runs his tongue up the side of my face—from my jaw to my temple—in a long, languid stroke. Panic embeds itself in my throat, sharp as a knife blade.

"*Stop*, Ashton. Enough," I shout, wriggling against his grasp with every ounce of energy I can muster. But he only laughs at my plight as if *this* is the game. He jerks my face back toward his with a rough grip of my chin and plants an eager kiss on my lips. Despite my struggles, he manages to force his ravenous tongue into my mouth, stifling my cries.

I pull back, as far as my neck will allow. But it only exposes my neck for the taking, which he devours despite my pleas. With my free hand, I grasp his face, trying to push him away. But he doesn't budge.

When I shove him, he captures my arm with a violent grip, and I wince at the pain it elicits. But when my free hand strikes a solid blow to his cheek, he recoils and looks me square in the eye. His are glazed in his drunken state but also ablaze with fury.

"What in the hell is your problem?" he yells, and I withdraw at his brutal tone.

He yanks at the bottom of my shirt, pulling the hem away from my body and shoving a hand up under it. When he grazes my stomach, I scream as loud as my lungs will allow. He slaps his other hand over my mouth in seconds.

Sharp pricks dig into my back and shoulders as I scrape against the hedge behind me amid my struggles. In my state of panic, I shove him against his chest, arch myself backwards, and swing at his face. Two fingernails catch his cheek, tearing his flesh open in small linear marks near the jawline. He reels back around to face me so slowly that it gives me pause, fear pinching my throat and robbing me of breath. His tenebrous eyes widen, stunned, and he wrenches my striking hand. "*You fucking bi—*"

"HEY."

Pure venom pierces the darkness, followed by rapid footsteps on gravel. Before Ashton can turn around, he's yanked away from me with violent hands.

James.

Ashton stumbles out of his grasp, taking a bumbling step backward. James jerks forward and lands a single sharp blow to the bridge of Ashton's nose with his forehead. A harsh cry penetrates the night as Ashton covers his face and staggers in agony. James rushes him, grabs him by the collar, and lands a fisted blow to his face. His knees buckle and he hunches over in a daze, clutching a hand over his bleeding nose once again.

James grips him by the hair. "Can you understand me clearly?" he demands, his eyes never leaving Ashton's and his tone blazing.

Ashton doesn't say a word. Only his heavy panting fills our corner of the maze.

He yanks harder, his grip tight at the root, and Ashton, his face streaked with blood, winces in pain.

"I asked you a question," James roars, lowering his face to mere inches from Ashton's.

He nods, his face pain-stricken and his nose oozing blood.

"Good. Now listen to my words, and don't you ever forget them. That woman right there..." James nods in my direction again. "Does not *fucking* belong to you." His threat penetrates the labyrinth in a low, menacing growl. He then releases his grip by throwing him to the ground face first.

He lands on all fours, grunting in pain.

"Now get the hell out of here," he shouts, pointing toward the hedge junction.

Ashton heaves himself to his feet, covering the back of his hand in his blood as he runs it through the mess from his nose.

"What the fuck's your problem, man?" he sneers, his breath staggered. "I thought letting loose was all part of game night."

"And you thought that meant the women were fair game to you?" James clenches his fists. "Even *mine*?"

Mine.

He straightens and squares his body with James. "We left our inhibitions at the door, right? If you already staked a claim on this bitch, all you had to do was say so."

James lunges at him, his glasses falling off as he tackles him to the ground. In a split second, the two are nothing more than a tangle of bodies, swinging punches and rolling on the gravel. A series of grunts and cries fills the dead end of the maze as they land one blow after the other.

My pleas for them to stop go unacknowledged as I grab at James's shoulders while he straddles that fucking prick. As much as I hate him, I don't want to see Jenna's night ruined because of this, and I don't want James to have regrets later. Ashton is clearly drunk and making piss-poor decisions as a result. And hell, we have a wedding to attend in a week's time.

This needs to end.

Now.

"James, *please*," I beg for the thousandth time.

He drops his arm, his chest heaving. There's a gash across his cheek and a cut on his upper lip. Ashton did not fare so well. His nose is still bleeding and there's a laceration across his left eyebrow. He has a swollen lip and what is likely to be a hell of a lot of bruising come morning.

James climbs off him and reclaims his glasses nearby. Ashton rolls onto his side with an achy groan and pushes himself up, stumbling to his feet.

"Just get the hell out of here," James orders, his tone even but firm. Powerful. "Go find your partner, finish the game, and treat her with the goddamn respect she deserves. Got it?"

Ashton squints in response and huffs, running the back of his wrist under his nose.

But he doesn't say a word, only spits on the ground near James's feet before turning away and heading toward the hedge junction.

"Oh, hey, Ashton," James calls out, taking several steps in his direction.

Why would he call him back here? My throat tightens all over again.

Ashton pauses and spins around.

"If you ever lay a hand on her again, if you ever so much as *look* at her with ill intent, I will kill you. Do you understand me?"

A choking sound escapes his lips—*or was it a chuckle?*—then he skulks off. Making a right at the junction, he leaves us behind in our strip of darkness.

In a handful of strides, James is on me, capturing my face in his hands.

"Are you all right?" he asks, his face contorted in agony.

"I'm fine, really."

Despite my reassurance, his eyes are molten.

"You found me." I give him the biggest smile I can muster, my poor attempt to lighten the mood.

He leans in close, his lips nearly grazing mine. I wait for his kiss, my heart damn near bursting from my chest.

But it never comes.

Instead, he pierces me with a look, his pupils dancing with an intensity I've never seen, my face caged in his hands as he eye-fucks me with abandon.

Releasing me from the prison of his gaze, he gives me a slow once-over. His attention lands on my flag belt and remains there for several moments. With one sharp tug, he yanks it from my body, snapping it in half.

"Wait, wha—" I start, taken aback.

"Stay here," he barks.

Riddled with confusion, I watch as he hurries away and disappears into the maze of elongated shadows, my broken flag belt in tow.

Chapter 9

James

Before my run-in with Ashton, I heard screams and knew they were hers. I can't describe what happened to me at that moment; a fury not felt in years consumed me until I was damn near sickened by it. All I could think about was destroying the cause of those horrible sounds. I followed her cries, twisting and turning through the maze to no avail.

As I rounded a corner, desperate to reach her, Keith appeared in the distance. "What is that?" he asked, rushing toward me.

"It's Evie," I roared, refusing to waste even a second answering questions. "Help me find her. Please." Running as fast as my legs could carry me, I barreled past him, making a left at the next split. He kept pace behind me, our footsteps crunching against the path.

Then, in an unexpected turn of events, the sounds stopped, and my heart sank.

Hugging the hedge line as I ran, I listened and prayed for Evie to make any sort of noise so I could track her farther.

But there was nothing.

Keith stood beside me, back straight, head swiveling, eyes searching.

A stymied scream cut through the silence.

"This way," I commanded. Keith followed close, but a *Y* split in the maze forced us to come to an abrupt halt. We darted glances left, then right.

"I'll go this way," I pointed right, "and you head that way, yeah?" I directed him left, and he nodded in agreement.

A sharp *slap* ripped through the night air then. Quick but distinct.

It led me exactly where I needed to go.

I didn't have to travel far before I turned a tight corner and stumbled upon Ashton with his back to me.

And his hands all over Evelyn.

To say I blacked out would be inaccurate, as I remember everything. Maybe too well. A blinding rage bubbled up inside me at how Evie struggled against Ashton's hold, the way those fucking hands gripped her trembling flesh...

It made me want to kill him. *Truly* kill him.

But when Evie's cries suddenly bore *my* name, begging me to stop as I straddled the asshole and pummeled him, I conceded to her pleas. My name on her lips in that manner was pure agony.

So I freed him as she begged, as much as I hated doing so.

He didn't deserve it.

When Ashton disappeared into the night, my instincts to protect her transformed from a blind rage to one of almost paralytic concern. And uncontrollable desire.

I wanted to hold her in my arms until the shaking subsided, kiss her mishandled flesh, and whisper words of reassurance. At the same time, I wanted to take back what's *mine.* Rip her clothes from her body and ravage her until she fell apart in my arms; until her only fear was whether my seething cock would tear through her as I fucked her senseless right there on the gravel.

I wanted her to scream as I dared her to beg me to stop.

I wanted her to cry out in an unadulterated pleasure that would leave her begging for more.

With those polarizing urges—concern and desire—tearing me in two, I responded the only way I knew how. I tore her flag belt off her body with one quick yank.

"Wait, what—" she shrieked, but I didn't pause to explain nor meet her gaze. Instead, I took off in the direction I came, stopping at the Y-junction where I last saw Keith.

Eager to start playing this game by *my* rules.

⋅⊰⊱⋅

I HOLLER FOR KEITH.

In a matter of seconds, he appears at the junction, out of breath and wearing a deep frown.

"Did you find her?" he asks, resting his hands on his knees and doubling over.

"Yes. She's okay. But take these." I remove my flag belt from around my waist, all five flags hanging from it, and hand it to him.

He hesitates. "Why are you giving me these?"

"Because we won't be needing them. Give our flags to the other players when you see them. Or throw them away. I don't give a shit."

"But you have them all. You two could easily win this—" His eyes widen with confusion, but then narrow in on the gash across my cheek. "What the hell happened?" he asks, waving a hand at my face.

"It's nothing to worry about," I reply, protecting Evie the only thing on my mind. In every sense of the word. My voice is steady, even though my insides are the opposite. "Ashton's a dick when he's drunk."

"Did he hurt her? Is she okay? We heard scream—"

"She's fine. And I don't think he'll be a problem anymore. But I don't know if Evie wants anyone to know about this, and I need to get back to her. So please, take these"—I hand the belts out to him again—"and promise me you'll keep this on the down low. For now, anyway."

I'm several steps away when he calls out from behind me.

"Hold up a second."

I pause to face him.

"What do you want me to tell David and Jenna? They'll take one look at you and have questions."

"I don't know yet. Just follow my lead when the time comes, okay?"

He acquiesces in a subtle nod. "I'll play dumb for now, man. Just promise me something..." He clears his throat. "The next time that asshole touches one of our girls, you'll let me know immediately. If he lays a hand on Evie or anyone else, I want a piece of that prick too."

A ripple of calm subdues my rage, and I reach my hand out to Keith for a quick handshake. "It's a promise."

Evie is right where I left her, rubbing her bare arms against the biting air. A look of relief washes over her face when we lock eyes.

"What's going on?" she urges as I stalk toward her. "Why did you take my belt—"

"Because we're forfeiting."

"What do you mean, we're for—"

I silence her with my lips, pressing them hard against hers, consuming her with a violence reserved only for taking back what's mine—we haven't spoken the words, but I know it and she knows it. She lets me take control, her body responding with a series of trembles, her moans giving way to blissful sighs. I pull her against me, my arms yet another obstacle she'll have to escape tonight—if that's her choice. But based on the way she exhales my name against my ear, her breath warm and wanting, I have no doubt she'll give in to the challenge.

My fingers trail along the small of her back, across the sliver of exposed flesh from her knotted top. Her breath hitches in unison with mine with each pass of our tongues, my boner raging hard and eager against my shorts.

I pull away and sink into her lascivious eyes, captivated by their illumination in the staggering darkness. "Did he hurt you, Wats?" I run my thumb across her cheekbone, terrified at the possibility but unwilling to go a moment longer without knowing.

She studies me with a moroseness that rattles me to my core. Nonetheless, she responds with a simple shake of her head.

"Where did he touch you?" I demand. "The truth."

She doesn't answer. Instead, she slinks her hands around the back of my neck and tries to pull her lips to mine, clearly avoiding my questions.

I stop her.

"Evie, please. I need to know."

"James," she whispers, her gaze averted to my chest. "What does it matter? You're here now. You found me."

Her expression is calm despite the way her downturned eyes slice through my entire being. And I can't resist any longer. I kiss her, consume her, and rob her of every breath until her moans echo against the walls of our little slice of labyrinth.

"Listen to me." I grab her chin and force her to look at me. "I will *always* find you. Don't ever doubt that. Don't ever doubt me.*"* She shudders and sucks in a deep breath.

"Do you promise?" Her voice is almost childlike in its inno-cence—like my good little girl.

"I promise."

With a force that makes her wince, I devour her lips, but she returns each kiss with grace and fervor. My glasses steam over as the heat of our breaths coalesces with the air's chill.

I force a hand under her tank top, shoving it up her torso and freeing her perky breasts from the built-in bra. Her nipples stand erect beneath my touch, desperate for attention. She groans against my ear as I pinch one, then the other, and nip at her neck with my teeth.

As I bring my mouth back to hers, she pulls away to grip my jaw. Turning my face to the side, she slides her tongue along the rim of my ear and nibbles on the lobe.

She moves down my neck, her mouth landing at her favorite spot—and now mine—my Adam's apple. When she presses her lips to it, I swallow hard, teasing her. But she holds tight, her lips never abandoning my skin as my Adam's apple shifts. One sharp tug of my hair later, she exposes my neck, which she takes for herself and sucks—so...very...slowly. Tracing around it in small circles with her tongue, she mouth-fucks my apple into submission.

When she grasps at the front button of my shorts, I grab her hand to stop her, shaking my head.

"You first," I whisper, meeting her wild eyes once she's freed my neck from her lips.

I find her butt with a wandering hand, reveling in its suppleness and the way my palm fits around it. She likes it, my hands on her ass. I can tell by the way she digs her fingers into my chest and nestles her face into the crook of my neck, planting small kisses along my collarbone. I stop holding in my groans. With Evelyn, such an endeavor will always be pointless.

My hands drift from her bottom, and I bend low. Her breath catches as I grip her thighs and lift her off the ground, forcing her legs around my waist. She grasps at my hair, hanging on by the roots as I lower her onto the smooth gravel stones at our feet.

I sink into her neck, planting firm kisses along every square inch, running my tongue along her throat and down to her cleavage. She massages her fingers through my waves as I push her top up and over her head and toss it to the side. When the cool air hits her skin, her nipples harden to points, which I take into my mouth without a moment's hesitation.

With her hands still buried in my hair, she quivers with each pass of my tongue. I grope her straining peaks, caress them, and take them deep into my mouth, sucking the life out of them, wanting to leave them bruised and marked—*mine*—as a subtle reminder come morning.

She arches against me as I snake my way down her torso, dragging my tongue along her flesh. Kneeling before her, I yank each of her tennis shoes off her feet, not bothering with the shoelaces—I'm far too impatient—and drop them, one after the other. I pull the waistband of her leggings down in one swift motion, turning them inside out as I go. Her naked body trembles—from the frigid air? From her arousal? From the sudden vulnerability of lying naked in front of me? I can't be sure.

Maybe all the above.

I press my forehead to hers, and she places her hands on my cheeks, breathing in my exhaled air.

She shifts beneath me and wrenches my shirt off, then tosses it aside. The nip in the air is a welcomed sensation against my burning, aroused flesh.

Her panties are a thin lace, easily torn from her body if I want them to be.

And I want them to be.

With a swift tug, I tear them away, a conspicuous *rip* resonating down low. Her gasps are only a whisper away from my lips.

"You're with me now, Wats. You won't be needing them anymore."

A tremble takes her then, and she kisses me hard, forcing my head closer to her with a firm grip of my hair, consumed with a hunger that can only rival my own.

I discard her torn panties to the side and reach between her legs. Her pussy is wet and eager, desperate for the attention that has been teased all night long. I run my finger around her clit, swollen and ready, and she grips my face as she releases a series of erotic cries.

I can probably make this girl come in two seconds if I want, she's so ready. But I've waited long enough to tongue-fuck her, and I'm going to make it last.

For the both of us.

I drop down between her legs, forcing her bent knees even farther apart.

"Wait," she gasps, sitting upright and startling the hell out of me. "I still have my socks on." She blushes and shifts forward to reach for her ankle socks. But I grab her hand to stop her.

"So what?"

"It's just...I'm naked except for my socks. It's weird." She laughs.

"I left them on your feet on purpose."

She cocks her head in utter confusion. "Why?"

"Because they're the only article of clothing you have on that *isn't* in my way," I tease. I lower myself between her legs again, but she interrupts me.

"So you're going to eat me out while I'm naked except for a pair of socks, and I'm not supposed to find it weird?"

"Honestly..." I sit back on my heels.

She props herself up on her elbows, her messy ponytail brushing against her bare back and her porcelain legs still beautifully spread for me.

"I love it. You want to know why?"

She nods, biting her lower lip.

"Because it forces you to trust me, even if only a little."

She arches a brow.

"If you're self-conscious about it, it's because you're afraid of what I might think. That there's some level of judgment. But I'm the one who left them there, sweet girl. I'm pushing you to be vulnerable with me, forcing you to trust that I'm someone you *can* be vulnerable with in the first place."

Her lips curl into a cute little grin. "James, I'm lying here naked and spread-eagle in front of you in a creepy hedge maze in the middle of the night. How much more vulnerable do you want me to be?"

"And yet, it's the *socks* you're hung up on," I jest.

"All right, all right. Well played."

"We're leaving them on, Wats. End of story. You trust me, right?"

"Of course," she whispers, making my breath catch in my throat.

"Good." I sink back between her legs as she lowers herself onto the gravel.

In a split second, her body has abdicated itself to me. I lap her clit with firm, hard strokes, her thighs twitching and her pelvis bucking with each pass.

She holds my head between her legs, pulling at my hair and releasing sharp moans that become less controlled as I tease her clit with one swirl of my tongue after another. She's dripping for me, her wetness like pure butterscotch. I push one of her thighs lower with one hand, opening her up even more, and shove two fingers into her eager pussy. She arches her bare breasts in response.

Her moans evolve into cries, signaling her orgasm's approach. I quicken my tongue, tracing it around her clit, dipping it into her pussy alongside my thrusting fingers, and back out again.

As I focus on her sopping sex—clearly enjoying my touch but likely wanting to be fucked raw instead—footsteps sound nearby. I look up and past the curvatures of her figure, catching sight of someone standing in the shadows.

"Who's there?" I seethe at the thought that it might be Ashton watching Evie exposed this way.

She sits bolt upright, covering her exposed breasts with her arm and bringing her legs together.

I stand, my cock raging in my pants, and squint at the dark figure.

Figures. There are two of them.

"This isn't funny," I yell, irritated and horny as fuck.

One of them lets out a squeal of laughter, and relief soothes the tingling aftershocks of my firing nerves when I realize it's Lacey and Reese.

"Sorry. We just stumbled upon you two, well, making up your own rules to the game it seems," Lacey says.

Reese stares a bit too long at Evie, who is still naked on the ground near my feet.

"Beat it," I order, pointing them back the way they came.

They turn to leave, and I drop back down to my knees. "Lie back, baby girl. We're not done yet."

"But maybe doing this *here* isn't such a good idea." She hesitates, her eyes wide with concern.

"Fine. Stay upright," I prompt, ignoring her trepidation and sinking between her legs. An "*Oh God*" rushes past her lips and she collapses back onto the gravel.

Such a fucking good girl.

Her hips resume their bucking motion against my face as I lap her pussy raw. To hold her still, I force one of her legs open by pressing my elbow against her inner thigh, then splay my palm over her pelvis to steady her.

As my girl writhes in ecstasy, grabbing her own hair and gasping my name, another set of moans starts up close by.

Female.

Not Evie's.

I look up from between her legs, keeping my tongue right where it is, and spot Reese and Lacey still standing nearby against a hedge. He's kissing her neck and grabbing at her breasts under her shirt with a forceful passion; her mouth is agape as she cries out in pleasure. It's only a matter of time before Evie hears them and knows we still have company.

I shove two fingers back inside her and wave my other hand like an idiot, hoping to draw their attention. Lacey finally opens her eyes, notices me, and pushes at Reese until he turns my way. I motion for them to get the hell out of here. This isn't a designated orgy corner of the maze. This is for Evie and me, and everyone else can fuck off and find their own spots to hook up.

After several awkward seconds, they take the hint and leave our dead end, our little piece of this island where I'm going to tongue-fuck my partner until she erupts all over me, no matter how many times we're interrupted tonight.

As I resume my work, shoving a third finger inside because, well, that's just manners, I'm distracted once again by loud grunts and groans coming from multiple sources.

What now?

Sex noises.

Seriously?

Loud, unmistakable, and right on the other side of the hedgerow. Evie's eyes burst open as she hears them too.

"Is there someone fucking over there?" she asks, her voice sharp.

"Certainly sounds that way," I grumble from between her legs. "Probably Reese and Lacey, pissed we made them leave so they're trying to be disruptive."

"They're awfully loud. Like they're trying to outdo us," she ponders, rising to her elbows and meeting my gaze.

We look at each other for a good long while, plotting our next move silently.

"Are you thinking what I'm thinking?" she asks.

God, I want to shove my dick right into that smirk.

"Absolutely," I say with an eagerness I can't control.

She giggles and falls back to the ground as I get back to work. I thrust my trifecta of fingers in and out of her harder than before, an odd sense of competitiveness rising inside me.

With a hand tangled in her hair again, she arches her back with each pass of my tongue, expelling her cries toward the heavens.

She's close. Very close.

"Make it loud, baby girl. We can outdo them. *Scream for me.*"

I bring my tongue, taut and firm, across her entire sex, then loop it around her clit, all the while shunting my fingers into her. My arm aches from the repetitive motion, but I don't give even the smallest of shits.

We're going to win.

Evie's cries mix with the *uh, uh, uhs* coming from the other side of the hedges, Lacey clearly getting fucked by Reese and loving every second of it. As much as I want to fuck Evie, I want to wait until the games are over and she and I can ravage each other without prying eyes or some pre-established time limit.

Regardless, the erotic sounds of the lovers next door impel my cock to pulsate with pure aggression, thus causing precum to soak into the front seams of my shorts.

When my girl comes undone and lets out her highly anticipated screams, she does not disappoint.

My little Watson is as competitive as I am.

Her outburst hits its max as I shove my pinky finger into her other, puckered, entrance. Her legs twitch against my face, and her hips buck, almost in agony. I lap up my victory with my fingers still trapped in her tight holes.

Her body shakes as she comes down from her orgasm, and I free her from my grasp.

Lacey's moans of passion subside as Evie basks in her own afterglow. I place several delicate kisses beside her bellybutton, and goose bumps grace her skin against the tickle of my touch.

When I shift away to look into her eyes, she sits upright, reaches for me, and brings her lips to mine in a soft, almost virginal, kiss.

The strawberry taste is long gone, but this time I taste *her,* au naturel, and it's everything.

I stand and extend my hand to help her up. But she doesn't take it. Instead, she shifts to her knees in front of me and moves to unbutton my shorts, her hand grazing across the tented part of the material.

She peers up at me with those piercing eyes, taunting me, begging me to fuck her as she pulls the zipper open with a soft *purr.*

But as the zipper meets its end, I grab her hand. "Let's focus on you for now, okay?" I hate myself for saying anything that stops this woman from devouring my cock. But I don't want her to think she owes me.

She stops as I instructed, her naked porcelain body—minus her feet, of course—poised in front of my raging boner. But she doesn't stand. Instead, the storm in her eyes is cycloning out of control as she examines me through her lashes. "One thing you really ought to know about me, partner," her lips twitch into a flirtatious smile, "is that I can be very stubborn."

Before I can formulate a response, she yanks my pants and boxer briefs to the ground in one quick motion. I nearly jump at the assertive way she disrobes my junk, but what can I say? I fucking love it.

My cock stands at full attention before her as she licks her lips. The way she bites the bottom one reminds me of the Rocky Horror T-shirt she wore earlier in the night.

She opens those rosy lips wide and takes me in with abandon, far from virginal now. Jesus. My groin aches with each pass of her tongue and pull of her puckered lips. She teases at taking in my entire length, giving special attention to the head, and making me shake like a goddamn leaf.

"Holy fuck." I moan, watching her bob along my shaft. She caresses the contours of my abdomen with one hand while she pulls on my shaft with the other. I'm amazed at her delicate touch, especially considering her mouth is anything but.

I arch my neck, then look back down at her, then back up again as my brewing orgasm draws nearer, my balls tightening.

When precum leaks from my cock, she licks at it with a twirl of her tongue, pulling animalistic cries of pleasure from my chest.

Will she swallow when the time comes? She seems awfully comfortable with my precum dripping down her throat. Or...

"I'm gonna come, baby," I rasp, my breath quick and shallow.

She picks up her pace, and I grab her by the back of her head, forcing her lips as close to the hilt as I can get them. She groans as I fuck her throat, my balls twitching with each pass. Before it's too late, I pull her off my cock and tug on her hair until her gaze meets mine.

"Lie back," I instruct.

Her eyes widen with surprise, her confusion apparent despite the shadow that encases us.

Barely in control of my breathing, I pant, desperate for prurient release. "In case you didn't know," I say on a quick exhale, stroking my cock. "The others are playing the game tonight for points. *I'm* playing to get what I want. Now lie back and open your mouth for me."

Her gaze remains fixed on mine.

"Now," I bark. I'm so close to orgasm.

She does as instructed, her naked body once again sprawled before me. I step out of my fallen shorts, stand over her, and straddle her beautiful body as I hold my cock above her chest. I continue tugging with rapid strokes, as I have a thousand times in the past.

Her look of surprise morphs into one of a sly little minx, her lips quirked in a smile and her body patiently waiting for my seed as she props herself up on her elbows.

My orgasm teases its way to full eruption with each pass of my hand, my groans giving way to a carnality outmatched by past sexual endeavors.

When she parts her lips, ready and eager to catch my ejaculate from afar, I erupt with an intensity far beyond my imagination. I come on her naked body—in and around her open mouth, coating her chest and neck. She swallows what does make it into her mouth and licks her lips without breaking eye contact. The torrent of lust she bestows upon me damn near tears me in two.

As my climax ebbs, she sits upright and takes my erection into her mouth. She sucks—no, *pulls*—the last of my cum from inside me, swallowing it deep as her moans reverberate against my tender flesh.

My cum drips down her chest as she pulls away and lies back on the gravel with an arm behind her head. She runs her fingers through my mess, dragging it over her nipples in little concentric circles.

Goddamn, I want to fuck this woman.

But the night is far from over.

Undoubtedly, our hour in the maze is up, or about to be. It's only a matter of time before they send people in for us.

And we still have to find our way out.

"You know," she says, interrupting my thoughts. "It's a good thing you're cute." She pauses as she regards me with a teasing squint, the finger on her nipple falling still. "Because you have *terrible* aim."

I barely notice her cocky grin before I've hoisted her to her feet with a firm pull at her elbow. "Not when it counts," I growl, and capture her mouth in an unbidden, punishing kiss. She presses her body against mine with an insatiable need, the cum on her breasts painting my skin as I devour her. The lingering musk on her lips sends my mind spiraling, and I'm overcome with the desire to lick it off until her natural flavor returns.

With the slyness of a little brat, she bites my lower lip, holding it captive in her teeth. I chuckle despite myself and allow her to tug for as long as it pleases her. A soft, dulcet moan flows between us as she releases me from the slow drag of her suckling, pursed lips.

The chill of the night air disappears as I fall like a comet—fervid, unstoppable, and quicker than the blink of an eye—into the starlight that dances in her eyes. Tremulous yet surprisingly calm from the warmth of her form against mine, I search them for the storm clouds that haunted me upon our first encounter. But, much to my relief, they possess the vivacity of a meteor shower and the clouds are nowhere in sight. I'm transfixed by them—speechless, breathless, weightless—daring to transform this hedge maze into my grave as I beg the universe to leave me here forever.

"All you alright?" she asks with a soft smile, caressing the nape of my neck.

A slight nod is all I can muster.

She dots the tip of my nose with a single kiss and nestles herself against my chest, my heart taking flight as our naked flesh presses against one another. For several moments we bask in the stillness of our embrace.

When a shiver rakes through her, I'm pulled from my euphoria, now aware of how cold she must be at this late hour.

"I don't mean to be a buzzkill," I whisper, my chin resting on the crown of her head, "but we have to tell David and Jenna about Ashton."

Her smile fades in an instant, and she takes a small step away from me.

"When they see this," I gesture to my face, "and Ashton's face, they'll wonder what happened."

Her shoulders slump as she sinks into herself. It's almost enough to make me regret hitting that piece of shit in the first place.

Almost.

She shakes her head. "We can't tell them. It would crush Jenna. This whole night is so important to her..." She looks away, falling silent for a long moment. "She'd be devastated. I don't know how well she knows Ashton, but I can see her blaming David for not knowing what kinds of friends he keeps. The whole thing would be such a mess." She runs a hand through her tousled hair, her ponytail hanging loose and crooked.

"But if Jenna finds out the truth from someone other than you, imagine how much more devastated she would be."

"I know." She releases a heavy sigh. "I will tell her, James. You're absolutely right. Just give me until after the wedding. I can't bring myself to spoil anything before then. She deserves to enjoy this time. I truly think she'll understand why I didn't say anything tonight. She's always been understanding when I don't feel comfortable explaining..." She trails off, attention fixed on her hands as she twists them around each other.

My stomach is as knotted as her fingers, the curiosity biting at my insides like a rabid dog. But I concede. It's the least I can do for her. With a tender voice, I reply, "All right, Wats. Maybe you're right." And, as I instructed Keith earlier, I tell her, "When the time comes, just follow my lead, okay?"

Her face relaxes, a subtle glint of starlight still illuminating her eyes. Perhaps she's fighting back tears. Or maybe it's from a newfound sense of relief, knowing I'll look out for her. I hope it's the latter. Because the overwhelming desire to protect her has, in an instant, become my new truth. Like an early autumn tropical storm tearing through my mind, my judgment, my heart and soul alike, all sense of a life in which I'm not protecting this woman, vanishes in the blink of an eye.

Perhaps I have Ashton to thank for that.

Fuck if I'll ever thank that asshole for anything.

But it doesn't make my feelings any less real. Evident by my rapid heartbeat and restless desire to pull her to the ground and take her in every way our bodies crave. She has, undoubtedly, transformed my sense of self into something altogether new, something I was unaware I even needed.

Something that must be protected at all costs.

I grab my balled-up T-shirt and clean her up as she fixates on my neck. Once every article of clothing is accounted for, we stumble in the darkness as we dress.

"Come on." I extend my hand.

She takes it without question, and together, we make our way back into the thick of the maze—ensconced in moonlight and a myriad of shadows.

Chapter 10

Evie

James leads me away from the dead end, my little corner of heaven. For the first time since entering the labyrinth, my nerves are quelled, and my trepidation has subsided. Being reunited with him leaves me feeling secure and reassured. Safe.

With each twist and turn and dead end we encounter, my mind is surprisingly at ease. I'll stay here forever, as long as I'm with him.

After what feels like an eternity of backtracking and winding our way in and out of hedgerows, each identical to the last, James exclaims on an exaggerated exhale, "Finally. We made it." The wrought-iron archway is straight ahead. Holding my hand with one and carrying his crumpled, soiled shirt in the other, he pulls me toward it, a new burst of energy consuming us, and I can't help but laugh.

As we emerge from the maze, we're greeted by all the teams with a brief applause and obnoxious cheers.

Jenna hurries over, giving James a dramatic once-over as she surveys his shirtless figure. "Well, well, now I know what kept you two," she teases, making me go hot all over.

"What can I say? When the mood strikes…" I shrug at Jenna.

She homes in on James, who give my hand a gentle squeeze when she grips his chin and turns his face for a closer look at the gash across his cheek. "Okay, now I really need to know what the hell happened in there. Ashton is like a brick wall, telling me to 'just ask Prince Charming.' What happened? Why do you both look like the maze chewed you up and spat you back out?" Her hands are planted on her hips.

James and Keith exchange nervous glances, making it apparent that he knows at least some details about what transpired, and my stomach performs a nervous flip.

"You did tell us to protect our partner's flags by any means necessary," James remarks. "Ashton came for Evie's flags. And let's be honest, he has a rather punchable face, so it was merely an opportunity I couldn't pass up."

"Man, fuck you," he barks, taking an aggressive step in James's direction.

David reacts, stepping in front of him and extending a hand toward his chest. "Whoa, enough. What in the hell is going on?"

"This guy's a fucking prick, that's what," Ashton sneers, his eyes narrowing.

"If you don't like the rules of the game, then don't play, asshole," James taunts, striding toward them and pointing a finger in his direction.

Heather steps closer to Ashton's side. "What were you thinking, James? You had no right—"

"Maybe Ashton had it coming. You ever think of that?" Keith interjects, glaring at Heather, his arms folded across his chest in silent reproof. Steph eyes him, confused.

Heather sneers, her lips curled in disgust. "How would you know? Were you there? If so, why didn't you stop—"

"Enough, all of you," David commands. "To be fair, James, we didn't exactly give you the go-ahead to punch the other players to protect your partner's flags. But Ashton, you got your licks in too, so can we just chalk this up to alcohol and misunderstanding and shake on it already?"

Neither James nor Ashton moves. They only hold each other's stare like wolves baring teeth amid their unquenchable thirst for blood.

"Come on, please. It's just a game, and it was a stupid thing to fight over. James and I forfeited anyway, so what does it matter?" I fix my gaze on Ashton despite my desire to look anywhere else. If he backs down, then maybe James will too. And I need Ashton to know that I have no intention of bringing up what really happened in the maze tonight.

He takes a step back, his body relaxing as he slinks alongside Heather. I loop my arm around James's and pull him toward me.

"We're not leaving here until you shake on it. I'm serious." David's tone is gruff as he runs an irritated hand over his beard. "The night isn't over yet. I need you all to get your shit together."

James makes the first move, taking a step in Ashton's direction with a calm demeanor. Ashton remains planted in place, but when he exchanges glances with David, he exhales heavily and steps toward James.

After several awkward seconds, he takes James's outstretched hand, and the two of them shake as a proclamation of peace.

The tension among the group dissolves as James rejoins me. Yet, the residual awkwardness in the air keeps us all from speaking.

After a long, uncomfortable moment, Jenna claps, forcing us away from the unpleasant silence. Turning to my partner and me, she grins and says, "It should come as no surprise that you lost this round big-time. On top of your admitted forfeit, you don't even have your belts on anymore." Her focus drops to our waists. "But... something tells me that you don't mind so much." Her smile turns impish. She's enjoying this way too much. But it's Jenna. She adores teasing. It's like oxygen to her.

"Who did win?" I ask, ignoring her banter.

"Oh, Steph and Keith, by a long shot," Jenna replies.

"Good for them," James says with utmost sincerity.

As a group, we leave the hedge maze and follow our hosts back toward the manor.

When the path levels out closer to the gardens and we're no longer single-file, I wrap an arm around James's waist and pull myself close. I graze his bottom, brushing against something in his back pocket. We pause on the path, and he reaches behind him to remove the object. It's a red bandana. One from my belt, no doubt.

"A souvenir?" I joke.

"Not exactly." He laughs, running a hand through his disheveled waves. "It's for later."

"Later?"

He eyes the rest of the group, who have gone on ahead without us, and waits for them to gain some distance. He then grabs my wrists and holds them together, draping the bandana over top of them.

"*For later*," he repeats, his smoldering gaze narrowing in on me.

My pulse accelerates to an alarming rate. The idea of being tied up and surrendering to James makes my body ignite with unspeakable desire.

"In case you didn't know, Evelyn," he explains, the use of my full name reiterating his intentions, "I *will* be fucking you senseless before the night is through."

Umm...okay. Where am I? Who am I? What's my name again?

My panties are MIA, stuffed into one of James's pockets—now *that* is likely a souvenir—so I have very little way of hiding the intensity of my body's carnal demands as he torments me with his words.

He returns the bandana to his pocket, holding my gaze, waiting for me to respond. But for all the sensations that are unfurling down below, my mind is devoid of words. Other than *um, yes please*—which would sound ridiculous out loud.

"Have I made Miss Evelyn speechless?" he jests, adding, "Hopefully in a good way."

I give him a crooked smile, words flooding back into my

consciousness. "Clean bill of health?" I ask, thankful that my embarrassment is obscured by the darkness.

He leans away from me and releases a hearty laugh at my awkward yet necessary question. "Sure thing, Wats. You?"

"Absolutely." I extend my hand. His knuckles are starting to swell, but his palm is rough and warm and at home against mine as we shake on the trust of our affirmations.

⚜

UPON OUR RETURN TO THE MANOR, JENNA ANNOUNCES A one-hour interlude to give us a chance to "freshen up, grab some drinks, eat something, relax..."

James and I head upstairs to shower in our respective rooms, agreeing to recommence downstairs in a half hour. I have just enough time to wash James's spunk off me, change into a pair of jeans shorts and a form-fitting heather-gray shirt, go barefoot under Jenna's advisement, apply a basic amount of makeup, and throw my hair up into a messy bun before making my way downstairs.

My stomach growls with voracious irritation. Luckily, James is camped out near a replenished buffet table in the ballroom with most of the other wedding party members.

Ashton stands off to the side, away from the table, engaged in a conversation with Heather. As I cross the room, I notice early stages of swelling around his eye and a split across his nose, which Heather caresses as he speaks. The mere sight of him turns my stomach to stone. Just the thought of the wedding next week concerns me. But I'll be damned if I'm going to allow anyone to ruin Jenna and David's big day. So I'll ignore his egregious actions and his inability to take no for an answer.

For now.

I inhale several bite-size goodies and an entire small plate of fruit. James is chowing down on a small mound of pineapple pieces he has piled on his plate. He sticks a fork in one and offers it to me. "Would you like some? Or do you only stick to historically forbidden fruit?"

"I mean, the more forbidden, the better, right?" I flirt. "But I never say no to pineapple." I bite the piece off his fork and savor its sweet juices.

Heavenly.

"Besides, pineapple makes your cum taste sweet," I inform him.

"Now that I *did* know. Why do you think I grabbed it all?" He nods at the large helping on his plate.

"Always thinking ahead," I reply, pointing to my temple.

His smile goes crooked, and a frisson of excitement pierces my belly.

"I like it, by the way." I nod at his shirt. "Led Zeppelin is one of my favorite bands." The cotton tee bears the famous Icarus image, white against black fabric.

"No kidding?" He pulls on the hem and examines it, as if reminding himself of what he's wearing.

"Yeah, my dad loved Zeppelin, Fleetwood Mac, The Rolling Stones...heck, even Johnny Cash, and of course, your favorite, Elvis." My heart blossoms with a delicate warmth at the memory of the escape room. And of my father. "They hold a soft spot in my heart, I guess."

"He had great taste," James replies.

"Do you have a favorite?" I ask, motioning to his shirt again.

"That's hard to say. You can never go wrong with 'Stairway.' And the first thirty seconds or so of—"

"'Good Times Bad Times'?" I cut in.

"Yes." His grin widens. "How did you—"

"Because the opening of that song is epic. Plain and simple."

His eyes bounce between mine in a comfortable silence.

"Is that your favorite, then?" I ask after several unspoken beats.

He shifts the plate to his other hand. "I don't think so. Not when there are so many other great choices. Honestly, I may have to go with 'Fool in the Rain.'"

"Aw, I love that one too," I coo. "It's painfully overlooked if you ask me."

He offers me another piece of pineapple, feeding it to me in a way that I could have made sexy if I wasn't starving.

Ashton shifts into my field of view, and I pivot to match, keeping my back to him as much as possible. James, on the other hand, shifts every so often to ensure he *is* facing him, never letting him out of his sight, I suppose.

It would provide the comfort it intends if it wasn't so distracting. Each shift of James's body only reminds me that Ashton is behind me somewhere.

I just want to forget about him.

Although the delectable pineapple and the way his Zeppelin shirt fits snugly around his muscular arms serve as lovely distractions, I'm anxious for the next game to begin. Because once they're over, I won't have to be in the same space as Ashton anymore.

And I can finally sink my teeth into James.

Now there's a distraction I can get behind. The thought sends a throbbing heat between my legs, thumping to an erotic beat and hungry to be pounded into submission.

James reaches for another piece of pineapple, picking it up with his fingers this time.

"Oh, wait." I touch his arm as he brings the fruit to his lips. "You don't want to eat that one."

He pauses, his mouth agape. "What? Why not?"

"Because I already licked it," I tease, trying to maintain an even tone.

Confusion is cemented across his face. "Huh?"

"I licked it," I repeat. "I grabbed it from your plate and licked it when you weren't looking," I lie. "Which means it's *mine* now, right?"

His hand is still frozen midway to his mouth.

A rolling boil of laughter threatens to burst forth from my lying lips. "Isn't that how it works? Did you claim things like that when you were a kid? If you licked it, that meant it was yours." I cock my head to the side and trail a visual path from his face to his groin. My gaze remains fixated on his crotch, and my coy smile broadens even wider when it twitches inside his pants.

The piece of fruit falls from his grip. It misses the plate entirely, and he fumbles to catch it, but instead, he drops the entire plate. The *crash* echoes throughout the vast room, and all conversations come to an abrupt halt as everyone stares at us.

James is frozen, flushed, and looking at the floor in horror.

Stifling a laugh, I grab a stack of napkins from the buffet table and kneel to wipe up the mess. He falls to his knees beside me.

As we push the food into a pile, I peek up at him. "My, my, my, Mr. Pierce. I do believe you're blushing."

"You are *so* gonna get it," he replies, a grin spreading across his crimson cheeks as he pushes the mess around. "And besides, Wats, you know that works both ways, right?"

"What does?" I ask, already knowing the answer but wanting to hear the salacious words from his lips.

"I've licked you too. Which means she's also mine." He nods toward the eager space between my legs, and it clenches in response.

My mind reels with three tantalizing words replaying on a loop to the point of dizziness:

Licked.

Claimed.

His.

I can flirt with him all night. For a moment, I think I may be granted the opportunity. But as I start to forget where I am and why, bathing in the seduction of my partner's gaze between swipes along the mucked floor, Jenna enters the ballroom and makes a beeline straight for us.

"Oh, leave that," she cries.

We ignore her and pile the pieces on James's plate.

"Seriously, don't worry about it. We'll have it cleaned up," she says.

"We don't mind, Jen," he says. "It's almost picked up anyway."

We scoop up the remaining pieces of fruit, and I wipe the floor as Jenna takes the plate from us.

Once back on our feet, James grabs me by my lower back and pulls me close, pressing his forehead to mine. My heart flutters with the anticipation of a kiss. But when his lips find mine, no amount of anticipation could prepare me for the erratic way the butterflies in my stomach flit about. The kiss is brief, but it's everything; everything I want and need—not just tonight, but every night.

When Jenna reenters the ballroom, she motions for everyone to gather around with an exaggerated wave of her arms. "Now that we're all refreshed, rehydrated, relaxed...how about we begin our final round?" she asks with a peaked voice. "Follow me."

As we gather in the foyer, we arrange ourselves in a semicircle around Jenna and David as they instruct us on the final round.

"For the night's fifth and final round," David begins, "everyone will participate in a classic game. One that's familiar to all of us and has the simplest rules imaginable. A game of hide and seek."

The murmurs that ripple throughout the group are a mix of excited and anxious. The manor is enormous, so seeking one another out within its walls is daunting at best. But the rules are simple, and it will certainly be anyone's game this time. No strategy to help us win, no stamina required to outrun our opponents. Simply a child's game of hide and seek.

How hard can it be?

"Teams will be split up," Jenna states. "The ladies will come with me, and they will be hidden somewhere inside the manor. Guys, your task is as simple as being the first to find your partner. When you find her, the two of you will return to this very spot and ring the bell like before, and the points will be awarded based on the order in which the teams complete the round."

James gives me an assured look.

"The ladies will not be choosing their own hiding spots. They will be hidden in predetermined locations. You'll have one hour to find them once we say go." She pauses as she skims the cluster of onlooking faces. "And if you find someone who is *not* your partner, you cannot give away her location. I don't see why you would since that would only give your opponent an advantage. So leave her there and only seek out your own partner."

David chimes in. "The only areas that are off limits are the guest quarters upstairs. Everywhere else is fair game."

Being hidden in such a place is unsettling. But something about knowing it'll only be James looking for me this time rouses an excitement I can't wait to explore.

"So ladies, if you'll all follow me." Jenna waves a hand. "And guys, you'll follow David out onto the front porch."

I step away from James, my body cooling when his arm slips from around my hips. "Good luck," I whisper, then turn to join the other girls as they gather around Jenna.

But I don't make it more than a step before James grabs my arm, pulls me toward him, and captures my mouth in a firm, ravenous kiss. Heat radiates from my skin, my nerves blinking alive.

He kisses me with unprecedented urgency, as if there is a chance he may never see me again. It's ridiculous; this is only a game, after all. But the desire that tumbles inside me obscures all logic, and I return his kisses with brash exuberance.

Everyone must be staring, but I don't care. Or maybe they're all gone and we're the only ones left in the foyer. It's impossible to tell; all sounds around me fade into a dismissible white noise. The world has fallen into bright specks of light akin to fireflies dancing at dusk.

When he pulls away, his hands cupping behind my ears with a

delicate touch, he locks on to me and asks, "You remember what I said to you in the maze, don't you?"

I quirk a brow with uncertainty.

"I'll always find you, Evie," he whispers. "Just as your eyes always manage to find the starlight, I will always find you. Now go, let them try and hide you from me. We'll be reunited before you know it." His aplomb makes white hot coils of arousal tighten inside me.

I respond with a full-lipped kiss to his cheek. "I'll see you soon."

He teases a smile and replies, "Ready or not, here I come."

I back away with a grin and flushed skin and turn toward Jenna and the girls, who are, in fact, waiting for me and, yep, they're staring. Any other time, any other weekend, I would have been embarrassed. But here, now, with him, I'm anything but. Because the reward of being with James, in his arms, his lips on mine, his erection digging into my hip, far outweighs the risk of what others may think.

We're supposed to be existing in a judgment-free zone anyway.

Jenna's giddy, and she's on the verge of one of her famous squeals. But the playful side-eye I shoot in her direction forces her silence.

In the kitchen—oddly modern and bright compared to the rest of the manor—I perch myself against the beautiful marble island, waiting for further instructions.

One after the other, staff members enter the kitchen bearing handcuffs made of thick red rope, and multiple strips of black fabric bands. The women stir, their discomfort obvious as whispers dance through the group.

"You'll each be given an escort to your designated hiding spot." Jenna motions to the line of staff members behind her. "Once there, the staff member will bind your hands, feet, and mouths, and then blindfold you."

"You can't be serious," Heather protests, her mouth slack.

"Yeah, that's *insane*," Steph agrees.

Ami's face is pinched. "No way am I doing that."

My nerves are too frayed for me to speak.

"I know it seems scary. But I'm telling you, the hint of fear will lead to a rush of adrenaline you can only imagine once you're found. There's a reason we chose this as the last game. We want you to ride that adrenaline high with your partner any way you see fit once the games are over."

"They're trying every possible avenue to get us all laid," Lacey laughs.

"Hey, I'm not complaining. Keith is hot," Steph remarks, fanning herself with her hand.

Jenna grabs a rope handcuff from a staff member, a straitlaced woman with her hair in a tight bun and a no-nonsense look on her face—the woman I ran into upstairs at the start of the evening.

"Would it make you feel better to see how these work?" Jenna presents the red cuffs for all of us to see. "You can remove these yourself if you need to by pulling your hands apart, like so." She inserts her wrists into each loop.

The lady with the bun steps forward and tightens them at the two cinch points in the center.

She holds her bound wrists up, then separates them with a quick yank. The loops widen, and she removes her wrists with ease. "Once they're off, you can easily remove all other restraints. We'll be using these satin bands to bind your feet and to cover your mouths. And then we have blindfolds for your eyes that slip over the top of your head."

The impenetrable silence is riddled with uncertainty. As nervous as I am that this round may bring about fears I haven't had to deal with in years, the prospect of being bound and discovered by James consumes me with an arousal I never would have expected.

Once again, the line between the phobia that has plagued me my entire life is blurred with that of pure eroticism. But how can being trapped and unable to escape—a fear that, in the past, has led to paralytic fits of terror—suddenly become the source of unshakable desire?

The longer Jenna explains the process, the more tantalizing it feels. The wave of ecstasy in my belly is proof enough. I have never been voluntarily robbed of so many senses all at once, as well as my ability to *move*. But James untying my restraints, frantic as he rescues me from my temporary imprisonment and soothing me with his velvety voice? Even scooping me into his arms and carrying me off to finally devour my begging flesh? The thought nearly knocks me off balance and sends me straight to my knees.

Jenna is right. This could very well lead to an erotic conclusion to the games.

The staff members join us at her request.

A lanky young man with a trimmed black beard and long black hair pulled back in a low ponytail stands beside me. He's dressed like the other staff members, in a black and white suit with a white bow tie—a chic butler-style outfit that he pulls off nicely.

As the other ladies leave the kitchen with their escorts, mine looks at me and says, "We'll wait here, miss, for the others to clear out."

"Why?"

"Because your hiding place is just over here." He points to the rear entrance on the kitchen's opposite side. With a hand on my elbow and a hint of displeasure that causes his nostrils to flare, the man escorts me out of the kitchen and toward my hiding spot.

Inside the narrow hallway, I spy two doors.

My escort opens the one on the right and reveals a large yet dark, empty walk-in closet. An old broom cupboard, no doubt.

"No way," I say, a frisson of fear rippling through me.

He reaches in and pulls a white string hanging from the ceiling. A single bulb illuminates the space with a cone of golden light.

It appears smaller lit up than it did in the dark. The only thing I can see now is an empty metal shelf unit at the far end. The rest is empty. The floors are the same hardwood as the hallway outside, dark and polished clean.

The man breaks the silence. "All hiding places have been thoroughly cleaned in anticipation of the arrival of tonight's guests."

"Oh, it's not that," I reply, still peering into the closet.

"You're afraid of the dark then?"

"Well, not exactly." I release an exhausted sigh. "It's kind of hard to explain."

And I'd rather not.

He hesitates for a beat. "I know it's none of my business, miss, but my father once told me that facing your fears and conquering them is the closest you'll get to being truly invincible. Our weaknesses *are* what lead to our own demise, after all..." He trails off, looking away as I turn to meet his gaze. "For what it's worth, anyway."

"No, you're right," I whisper. "If only it were as easy as it sounds."

"Yes. But it's only for an hour, tops. Plus, there are a dozen people here who know your whereabouts. You'll be fine."

"Will you promise me one thing?" I ask, fixing my gaze on him. "Just please promise me you won't lock me in there." I nod toward the closet.

His eyes widen and his nostrils flare. "Of course not. We won't lock anyone up *anywhere*. This manor is filled with priceless antiquities, and we have worked far too hard to preserve its history and integrity to risk having guests break open doors and cabinets and who knows what else, all for the sake of a silly game."

I'm not sure how, but it seems I've offended him, and it makes me fall silent.

After a long stretch of silence, he asks, "Shall I, then?" He motions with the items still in his hands while maintaining his wooden composure.

I nod, then, with a deep breath, I step into the closet.

"Down on the ground, please," he commands.

I comply, sitting on the floor with my legs outstretched. A small shudder radiates through me as my body reacts to the closet's chill.

He binds my legs first, and I hold back a slight gasp when he yanks the final knot tight against my bare ankles. "Hands behind your back."

I reach both hands behind me, and he gathers my wrists together, slipping the cuffs around each one. In a cautionary measure, I pull my wrists apart to see if they will loosen. Much to my relief, the cuff holes widen, and the entire thing nearly falls off my hands.

"Already eager to be removed from your restraints," he comments, his voice sharp. He cinches the cuffs tight around my wrists again—almost punishingly—and I can't hold back the wince that crinkles my face at the discomfort.

Or the fear that tingles the nape of my neck.

He shifts behind me.

"Open up," he orders, holding the silk headband. His use of the word *miss* is long gone.

He presses the silk material hard against my parted lips and fastens a knot that digs into the back of my head. It isn't painful. At least not yet.

"Comfy?" he asks, his professional demeanor fading away while he admires his handiwork.

I shrug. As comfy as I can be, considering.

From the empty shelf unit off to my right, tucked farther into the closet's dark recesses, he grabs the red satin blindfold with a black lace overlay. It's beautiful—classy, in a way. But I'm not afforded the opportunity to admire it beyond a simple glance before the man places it over my eyes and secures it behind my head.

The darkness is quick and unforgiving. This is not the first time I've ever been blindfolded. Hell, it's not the first time I've been blindfolded tonight. But huddled in the small encapsulating space in which I'm imprisoned is the closest I've come in a very long time to receiving a visit from my inner demons.

Dread grips me low in my gut and permeates every fiber of my being. Before this round is over, I fear my demons will force me into a witching-hour dance, undoubtedly performed over my father's grave. The rhythm of my racing heart will serve as the beat, and the clasps of my twirling bodice will glisten in the moonlight as they spin me round and round. The panic of being lost forever in that endless night will consume me until I'm nothing but a shell of my former self.

My nerves coil into a tangled mess of fear and adrenaline as the ponytailed man turns out the light with a noisy pull on the string and closes the door behind him. The sliver of light below my blindfold is snuffed out, and the darkness—that familiar, terrifying darkness—envelops me just as it did all those years ago.

I shift against my restraints, failing to find a comfortable position. Eventually, I give up my quest and lean my head against the wall and wiggle my ankles to encourage blood flow to my feet.

In an attempt to distract myself, I think of James and which room he might be in right now. Is he at the desk in the study? That beautiful mahogany desk; ornate, well built, sturdy. I imagine him bending me over it, yanking my shorts and panties off, and smacking me hard on each ass cheek. The way they'd turn a rosy red and how he would bend down to kiss them better. I can almost feel him thrusting a finger into my eager void, leaning low to moan in my ear, calling me his "good little girl," then spreading my cheeks to thrust his cock deep inside me. The papers soaring to the ground, the desk shifting across the floor with each aggressive thrust. James yanking my hair with passion and anger, pulling me up to meet him as he fucks my ass hard and deep. I relish the thoughts of pain mixed with the pleasure; the unforgiving nature of a man taking what he wants until I come apart at the seams.

A distinct wetness pools between my legs and my clit pulsates to the same beat as my fearful heart. I want nothing more than to remove my cuffs and rub one out right here, right now.

Tipping forward and to the side, I edge away from the wall so I can shimmy out of the rope cuffs. I want to touch myself to thoughts of James and his strong, calloused hands, his aggressive lips, and *holy shit*, that tongue.

I pull my wrists apart to loosen the cinch points.

But the restraints don't budge.

What the fuck? My throat tightens in an instant.

The rope burns my flesh as I yank harder, forcing a wince from behind my gag, which is now a soaked mess rubbing the corners of my mouth raw.

A force a deep inhale through my nose. *This is only temporary*, I repeat to myself. In less than an hour, you'll be out of here, and back in James's arms.

As I pull against the cuffs again, footsteps—faint yet distinct—echo in the distance. Finally, the guys are making their way toward the back half of the manor.

Craning my neck, I listen for voices, anything indicating that James may be nearby. But instead, all I hear is a single set of footsteps drawing nearer.

And they're much too light-footed to be James.

Perhaps it's the darkness playing tricks on me? Maybe it *is* James.

Or maybe it's my imagination. Maybe I'm making it all up, like my crazy papa. Or maybe the monsters are real after all, as he always claimed. And maybe they've finally found me...

The demons bow low at the waist, perched on my father's grave, asking me for a dance.

With each plodding step in the hall, my trembling intensifies. Despite the blindfold, I shut my eyes and beg for them to disappear —for my demons to cease their evil requests.

Ragged gasps press against my gag as my heart nearly bursts from its bony cage.

Louder the footsteps grow as tears brim in the corners of my eyes and soak into the blindfold. I prepare for the scream billowing in my chest—the one for my father, which I haven't felt in years.

Papa's name dangles from the tip of my tongue as the closet door whips open with a high-pitched *creak*. A small band of light appears at the bottom of my blindfold.

James?

I can't call out to him. I can't even move.

With bated breath, I wait for the man to rush inside. For hands to tear my blindfold off and pull the gag from my mouth.

But there are no sounds at all.

I groan in a failed attempt to speak.

Is he just standing there?

There's a faint sound of breathing.

Deep.

Calm.

Unhurried.

It's not James. It can't be.

After several silent moments, the closet door creaks closed, enshrouding me in darkness all over again.

But the sound that follows is one I've avoided since I was a child.

One my demons feast upon.

And tonight, they're having their fill.

The sound of the closet door lock engaging with a sickening *click*.

Trapping me inside.

CHAPTER 11
JAMES

"I hope you all have been paying attention to your surroundings since you arrived," David announces once we're all gathered on the front porch. "It will come in handy this round."

The air is cooler than it was when we returned to the manor an hour ago. Or maybe being surrounded by hedges made it feel warmer. Honestly, I don't give a shit about what the night air feels like while in Evie's presence. The woman is a distraction of the best kind.

Where are they taking her? How long will she be left alone before I find her? I promised I would find her. Before the clock runs out; before we have to forfeit the round and the staff have to recover her.

I will never stand for that.

She's *mine* to find.

Mine to keep.

"As a reminder, the guest quarters upstairs are off limits, but everywhere else is fair game. The ladies are not hidden where you cannot get to them. Meaning, they are not behind locked doors or inside locked cabinets or secret passageways—"

Reese releases a sharp gasp of intrigue. "Wait, are there actually secret passageways inside the manor?"

"There are. But we've only got an hour to work with, so we don't expect you to locate them...or do we...?" David teases with an ominous smirk.

A hum of intrigue spreads through the group. "So please, do not break into anything to gain access. If it's locked, it stays that way. Capisce?"

"Got it," Mark replies as the rest of us nod in agreement.

"When the ladies are hidden, we'll return to the foyer."

The manor's enormity could make this round the most daunting of them all, so simple in concept yet endless in its play. Fortunately, my girl is deliciously tall. There are only so many places they can hide her.

My balls clench at the thought of those incredible legs. Soon they'll be wrapped around me, forced apart at the peak to accommodate my insatiable hunger.

I move behind the others in a desperate attempt to hide the boner I can't seem to control tonight. By the time David is given the okay by a staff member who makes it even more dramatic by whispering it in his ear, my hard-on has dissipated, and I'm ready to take on game night's final round.

"It sounds like everyone is hidden," he announces once the staff member has stepped back. "Let's head in."

We shuffle back inside, the crickets' songs fading as we leave them behind in their nightly splendor.

"On my count, you'll begin your search." David raises his hand above his head. "In three...two...one. *Go.*" He whips his arm down like a tomahawk, and we take off in all directions. However, my attention shifts to Ashton, who beelines for the library.

I'm hot on his heels.

He makes his way past the velvet couch and oak coffee table, straight to the bookshelf adjacent to the door. He skims the books, unaware that he has company as I creep up behind him. When I grab him by the collar of his shirt, a startled cry escapes him.

And another when I shove him face first into the wall of books.

He whips around to face me.

"What the fuck, man?" he barks.

"Listen, asshole. You and I are going to do this last round together, you hear me?"

His face contorts as he yanks himself out of my grasp, knocking my arm away and readjusting his shirt.

"What for?"

"Because there's no way in hell I'll risk you coming across Evie before I do. If I even think about what you might do if you find her first, I'll end up fucking killing you out of spite. So here's what's going to happen. Where I go, you go. Understand?"

"Screw off," he bites, turning back to the books. I allow it without so much as a word. He's looking for something. Maybe it'll benefit both of us.

Ashton reaches for the copy of *Paradise Lost* submerged among the sea of books. He pulls it toward him, and a loud *clank* sounds from somewhere behind the bookcase. A pivot point appears in the bookshelf's frame as he pulls it open and swings it wide like a heavy door, revealing a dark passageway on the other side.

"What the fuck? How did you know this passage was here?"

He gives me a condescending sneer. "This was my escape room. Heather and I discovered it by accident. When we opened it, a man came in and told us it wasn't part of the escape room and to leave it shut."

"Why would they hide one of the girls there?" I ask, taken aback by how dark the narrow passage is and plagued with concern that Evie may, in fact, be hidden in there. "David said he didn't expect anyone to find these."

"Because, genius, they know now that at least some of us are aware of its existence. I told Keith about it too. If someone *is* hidden back there, it'll probably be Steph or Heather since we're the only players who know about it. Why do you think I came straight to the library?"

"Okay. How are we going to find our way through this thing? It's pitch black." I crane my neck, taking in the musty space from the safety of the doorway. A cone of light from the library illuminates the concrete floor and a line of unlit sconces on the walls.

"*We* are not going to do anything." Ashton's voice echoes between the narrow walls. "I'm going in to find Heather. You can fuck right off."

"Maybe you didn't hear me the first time, but I'm not letting you out of my sight. Now help me find a damn light switch or something."

We stick our heads into the passage, neither of us trusting the other to enter first. I run my hand along the nearest wall but am met with only the rough texture of aged brick. Ashton does a half-assed search of the opposite wall from the doorway.

"It'll be easier to find the light switch if you actually *go in*," I growl, grabbing him by his arm and shoving him into the passageway. He stumbles and lands against the opposite wall with a dull *thud*.

"Such a dick," he mumbles, then turns away from me and runs his hand along the wall.

I step in after him, the open door providing enough light for our eyes to adjust. I run my hand along the dark wall, the dampness sending a chill through my arm. It's cold—*too* cold. Hopefully none of the girls are hidden in here.

My hand bumps the doorframe. A second later, it's met with some sort of plate.

A switch.

With a flip, the sconces illuminate the passage in a soft, warm glow. The hallway spans into eternity, the far end enveloped in darkness despite the new source of light.

"Ladies first," I tell him, tipping my head toward the black abyss.

He flips me his middle finger and proceeds.

Our steps echo against the concrete as we walk single file toward the unknown. Drops of water plink into small pools in the distance, and the farther we get, the mustier the smell grows.

I give the doorway a glance over my shoulder, surprised to see that the cone of light from the library is now merely a sliver.

"There," Ashton calls, his voice booming up and down the hall and startling the shit out of me.

I see it too. My pace quickens to match his.

We come to an abrupt stop in front of a crumpled shape on the floor.

A woman, blindfolded and bound, sitting on a blanket. She's curled up in a ball with her knees drawn up to her chest, her blond hair protruding out from under her blindfold strap.

Steph.

"What the fuck?" I curse. "They're blindfolded and tied up?" A pit forms in my bowels. Knowing that Evie is compromised in such away, and alone, makes me as nauseous as it does enraged.

"David and Jenna are twisted," Ashton comments with a chuckle. "But you have to admit, it's hot."

"What the fuck is wrong with you?" What I'd give to beat him to a bloody pulp and repress the sickness invading my gut.

Steph moans against her gag, alert and anxious. I crouch in front of her and remove her blindfold.

"What are you doing?" Ashton sneers.

"We can't just leave her like this."

"She's not our partner. She's Keith's problem."

"How in the hell will he find her if he doesn't know about the secret passage?" My pulse ricochets against my temples.

"He knows about it, dumbass. Remember, I told him after the escape room round was over?"

"But did you tell him how to find it? How to get in?"

"Well...no."

"God, you really are an idiot," I reply with an exasperated sigh.

I pull her gag away from her mouth, and a slight smile emerges as she takes in a deep breath.

"Are you okay?" I ask.

"Yes. But it's cold in here." She's dressed in a yellow tank top and jean shorts. The blanket beneath her is clearly meant to provide comfort against the cold concrete. I debate removing it to wrap around her but figure it's better off between her and the floor.

"Give her your shirt," I order Ashton.

"Why the hell—"

"Just do it," I shout, sick of his shit and making Steph jump in surprise.

With an exaggerated sigh, he doffs the twill button-up shirt he's wearing over his T-shirt.

He drapes it over Steph's shoulders, and her shivers ease a bit. "Come on, we're wasting time," he gruffs.

"We should get you out of here," I tell her, ignoring Ashton's bullshit. I reach for the ties around her ankles, but she pulls her legs out of my reach. "No, don't. If you free me, then we'll lose this round."

"Steph, I can't just walk away and leave you in this miserable place." I examine the ceiling in the low light.

"It's all right. Really. Go find your partners." There isn't even a smidgen of concern in her tone. "Besides," she says, "these rope cuff things are self-removable. I just have to pull my hands apart if I need to. I'd show you, but I don't think I'd be able to get them back on..."

A ripple of relief hits me knowing Evie can escape her restraints if necessary. But she's still blindfolded and bound and waiting for me to find her. It worries me in a way I could never have anticipated going into tonight's festivities. This partner of mine has crept her way into my heart and settled in nicely. But as concerned as I am for her, the very idea of this round of the games is also painfully arousing.

Ashton was right.

Dammit.

A vision of Evie comes to me, unbidden. Strawberry lips parted by a silk gag, her breathing heavy against the delicate fabric. Subtle red marks on her wrists from the way the rope restraints rub against her tender flesh. The red blindfold with sexy lace overlay is enough to make me want to tear down every wall of the manor just to find her and slay her body once and for all.

Where is she? Is she frightened? Is she screaming for me? Is she fighting against her restraints?

Don't worry, Wats. I said I would find you. And when I do, I will take you in every possible way. You'll scream my name, yearn for me, beg me to fulfill even your darkest desires. You'll plead, and you will receive. And I'll send you frolicking among the stars.

I secure Steph's blindfold as Ashton replaces her gag. Then I give her shoulder a reassuring touch before I turn my back to her.

Back at the entrance, I give Steph one final glance. Her small silhouette, balled up and waiting to be found by her partner, is unmistakable, despite the distance. Leaving her in here makes me queasy. It feels wrong in so many ways. But it's all part of the game, and no one said the games would be easy. We agreed to surrender ourselves to David and Jenna tonight. And I trust them not to steer us wrong.

Ashton reaches for the light switch, but I grab his hand before he can flood the room in darkness.

"Don't," I say in my sternest voice. "Leave it on."

He obliges, and after we've stepped back into the library, he closes the secret door, hiding her once again.

After a fruitless search behind the billowy curtains that hang along the far wall, we exit the library and make our way out into the foyer.

"Should we check upstairs?" Ashton asks.

"We haven't finished searching down here yet."

"You know, we'd cover a lot more ground if we split up," he sneers.

"You're stuck with me. Suck it up, princess."

He gives me the finger again, holding it close to my face, then points toward the billiard room. I ignore his antics in lieu of keeping up with him as he crosses the foyer. Keith emerges from the lounge to our right, a smile splitting his face when he sees us.

"No luck yet either, I see," he calls out. I shake my head. "There's something you need to know…" I can't stand the thought of Steph being stuck in that dank passage a moment longer. But Keith is a competitive guy; he'd hate to win unfairly.

His brown eyes flare with curiosity.

"I won't give it away, but"—I hook a thumb over my shoulder toward the library—"John Milton…The Garden of Eden."

He responds to my ambiguity with a look of confusion.

"Who's John Milton?" he asks.

"That's all I'm going to say. Find it in the library, and you'll find what you're looking for."

He gives me a nod of understanding, his brow relaxing. "Thanks, man. I owe you one."

"Hey, one last thing," I call as he takes off. "Have you seen Evie? You don't have to tell me where she is; I just want to know if she's somewhere on this floor."

He stops midstride and lets out a quiet sigh. "I've only searched the lounge, the parlor, and the study so far, and I didn't see her."

Adrenaline bubbles inside me as the grandfather clock ticks beyond the stairs.

"Okay. Thanks, Keith."

When I enter the billiard room, it's empty of players. I search behind the bar and open every cabinet, even the ones that are too small to house a human. "I'm Sexy and I Know It" earworms its way into my head as I pass the circle of chairs from tonight's striptease game and head over to the bank of windows.

I push open the first heavy curtain panel. Craggy tree branches resembling skeletonized fingers scrape against the window, dancing in the night breeze. The ominous sound sends a quiver to my tailbone.

The billiard room is a bust.

As I rush to the door, I dread the possibility that Evie is hidden inside a secret passageway I know nothing about.

Secret passageway.

Wait, where the hell is Ashton?

He must have slipped away while I was talking to Keith, and I've been too fixated on finding Evie to notice.

Fuck, fuck, *fuck*.

A vat of bile sloshes in my throat as I run into the foyer in a panic. I scan every room I pass, looking for signs of him. I poke my head into the lounge, the study, the ballroom, the dining room.

Nothing.

Footsteps thump on the grand staircase behind me, and I make a mad dash to see who it is. It's Mark, his arm around Ami, who's giddy and reveling in her newfound freedom. Before long, the hotel bell chimes, announcing their first-place victory.

It's the least of my worries.

I round the corner beyond the staircase and make my way to the kitchen.

Ashton's smug face appears as he meanders toward me.

"What the fuck?" I bark, enraged.

"You're not my keeper, asshole," he scoffs.

I reach him quickly and get in his face. "I'm really going to enjoy beating the living shit out of you after the wedding." I can practically smell his blood on my hands.

"Threaten me all you want. I'm the only one who knows where Evie is." With that, he races past me into the foyer and out of view.

My chest seizes up, locked in a vise grip.

He found her? If he laid even a hand on her, so help me God…

The urge to follow and beat him into an unrecognizable mess is hard to ignore. But instead, I pause, gripping the kitchen island and bowing low to steady my breath and level my head.

Finding Evie is my priority right now.

Pull yourself together. He wasn't out of your sight for long. If he already found her, then she must be close by.

The adrenaline coursing through me makes me damn near weightless as I whip open every cabinet, every pantry door.

Nothing.

Ding.

The bell in the main hall rings again.

Another victorious pair.

I exit the kitchen through the door on the opposite side, emerging into a hallway that feeds into a little bump-out room. The room is surrounded by windows on three sides and contains a small round cherry wood table. I bend low to peer underneath it, then check behind the flowing curtains and inside the hutch against the far wall.

The more futile my searching becomes, the more my composure wanes. Defeat grows inside me, destroying everything in its wake like a cancerous lump.

I hurry back into the narrow hallway and stop at a pair of doors along the wall opposite the kitchen. The one on the left is unlocked. It leads to a dark, narrow L-shaped staircase abandoned from another era. Unlike in the secret passage, the light switch in the stairway is easy to find right inside the door. With one quick flip, the space is illuminated with an ominous *crackle*, and I race to the top two steps at a time.

At the top of the stairs are two more doors.

At random, I throw open the one on the right. Inside is a stark, simple room, seemingly untouched in decades. There is a single twin bed against the far wall, made up with basic linens to include a thin, white lace throw. A wooden writing desk bearing an oil lamp with pink roses painted on the glass shade stands near the bed, a solid wooden chair tucked into the desk's void. Opposite the bed, next to a small wardrobe, is a simple wash basin, weathered and worn. There are no closets—only the simplest of furniture and not much else.

I fall to my knees and peek under the bed.

Nothing.

I throw open the wardrobe doors.

Empty.

The other door leads to an identical room that is displayed in a mirror image.

No sign of Evie there, either.

Ding.

A third victory.

Once I make it back down the cramped stairwell, I reach for the second door's handle.

Locked.

Fuck.

My head is spinning.

I hurry back into the kitchen and turn every which way, overwhelmed with anxiety. Knock it off, James. Stop. *Think.*

I'll never find her if I let my senses fail me.

Out in the main hall, the victorious teams are gathered, chatting to one another. Ashton and Heather are not among them. The thought of Ashton with Evie, even as I'm searching for her now, is too much to bear. I force it out of my mind and race to Keith and Steph.

"Hey," I call, hiding the torment in my voice, "I don't give a shit about winning this thing. I just need to find Evie, and I need to know where Ashton is. Have you seen either of them?"

Keith's eyes widen with concern, Ashton's twill shirt balled in his hand. "No, the last time I saw Ashton, he was with you."

"He went upstairs a few minutes ago," Mark chimes in, his hand on the small of Ami's back.

"But did any of you see Evie? I'll forfeit this game if need be. I just need your help."

They all shake their heads as fear clutches my heart.

"I owe you one, James. And I wish I could be more help," Steph says with a look of genuine sincerity. "We convened in the kitchen with Jenna for our instructions, but when we were escorted by the staff to our hiding places, Evie didn't come with us."

"What do you mean she didn't come with you?" A flitter of hope sends a tingle up into my neck.

She looks up at Keith then back at me. "I don't know what happened once I was escorted into the library. But I can tell you that she stayed behind in the kitchen with her escort, at least for a time."

As I take in a sharp breath, a new surge of energy whisks its way through my core. "Thanks. Really." I run back to the kitchen as beads of perspiration form along my brow line.

I push through the kitchen door and scan the space again. I swear I've searched every inch of the room. Even the old rooms at the top of the narrow stairs. Where else is there?

Other than that locked door in the hallway.

But David said that the girls would not be locked inside anywhere.

Changing my strategy, I go back to the breakfast nook and search for seams in the walls, trapdoors in the floor. If it's too obscure, Ashton would never have found it so fast.

Time is working against me, slipping through my fingers, same as Evie. In twenty-two minutes, the time will be up, and the staff will reveal the location of my beloved partner. But I won't stand for that. I told her *I* would find her, goddammit.

I run my hand along the hallway wall, inching my way back

toward the doors near the kitchen: one locked and the other leading to the creepy stairwell. I trace my fingers along the aged floral wallpaper, searching for seams that lead to something unseen.

As I work my way closer to the kitchen, a faint yet unmistakable tinning noise, like metal smacking against metal, whispers through the narrow space. I press my ear to the wall, but it does little to improve the sound.

When I knock on the plaster, the tinning noise sounds again, this time repeated in a rapid pattern.

I rush to the locked door and turn the knob and yank.

It doesn't budge.

I pound against the solid oak, hollering her name.

"Evie?"

Then a muffled sound—a stymied voice.

"*Evie.*" I grab the knob again, pulling and twisting with all the strength I can gather. But the fucking door won't open. I shove my shoulder into it, then pull on the handle and ram into it again. I repeat the same desperate actions over and over despite the pain lancing through my shoulder.

"Sir, what on earth—" a staff member calls out to me.

"There's someone in there. I can hear her." I ram into the door again, my shoulder screaming in response.

"Sir, please, stop. If the door is locked, there's no one inside, just as you were instructed—"

"Then where the hell is she?" I demand. "Get the key *now*."

"The time has not run out yet, and the game is still at play." Her firm voice grates on my nerves.

"I don't give a shit. Either open this door and show me what's inside, or I break it down."

She takes several steps back, cowering. "I'll get the key. Just please give me a minute." She hurries from the room.

I knock again.

"Evie?"

The tinning sound rings out again, quicker this time.

"Evie, I'm here. I'm waiting on a key, and then I'll get you out."

Silence.

People gather behind me, feet shuffling as they pile into the narrow hallway.

"What's going on?" Mark asks.

When I turn, I'm greeted by a sea of agape faces.

Jenna pushes through the crowd before I can answer. "James, what is it? What's going on?"

"There's someone locked in here. I think it's Evie," I reply, my focus locked on the door.

"That can't be. They weren't supposed to lock anyone in anywhere. And this isn't even Evie's hiding spot."

"Then where is she? Someone is in here, and it has to be either Evie or Heather. They're the only ones unaccounted for. So if she's not in here, then where?" My patience is stretched as thin as the precious silk gossamer of a garden spider.

"I don't know. She was supposed to be hidden in one of the old servants' quarters upstairs—"

"She's not up there. I checked." My voice is stern. "And I'm done waiting for this fucking key." I spin to the group. "I need a hairpin. Or a paper clip. Or both."

Looks of confusion are exchanged before anyone speaks.

"Here." Wide-eyed, Ami reaches into her hair and removes a pin from her bun. It's long and adorned with a lotus flower on the top.

"Thanks," I reply when she hands it to me. "Do you care if I ruin this? I have to break it in half to use it."

"No, go ahead. I have others." The urgency on her face is rivaled only by my own.

I pull the prongs apart, bending them back on themselves until the pin snaps in half. Holding one straight piece in my mouth, I bend the other into an L shape, then shove it into the bottom part of the lock as I work the straight pin into the top.

Jenna releases a deep exhale and mutters, "Where in the hell is David?"

"Time's up. He went to look for Ashton and Heather," Reese replies.

"Evie?" I call as I maneuver the pins. But there's no responding sound. No movement. Nothing.

My heart rate accelerates as I double down on my work.

"Where did you learn how to do that?" Keith asks.

"Military," I reply. I suck in a steadying breath and focus on my task.

With a strained voice, Jenna asks, "Are you *sure* you heard someone in—"

The lock gives a distinct *click*.

I twist the knob, ignoring everyone and everything around me. Nothing else matters. Only getting inside.

A shaft of light from the hallway illuminates the room. Evie is near the back, propped against an empty metal shelf.

"Evie," I cry, falling to my knees beside her and pulling her blindfold off.

Her forehead is covered in perspiration, and tendrils of hair are stuck to her brow. I pull the gag away from her mouth and let it fall around her neck. Her eyes are wide and panicked, and her breathing is concernedly rapid.

Jenna follows behind me and kneels beside us. The rest of the group stands in the doorway gawking, helpless.

"She's having a panic attack," Jenna exclaims.

"Evie," I call out, ignoring Jenna. I cradle her face and run my thumb across her lips, parting them to give her more air. "It's James. You're okay." I keep my thumb in place against her bottom lip and hold her cheek to keep her mouth open.

Jenna shuffles around to Evie's back and manipulates her wrist restraints. "What the—" she mutters under her breath. "They're locked."

Still looking at Evie, I ask, "What do you mean they're locked?"

"Gimme a sec."

I maintain a firm hold on Evie's gaze as tears threaten to spill down her cheeks. Her panting is hot against my thumb, her chest rising and falling in rapid bursts.

"Hey, Watson…" I start. "You and I are going to tackle this together, okay? We'll take some nice, deep breaths, yeah? In through the nose for five seconds and then out through the mouth for five seconds, got it?"

There's a pause before she nods.

Jenna lets out a stream of obscenities as she tries to undo Evie's restraints.

"All right, in through the nose…" I inhale—slow and deep—and she follows suit. After a five-second count in my head, I exhale from my mouth. Evie's warm breath grazes my thumb as she does the same.

"Good girl," I tell her, and her breath hitches.

I breathe with her again, prolonging the length of each inhale and exhale. Her breathing evens out with each round.

"Got it," Jenna exclaims, releasing Evie's cuffs and dropping them to the floor. "There was a tiny latch on each cinch point that I could hardly see in this light. I didn't even know the cuffs had those."

Ignoring Jenna, I grab Evie's hands and rub her wrists, red and raw from her struggles. I place a single kiss on each one, feeling her pulse against my lips. Even though her breathing is leveling, her heart is still racing.

I remove the ring from her middle finger with relative ease.

"Hold out your hand."

She does as she's instructed, and I place the ring in her palm.

"Rub it like this." I curl her fingers around the item, forcing her to feel its shape and dimensions. "Keep taking deep breaths with me, in through your nose and out through your mouth. While you do that, work it through your fingers. Rub it, feel it. Get to know the shape, the weight, the smoothness. Let it calm you."

She rubs it between her thumb and fingers, taking in deep breaths as she goes. In the meantime, I remove the restraints from around her ankles, which come off much more easily than her cuffs did.

Once her legs are freed, she shifts into a cross-legged position, wincing as she gets situated. I reach for her wrists, noting her slower heart rate.

Jenna's shoulders go slack. "I'm so sorry. I don't know what happened. They weren't supposed to hide you in here. And they were never supposed to lock you in. I had no idea the cuffs could even lock up like that..." She runs a hand through her hair as she rambles.

"It's all right," Evie mutters in a whisper.

"Who put you in here? Do you remember? I'll get to the bottom of this. None of this is okay—"

Evie cuts her off. "It was a guy. He had long black hair pulled back into a ponytail. A dark beard. It may have been an accident, though, Jen. I honestly don't know..."

"I know who you're talking about. Marco. Younger guy, right?"
She nods.

"I have to let David know. But first, what can I do? What do you need—"

"Leave us," I demand, my voice low but rough.

Jenna looks at me, eyes wide in bewilderment. "What? I'm not going to leave her—"

"I said leave. Please." I spin, addressing the gawkers, an assortment of heads still peeking through the door. After several awkward beats, they clear the area. Everyone except Jenna.

"She's my best friend, James. I got her into this mess, and I'm not leaving until I get her out."

"Jenna, she's all ri—"

"It wasn't your fault," Evie says, placing the ring back on her finger. "I wasn't locked in initially, although I think my cuffs were locked from the beginning. I'm not sure if that was intentional or..." She shakes her head.

Jenna and I exchange glances.

"After Marco left, someone found me. The door opened, and I could hear someone breathing. They didn't come in; they just stood there watching me."

A seething rage rumbles in my chest. It was Ashton. It had to be. I'm sure Evie knows it too. But how did Ashton get a key? Undoubtedly, she's sparing Jenna's feelings by not saying too much.

"Eventually the person left, but when they closed the door, the lock clicked. I tried to undo my cuffs, then, and that's when I discovered they were locked. I managed to scoot over to the shelf and bang my ring against the metal. I don't think the sound was very loud, though..."

"It was loud enough," I assure her.

Jenna puts a comforting arm around her friend, who sinks into her embrace. "I'm so sorry. I never meant for this round to go this way."

"It's okay. It wasn't the small space, or being bound, it was the sound of the lock, like always. And it wasn't your fault, so please don't beat yourself up over this. I'm all right." She throws her arms around her friend and holds her in a long embrace.

When they pull away, Jenna's eyes meet mine. I raise a brow at her and subtly tilt my head toward the door. She gets the hint and gives me a quick nod of acquiescence.

"I'll leave you two," she says, standing and brushing her head against the light string that dangles from the ceiling. She gasps, startled. "Oh shit, there's a light in here?" She giggles, tugging on the string and illuminating the closet. "Having this light on would have made the last few minutes a hell of a lot easier." Her energy is lighter. She's back to the Jenna we all know and love.

"Shall we wait on you two lovebirds before announcing tonight's winner?" she asks, pausing at the door.

"Nah, go ahead. It's safe to assume we did not win tonight." I chuckle. The sense of calm that takes root is damn near euphoric.

Jenna glances between Evie and me. "You never can tell," she replies, her lips turning up in a playful smirk before she disappears out the door.

Alone, finally.

I turn my attention to Evie. She's a little peaked, but no longer panicked. Her eyes are puffy from the tears, or maybe from being tired. Perhaps both. It has been a long night.

But it's far from over.

She opens her mouth to speak, but before she can utter a sound, I capture her mouth with mine. The taste of strawberry is long gone, wiped away with the passing time and the silk gag that now hangs around her neck. But her natural taste is even more delectable, and I devour it like I need it to survive.

Her breath hitches against mine as I lap her up, her taste, her tongue, her naked lips. I entwine one hand in her hair and yank her head back. As I suck on her jawline, she gasps, prompting me to trail rough kisses down her porcelain neck. Her liberated mouth releases substantial moans that echo across our dimly lit chamber.

She lowers onto her back as I grab at the hem of her shirt and push it up and over her bare breasts. No bra for my partner in crime. She heeds my instructions nicely.

Such a good girl.

I take one of her erect nipples in my mouth, pinching the other with a free hand. As I suckle, her moans become cries, and her hips buck beneath me as she arches her back to farther shove her tits in my face.

Taking a risk considering recent events, I push her fallen gag aside and wrap my hand around her throat. She responds by grabbing her hair and arching her back even higher. Her tits aren't much more than a handful, but they're perfect. With one in my free hand, I take the other in my mouth and nibble its tender flesh.

She cries my name between moans and writhes beneath me. My cock, throbbing and erect, leaks in response.

I unfasten her shorts and release the zipper. With one quick tug, they're at her ankles, and fuck, she's pantiless.

Very good girl.

I run my tongue against her slit, dragging it from her taint to her clit and pulling a ragged cry from deep inside her. Groans of my own arousal hum against her sensitive flesh, the vibrations sending her bucking like a wild animal.

"Oh God, James. Please."

I chuckle against her clit.

Not yet, baby girl.

"*Please*, James."

I drive my pointed tongue deep inside her, her butterscotch dripping down my chin and covering my nose.

With a hand against her abdomen, I hold her still while I wrap my other arm around her leg to keep her close. She entwines her fingers with mine on top of her stomach. The tenderness of the moment gives me pause, and my heart cries out at her touch.

"What's wrong?" she asks.

"I want you, Evie. Now. But not here. Considering what just happened…"

She sits upright, and I kneel forward to meet her.

Taking my face in both hands, she says, "James, I want you too. Right here, right now. I was scared for a while, yes, but you found me. Just like you said you would. You found me…in here. And this is where I want to have you." She plants a hard, passionate kiss on my lips, stealing my breath, our moans coalescing into one single harmonious note.

Pulling away, she says, "For the first time, that is. After this, we're taking things upstairs."

We share a laugh, and she moves to undo my pants. In a matter of seconds, I'm naked right along with her, and my tongue is raking across every inch of her body.

I hover above her, kissing her lips and caressing her cheeks. She strokes my jaw with one hand, and with the other, she strokes my erection. I let loose a feverish groan against her mouth as she takes my bottom lip between her teeth, nibbling it as she teases my swollen cock.

Jesus fuck.

Precum trickles from my tip and into her palm, and she rubs it along my shaft like warm lubricant. When she licks it off her hand, dragging her tongue from the base of her palm to the tip of her middle finger, my cock jerks at her entrance.

She sticks out her tongue, now bearing my seed, in a silent offering to me. Taking it, I lean in and suck the salty musk from her. As I swallow it, I shove my cock deep inside her, pulling a sharp cry from her throat.

Buried inside her tight sheath, my cock pulsates with arousal, my length finding her end with ease. She buries her face in my neck, her cries like music to my ears.

She trails her fingertips down my back and grabs at my ass, pushing me deeper. The little vixen is tempting me to push beyond the boundaries I know I can't break.

Unless she wishes to be broken.

Judging by the way she grips my ass and screams "Oh God, *harder*," she wants me to penetrate her beyond her own anatomy and defile her entire core.

And what my Evie wants, she gets.

Each thrust is more aggressive than the last, and her body responds exactly as I want—with her back arching high and her breasts jutting up and into my chest. She shifts her long legs up my back, lifting her pelvis off the floor so I can ram against her end. My explosion is seconds away, but I want her to come first.

I kiss her hard and press my forehead to hers.

"Come for me, Evie," I pant. "Be a good girl now." I lower my hips, bearing my pelvis down onto her with every ounce of strength I have.

In less than a handful of thrusts, my Evie comes undone. She releases my hair and bites down on her own forearm to stifle her cry as she climaxes around my cock. With each pulse of her aftershocks, I unravel.

As her cries subside and she releases her arm from between her teeth, I press my lips to hers and come deep inside her. My cries tumble against her lips, which she traps in her teeth as she bites her bottom lip.

I collapse against her, my head resting on her unsteady chest. Her heart races the same as mine, and together, we share the rhythmic pleasure of our afterglow.

In time, her body relaxes beneath me. She twirls my hair between her fingers while I run my hand along the swell of her hips. A bead of perspiration trickles from my brow and lands above her breast.

My cum drips from inside her and smears onto my stomach, the warmth oddly soothing. I reach between our naked bodies and wipe at the wetness. It's a delicious mixture of her butterscotch musk and whatever the hell I taste like. I raise my head to look at her, and she meets me with the most incredible doe eyes, loving and tender, beyond anything I have ever seen.

I bring my coated index finger to her lips. "Would you like a taste?"

The seafoam in her eyes glistens as she responds with a soft smile and a single nod.

As I paint her bottom lip with the wetness, her tongue traces along, savoring each little bit. Blood rushes to my cock all over again as I move to taste the remnants of our release on my finger. But instead, my goddess-in-heat grabs my hand and takes my finger into her mouth, sucking its length. It's a familiar sensation by now, but one I can never get enough of. She twirls her tongue and releases me only when she's damn good and ready.

Take it as long as you want, sweet girl.

I anticipate her release of my finger, especially the *pop* that follows. Perhaps it's the cute little noise that excites me the most. Or the way her lips pucker to ensure its audible release from her mouth. Maybe it reminds me of a mini orgasm for my finger? Who knows. But the more she sucks, the more I know that little *pop* is coming, and then I—

Pop.

Fuck yes.

My cock wants her again. *Needs* her.

I kiss her hard, our lips smacking together as her breasts press against me.

"James," she says, pulling away to look me square in the eye. "Take me upstairs." Her eyes are on fire. She isn't asking; she's demanding.

"As you wish, baby girl."

We don our clothes, haphazard in our attempts. I don't even bother with my shirt, choosing to sling it over my shoulder instead.

Speaking of slinging things over my shoulder...

Her shorts aren't even fastened when I bend low, grab her around the waist, and toss her over my shoulder like a sack of grain.

"*James*," she squeals.

"Be a good girl and trust me," I chuckle.

I carry her out of the closet, through the kitchen, and into the main foyer.

Where everyone is apparently still gathered.

Shit. Well, this is awkward.

I thought for sure they would have retired to their quarters or to the lounge for drinks by now. But nope, apparently now is the moment Jenna and David are announcing the winning team. It must have taken David longer to find Ashton than I thought. And of course, it's right as I'm carrying my partner to the grand staircase and up to my room. With her face only inches from my ass, no less, and her giggles echoing up and down the main hall, oblivious to the crowd before us.

I freeze under their impenetrable stares. Silence stills the foyer for what seems like an eternity, until Jenna breaks out into an uncontrollable fit of laughter. She slaps a hand over her mouth, but it does little good in a room so vast and silent.

"What's going on?" Evie asks, confused considering her field of view is limited to my ass.

"Nothing much, honey bunch. We have company is all." I slap her bottom, and she lets out a playful laugh.

"'Scuse us," I say, affecting calm as I carry Evie past the rapt crowd and toward the stairs.

"Have fun, Evie." Jenna giggles. She shifts her weight against my shoulder to wave at Jenna while I traverse the steps.

The group below rustles, perhaps talking about us. Perhaps praising the winner. Either way, we pay it no mind.

With my little minx slung over my shoulder, I hurry to my room to devour her until the morning light.

CHAPTER 12
EVIE

All I can see is the way his shorts hug his cute little ass.

Those cheeks are so close to my face, I want to take a bite out of them every time I swing in their direction. But I can't reach them with my mouth alone, so I slap his taut glutes instead, playing them like a set of bongos as he carries me to his room.

With each rhythm I beat, he responds by slapping my ass, which only encourages me to keep my little solo number going even longer, harder, and faster.

I can do this all night, Sherlock.

I'm interrupted, however, when he throws his bedroom door open and flings me onto the bed. I land with a bounce and a gleeful cry.

Standing at the foot of the bed, he pulls my legs until my body is below him. He leans in close, looking up at me through his lashes, his lips upturned in a smirk as he pulls my unfastened shorts off and throws them to the floor.

I sit upright and tug at the hem of my shirt, but he grabs my hands to stop me.

"Tsk, tsk, tsk," he sasses, shaking his head and wagging a finger at me. "*I* undress you, Wats. No one else. That includes you."

My stomach flips at his commanding voice, and I drop the hem of my shirt. With both hands, he pulls it up and over my head.

"And what about you?" I tease. "Do I get to undress you?"

He pauses, pressing his lips together as he studies me, then says, "Yes. But only with this." His thumb find my bottom lip, parting it from the other.

"I've already seen a button on that beautiful tongue tonight. How about another? And a zipper too?"

My pussy aches at his words, ready to play. He palms the back of my head, forcing me off the bed and onto my knees before him.

Taking the front button of his shorts in my mouth, I pull on the tab of material above it with my teeth. Using my tongue to push the button through its hole, I make slow progress. It's trickier than it looks.

The front of his pants bulges, the fabric pulled tight by his erection, making the endeavor even more difficult.

But as my saliva soaks into the material, it loosens up a bit. I continue my ministrations, and before long, I manage to push the button through. In response, he flexes his cock and groans.

The zipper is a piece of cake compared to the button. I hold it between pursed lips and pull it down on the first try. I then bite the bottom hem of one leg and tug as hard as I can. A few grunts later, the shorts crest the hump of his ass and fall to the floor around his ankles.

Until now, I haven't noticed his lack of underwear. Either he chose to go without like I did, or he forgot them in the closet and the staff will have a surprise waiting for them come morning.

His erection is at high mast and staring me down.

I eye him from below, victorious in my endeavors.

"Such a good girl," he praises, making my heart flutter as he watches me. "Do you like being my good girl?" His tone is firm, his demeanor almost regal.

I nod so quickly my head nearly shakes right off my neck.

"Then show me." He cups my cheek and shoves his thumb into my mouth. Before I can suck, however, he growls "open wide," and shoves his cock into my mouth with one audacious thrust.

My sharp inhale is hoarse and unfulfilled. It's impossible for me to take in air around his cock at it slams the back of my throat.

He guides my hands to his ass cheeks. Then with one hand gripping my hair, he fucks my mouth and throat with abandon. I inhale quickly with each outward pull, giving my burning lungs what they crave. After each thrust, I suck past my puckered lips, dragging my tongue along his shaft and drawing circles with it around the crown.

As he throws his head back and releases guttural moans, all I can see is that prominent Adam's apple. It makes my pussy squirm with delight.

He quickens his pace, crying my name each time his dick bottoms out in my throat.

He's so close.

Which is why I'm startled when he suddenly pulls away. Saliva drips down my chin as he pulls me to my feet and flings me face-first onto the bed. With my feet still on the floor, my body bent over the foot of the bed, he positions himself behind me. He teases my entrance with his cock and runs a hand over my bare back.

He slaps my ass cheek...

Once.

Twice.

Three times.

Each time harder than the last.

I squeal with delight at the sting that scorches my flesh.

And at the pleasure, the dominance...the power behind it.

"You have a beautiful little asshole, you know that?" he says gruffly.

My face flushes with molten embarrassment, surely as red as my ass is. I have never in my life received such a compliment. Thank God he can't see my face right now.

But my chance to dwell on it evaporates almost instantly when he slicks a finger through my juices, teasing my center, then—"*Oh God, yes*"—hooks the tip of it into my ass as he thrusts his cock deep inside my pussy.

With each violent thrust against my backside, his pelvis rams his finger into my other entrance even deeper, consuming me in a whirlwind of sensations that makes my body hum with sinful pleasure.

My feet have no traction on the floor. I'm anchored to the bed only by his ramming cock and invasive finger. I cling to the bedding for dear life as my feet slip on the polished hardwood. But even more so, I grip it out of pure passion as the man who has waited all damn night to fuck me raw takes me for his own.

The bedding, balled in my hands, dislodges from its corner mounts as the bed rattles.

I try to bury my screams in the mattress, but I want to be closer to James, so I push myself up but can't find traction with my feet.

He grips my hair hard by the root, a dull sting on my scalp forcing a cry from my throat. In a flash, the heat from his breath is raking across my neck as my arched back presses into his chest.

"How far can you take it?" he growls in my ear, removing his hand from my hair to grab me by the throat.

"Take what?" I ask between cries of pleasure, my voice ragged and pinched.

"*This.*"

He shoves his finger all the way into my ass, fast and unforgiving, not stopping until it reaches its end. I spasm against it and release an uncontrollable scream of pleasure against his jaw.

Our perspiration mingles as our faces press together, his breath becoming mine as I cry out in an orgasm that rips through my body. My vision blurs and my flesh quivers as ripples of electricity radiate from my core to my fingers and toes.

My throat is raw, but no longer held captive by James's masculine hand. He rams into me faster than ever, gripping me by the swell of my hips, the headboard slamming into the wall and the canopy swaying above our heads in a rhythmic dance that matches our own. Amid his powerful claiming, I fall forward onto the bed in almost an act of contrition, unable to hold myself up against his jackhammering any longer.

As I sink my teeth into the crumpled bedding, fighting the screams of sheer pleasure that spill from the recesses of my throat, my vagina clenches against his engorged member.

James cries out. "Oh *fuck*, Evie."

His cock flexes inside me as he fills me with cum. As he empties himself, his cries devolve to moans, and I bear down around him to finish him off entirely.

For several moments, he remains inside me, both of us reveling in the stillness despite the aftershocks. He pants, same as me, his grip still firm on my hips. We're connected, a single person if only for a time, hooked together by aching flesh and white-hot ecstasy.

He pulls out and steps away, freeing me from my pinned position against the bed. But my unsteady legs shake, and as I slowly sink to the floor, he bends low and wraps an arm around my waist, hoisting me up and onto the mattress. I scoot toward the headboard, sitting against a stack of pillows, admiring the view of my naked Adonis partner—the Sherlock Holmes to my Dr. Watson.

The very reason my legs are shaking, and my vagina is singing her little pink heart out.

He rounds my side of the bed and places a firm, loving kiss on my lips. "Be right back."

I rest my head against the headboard as he saunters off to the bathroom, listening to the running water and admiring with a chuckle how badly we skewed the canopy drapes overhead.

James returns, crawls under the covers, and pulls me to him. His racing heart pounds against me as I cuddle against him, and I wonder if it's from exertion or from our embrace.

I trace circles around one of his hard nipples in a daze, reveling in the way his fingers tickle my shoulder as he holds me.

"You know, I'm starting to believe you may not have actually been a soldier," I tease, propping myself up with an elbow to face him.

"Is that right?"

"To be perfectly honest, I've never seen a soldier with so few scars. Aside from this one"—I stroke the linear scar that stretches at an angle across his shoulder. "You're far too pristine." I examine his body, taking in every dip, every crevice, then focus on his cock, which, of course, he flexes for me.

He mirrors my position, propped on an elbow.

"You've seen many naked soldiers, have you?" he teases.

"Not exactly." I drag my attention back to those piercing eyes. "But I've certainly pictured a few. Tattered, ragged, worn..." A dramatic sigh flows from my parted lips.

"Maybe I'm not so scarred and tattered because I'm just that good," he says with a smile. "Maybe you should see the other guys."

A drop of perspiration catches my eye as it glistens across his chest. I want to cover myself in it. His natural scent sends me into an inescapable state of arousal. Combine that with the sweat and the smell of sex in the air, and my pussy is already begging for more.

"Check this out." He sits upright and bends his right knee, moving it in my direction. "See that?" He points to a gnarly scar on the side of his knee, shaped like a fishhook but larger.

I heave myself up for a better view and gasp. "How did I not see that before?" I trace my fingers over the repaired skin.

"To be fair, I've either had pants on, we've been in dimly lit areas all night, or you've been on your knees...umm," he lets out a sarcastic small cough, "looking elsewhere."

I roll my eyes and press my palms to my heated cheeks. "What happened?" My voice is quiet, timid. I don't want to pry.

He straightens his leg and adjusts to face me. "It was during a deployment. I was part of a provincial reconstruction team in Afghanistan back in '06. An IED went off inside a parked vehicle near my station at a local courthouse in Ghazni. A piece of shrapnel caught me. It hurt like a sonofabitch."

"My God," I reply through a shaky exhale. "Was anyone else hurt?"

He bumps the underside of my chin with the crook of his forefinger. "We didn't lose any soldiers, although several of us were injured, some rather severely, in fact. But unfortunately, a few civilians did not make it."

"But, as a pilot...?" Words escape me.

"I served as a combat pilot during active military operations. I also trained to be a special warfare airman between deployments. When I went back overseas, the recon team was my primary objective."

"When did you enlist?"

"Shortly after 9/11."

An invisible string cinches my stomach into a painful knot.

"I never planned to join the military. I was a huge nerd in high school. I was captain of the chess team for crying out loud, remember?"

He's so endearing that I damn near throw my arms around him and kiss him right then and there. But I want to hear more, so I suppress my urges and watch him as he continues.

"On 9/11, I was going to school in Boston. The attacks in New York were so close by, though, and the aftermath was so devastating. I couldn't sit behind a mountain of textbooks anymore. I felt like I had to do something." He rubs a hand over his jaw and sighs. "So I finished out the semester and enlisted less than three months later."

"How old were you?"

"Almost nineteen."

So young.

"Enlisting was the best decision I ever made." He grabs my

hand, the warmth of his touch stirring that kaleidoscope of butter-flies inside me. "The next being the decision to come to the island of Eden's Green for my buddy's bachelor party. Or whatever this is."

His flirtatious words sing between us.

He leans in and plants a soft kiss on my lips. It's close-lipped but full of want, and we sink into the pillows together.

After several minutes of soft kisses, caressing touches, and tender sighs, he pulls away from me and asks, "If you could try anything, Evie, with me, what would it be?"

Morbid curiosity brews inside my belly at his question. "What do you mean?"

"Like bedroom stuff. Is there anything you've wanted to try but never have? Any cherries I can pop?" He grins at his own stupid innuendo and flicks both brows.

"I don't know..." It's hard to focus on anything other than that smoldering look he's giving me. "Something tells me you have a thing or two in mind, though." I raise a sarcastic eyebrow, and he brushes it off with an uneasy laugh.

"Nah, I'm just...well, maybe, yeah."

"I knew it," I exclaim, sitting bolt upright. "Spill it. I want all the details."

"Hey, I asked you first." He props himself up on his elbow again and rests his cheek in his hand.

"Fair enough." I pull my knees to my chest and study the askew canopy as I ponder my answer. "Hmm, do I have to pick just one? Because there are a few things..." I trail off.

His eyes dance with excitement, bouncing between mine. "No shit? Now's my turn to tell *you* to spill it."

"But we have to make a promise to each other right here and now. No judgment. No matter what," I say.

"Of course." He recoils. "Should we shake on it or something?"

"Meh. I mean, we can *fuck* on it if you want..."

"Um, yes please."

I catch his semi forming from out of the corner of my eye. To be perfectly honest, his cock has a terrible poker face.

"But in all seriousness, tonight may have tapped into some, um, urges I've never thought about before," I admit.

His grin gives way to a more earnest expression.

"For instance, when I was in that hedge maze..." How do I explain my desires in a way he'll understand when I don't entirely understand them myself? "There was something about being in there all alone, but...knowing you would, you know, look for me...*just* me." I avoid his gaze and hope he'll say something. But he remains silent, so I go on. "Like, I spent the whole time wishing the rules were just a bit different."

"How so?"

"I wanted to compete against each other. I wanted the point of the game to be me running and you chasing. The idea of being lost in there and being, I don't know," I wave my hands in front of me, "*hunted* was damn near electrifying." I drop my hands to my lap and heave a deep breath. "Does that make sense?"

His lips upturn in a sly crooked smile.

"It's funny you say that. It aligns almost perfectly with what I was going to say when you spun the question back around on me." He runs a gentle finger over my forearm. "While I was in the maze, I captured all the other flags early on. Some of the ladies stuck together, which made it easy. So I spent most of my time looking for you. And the chase of it, turning each corner, wondering if you would be there, fantasizing about what I wanted to do to you...Let's just say I had an erection for most of that round." He laughs at himself.

But the levity quickly disappears, and his tone turns serious, somber even. "Of course, I never expected to find you under the circumstances that I did." He studies the bed, averting his gaze.

Ashton.

"Can I say something?" I ask.

"Of course." He grabs me by the hand. "You don't need my permission."

I suck in a deep breath, my heart rearing up again. "I need to know that I can speak freely about Ashton with you."

An uncomfortable energy permeates the air around us. "What about?"

"There's something you need to know…"

The color drains from his face, and his brow furrows in concern.

I wish I could forget all about Ashton and move on. But despite knowing James for such a short time, it feels wrong to keep what happened in the ballroom a secret any longer. "I need to know that I can be honest and not worry about you rushing out of here to kill him."

"That's a tall order."

Trepidation makes my palms go clammy. He's right. How can I know how he'll react? A lump lodges itself deep in my throat, and I try to swallow it down to no avail.

"You can tell me anything, Wats. But, I'm not going to lie, you have me nervous as hell right now." He runs a tremulous thumb across his lip.

"Earlier, when we were all in the ballroom during the first round of games…" Fuck. I want to meet his gaze, but it's all too much. Maybe I should wait until later? After the wedding, maybe?

Jesus, Evie. It's too late now.

"I know something happened while I was checking blindfolds." James breaks the silence. "I could tell by your posture. The way you were standing there. What happened?" There's a shimmer in his eyes I haven't seen before.

"While I was standing there with my blindfold on, someone came over to me to check it. And they touched me. It all happened so fast. He reached under my dress and pinched my bottom, *hard*. It startled me, so I lifted my blindfold. And it was

Ashton." My heart races, hammering in my throat, and I fear I may choke on it.

He sits upright and runs an irate hand through his hair. He won't look at me. Instead, he stares past me, fury brewing in his ardent eyes. "You should have told me when it happened," he scolds, holding a tight fist up to his mouth, his elbow propped on a bent knee.

"We had only just met. I panicked. Like I said, it all happened so fast, and I didn't want to make a scene...we'd all had so much to drink, even then—"

"Stop." His tone is sharp but cracks at the end.

I recoil in confusion. "Stop *what*? Stop talking?"

"Stop making excuses that may prevent people from stepping in and protecting you. Why do you feel the need to protect everyone but yourself? Even the people who hurt you?"

His words bite, painful and raw. The sting catches me by surprise.

"I'm not trying to protect *everyone*," I argue. "I was trying to protect Jenna...and you."

"I don't need you to protect me, Evie." His face is flushed with frustration. "That's not your job. It's my job to protect *you*. And I'm losing count of all the ways I've failed at that tonight." He removes his glasses and rubs the bridge of his nose.

"Listen to me." I grasp his arm, using it as leverage to scoot closer to him. Gripping him by his cheek, I pull him to face me.

He doesn't fight it. He scrutinizes me, his eyes never leaving mine, watching, waiting for my explanation.

"Every time I was in trouble tonight and needed someone, *you* were there. No one else, only you. Every time I was lost, *you* found me. So don't think for one minute that you failed me. That's utter bullshit. You have been there for me more in the last twelve hours than most people have my entire life. I've been an orphan since I was eleven. I grew up with so few people in my life. But you...you make me feel, for the first time ever, like I'm worthy of protection." I look away, staring down at my lap instead. Shit. I may have opened a can of worms that will lead to a whole slew of questions I'm not sure I'm prepared to answer.

But he responds by reaching for my hands and holding them in his, his demeanor relaxing a bit as he faces me. "I will always protect you, Wats. You are worth protecting...more than you'll ever know."

I fight back a smile, but my stomach flips at the warmth of his words. "I've said it before, but I will say it again...I will always find you. You will never be lost as long as you're with me."

"I know," I whisper. "You make me feel safe. Take comfort in that."

"I'd take more comfort in knowing that I had beaten his fucking ass to a bloody pulp after he put his hands on you."

"You did, though. He paid for it when you let him have it in the maze. I'm not sure why it still upsets you—"

"Because, Evie, he put his hands on what's *mine*." He runs the back of his hand over his mouth as his shoulders slump, the fury in his expression beginning to fade. "I'm sorry." His tone is quieter, more even.

"It's okay."

"No, it's not. It's not right for me to dump my feelings on you like that."

"Feelings?" I have to know.

But much to my chagrin, he shakes his head without looking up.

"Don't do that. Don't start something you have no intention of finishing. If there's something you want to say, then say it."

"What do you want me to say, Evie?" His exasperation outshines my own.

"Whatever is clearly on your mind." I turn and scoot back so I can see him better. My feelings for him are taking me by storm. And if he reciprocates them even a little, I'll feel more validated with how quickly this man went from stranger to partner to lover to...well, something else entirely; something even more amazing.

"Okay, fine," he quips, shifting his body so it's square with mine. "Here goes." He slaps his knee. "What if I told you I never want another man to touch you ever again? That you have been in my every thought since the moment I saw you coming down those stairs at the start of the evening? That I want to mark you, *claim* you, as my own so that no one ever lays a hand on what's mine again?" He swallows hard and clears his throat. "What if I told you that, since the maze, I've plotted Ashton's death over a dozen times in my head? That the idea of tomorrow terrifies me because I don't know what'll happen between us when we step off that ferry and return to our normal lives?" He balls his hands into fists, but the look on his face isn't full of anger; it's fear. "What if I told you I wanted something more with you? Permanent. Is that what you meant when you asked me to tell you what's on my mind?" He looks away, his breathing rapid as he runs a hand down his face.

My jaw drops as I absorb his words. Despite the quivering that rampages my body, I'm relieved to hear my own feelings validated through his proclamation.

"I—" Where do I begin? "There's no reason to worry, James. You already have me."

His shoulders sag with relief. "What are you saying?"

"I don't want this to be over come morning." I pause and wait for him to look at me. When he does, I go on. "I want you, James, and you can take extra steps to claim me if you want, or don't, because it won't change the fact that you already have me."

Riding the moment like a surfer on a rogue wave, we lean in and kiss each other hard upon the lips. One tongue sashays against the other, and his hand is hot against my throat. Blistering, in fact. It makes my toes curl with pleasure.

"You're giving yourself to me, then?" He groans against my open mouth.

"Yes," I exhale.

"Completely?" He pushes me onto my back with his lips still on mine.

"Yes," I moan toward the canopy as he traces his fingers down my abdomen.

"Will you let me mark you, Evie? Will you let me chase you, hunt you down, and claim you as mine once I've buried my teeth in you?" He purrs against my neck, eliciting a sea of goose bumps across my body. But I can't respond. All the air is sucked from the room—and my lungs—as he shoves two forceful fingers into my pussy. I clamp down around the welcome intrusion as he breathes his possessive words against my neck.

"You don't have to ask." I barely manage to say out as he tongue-fucks my nipples until they're humming and raw.

"I want your permission," he breathes against my tits.

With my hands on his cheeks, I pull him up to meet my gaze. "Whatever you want to do, James, you have my permission. I want to try everything with you. I want you to ravage me, take me, make me yours." I moisten my lips with a flick of my tongue. "I'm giving you permission to not ask my permission."

That gossamer shimmer returns to his beautiful brown eyes. "As you wish, Wats." He dots a single kiss upon my lips then pulls away. "And just so you know, all this shit with Ashton is far from over. While you're having your little chat with Jenna after the wedding, he and I will be having our own, so to speak. No one touches you and walks away. I'd honestly kill him if I could."

"I know," I whisper against his lips.

I raise up on an elbow to meet his solid form. Grabbing his engorged cock, I duck low to catch his Adam's apple in my teeth.

"You seem to have a fascination with my Adam's apple," he chokes out with a ragged chuckle.

"You could say that," I reply, my heart singing at the sound of his laugh. "In fact, can I be perfectly honest?"

He leans away and studies me with that smoldering gaze that drives me wild. "No reason to stop now."

"I would do awful, filthy, disgusting things to get to know *this*" —I press on his Adam's apple with my thumb, and he arches his neck upward, his breath catching—"in a more intimate sense."

I kiss his throat. "With your permission, of course."

He squares his body with mine. "I need you to know. I want to claim you, but I don't own you, Evie. I want us to belong to each other, and that means you can do whatever you need to claim me as well, all right?"

I nod, my lips curling upward in a gracious smirk.

"Then this is how I want to claim you." I tip forward and kiss him, jamming my tongue in his mouth and wrestling against it. It's not a dance this time. It's an all-out war. Lips are bitten, teeth click against one another, and fingers smother breaths as they press against throats.

"My body is yours, Evie," he whispers as the taste of copper lands on my tongue. One of us is bleeding, and it strangely sends my clit on a pulsating rampage.

My flesh is reignited, a forest fire of desire raging across every orifice, ready to claim that prominent Adam's apple and consume its forbidden flesh.

I sit upright as James shimmies down away from the headboard and lies flat on his back. He places a pillow behind his head longways, following the line of his body, allowing more space for my knees on either side of his head.

I move into position, straddling his neck, when he says, "You know, with those long legs of yours, you'll have to practically do the splits to spread wide enough to lower you down that far."

Ignoring him with a coquettish grin, I brace myself with one arm against the headboard, inspect him for a long moment, and whisper, "Challenge accepted." I spread my legs wider...wider... wider...and lower myself onto him.

As my sex reaches his neck, he raises his chin, pronouncing his Adam's apple even more for me. Before long, I'm splayed enough that my clit has found James's own forbidden fruit.

Bullseye.

The mere contact of my most sensitive flesh against his apple makes my pussy ache with jealousy, dripping my wetness all over him. I'm gentle at first, not wanting to hurt him or compromise his air supply. My clit is sensitive enough already that I'm confident it won't take much pressure to send me over the edge. But he hooks his arms around my thighs and pulls me down. The tension at the apex of my legs forces a gasp from my lips as the pressure increases on my clit.

"Take it," he wheezes, still so commanding even when robbed of breath. "Don't you...dare...stop."

The force of his grip makes my clit sing as I find the sweet spot against his neck. I cant my hips to my own erotic rhythm, the headboard banging against the wall as I writhe against him. With my free hand, I caress his jaw, his mouth agape as he fights for breath.

I can't take my eyes off him. The sight of his rosy face as I fuck his neck sends me into a complete tailspin.

He removes a hand from my thigh and positions it underneath my ass. As my pelvis bumps his chin with each pass, he shoves his thumb inside my other entrance.

And I nearly come undone.

Staccato cries burst from my lungs as he rams his thumb inside my virginal entrance. And I wait with bated breath as my clit pulsates against the delicacy of Eden, knowing this is about to undo me in the most deliciously sinful way.

His moans morph into croaks as he holds me tighter with his free arm, the vibrations of his labored breaths shooting bolts of ecstasy straight into my vulva.

"Oh, I'm gonna come," I cry, head thrown back. "Oh Gaw—" I

explode against him, my legs shaking and my vision obscured by an endless sea of stars scattering across my vision like a meteor shower.

I collapse against the arm I have braced against the headboard. My breathing is beyond my control and my throat is hoarse and raw.

James releases my leg and shifts for a better view of me. I'm greeted with a smile, his face a crimson hue.

Extra points for not accidentally killing him.

His neck glistens as I climb off and assume my position beside him. I lap his apple slowly, now as red as its namesake.

"Does it hurt?"

"No, just a little tender, I guess." He exhales a soft, hoarse laugh.

I kiss it, and he swallows hard under my lips.

"Sorry," I whisper.

His breath stutters. "Please don't be sorry. That was the single most erotic thing I have ever experienced." He plants a kiss on the top of my head. "And now that you've had your fun being the dominant one, you know what's next, right?"

I peer up at him, confused.

He sits up and cages me between his arms and the bed.

"It's *my* turn."

In a flash, he sinks low, grabs my ankles, and yanks me toward the foot of the bed. A squeal of shock followed by giggles fills the room.

"Stay there," he commands. Scooping his shorts off the floor, he rifles through the pockets and removes the red bandana. He then switches to a different pocket. To my surprise, he reveals the long satin restraint that was used to bind my feet inside the locked closet. My stomach quakes at the memory, but my pussy overrules it with her own excitement.

He starts with the red bandana first.

Overlapping my wrists, he wraps it around and secures them together. With a soft tone, he asks, "Is this okay?"

I respond with a reassuring smile.

After several tugs of the satin bind, his arms flexing and causing my nipples to go fully erect, he tears it in half, creating two pieces out of the long strip.

With a firm grip on my ankle, he pulls me closer to the edge of the bed. I wince in discomfort as he wraps a silk strip around one of my ankles. My skin is still raw from when they were bound earlier.

"You never should have shown me how far you can spread those amazing legs, sweet girl." My playful James from only a moment ago has vanished. His voice is gravelly and raw from the way I worked myself on his neck, which only enhances the savagery consuming him before my eyes. He's silent as he ties the other end of the silk strip to one of the posts at the foot of the bed.

With his attention set on me, he walks to the other post, grabs my other ankle along the way, and pulls.

My feet are tied to each post with so little slack that I'm practically in a splits position, my ass teetering on the edge and my legs spread to the max.

"I've been wanting to do this from the moment I saw you and those mile-long legs of yours. I knew if anyone's legs could be spread out between these canopy posts, *yours* could."

Heat coils inside my gut at the vulnerability of being so spread. I'm almost too spread out, my outer vaginal lips naturally spreading to reveal my pinkness underneath.

And he has a front-row seat to my exposure.

I reach down with my bound hands to cover myself. But he grabs them and forces them high over my head against the mattress. Bringing his face to mine, he commands, "Don't you dare feel self-conscious with me. I don't ever want to see you cover yourself up, understand?" His gravelly voice is nothing short of a growl, as if my sweet, nerdy partner has been taken over by a possessive, merciless monster.

And my body craves it in ways I never expected.

I need him, *ache* for him. Every passing second that he isn't subduing my pleading sex is a torture unlike anything I've ever known.

"Stay like this. No exceptions, understand? I don't have enough to tie your hands to the other posts, so just keep them above your head. If you lower them, I will punish you. Don't speak unless permitted. Not a beg, a plea, or even a whimper. Only screams of pleasure. I want them loud; I want them unobscured. I want the entire manor to hear them."

My skin is ablaze, and my clit is rock hard. It needs to be fondled, and the absence of touch makes me want to scream, and not from pleasure.

"Nod if you understand."

I obey, desperate for him to ravage me and ease my aching bits.

He leans in, and I close my eyes to receive the kisses I'm sure he's doling out. But he stops shy of my lips and backs away.

Locking his eyes on mine and pressing his index finger over my mouth, he says in a cruel yet lustful voice, "I'm not here for *these* lips. They can wait their turn."

He falls to his knees between my legs, which are shaking from being pulled open so wide.

I arch my back, desperate for his tongue. But first he runs his hands up my thighs from my knees to my apex, creeping up my flesh and leaving goose bumps in their wake.

Without warning, he removes his hands, and I'm devoid of touch all over again. I squirm against the bed, the discomfort unbearable.

I need to be fucked, *hard,* and I need it now.

A sharp gasp escapes my throat as he suddenly laps against my exposed pink flesh, from my taint to my clit and back down again.

My body bucks and my screams are already free flowing.

"So wet for me, baby," he says from between my legs, lapping at me like I'm a goddamn ice cream cone.

My view is all headboard as I arch and twist against his

torturous tongue, my legs pulled straight and shaking with abandon as they suffer their inescapable restraints.

The carnal desire for him to fuck me into oblivion sends my mind into a state of numbness that is unparalleled. The raw ache consumes me, my pussy clenching around a cock that isn't there, and my ass puckering with an urge for penetration that rivals the greedy little bitch in front.

"James, *please*." The torture is unbearable.

Just like that, he pulls back and stands to face me. "What did I tell you about speaking without my permission?"

My lungs quake with each weak breath, and a tingle of anxiety shoots up my spine.

He saunters over to the goodie bag on the nightstand—its contents unknown to me. My anxiety takes a firm hold at the base of my neck as he roots around inside.

He removes what looks like a small dildo. It's purple, slender, and about as wide as a large finger. Aside from the color, it resembles a real penis, with bulging veins and everything. He clicks it on, and a low buzzing fills the room.

"This should do nicely," he says, making his way back over between my legs.

He bends low over me and brings the little guy up to my mouth, the hum of its motor gradually increasing as it gets closer.

"Suck it," he instructs.

I part my lips and suck on the toy as if it's James himself. The vibrations are mild, and yet the entire lower half of my face goes numb after only a few moments.

He traces it down my chin and neck and across my chest, gliding across each nipple, the vibrations making them rock-hard and yearning to be pinched, sucked, teased.

Hell, this is a good start, though.

He continues the journey down my abdomen, over my belly

button, and, slowing his pace dramatically, he travels down my pelvis...

The expedition is slow, and my clit, the next stop on the pillaging path of vibration, swells to its max and throbs all over again.

James watches me as he teases my body in every way, his eyes aflame with lust and power and his lips curled in a devilish smirk.

As if he has all the time in the world, he glides the vibrator, one millimeter at a time, closer and closer to the top of my shaven slit. I buck and roll my hips in a desperate attempt to push that baby closer to where my body wants it most.

"Ah, ah, ah," he warns, pulling the device away as it reaches the top of my slit. "There's no cheating allowed on game night..." That smirk, *fuck*, I want to smother it with my pussy until it's snuffed into oblivion.

He presses on my hip with one hand, holding my writhing body still, which only causes that unshakable ache to root itself deeper.

"Close your eyes, Wats," he commands. "I don't want you to see. Only feel." He bounces the vibrator rapidly between his fingers like a pencil, one brow cocked. "Don't make me blindfold you."

The room goes black as I concede, and my heartbeat quickens at the sudden loss of one of my senses.

Robbed of my sight, the musky smell of sex is more noticeable than ever and the vibrator's buzz is almost deafening.

And I'm now painfully aware of the prolonged absence of his touch.

Where is he?

The anticipation of not knowing where I'll feel him next wreaks havoc on my nerves.

But I don't have to wait long.

He plunges the vibrator deep into my pussy, causing my lungs to seize with a shocking gasp. Its increased level of vibration shakes me from the inside out.

It isn't left in long. Only a split second, in fact.

Now coated with my juices, James works its entire length into my other entrance with a slow, purposeful shove. I buck my hips in shock, which makes me clench even harder against it.

Holy fuck.

Through clenching alone, I take it in deeper, writhing against its vibrational ecstasy. As I twist my hips, I arch my back against my restraints, luxuriating in the increased pressure of the little cock seizing inside me each time I struggle.

I'm mere seconds away from breaking the no talking rule. I'm desperate for James to fuck me straight until dawn, and I'm ready to beg for it.

But I don't have to.

Just when I think my body can't take another second of this torture, he places a hand on my abdomen and says, "Open your eyes, pretty girl."

The canopy linens appear above me once again as James positions himself between my legs.

"Look at me…" He bends close and pinches one of my nipples, turning it bright pink and sending a sting shooting through its tender flesh. I obey. Despite the vibrations radiating through my bottom and sending my pussy into a jealous rage, I'll lie still, as he commands.

His hot breath tickles my ear as he whispers. "Is my good little girl ready for me?"

I nod quickly.

With his open mouth pressed against my cheek and one hand grasping my bound wrists against the bed above my head, he rams his cock into my pussy.

The air disappears from the room with the initial thrust. The greedy bitch between my legs is more than ready to spread for him, accommodating every masculine inch until his hilt connects with my shaking thighs.

The tension of his ramming cock on the vibrator in my ass is absolute paradise. My body responds by clenching every muscle from the waist down. He grips my jaw with his free hand, his fingers digging into my chin and his nose still pressed against my cheek. Our moans mingle and our pants sync with each shunt of his hips. I writhe in my ravishment of him and every sensation he's bestowing upon me.

"*Uh*. I can feel it…*Uh*. I can feel it *through* you," he growls, his fiery breath scorching everywhere it lands.

I pant in response, but I don't dare utter a word. Beads of perspiration form along my brow line, and little tendrils of hair tickle my forehead.

"Scream for me."

My sex clenches as hard as my muscles will allow as my orgasm rapidly approaches. I want to scream *harder* and *don't stop* and *oh James,* but I'm afraid he'll stop entirely to punish me for speaking. So I release wordless screams into the night as my man commands.

"Oh God, Evie. Louder." Spurred on by my reaction, he moves faster, pounding into me harder.

That poor, poor headboard.

"*Uh*. I permit you to speak, sweet girl…*uh*. Let me hear your voice."

Of course he asks me to speak when all words have escaped me and I'm seconds away from exploding all over his tumescent cock.

"Say my name, baby," he cries out, his forehead pressed to my temple.

"James," I groan between pants, remembering words again. "Oh Gaw—*uh*, harder. Harder, James. Fuck me *harder*."

He thrusts with lightning speed until I tighten and explode around my welcome intruders. My screams are raw, animalistic, unrecognizable.

They combine beautifully with the grunts he releases against my sweat-soaked skin.

His cock twitches as he comes undone, spilling what seed he has left inside me while maintaining his fierce grip on my jaw and crying out against my skin.

We sound like a pack of wolves. Howling at a full moon; our own personal hail to hunt.

But despite my manic cries, tonight, he's the wolf and I'm his prey. I was sought; I was found; I was captured...and I was devoured.

Chapter 13

James

She releases a whimper as I free her ankles from their satin binds. The linear marks on her flesh are raw and red, much like I imagine her pussy to be at this very moment. My balls tighten at the thought.

My caress does little, I'm sure, to soothe the aching discomfort she must feel in her legs, but she arches her neck and sighs all the same.

Keep that up, and I'll leave these binds on your ankles and ram you all over again.

And that headboard. I plan to break it tonight. Krelborn Manor may have to bill me before my time here is through.

At that, I chuckle.

But I don't stop my examination. The farther up her leg I get, the closer I come to her beautiful peak, the more violent the shaking in her legs grows. And not from the vibrator in her ass. I pulled that out already and tossed it to the floor. Her legs were pulled so wide open for so long, and then she endured the weight of my cruel, rapacious cock. It's no surprise she shakes for me.

Once I've untied her ankles, I grab her by both hands and pull her up to a seated position. She mewls in pain as she brings her knees together.

"Are you okay?" I ask, my stomach knotted in concern. I may have fucked up here.

"Yeah, it's just…a little sore. A little raw, I guess. My legs are shaking like crazy." She lets out a small laugh.

A good sign.

"Here, feel." She pulls my hand toward her, splaying her knees and placing my hand alongside her peak.

The vibrations of her erotically strained body sear through my hand. It makes my head dizzy with pleasure, to know I fucked those vibrations into her. Blood rushes back into my cock.

"Can you stand?"

With great effort, she tries to scoot toward the edge of the bed, but her spent body is uncooperative. She reaches around me as I bend low next to her. I wrap my arms around her waist and help her to her feet. She claws at my arms as her legs fail her, so I stoop low to catch her before she falls and pull her close. With her arms thrown around my neck, she exhales a nervous laugh against my temple.

"I got you, Wats." I scoop her up and carry her away from the bed.

She holds tight to my neck for support, and her eyes gleam with relief.

"Should we get cleaned up?" I whisper.

She nuzzles her nose against my ear, my cheek, my neck, as I carry her toward the bathroom. Her subtle touches send goose bumps soaring across my body despite the warmth of her breath against my skin.

But when she places a soft kiss against the crook of my neck, it stops me dead in my tracks. She pulls back, those seafoam eyes regarding me, exhausted yet surprisingly flirtatious considering the late hour and the sexual prowess she has already delivered.

"You want me to fuck you again so soon, Wats? You can't even stand."

She doesn't respond, but she doesn't take her eyes off me. Only cocks a brow.

My body goes rigid, my cock included, when her breath grazes my ear. She captures the lobe with those incredible lips that resemble her pink perfection down below.

Goddamn, this girl knows how to rev me up.

In seconds, her nibbling turns to sucking. She's as aggressive with my earlobe as she is with my cock and perhaps twice as eager. This girl clearly wants to be fucked again.

Message received, sweet girl.

For a minute, I forget which appendage is which. The way she takes my ear in her mouth makes my balls clench and my cock spring to its upright and ready-to-serve position.

Even my asshole puckers.

"You're so gonna get it," I exhale, my heart weltering against her.

She giggles as I rush her into the bathroom.

The tile is frigid against my feet as I cross over to the claw-foot bathtub against the adjacent wall.

Her eyes widen and she releases a startled cry as I lower her into the tub and her bare back meets the cold porcelain.

"You all right?"

"It's just cold," she laughs.

I spin the shower head toward the wall, then turn the water on. Waiting for it to warm up, I stand inside the tub between her legs, beholding her beautiful naked body. When she smiles up at me, ignoring my boner and looking into my eyes, my heart nearly gives out on me.

"How are your legs?" I ask.

"Still shaky. They're regaining feeling, so they're tingly. It feels weird, but I'm also kind of enjoying it."

Such a horny girl.

I give her my best flirtatious smirk, and she responds as I want her to—by reaching out and caressing my erection.

But I stop her.

She furrows her brow initially, then concedes to my whims and regards me with heavy eyes as I admire her from above. She's somnolent, that much is clear. But that cocky little side-grin of hers tells me she's not quite ready for bed.

The water is hot now, so I rotate the shower head in our direction and soak my face in the steady stream. I turn to face her, but she's back on her feet and spins me away with a soft grip on my shoulders. The water bounces off the back of my neck as her lips press against the space between my shoulder blades. Her kiss is so soft that I almost mistake it for a phantom tremble. But when her tongue rakes along my tattoo—an open-winged bald eagle that spans my entire upper back and shoulders—blood rushes at full-speed into my cock.

Slowly her lips, in tandem with her tongue, make their way from the apex of one shoulder, across my back, and to the apex of the other, licking the warm water straight from my skin. She presses herself against me, reaching around my chest to caress my nipples, erect despite the heat from the steam around us. With each pinch that follows, my cock bobs with desire and my guttural moans absorb into the shower stream. I'm caged in by her; a cage I never want to escape.

Everything goes dark as I brace myself against the tile wall and close my eyes against the sensations that bombard my body. Her lips tickling my back, her fingers pinching my nipple, her other hand stroking my cock; the water providing a lubrication that makes my stomach tumble, all while cleansing my past away and clearing the path for Evie.

My future.

A slight tingle radiates from my back when her finger traces the long, linear scar that cuts through the eagle's wing on my right shoulder. As water pelts the back of my neck and steam envelops us in a world devoid of oxygen and judgment, I press my forehead against the cold tile and inhale the droplets that coat my lips as she works her magic.

She has seen my other scars. Hell, she may have even seen this one. But despite it being on the back of my shoulder, often out of sight, it's never out of mind. It was the worst of my wounds and took far longer to heal than the others. And every time I see it, I can't shake the screams that tease at my memories; the deafening explosion and the sharp ringing that immediately followed. The blood, the tears, the wailing of civilians as they held their deceased loved ones.

I remember how paralytic the bombing was; how everything went black. For a time, none of it felt real. It seemed like a nightmare that pierced both flesh and certainty, planting doubt in my head as to whether I was even alive.

Now, no matter how hard I try, I can't silence the urgent voices of my comrades pleading for me to open my eyes. The way they shook me, pulling me back into a world I wasn't sure my soul was even part of anymore.

I never draw attention to my scars. Ever. But with Evie's tongue tracing in intimate detail the entire length of the one on my back, for the first time in my life, my knees are quivering. Far beyond my control and threatening to drop me into this woman's arms for good.

But I welcome it.

She may not realize it, but this moment has brought me closer to her than I ever could have imagined.

Because she sees me. Like no one else ever has.

The idea of losing this feeling has my stomach all twisted up. I can't lose it.

I won't.

A pull of pure desire rakes through my spine, and I shiver beneath it.

"Are you all right?" she asks, her hand pressed against my back. "You're shaking."

I inhale deeply. "Please," I beg against the tile wall. "Don't stop."

She traces my scar with a delicate finger, so faint that it tickles.

I can't control my salacious urges any longer.

After turning to face her, I bend low, reach for her legs, and hoist them around my waist. Understanding my intentions, she loops her arms around my neck and holds on as I lift her.

I prop her against the slick side wall, the hot water pelting us both. Her moans echo within our little slice of heaven as I bury my lips in her neck and suckle her sweet skin, as she did mine. Her head thrown back, she exposes her neck to me, and I devour it like an alcoholic at an open bar. She said I can mark her, so that's what I intend to do.

Ever so lightly, I bite along the crook of her neck, leaving ghostly traces of teeth marks on her flesh. Her cries reverberate against the shower walls, and I pull away, afraid the pain has outweighed the pleasure for her. But my goddess grabs me by the roots of my soaked hair and shoves my face back into her neck.

I kiss the marks I've created, then bite her again. This time, she lets out an animalistic cry, sharper than before. With each mark I make, I'm increasingly aware of how her legs shake against my waist.

I press my body even harder against hers as I fight to maintain my balance against the slick tub floor. Freeing my hands as I pin her to the wall, I pinch her nipples until they're as red as her pussy.

But it isn't enough. It seems my sword is as insatiable as her sheath, and he aches for her all over again, even though I'm not certain I'll be able to come again tonight.

"Guide me in, baby girl," I command, pressing my forehead against hers and breathing in the steamy air.

"That's it," I hiss, shutting my eyes as she snakes one hand between us and brings my tip to her entrance.

As the tip of my cock breaches her, I hold it firm. She wriggles between me and the wall, desperate for me to quell the tortuous ache in her core.

But she surrenders to me like a good girl. We'll do this my way. Millimeter by millimeter, I tease my cock into her, so slowly that its movement is virtually undetectable.

"Please, James, please," she cries out, her nails clawing deeper into my neck and back.

I give her another fraction of an inch.

So. Very. Slowly.

She writhes to the best of her abilities, but her movement is restricted against the wall. I grope her breast as I bury my face in her neck.

As I drag out her desperation, I savor every gasp, every trickle of water that races down my back, every stifled breath filled with steam and lust, every tight inch of her.

I'm granted the pleasure of her pulses as the head of my cock spreads her pink walls open. Then, my shaft, smooth and engorged, revels in the tightness and the fluidity with which she squeezes then releases around it.

A sharp pain sears my back as she digs her nails into me. She flails against me, her grip slipping against my soaked skin.

"*James*," she cries out, squeezing my hips with her thighs with an intensity that is sure to leave bruises come morning.

"Fight and claw all you want, baby girl. I'll only drag this out more. I want you to feel every...single...inch."

"Harder. *Please*."

Such music to my ears.

"I want to feel every single inch of you too, Evie. I won't stop until I've felt it all. You surrendered yourself to me, remember? I'm simply taking what's mine..."

Her pussy clamps down around me for a split second before relaxing, acquiescing to my whim. "It's yours."

No more nails in my back, no more pleas. Instead, she presses a hand against the tile above her head. There's nothing to grip up there. This is merely an act of capitulation.

Perhaps she thinks it will urge me to ram my cock the rest of the way and fuck her blind. Not yet, Wats. Not yet.

Almost there.

"I can feel it," she moans, head thrown back. "I can feel all of it. All of you."

Her words sing in my ears on an endless loop, penetrating my soul with as much abandon as I'm penetrating her. Every time it seems like we can't be more connected, another moment like this arises and surprises the hell out of me.

I finally reach her end, my hilt pressing against her peak.

"I can feel you too, Evelyn."

She cries out into the swirling steam as I say her full name, and I send up a silent prayer that it means the same to her as it does to me: she's my entire world, and every square inch of her belongs to me.

Faster and faster, I shunt against her, groaning into her neck as she screams *harder*.

"Come for me, Evie," I demand. She meets my thrusts, and I flex my pelvis to give her the hardest possible surface to grind against. Her legs haven't stopped shaking, vibrating against my hips as my body rakes against her clit.

"Don't stop," she cries.

The floor is slick, and the oxygen is depleting the longer we stay in here. But goddammit, take my air or force me to fuck her while standing on a sheet of ice, and it will not change the fact that my Evie comes when she wants.

And she does.

Her pussy contracts hard, and she releases her orgasmic cries into the steamy whirlwind as I ejaculate against her cervix, my mini orgasm catching me by surprise.

I can't remember the last time I came this many times in one night. She makes me feel like a teenager again. Hell, I wasn't even this randy back then.

With her arms around my neck and her legs hooked around my waist, I shut the water off, snatch a towel off the hook, and carry her back to the bed.

I dry her off the best I can, running the terry cloth over her skin and squeezing it around her wet hair.

She looks at me with exhausted, smitten eyes.

I'm locked in.

After my own pat down, I toss the towel to the floor and crawl into bed beside her.

She reaches for me.

"Goodnight, Watson," I whisper, pulling her into my arms as her eyelids droop.

"Goodnight, Sherlock," she whispers back before drifting into a much-needed sleep.

CHAPTER 14

EVIE

lick...

    Click...

    Click...

The footsteps draw near.

Click...

Click...

Closer now. Snaking their way down the hall.

The metal toe plates on the bottom of his shoes click with each calculated step as he approaches my room.

Click...

Click...

So close, so palpable.

He stops at my door, the sudden silence making my hair stand on end. But only a moment passes before my door is thrown open with brutal force. The hinges barely creak before it slams into the wall behind it. I jump, forcing a suppressed cry against the hand I hold over my mouth.

Click...

Click...

Click...

His footsteps quicken, their intensity growing as he enters my room.

Papa, where are you?

Click...

Click...

Click...

He crosses over to my bedroom closet and throws the doors open, then shoves my hanging clothes aside.

Now silence.

I can't see him from where I'm hidden, but abject terror keeps my eyes screwed shut all the same.

What is he doing?

The awful clicking noise returns.

Closer than before.

Click...

Click...

Click...

It should grow fainter. He should give up his cruel search and leave me in a pool of my own dread and despair.

Click...

Click...

Instead of retreating, his footsteps slow as he nears the standing wardrobe on the far side of my bedroom.

Where I'm lying, locked inside.

My cheek presses against the cold wooden grain as I lay on the wardrobe floor. Horrified, I peek through the crack beneath its heavy oak door. If it wasn't for the light seeping into my bedroom from the hallway, I would be met with nothing but darkness through the sliver of space.

The air inside the wardrobe is so close—heavy even—that I'm damn near suffocated by it.

I shut my eyes and force myself to inhale slowly through my nose, a trick I learned long ago after the first few times Papa locked me in this very prison. But this time, it does nothing to soothe my racing heart.

Click-Click.

He comes to an abrupt halt in front of the wardrobe door, mere inches from me. His shoes—those horrible fucking shoes—are barely visible through the crack. From what I can tell, they're loafers; a deep red color bearing a weird reptile-like pattern. Not a snake. These are different from the snakeskin boots I've seen. They're more akin to a crocodile or an alligator or a lizard.

They're unlike any shoes I've ever seen.

And they do not belong to my father.

He taps a foot in rapid succession...

ClickClickClickClick...

As if trying to drive me to the brink of madness.

Papa, where are you? Please.

He pulls at the knob on the wardrobe door, and I squeeze my mouth so hard my jaw screams under the pressure. Tears stream down my face in agonized silence, trickling sideways down my temples and onto the wardrobe floor alongside my cheek.

It's locked. I know that for a fact. My father has locked me in here so many times I eventually stopped checking the inside latch altogether.

He always comes to let me out.

Always.

But this is not my father.

As he jostles the door, coats rustle above me and the wood groans as the wardrobe shifts against its mounts.

The door doesn't budge.

After a brief reprieve, the shaking resumes. The walls rattle and the hinges squeak under the man's attempts to throw my wooden tomb wide open.

From which I cannot escape.

I'm trapped in there. All thanks to Papa.

A coat falls free of its hanger and lands on me. I let it cover me as

I pray for Papa, and for the man to give up his search and leave me here.

When the shaking finally subsides, I open my eyes, hoping the coast is clear so Papa will return with the key to free me. But even through my tears, those red shoes remain.

And this time, they are accompanied by a pair of knees covered in dark slacks as he crouches low.

Any second, he will see me through the crack beneath the door. He'll know I'm in here. And there will be nowhere for me to go.

Papa, please, where are you?

Papa locked me in here only minutes ago. He placed his hand over my mouth to silence me as he yanked me from my desk. Per usual, he instructed me not to make a sound, lest the monsters find me and take me away.

The wardrobe's lock clicked into place as Papa trapped me inside, as he had a thousand times before.

But this time is different. Seconds after my father locked me in, the silence of my imprisonment was disrupted by harsh yelling in the distance, followed by a series of screams.

As terrified as I was by them, it was the silence that immediately followed that sliced me in half with panic.

I grit my teeth, waiting to be discovered by the faceless man as he peers through the crack under the wardrobe door. Perhaps I will be met by the sound of cruel laugher after he realizes he has found exactly what he's searching for.

Me.

Blood pumps through my veins at such a maddening pace that I'm deafened by it. I wait with bated breath and clenched eyes, not wanting to see any more of the stranger who hovers inches away. But they're forced open with a jolt and I cry into my hand as the wardrobe shakes all over again. I stiffen as my wooden cage closes in on me.

I want to scream until my lungs give out; to beg for Papa to stop this man.

To save me.

I push the fallen coat off and scoot to the rear of the wardrobe. Then, I push on the trapdoor in the back, yank it open, and curl up inside. Despite the pitch dark, I know the secret compartment at the back of the wardrobe better than I know my own bedroom. It's a space large enough for me if I pull my knees to my chest—my own waking nightmare. I despise the wardrobe, but I hate the hidden compartment, built by my very own papa, even more.

My prison continues to shake against its mounts on the wall. As I close the trapdoor, locking myself in my very own pit of hell, I'm overwhelmed by the sensation of falling.

Papa, please.

I don't want to open my eyes. But in an instant, I'm consumed by the idea that my eyes may never open again; a sensation I can only imagine is far too similar to dying.

As my entire world shakes around me, I concede to death—surrender to it—willing it to take me.

In a flash of panic, I open my eyes. Wide.

Above me, beautiful white lace is draped across a dark canopy bed frame.

No rattling walls.

No locked doors.

No red shoes.

Only James, as he shakes me by the shoulders, shouting my name. His voice is filled with a fear not unlike the scream that rang out shortly after Papa locked me inside...

"Evie. *Evie.* Look at me. You're all right. I'm here..."

I want to scream from the shaking. Haven't I endured enough? But I can't move, can't speak. And a wave of panic consumes me all over again.

He releases my shoulders, and the shaking of my nightmare

visions evolve into the present. His hands scorch my flushed skin as he cups my face in his hands.

"Evie, look at me, please."

Papa, please.

He lowers his face to mine, but my focus is still locked on the floating canopy linens, almost ethereal in their delicateness. Nothing like the stifling wardrobe, where the air is as thick as oily pitch and just as suffocating.

I can't move my limbs, no matter how I try. Even my fingers are frozen stiff.

Panic holds me with an unrelenting grip, my breathing labored and shallow.

James holds my hands. "It's all right, Evie. It's James. You're in my room. You're safe. Take a deep breath. Breathe with me. Breathe…"

He sucks in a deep breath and raises my hand to his chest. I want to turn my head to see him, but my neck is failing me. The tears, now dry against my temples, itch along my hairline. I'm aware of every breath, every beat of my racing heart. I want to follow his instructions, but when I try to move my toes or bend my knees, my body refuses to cooperate, and terror forces a new batch of tears to cloud my vision.

"Don't move. Just breathe. One breath at a time."

I'm trapped.

"It's all right, Wats," he murmurs, running his hand up and down my arm and wiping new tears from my temples. "I know you're scared, but you're okay. I'm here and I'm not going anywhere."

I'm battered and broken like a ship in a midnight storm, merely pieces of what I was before. But his voice is like a beacon of light through the dark waters, calling me to shore.

With each pass of his hand along my arm, with each comforting sound that escapes his lips, the blood ebbs from my eardrums; movement trickles back into my limbs and my breathing evens out.

The crashing waves subside with the outgoing tide.

I blink. My eyelids, thankfully, are cooperating, and the last bit of tears fall silently down the contours of my face.

His sigh of relief is loud and full. And when he kisses my lips, I welcome the touch with every piece of me.

But I can't reciprocate. My limbs tingle as they slowly regain movement, but my lips don't move the way I want them to.

He pulls away and runs his thumb along my cheekbone. "Are you okay?"

"Yes," I rasp.

"Can you sit up?"

When I nod, he runs an arm around my back and helps me into a sitting position. I scoot back against the headboard, relying on him to help me.

He climbs off the bed, grabs a drinking glass from the night-stand, and fills it in the bathroom sink. Once he returns, he brings it to my lips. "Let me help you."

The water is refreshing against my inflamed skin. My senses return one after another, and my limbs respond to my attempts to move them. As I work past the night terror that still has me reeling, the horror I've experienced is replaced with embarrassment.

James has witnessed my sleep paralysis.

Fuck.

I must look like such a basket case.

Bile rises in my throat, daring to scorch my insides to match my outsides. I swallow hard against it.

I don't want to be here. I don't want him to see me like this.

Small ripples radiate across the water in my glass from my shaky grip. James still has one hand on it to keep it from spilling.

After several silent moments, he asks, "What was that? I woke up to you making these choking sounds. Your eyes were open, but you wouldn't look at me. You looked like you were awake, but it was like you couldn't hear me or even move. And you looked so scared..."

I can't bear to meet his gaze. I'm so humiliated, and my face is burning hotter than ever. I'd welcome being locked in that horrible closet if it meant sparing me from this inevitable conversation. "I don't know what to say. I'm sorry..." I pull in a deep breath, trying to give my lungs what they so desperately need. I can't take my eyes off the glass in my hands. And I don't want to. "I'm sorry if I scared you."

"Jesus, don't apologize. I just..." He scoots closer to me and ducks his head, willing me to look at him. But I refuse. "Has that ever happened to you before? What was it?"

"Yes," I whisper. "Not for a long time, though. I..."

He waits for me to continue, holding my hand and running circles over the top of it with his thumb. But I can't. I have neither the words nor the desire to let this man into the darkest recesses of my mind.

"I don't really want to talk about it."

"Why not?" he asks. "You can tell me. Maybe the best thing for you to do would be—"

"What?" I glare at him, irritated by his presumptuousness and overwhelmed with embarrassment. "What should I do, James? *Please* tell me how you can fix this. Oh wait, that's right, you can't. No one can." I leap off the bed, set the glass on the nightstand, and begin searching the room for my clothes. I'm suddenly aware of how naked I am, and it only enhances my vulnerabilities.

"Whoa, what is happening right now?" he asks. "Why are you upset? You had some weird panic attack in your sleep, Evie." He motions toward my side of the bed. "I have every right to want to know what's—"

"No, you don't. It's not that simple. And I don't want to talk about it." When I spy my shirt on the floor near the foot of the bed, I stomp toward it and pull it over my head.

He moves to the edge of the mattress, throwing his legs over the side and looking for his own clothing. "After everything, I can't believe what little regard you're giving me, giving *us*," he mutters, fuming.

I yank up my shorts and glower at him. "What us, James? You hardly know me."

"I'm trying, Evie." His fiery eyes square on mine. "Christ, don't you see that? I'm trying to know you, to know *all* of you, but how can I if you won't let me in?"

I head for the door, but his next words make me freeze.

"Was this your plan all along?" he asks.

I whip around to face him. "Was *what* my plan?"

He pulls on a pair of pajama pants from his open suitcase on the floor. "To use me for a night and then run out of my life as quickly as you entered it? To go our separate ways after we set foot off that ferry today? Was everything you said last night all a lie?"

I'm stunned silent. Why would he ever think such a thing? What have I said or done since the moment we met to make him think it? "Of course not. How can you say that?"

"What in the hell am I supposed to think? Because guess what, baby girl, I'm confused as hell right now. If your plan was to keep seeing me once we were back on the mainland, then you must know that whatever *that* was just now"—he waves a hand toward the bed —"would need to be explained at some point, right?"

"Honestly, no. I don't see why it has to be discussed at all."

His eyes widen, little embers of light dancing in his irises.

"Now it's my turn to ask how *you* can even think that." His voice is calmer now but direct, his stance squared and his feet firmly planted. He's a soldier through and through; unshakable.

"I don't think it's too much to ask, James. It doesn't change the way I feel about you, and I would hope it doesn't change anything for you either."

"But it does, Evie. Not the way I feel about you, but it has me questioning us. How are we ever supposed to be together if you don't trust me enough to let me in?"

My heart flutters at his words—*be together*—and I force myself to quell the butterflies that flit about in my riled stomach. I have no idea what to say. My mind is still trying to catch up.

Instead, I berate myself for having another goddamn episode. In front of him, no less. First, a panic attack, then sleep paralysis. Jesus. It's a wonder he's still here at all. But regardless, these are my experiences, my triggers, my trauma. It's only right that it be divulged on my timeline.

He folds his arms and finally breaks the painful silence. "Are you implying that something traumatic happened to you when you were younger and it now causes these, I don't know, these *episodes* that you don't want to talk about?"

The way he uses the word *episodes* feels dismissive in a way that sends me reeling.

Dick.

I fasten the button and zipper of my shorts without even a glance in his direction and head for the door.

"Evie, *stop*."

The sharpness of his tone gives me pause. But I refuse to turn around. Instead, I wait for my breathing to steady.

"Don't feel bad, James," I tell him without so much as a glance over my shoulder. "It isn't personal, I swear. This isn't something I tell anyone."

"Yeah? And how's that working out for you?" His voice is cruel, masking the frustration and heartache I know is brewing below the surface.

I shoot him a pained look and fling the door open. He leaps

forward and runs toward me, pushing the door closed before I can walk through.

"I'm sorry. It was a stupid thing to say. Please don't leave here upset. Let's talk about this."

"Just get out of my way, James."

"I'm not going to step aside and let you leave here pissed off at me." Although his voice is calm now, he looms over me, his bare chest heaving with deep, rapid breaths.

"You'd never believe me. I told someone once, long ago, and it was the worst mistake I ever made. I can't handle the thought of seeing that same doubt in your eyes. You mean the world to me, and I won't jeopardize what could be something great, all for the bull-shit that still creeps into my dreams every now and then."

I wait for him to respond. But what is there to say, really? There's nothing he could say to—

He tips forward and kisses me hard, catching me off guard and making me wobble. With his hands on my upper arms, he steadies me, and I let him press his body against mine. I moan against his touch and run my fingers down his bare chest while he places open-mouthed kisses down my neck.

"Please," he moans against my collarbone.

I expect him to beg me to stay. To say we can forget everything and start the morning anew. But instead, as he drags his kisses back up my neck and along my jawline, he says, "Let me in."

Arousal pools between my legs as his breath tickles my skin. I want to let him in. More than anyone ever before. I care for him in a way I never expected. But my feelings for him are precisely the reason I have to keep this to myself. If I tell him about the darkest time of my life and he doubts its authenticity, I'll never truly trust him, and I'll lose him forever.

"I can't, I'm sorry," I reply, pulling away from his embrace and reaching for the door. "I'll tell you anything you want to know,

James. Anything." I stare into his eyes. He looks as morose as I feel. "Just not this."

I open the door once more and release a startled gasp as I come face to face with Jenna.

"*Jesus*, Jenna, you scared the shit out of me," I scold, clutching my chest. "How long have you been standing there?"

"Not long," she replies, her eyes wide with surprise. "I came by your room looking for you, but you weren't there, so I figured you might be in here." She looks past me and up at James, who has sidled up behind me. "What's wrong?" Jenna's eyes bounce between James and me, clearly sensing the tension in the air.

"It's nothing. James and I...we just...I...you know what? It's fine. What did you need me for?" My words are more clipped than I intended, and my insides churn with a rush of guilt.

"Just letting you know that brunch will be downstairs at eleven, and the ferry leaves at one. And I wanted to give each of you..." She reaches for the pocket of her plaid pajama pants but stops abruptly. "You know what? It can wait."

"You sure?"

She nods and puts on her best fake smile.

She isn't fooling me. But I'm too emotional to ascertain Jenna's intentions right now. "Okay, then." I push past her, leaving her stranded in the doorway with James.

When I near the hallway junction, I stop and peer over my shoulder. I only catch a glimpse of Jenna as she steps into James's room and closes the door behind her with a soft *click*.

CHAPTER 15

JAMES

What the hell just happened?

My room is frigid in Evie's absence. I want to run after her. Grab her by the shoulders and force her to face me. I want to shove her against a wall and fuck her until her screams wake the entire island. Thrust inside her until she's on the brink of climax, then stop shy and demand she tell me everything. I want to make her beg to be finished off, bring her the combination of pain and pleasure that will force her to give me the answers I crave.

My cock jerks at the thought. But then I remember the look in her eyes as she lay, unmoving, eyes open and fixed above her, tears streaming down her temples. She looked terrified, and no matter what I did, no matter how I shook her and called her name, she wouldn't move, wouldn't speak.

Aside from my sister, I have never worried about another person like that. Not even during David's roughest times. I knew how much I cared about her when I caught Ashton putting his filthy hands on her in the hedge maze. But this was something different, something far more sinister and raw. She was suffocating against a paralytic affliction, and I was overwhelmed with the desire to free her from her own mental clutches. I wanted—*needed*—to protect her, no matter the cost.

I will convince her to confide in me. And no matter what she tells me, I'll listen. I'll believe her. And I'll comfort her.

Because I love her.

Wait, *what*?

The notion rushes over me like a tidal wave. Holy shit. I race to the door, eager to make my way to Evie's room. But the sound of Jenna's voice stops me dead in my tracks. "James, can we talk?"

Shit, I forgot she was even in here.

"I need to talk to Evie. I'm sorry, I can't stay—"

"Good. And I don't want to keep you. But I need to tell you something before you go to her."

My impatience far supersedes my confusion.

As Jenna steps toward the center of the room, I'm increasingly aware of the smell of sex in the air and the state of my horribly tussled bedsheets.

"Listen. I know Evie better than anyone. I can tell something happened this morning that she doesn't want to talk about. And I can guess what it is. It's literally the only thing she clams up about. I probably shouldn't tell you this, but you deserve to know. She suffers from night terrors that sometimes lead to sleep paralysis."

"Is that what that was? She was so..." I can't articulate what I saw or how it affected me. "You've seen it happen to her before?"

"Only twice. She and I are very close and have spent a lot of overnights together. They can be triggered by stress, but even she can't pinpoint exactly what brings them on. She said she hasn't had an episode in years."

"I don't get it. Why wouldn't she just tell me this?"

"She probably doesn't know how. They start as nightmares that eventually consume her to the point where she's temporarily paralyzed. And she can't tell the difference between being asleep and awake. But honestly, as far as *what* she's seeing during these episodes, I have no idea. She's never told me..." Jenna sighs, her forehead creased with concern.

"She said she told someone a long time ago, and it was the worst mistake she ever made." I study her face for answers.

"She's probably referring to her ex-boyfriend, Connor. Things ended very suddenly between them. But I don't know." She shakes her head.

"What else can you tell me?" I'm desperate. Even if I go over there and beg Evie to divulge the content of her nightmares, there's no guarantee she'll oblige. Maybe all I'll ever learn is what Jenna tells me right here and now.

"All I know is that when she was little, her father would lock her in her closet. He'd scoop her up, any time of day or night. Sometimes she would be sound asleep in her bed, other times she would be playing or eating. It didn't matter. He would put her in her closet and leave her there. Sometimes for hours. He claimed there were monsters in the house, and he was protecting her from them. And he warned that if she screamed for him, the monsters would hear her, and then he would be helpless to save her. So she would lie inside, crying silently for hours on end, trying everything in her power not to make a sound."

What the fuck? Monsters? Was her father crazy? What else did he do to her? The questions compound on themselves, and the beginnings of a headache brew behind my eyes.

A heavy sigh makes my lungs go slack. "Did he touch her?" I have to know. My face goes hot and burns all the way down my neck awaiting Jenna's answer.

"No. At least not that she's ever told me. But I do wonder sometimes..." She trails off, releasing a long breath that mirrors mine and peering off in the distance. My mind races a mile a minute as I attempt to piece everything together. But when she puts a comforting hand on my arm, my mind settles under the warmth of her gaze. "She's a good person, James. And she cares so much about you. She's clearly afraid of losing you. I mean, you only just met. This is a lot."

I scowl at her presumptions. "I'm not going anywhere, Jenna. If that's what you two are afraid of, don't be. I'm crazy about her. I only want the truth."

She smiles wide as she throws her arms around my waist. "I'm so happy to hear you say that."

I suppress a laugh.

"This is so amazing," she says, pulling away to look at me. "And it's the perfect segue to what I came here for." She reaches into her pants pocket and presents me with a folded sheet of paper. "I was hoping to give these to you both at the same time, but this can't wait any longer. Open it."

I unfold the sheet of paper as Jenna explains. "It's the wish she asked for last night. The one that went into the lockbox after dinner. I read through them after the games ended, and I couldn't help but notice how similar yours were. I thought maybe you'd like to read hers."

"Do you think she'd mind?" I ask. I'm nervous about what it might say. But I'm also tortured by my curiosity. I want to know the secret that eluded me all night long.

"You need to read it. And if it makes you feel any better, I have every intention of showing her yours when I leave here."

I divert my attention to the paper.

Finally, I hold in my hands Evie's answer to the question Jenna posed at dinner:

One thing your heart desires...

I read her answer slowly, savoring each word. It's a poem—of course, my darling English lit nerd—and it reads:

> A fervent kiss upon my lips
> And a night of carnal sighs
> A promise made within a whisper
> Of no more sad goodbyes
>
> A second chance at love unveiled
> My fate sealed on a whim
> My heart revels in pure desire
> What I want, dear friend, is **him**

My heart swells at her words, which are far more eloquent than my own. Within hours of meeting, she was willing to take a chance on me; to open herself up to the idea of trusting me with her heart.

I fold the paper and hurry for the door. "I'm sorry, I have to go."

"Wait, let me talk to her first. I want things to work out between you two, but she's upset and probably more embarrassed than anything."

I look at her, dumbfounded. No way will I risk waiting another second.

"She can't go anywhere," Jenna insists, as if reading my mind. "She's trapped on this island until one o'clock, like the rest of us. Give me a twenty-minute head start, okay? Then come over there and sweep her off her feet." Jenna's got her childlike charm turned all the way up; it's surely the same charm that won over David, not that I can at all blame him.

I acquiesce with a single nod.

"Thank you." Her smile is warm and relieved. She throws her arms around me in another quick hug and rushes from the room, leaving me alone with Evie's note and twenty solid minutes to devour it over and over again.

CHAPTER 16
EVIE

"Evie, open up. It's Jen."

When I crack the door open, I'm met with Jenna's concerned face. She's got a hand on her hip, which means she's more than concerned—she means business.

"What's going on?" she pushes on the door and saunters past me into my room.

"It's nothing. I'm fine," I lie, refusing to meet her gaze.

"Bullshit. You look like you're about to cry. What happened?" Her face is flushed with concern.

"I just…" I shake my head in frustration. "James and I had an argument, that's all. Really, Jenna, everything's fine."

"You've never been a good liar. Everything is clearly *not* fine." She waves a hand at my splotchy face.

"I heard you arguing." She sighs. "I don't get it. You hit it off so well." Her shoulders slump as she looks at me, silently begging me to explain.

"Yeah…I know." I study my bare feet as I cross my arms in front of me.

She steps into me and grabs me by the shoulders, then pushes me over to the bed before lowering herself beside me. "What's going on with you, Evie?" she demands. "The truth now."

She sounds like James.

"I just, um…" I fight to steady my pounding heart. "I—I had a night terror. Woke up paralyzed. I'm still kind of reeling from it, I guess. It's been so long since the last one, and I was stupidly hopeful that they were over with for good." I tangle my fingers in my lap and focus on the floor in front of me. "The doctor told me they often dissipate with age. So to have one so out of the blue like this, and in front of *him*. God, Jenna, I'm so embarrassed." I drop my face into my hands, an uncomfortable yet familiar warmth creeping into my cheeks.

She puts an arm around my shoulders. "There is nothing to be embarrassed about. He's so into you. And he's not the type of guy who'll jump to weird conclusions. Maybe if you told him—"

"Why, Jenna? Why is that my only option?" I leap off the bed, irritation tugging at my insides. Not at Jenna, but at myself for having another goddamn episode.

Fuck, I hate that word.

"I told him I didn't want to talk about it, but he kept insisting. I'm trying to put this all behind me and forget about it." I throw my arms up and pace the room. "How am I supposed to do that if people keep asking me to relive this shit?"

"Because we care about you," she replies, nearly cutting me off. And she's so calm it's almost irritating. "You've never even told *me* about the night your dad died. And you can deny it all you want, but I know something awful happened. Remember when you had a night terror at my house? I'll never forget it. You kept crying out for Papa in your sleep."

My mouth drops in shock, and I stop dead in my tracks. "You never told me that."

"That's right." The seriousness of her tone shakes me to my core. "Looks like we're both a bit guilty of not divulging what we should."

Touché.

"It scared the shit out of me. But you didn't want to talk about it, and I respected that. But that's my reaction. James isn't me. He wants to know you on a deeper level. One I know you don't let just anyone reach. Not even me."

My heart plummets straight to the floor at the sadness in her expression. I reach for her, but she recoils, and it knocks the wind right out of me.

She clears her throat and continues. "This is part of how he gets to know you. I mean, hell, I'm sure he has some skeletons too. We all do."

"Yeah, except they don't usually come out the first night you meet someone," I mutter.

"Not usually, no. But like you said, you just met him. What have you got to lose?"

A pit forms in my stomach at her comment. "James, he…" I trail off and return to my spot on the edge of the bed, bringing my legs up and crossing them under me. Hunched over, I let out a quiet sigh.

"What's going on? And I want the truth." Jenna turns and squares her body with mine.

"I just…" Where do I begin? "James means so much to me. I don't know what's happening exactly, but I'm crazy about him, and if I lost him, I don't know what I would do." I examine my hands as another round of tears threatens to spill. "I know it sounds ridiculous. I mean, we met yesterday." I peer up at her.

"Oh my God," Jenna gasps, her mouth open in awe.

"What?"

"Do you love him?"

"What? Are you *crazy*? I've known him for less than a day."

"Evelyn Foster, I have known you for years. You're my best friend, and I have never seen you this worked up over a man. You *love* him."

"You're insane. I mean…he…he's…just…so…" I tip my head back

and study the canopy coverings, shaking my head in frustration and confusion and angst and...

Love.

How in the hell is this possible?

It's insane.

Am I in love with James? After one night? That doesn't actually happen, right?

Fuck.

I fall silent, desperate for the right words. Heck, desperate for *any* words. I can't seem to convey what I'm thinking or how I'm feeling. And the worst part of all is that there's no way he's in love with me. If there's even the slightest chance he reciprocates my feelings, then that would make him crazy, right? And do I want to be with someone who's as crazy as, well, *me*?

A burdensome sigh escapes me, and I catch Jenna grinning at me like an idiot out of the corner of my eye. "Stop looking at me like that. People don't fall in love in the span of twenty-four hours—*less* than twenty-four hours. It just doesn't happen."

"Call it love or don't. Either way, it doesn't change how you feel about each other."

Damn it. Deep in my gut, I know she's right.

"I paired you two up for a reason." She pulls my hand from my lap and holds it. "From the moment I met him, I knew he would be perfect for you. He's strong but gentle, and he has that adorable nerdy thing going on that you like. He's a reader, like you. And as an added bonus, he's taller than you, which is rare because you're a goddamn giant." She grins and squeezes my hand. "But I knew, deep in my gut, that he would be perfect for you. The way he talks about his sister and his niece...I mean, he lights up when they're around. I met his sister a couple of times while we were up in New York. He's so protective of her in the sweetest way."

Her expression turns serious.

"She confided in me one evening. Years ago, she was in an

abusive relationship with the father of her child, and when James found out, he went ballistic and let the guy have it." She presses her lips together and regards me for a moment. "She said he'd do anything to protect the people he loves; that the only time she ever feels truly safe is when he's around. And you deserve to have that too, Eves, finally; someone who will love you and protect you and treat you the way you deserve to be treated." Her eyes go soft then, a sweet smile breaking out across her face. "And James *is* that guy, I can feel it."

My heart races to a nonexistent finish line. He never told me that about his sister. And why would he? We've had no time to swap stories. But I've seen how protective he can be. The way he protected me from Ashton in the hedge maze.

Then it hits me. Like a goddamn wrecking ball, it strikes me broadside.

James will do anything to protect me.

Jenna's words replay in my mind: *he'd do anything to protect the people he loves.*

Loves.

Does James love me too?

My heart hammers, fierce and tumultuous, and I instinctively run a hand over my chest to protect it.

Jenna sighs. "I suppose I have my own confession to make," she hedges. She bites her bottom lip and tilts her head, but it takes several seconds for her to continue. "This entire night? We set it all up for you, Eves."

My stomach drops. "What?" I'm not sure how many more surprises I can handle.

"You're my best friend, and I adore you. And I wanted you to meet James. I figured if I arranged for you to meet in an environment where everyone was letting loose and acting silly, you could get to know one another better and hopefully more quickly; you know, without the formalities getting in the way. David doesn't even know my true intention. He thought we were throwing a combined bachelor/bachelorette party thing. Whatever you want to call it. In fact, he kept insisting that I partner you with Ashton, but I fought it tooth and nail."

A sickening feeling rumbles in my core. The thought of having to spend the entire night fighting off Ashton's unwanted advances makes my skin crawl. But not nearly as much as knowing there was a chance James may have been partnered up with someone else. Jealousy as powerful as an avalanche damn near suffocates me.

"I told David that if you weren't paired with James, game night was not happening at all." She waves her hands dismissively.

I gape in shock. Why on earth would she go to so much trouble? Probably because after several blind dates, I swore them off entirely, so setting us up for drinks may not have gone over well. But to go this far? It was probably the best possible way to force me into the same space as a stranger of her choosing.

She knows me too well. It's a blessing and a curse.

She knew she would have to essentially trap me.

On an island.

With no way to escape.

Damn, she's good.

Her gesture consumes me with appreciation and a love for my best friend who went to so much trouble to help me find happiness. And it worked. She thought James would be a terrific partner for me, and he is.

In every sense of the word.

But I can't shake the feeling that she's not telling me everything. Never has she tried to push me toward a guy with such tenacity. And the timing of it is off.

I can't hold it in any longer. "Jen, I have to ask you something."

She tucks her hair behind her ears in anticipation.

"The timing is terrible, I know, and I'm sorry. But ever since you got engaged, we haven't had a single moment alone, and I have to ask..." I take in a deep breath, my lungs aching as they stretch.

Her worried eyes are painful to look at.

"Is David the one? I mean, is he..." I drum my fingers against my leg, a nervous habit, and peek back up at her.

Her brow furrows, but she remains silent.

"You say you love him, and I believe you, I just...it's all happened so fast."

She shifts and raises a hand to interrupt me, but I don't let her.

"Coming from me, considering the last, what, twelve hours, it sounds hypocritical, I know—"

"What exactly are you implying?" she replies with a pinched tone.

"I-I know you're a spontaneous person. But you never have been when it comes to men. You've always made guys work for it. You joke about how much you love making guys pursue you, how you're worth the chase—and you are. With David, though, we met him in a nightclub, and two months later, you were *engaged*." I pause and study my hands again. "It's so unlike you."

"Um, the last twelve hours have been so unlike *you*." She bites at her bottom lip and peers at me through squinted eyes.

"I know, I know, I know, I know." I bury my face in my hands, my hypocrisy chewing at my insides. "It's just, you have to admit, the timing is weird. It can't be a coincidence..."

"What can't be a coincidence?"

"You're really going to make me say it, aren't you?" My fucking heart is about to send me into cardiac arrest.

She replies with merely a tilt of her head.

"*The kiss*, Jen," I blurt out. "Two weeks—"

"Evie, stop," she interrupts, putting a hand up to silence me. She uncrosses her legs and shifts away.

But I ignore her pleas.

"Two weeks after you kiss me, you tell me that you and David are engaged."

"Goddammit, Evie. I told you to *stop*. I don't want to drag that up again." She turns away, avoiding my gaze, poised to pounce off the bed.

"Why? Why can't we talk about it? We're best friends—"

"It's always been more than that for me, and you know it," she barks, her neck and face flushed to match that wildfire hair of hers.

"I-I'm sorry." I reach for her, but she shies away. The gesture pierces me with a sickening mixture of nausea and guilt. Her pain is something I will never truly understand. But goddamn, how I want to. I would have my body drawn and quartered if it meant sparing her the pain she's feeling right now.

She releases a labored sigh, her neck as blotchy as ever. But she remains silent. Too silent. It's driving me mad. My heartbeat deafens me as I wait for her to speak.

Please don't leave. Hit me. Scream at me. Curse my name. Just please don't leave this room. Not yet.

"I didn't know what I'd found with David when I first met him," Jen finally speaks, cutting through the tense silence. "But I always knew what I had with you. I loved you, Eves. I still do. And not in a *best friend* kind of way. It took me years to work up the courage for that kiss. And after I started seeing David, I was scared that I may never be granted the opportunity. But you made it clear you didn't feel the same, and I respected it. But why are you bringing it up again now? Here of all places? And a week before my fucking wedding?" She leers at me.

My stomach churns at my own audacity.

"I'm sorry." I press my lips together and regard her. "I just want to make sure you're marrying him for the right reasons. Because you love him. Not to, I don't know, prove that you aren't hurt by me anymore."

"That's an awfully bold statement," she scoffs. One large boulder after the other stacks itself on my chest.

After several grueling moments, her demeanor softens; her shoulders relax and her tone evens out.

"But it's an honest one, so thank you." She turns to face me again. "I do love David. Very much. He's driven, he's handsome, he makes me laugh…" She reaches for my hand and pulls it from my lap again. "He's not you, though." She studies our coupled hands. "And he never will be. I mean, you—" she chokes, her eyes red and brimming with tears. "You're my person."

My throat tightens with a rush of sadness and guilt. I yearn to reciprocate the feelings that haunt her. God knows I love her in every sense of the word.

Except the one way she needs from me the most.

And I despise myself for it.

I wrap her in my arms and pull her close, waiting for her to break down. I await the flooding tears and trembling shoulders. But they never come. She doesn't shed a single tear. Maybe she's wept enough already, coddling her broken heart in private, shutting me out of her grievance, since I'm the one who put it there in the first place.

But she doesn't pull away either. I sink into her warmth as I rest my cheek against her head and squeeze her a little tighter.

"I do love you, Jen," I whisper, and her breath hitches against my neck. "I'd do anything to be able to give you what you want. I'm so sorry that I can't be the person you need me to be."

She pulls away, her features soft and her voice tender. "Don't ever apologize for being honest about who you are. You've never once misled me, and it means the world that we never allowed the kiss to skew our friendship. You've always loved me for who I am, and it's one of the reasons I adore you."

I scoot even closer. "I adore you too. You know I do." I lean in and rest my chin on her shoulder, facing her side. "David is the luck-iest freaking man on Earth."

"He is, isn't he?" she replies in a playful tone.

I can't help but laugh as I shift my weight to see her better.

"Heck, who knows," she says. "Maybe in another life, it'll be you and me standing at that altar together." Her neck and cheeks redden all over again, but she holds firm my gaze.

"It's a deal." I reach for her hand to shake on it, but instead, she brings my palm to her lips and places a light kiss inside. It's the gentlest kiss I have ever received, and it steadies my racing heart.

"Are you feeling better about this James situation?" she asks, lowering my hand back into my lap. "He'll be knocking on that door any minute."

"He's coming over here?" I interrupt, confused by the sudden change in topic. My stomach flips from the dizzying combination of trepidation and elation.

"Yes, to talk things over and to inevitably steal you away from me," she says with a laugh. Before I can respond, she goes on, "And you really should talk it out. Give him a chance to understand what happened—"

I shake my head, "You're never going to let up—"

"Listen. Do you like this guy?" she interjects, slapping her knee as she shifts over to her sternest voice.

"Very much."

"Do you want to see him again after we leave this island?"

"More than anything."

"Then why are you fighting this? Shit, just go over there and tell him what happened when you were a kid. Tell him what these night terrors are like for you. Let him into your life beyond a simple night of games and flirtation. And if he doesn't accept you for who you are, then I don't want you with him anyway." She huffs and raises her voice. "If that's the case, I'll take the blame for it and admit that I made a terrible mistake and grovel at your feet. Deal?"

Maybe I should be angry, but she's impossible to be mad at.

Plus, she's right.

"But I don't think I made a mistake with this one. I really don't." She's gone pensive, yet she's still pushy. "And before you ask, no, I'm not pushing you off on James to prove I don't have feelings for you. In fact, it's the opposite. I think you two make a cute couple, and because I love you, I want you to be happy."

My heart sings. I honestly don't know what in the hell I would do without her. She's always pushed me out of my comfort zone, supported me through my best and worst moments. I hope to always show her the same level of loyalty and devotion she has shown me from day one.

If not, I'll die trying.

I clear my throat. "If I owe anyone an explanation about my night terrors, it's you."

She transforms into a blurred mess as tears well up in my eyes. With her arms thrown around me, she holds me close. These last few minutes have felt like an awakening. As hard as it will be to let James in, I know it must be done.

Because I love him.

And Jenna will continue to push me toward him every step of the way.

Because she loves me.

She pulls back and places a gentle hand on my shoulder. "Let's start with him, okay? You know where to find me when the time comes." She brushes a tear from my cheek. "And before I forget, take this." She hops off the bed and pauses in front of me, her arm outstretched.

I arch a brow in confusion and regard the proffered item.

"This is why I was looking for you. It's his one wish." Her mouth quirks into a subtle smile. "Read it," she urges. "It may surprise you."

As she reaches the door, she turns to face me one last time.

"Don't you dare set foot down those stairs until you've reconciled with that man." She squints at me. "And we better not see the two of you at brunch either, capisce?"

Capisce. That's definitely a word she picked up from David.

"I want you up here, kissing and making up." She leaves with a cocky smile, slamming the door behind her before I have the chance to refute.

I cross my legs beneath me, unfold the sheet of paper, and dive in.

Maybe I could come up with a more solid answer for you if she wasn't sitting across from me right now. She's a brainiac, quippy, stunning. And those eyes, Jenna. My God. I've never seen anything like them. I'm WAY too distracted to think of anything else right now.

So, to answer your question, I don't want or need anything else. Because from the moment you announced that Evie was my partner for the night, I already knew I had everything I could possibly ask for.

Her.

I read it twice. Then a third time and a fourth. Hell, I don't know how many times I read it. My heart stampedes, and an ache takes root deep inside me. I will fix this. Jenna is right, as usual. James is too special, and I'm so dangerously close to trusting him implicitly. But I have to know how he'll react once I let him in all the way.

It's time to find out. Because he's worth it. Jesus, we've only known each other for one night.

This is insane. So utterly insane. But for the first time in my life, it feels right.

He feels right.
I've fallen for him.
And I think he has fallen for me too.
For he and I wished for the exact same thing last night...
Each other.

Chapter 17

James

I give Jenna twenty minutes. That's what we agreed. Twenty torturous minutes. It's only enough time for me to freshen up, devour every word of Evie's poem on a loop, cement them permanently in my head, and fight the urge to go batshit mad as the minutes tick by.

When Jenna's time is up, I hurry down the hall toward room seven and knock on the door. With each second I wait for her, a weight expands inside my chest.

Come on, Evie.

The folded paper crunches in my fist. What passes as mere seconds feels like years, but finally, the door creaks open, and Evie peers at me with red-rimmed, puffy eyes.

I take a step closer and cup her face in my hands, the paper brushing against her face.

She throws her arms around my neck and kisses me hard. The taste of strawberry is stronger than ever—clearly reapplied since we parted ways a short while ago. Our tongues barely find each other before she's falling to her knees and pulling my pajama pants to my ankles, forcing a stiff breath from my lips. She leans in to take my raging boner in her mouth. But I stop her. She still hasn't told me what I want—no, *need*—to know, and I can't shake the feeling she's trying to distract me from the questions she knows are coming.

Besides, my girl likes it rough.

And she still needs to be punished for not letting me in.

"I want to see that ass of yours," I say, peering down at her clothed body. I pull her to her feet, and she mewls like a little brat.

"Get those pants off," I bark. "Now."

She complies swiftly, doffing all her clothing like my good girl.

I relish her naked body, contoured in all the ways that make my head spin and my cock throb. I bend low at the knee and pick her up, throwing her over my shoulder in one swift motion. She squeals loudly against my ass.

With ease, I fling her onto the bed and flip her so she's bent over the edge with her feet flat on the floor. She squirms playfully as I tie a piece of canopy fabric around her wrists.

With her bare ass facing me, rotund and ripe, I flatten my hand and slap her. She moans against the sheets with each smack, and before long, both cheeks are a beautiful solid red.

I rub the area after each smack before punishing her again. In minutes, that sweet forbidden nectar I crave glistens between her legs.

"You're a bad girl, you know that? Keeping things from me. Tell me what I want to know, baby girl. Tell me what haunts you. Or I won't stop punishing you."

She writhes under my slaps, her cries muffled in the bedding as her pleasure swells inside her.

But she doesn't say a word.

She arches her back, offering her ass to me in anticipation of the next smack. The wetness between her legs pulls me in with its hypnotic shimmer. It's beautiful.

I smack it.

She screams into the bedding.

God, she's so wet.

I want to torture her with pleasure and punish her for shutting me out. Like a cat in heat, she writhes with each slap of her pussy, pushing against my hand.

The sight of her squirming on the bed engorges my cock to the point of pain. I press it against her backside, teasing her entrance.

"Please," she begs.

"Please what, you disobedient girl?"

"Fuck me, James."

I tsk at her. "You still haven't given me what I want. So I can't give you what you want."

She groans, probably cursing my name into the crimson blanket that matches her ass cheeks.

"I want to tell you," she cries. "I want to tell you everything. I always did. I just didn't know how. I was about to go to your room to tell you when you came knocking at my door."

"Don't play with me, Wats." I land another smack to her pussy but keep my hand against her wet entrance this time. She shifts her backside against me in response.

"I said no more lies."

"I would never"—she groans against the sheets as I caress her pink, teasing her—"lie to you...my love." Her breaths are shallow like a whispering wind.

My love.

I roll her onto her back and her eyes widen as I scrutinize her. "You love me?" I ask, my heart shooting straight into my throat.

"Well, I...I just meant..." she stammers as she pulls herself upright. A look of horror is stretched tightly across her face, and it nearly makes me chuckle. Nearly. She drums her fingers against her bare thigh as she avoids my gaze.

I climb onto the mattress beside her. "I want the truth, Eves."

Her eyes pierce mine when I call her *Eves*. I heard Jenna use it, but I don't know how Evie feels about me using it. But then, her lips turn up into a rapt smile, and I heave a sigh of relief.

"You've never called me 'Eves' before." Her eyes ignite. "I like it."

"It's fitting in a way, you know? Your obsession with my Adam's apple…" I give her my best devilish grin. "And you've already seduced me beyond any possible hope for redemption…" I lightly pinch one of her hard nipples.

She laughs and grabs my hand, then takes one of my fingers into her mouth.

If she's hoping to distract me from her indelible 'my love' comment, it won't work. I'd never forget such a statement. Especially from her.

I lower her onto her back, my erection poking into her hip as I hover above her. Running my fingers through her dark hair, I plant a kiss on the tip of her nose. Then one on each of her eyelids. She smiles at me, giggles even, and I take her mouth, pressing a firm, loving kiss upon her lips.

I want her. All of her. And with the slip of her tongue only moments ago, giving me a peek into her true feelings, I know I'm closer than ever to having her completely.

"Say it," I beg against her flushed cheek.

"Say what?" she coos toward the canopy.

"What I know you want to say but are holding back from me."

A silence hangs heavy between us. "I can't, James. You know why I can't," she sighs.

I prop myself up on my elbow and trace around her belly button. "Let me guess. You've found yourself in a very unexpected predicament, haven't you? You're in love with me, but you're afraid to tell me. Maybe because you think it's too soon. Because you're still judging the hell out of yourself for letting this happen so quickly. Or is it because you're afraid I'll think you're nuts and run for the hills?"

Her eyes lance mine, and I scour them for the truth.

And I find it.

She loves me. I can tell by the way it sets that seafoam aflame.

I just wish she'd say it.

So I take the bullet for both of us. "I love you."

Her eyes widen as they shimmer. "You do?" She rolls toward me.

"Of course. And I know it's crazy, believe me, so I get why you're afraid to say it. And you don't have to." I fidget with the lace bondages around her wrists, running the material through my fingers. "I thought it might be easier for you to accept what you're feeling if you knew I felt the same."

Her shoulders relax, and a heavy sigh escapes her lips. "I don't know what to say."

"You do, you just don't want to." I breathe my words against her ear, my nose grazing her temple.

"But I do," she whispers, her body trembling against mine.

I place tender kisses on her chin and the corners of her mouth, moving up her cheek and along the side of her face. Her lips part and a delicate sigh resonates between us.

"I love you," she whispers against my Adam's apple. My cock jerks when she presses her lips to my flesh.

"I love you too, Eves. You believe me, right?"

She nods, peering up at me, silently willing me to prove to her how true my words really are.

She shifts to meet my lips and kisses me with a passion she has apparently been saving for this moment. With the thirst of a woman stranded in an ocean's expanse, she searches for my tongue. Her body quivers as I explore every curve—her breasts, her hips, her buttocks. I want to touch every inch, kiss every part.

So that's exactly what I do.

I trace my tongue down her body, starting where her pulse beats in her throat, and slowly down to her belly button. I land in the sweetness between her legs. It's the heaven of butterscotch and musk that I yearn for, and I lap up every bit of it. She writhes and cants her hips and yanks at her own hair as I tease her clit with figure eights.

When her mewls evolve into the cries she saves for the edge of climax, I flick my tongue against her clit and thrust two fingers deep inside her. She bucks wildly, biting onto the back of the lace restraints to stymie her screams.

I pull them from her mouth. "I want to hear you."

"Oh God, James. I want you."

"I love to hear you beg, baby." I tease further. "Don't stop."

"Please, James." Her panting is out of control, and the gasps she lets loose are rapid and ragged.

She's so close.

"Please *what*, my love?"

"Fuck me."

I climb on top of her and throw her legs onto my shoulders. Then, bending low, I fold her onto herself. "Will you let me in, baby girl?" I whisper against her lips as I shove my cock deep inside her.

She breaks the kiss and throws her head back as I pierce her anatomy, releasing a lascivious cry. Her wrists are still bound, but she claws at my hair anyway, and I push her legs closer and closer to her own chest with each thrust. I reach her end with ease, filling her completely.

Erotic cries are all that escapes her as the headboard destroys the wall behind it.

She clenches down hard around me and screams as she comes, her orgasm arriving faster than I expected. The tightness makes my climax come racing.

When she finally opens her eyes and looks directly into mine, her orgasm waning, I fall apart. With a burst of flickering stars obscuring my vision, I come inside her, an intense growl lodging deep in my throat.

She holds my face against her chest as I release her legs. Her heartbeat is like a hummingbird, rapid yet soothing against my ear as I fight to catch my breath.

I never want to leave. I belong here, in her arms.

I want to fuse into her and leave as one person, never to be apart.

We lie like this for a long time, surrendering to the silence, the only sounds our labored breaths, our beating hearts, and birds chirping off in the distance.

She's the first to break the silence. "I'm ready to tell you," she whispers. "If you're ready to hear it."

I raise my head and meet her gaze. "I'm always ready for anything with you, love. Don't ever forget that."

We sit upright to face each other. I release her wrists from their binds and caress the skin to encourage blood flow. It gives me a chance to speak before she can begin. "Jenna told me a little before I came over here. I hope that's all right. She meant well." I pause, gauging her reaction. Much to my relief, her brow relaxes.

"What did she say?"

"That your father used to lock you in a closet when you were little and leave you in there. Something about monsters? Jenna didn't understand it well enough to explain it."

She looks away. "My...My father started showing signs of mental illness when I was about eight. I didn't learn until well into my adulthood that he likely suffered from acute paranoid schizophrenia. I grew up without a mother, so he and I were extremely close. He was my best friend, in fact. But then he started having these, I don't know, episodes. Out of nowhere, he'd find himself in a complete state of panic and claim there were monsters in our house."

She looks back at me, her brow tight, and I urge her to continue with a nod.

"He would scoop me up and rush me into the standing wardrobe in my bedroom and lock me inside. He would cut the lights out, claiming he didn't want the monsters to find me. I was instructed not to scream or cry, or hardly breathe for that matter, if I could help it. It was important that I didn't make any noise or else the monsters would hear me. And I believed him. I really did." She examines her hands, which are held in mine, and pulls in a long, slow breath. Her apprehension radiates off her naked body.

"I never saw anything, obviously, because there were not, in fact, monsters in our home. I was at a weird age where it seemed absurd, but my father had never done wrong by me before. He always took care of me; he never hurt me. So, if he said I was being locked inside a wardrobe for my own safety, I believed him."

"How long would he leave you in there?" I ask, my stomach turning sour, but my mind plagued with curiosity.

She answers with the shake of her head. "There were times I was locked in there for hours until the coast was clear. He would disappear the entire time. I never heard a peep. The silence inside my wooden coffin was almost too much to bear sometimes. I used to press my ear to the door, desperate for the sounds of his footsteps, anxious for the moment he would free me. I had no way to use the bathroom, but I was so afraid that my father was right about the monsters, so I wouldn't call out to him."

Her shoulders shake as she releases a pained, ragged sigh. She pulls a pillow into her lap, which she uses to occupy her hands by twisting the corner of its case around one of her fingers.

"There were times I was so thirsty that I would lie there dreaming of pools of ice water. Early on, I had accidents inside the wardrobe, especially if I dreamed of water. But eventually I learned how to hold it. Every time he locked me in, I cried, even though he told me not to. I discovered very quickly how to cry in silence. And most importantly, I learned how to go somewhere else in my mind to avoid going crazy. Sometimes I would fall asleep until my father returned. But other times, I would have full-on panic attacks, convinced the walls were closing in on me and I would be crushed to death. The air would be so thick that I knew I was suffocating." Her voice breaks, and her eyes fill with tears.

I cup her cheek, and she nestles her face against my palm. I have no idea what to say. And maybe there isn't really anything to say. She just needs to know I'm listening without judgment. That, despite everything, is her biggest fear.

She kisses my palm, clears her throat, and continues.

"Each time he let me out, he would tell me that the coast was clear. He'd scoop me up and carry me to my bed or to the couch and hold me. I never knew how to process it. He loved me, I was certain of that, but then he would be so spontaneously cruel. And on top of that, he would say it was for my own good. The most confusing part, though, was how he was always so gentle. Especially after he locked me away."

"I don't know what to say, Evie. I'm so sorry."

She makes eye contact, finally, before looking away again.

"You said your father passed, though, right?" I ask.

She nods. "I was eleven when he died. This is the part I dread telling you." She sucks in a long, deep breath.

I pull her into my lap and cradle her in my arms, and she buries her face in the crook of my neck.

Tracing her fingers up and down my forearm, she says, "By the time I was eleven, my father's episodes had become much more frequent, but I still never knew when they were coming. Even after years of enduring it, I never figured out the warning signs." She nuzzles my neck again. "And his paranoia had reached an all-time high. He built a secret compartment in the back of the wardrobe, convinced the monsters might break in and find me. So he dug a hole in the bedroom wall and bolted the wardrobe directly in front of it. There was a hidden door in the back with a rope pulley so I could get in and out of the secret compartment, but I was still locked inside the wardrobe itself, so it made little difference. Not that he ever understood, despite my tears and endless pleas. I feared that compartment more than hell itself. It was just big enough for me if I pulled my legs up to my chest, and I wasn't allowed to open the trapdoor until he knocked on the side of the wardrobe three times."

She shifts in my lap, adjusting herself to face me better. I run my fingers through her hair as she draws the pillow up against her chest and takes in another long, steadying breath.

"One evening, I was doing homework at my desk when my father burst through the door in a panic, yanked me by the arm, and tossed me into the wardrobe. Before shutting the door, he held a finger to his lips in a *shh* motion like always, reminding me not to make a sound, then pointed toward the secret compartment in the back.

"It started out like every time before, really, except this time I did hear voices inside the house. I couldn't make out what they were saying, but they sounded angry. It went on for several minutes, and then I heard what sounded like a man screaming, followed by weird shuffling noises, and then silence. I can't even begin to describe how terrified I was. I started to think that maybe my father's monsters were real. I was old enough to know better, but my imagination ran rampant in that wooden box."

She shifts again and hugs the pillow against her.

"And then I heard more scuffling, and the sound of doors opening and closing. Then a bizarre set of footsteps echoed in the hall. They made a clicking noise, like tap shoes almost. Like the metal plates people put under the toes and sometimes the heels of their shoes, you know, like boots or loafers?"

I nod. I know exactly what she's talking about.

"The footsteps grew louder, like someone was coming closer to my room. And then they were *inside* my room. Whomever belonged to those footsteps went to my closet and pushed my clothing aside. I can still remember the sound of the heavy hangers sliding across the bar. He was looking for something.

"Then he stopped right in front of the wardrobe. He tried to open it, but it was locked, of course. So he shook it. Violently. I've never been so scared in my life, and it took everything in my power to not scream. My father had always told me he locked me up because something was after me. That it was for my own safety. And for the first time in my life, I realized it was true. I silently begged for my father to come and stop the man before he could get me. But Papa never came. I was trapped. The walls continued to shake, and I thought for sure he would rip it right from its mounts and knock the whole thing over. I clutched my hand over my mouth to muffle my screams. I just wanted everything to stop shaking..."

She pulls herself upright in my lap, throwing one of her arms around my shoulders for balance and covering her face with a shaky palm.

"Hey, it's okay," I murmur, running my hand up and down her thigh in a soothing motion.

She takes another deep breath and lets it out slowly. "I was lying on the floor of the wardrobe, squeezing my eyes shut, begging for the shaking to stop. Finally...it did."

"And that's when the tapping started. He tapped his foot really fast, like *tap, tap, tap, tap, tap...*" She pats her hand against her leg to mimic the speed. "Through the crack under the wardrobe door, I could see his shoes. I'd never seen any like it. They were dark red with a weird pattern that looked like reptile skin or something. It terrified me. He shook the wardrobe all over again, and I used the deafening noise of it all as my chance to shuffle into the secret compartment.

"Once I was inside, there was a loud noise like wood splintering into a million pieces, and I just knew he had broken through the wardrobe. The only thing between him and me was that awful fucking trapdoor. I prayed for the man to give up his search and leave me there. But even more so, I prayed for my papa to come and rescue me. Before long, the sound of cracking wood stopped, and the distant voices and shuffling noises disappeared from the house and never returned. And neither did Papa."

"You mean he never came for you?" I ask, sickened with concern.

"No. Because, as it turns out, he was dead."

"Wait, *that's* when he died?" Thankfully, her attention is still locked on the headboard, because I can only imagine the look of horror on my face.

"It was. The police said it was suicide."

"The police?" I ask, my head swimming, desperate to fill in the gaps of the story.

"Yes. They're the ones who found me and let me out. I had been locked inside for two days—"

"Two days?" I cry. "What the hell—"

"According to the police," she explains, ignoring my cries, "my father had hanged himself with a belt from the showerhead in our bathroom. I didn't believe them then, and I still don't." She draws her legs closer to her chest.

"I stayed inside the secret compartment far longer than I should have. I was just so scared of making a sound, thinking that the man with the weird shoes would hear me and steal me away or worse. I couldn't see anything from in there, only hear the impenetrable silence from the other side of the little door. So I waited as long as I could before scooting back into the main part of the wardrobe. Much to my dismay, it was still locked. There was a hole in one of the doors, about the size of a softball, and there were pieces of splintered wood on the floor among my fallen coats.

"I wanted to break free, and I may have succeeded if I tried early on, before the lack of food and water made me too weak. But honestly, fear is what kept me from trying; fear of who might be out there waiting for me. Was it the monsters? A man in reptile shoes who wanted to hurt me? Plus, my father always came for me. And I thought he still would, even days later."

She gulps in air and toys with a small lock of hair near my right ear. She idly twirls it between her fingers, and I pull her even closer to my chest to grant her easier access.

"They took me to a hospital, and that's where the detective told me my father was dead. I told him someone else had been in the house. I told him about the voices, the red shoes, how someone tried to break open the wardrobe to get me. But he didn't believe me. He said there were no signs of forced entry. That everything pointed to suicide. And because I admitted that it was my father who locked me in there in the first place, they had even less reason to suspect foul play. He even suggested that I imagined it all because I was delusional from being locked up in complete darkness without food or water for so long. He implied that I was the one who punched a hole in the wardrobe door out of sheer panic and desperation."

"Jesus," I mutter under my breath.

"I never saw my father's body. The state cremated his remains...I never got to say goodbye."

"I'm so sorry, Eves." I squeeze her tight, breathing in her scent as I nuzzle my nose along her neck.

"Over time, I wondered if maybe I had imagined it. I couldn't make sense of it, and no one believed what I saw and heard. But no matter how hard I tried to convince myself that maybe it was a weird dream, I knew in my gut that what happened that night was real.

"My next of kin was my father's sister, Rose. She came out to Seattle to get me, and three days later she had me enrolled in a boarding school outside the city and then flew back to Boston. I protested. I didn't want to leave the home I shared with my father, but she insisted that enrolling me at Saint Jermaine was for my own good because I would be safe there. By then, I was so sick of hearing people say they were doing things to keep me safe. I didn't under-stand any of it. It just seemed like a way for people to excuse their cruelty.

"So, I attended Saint Jermaine until I graduated at eighteen. Then I ended up on the East Coast for college."

"Did you ever look for your aunt?" I ask.

She hesitates for several moments, her head tilted as she regards me, before returning her attention to the bedding. "I thought about it. But there was nothing she could say to me to make me want a relationship with her. So I chose to leave it in the past."

"You know…" I begin. "I'm glad you told me all of this. It certainly explains a few things."

She reels back, her eyes narrowing.

"N-No, shit. I didn't mean for it to come out that way. All I mean is, now that I know how your father would show you kindness following his cruelty, I can see why you keep making excuses for Ashton's behavior."

"I don't follow."

"Every time Ashton laid his hands on you, you made an excuse or shrugged it off. You would downplay the situation and say things like 'he's drunk; he didn't know what he was doing.' Even when that Marco guy locked your cuffs, you were quick to assume it was an accident. You shift the blame away from where it truly belongs. Your father was spontaneously cruel without reason or warning. But afterward, he would dote on you. It's no surprise that you may have a hard time realizing that a person's sole intentions are, in fact, to hurt you."

She looks rattled as she shifts in my lap and squints at me. "Are you implying that I don't know the difference between being hurt and being loved?"

"No, not at all. But until you truly find peace regarding your father, not just the circumstances surrounding his death but also the way he treated you, you may be more vulnerable to being hurt by others. Because you may end up excusing the behavior, you know?"

"And how am I supposed to do that? No one believes me when

I tell them what happened." She fidgets, twisting the corner of the pillowcase around in her fingers until they're purple.

"And they may never, Eves." I grab her restless hand and untangle the fabric. "But I do. Let me help you."

She shifts in my lap and faces me. Throwing her arms around my neck, she holds me in a tight embrace. Her breasts press hard against my chest, but my body is more consumed with surprise than arousal at the moment. She holds me for several moments while our chests rise and fall in a synchronized rhythm.

"Thank you," she whispers.

My heart tweets at her words. "Why are you thanking me?" I tilt my head back to look her square in the eye.

She shakes her head. "Years ago, I confided in someone I loved. I told him I thought my father had been murdered and that it was made to look like a suicide. About the wardrobe and the clicking red shoes..." She trails off, tears glossing over her eyes again. "Not only did he not believe me, but he even went so far as to imply that I was crazy and could have even inherited my father's schizophrenia. He told me that it would explain why I saw things that weren't there." She creates air quotes as she speaks.

"It was the first time in my life anyone had planted that kind of seed in my head. I know what I saw that night, but when he said that, I started to fear that maybe he was right. And that kernel of an idea evolved into paranoia, which is exactly what my father suffered from—paranoia and delusions. We broke up that same week," she whispers, ducking her head and picking at an invisible speck on the bedding beside us, "and I spent the next eight months seeing a therapist. I wanted a professional opinion." She buries her face in her hands again.

"You know, I saw a therapist after my last deployment. For a few years, actually. They can really help with trauma if you let them."

"You did?" Her voice no longer catches when she speaks, and

the redness brimming around her eyes begins to fade. I give her a nod of reassurance.

"My therapist helped me out tremendously, and I've since been checked out by many doctors who have assured me that I exhibit no signs of schizophrenia or paranoia. I believe them. It just took some time to get that horrible idea out of my head."

"What about your sleep paralysis? What do the doctors say about that?"

"It's probably triggered by the trauma of being locked up for so long that last time. They said it should likely subside over time, but it may never go away completely. But," she peers down at her lap, her face still flushed in a rosy color, "I'll never forgive him for planting that seed in my head. And after that, I swore I would never tell anyone. Not a soul. I couldn't risk doubting my own mind ever again.

"I had to explain some of it to Jenna when she witnessed my sleep paralysis for herself. But I couldn't bring myself to let even her in completely."

I pass my thumb over her cheekbone, causing a void in the pinkness of her flesh. "So why now? Why me?" I whisper. "Like you said, we've only known each other one night."

She shrugs. "I don't know. There's something about you that makes me feel safe. You have a comforting quality I can't explain." She presses her forehead against my cheek, and her breath warms my neck.

"Maybe on some subconscious level, the fact that we've only known each other for one night almost makes it easier. Like, if I did call you crazy or think you were lying, maybe it would be easier for you to dismiss my opinion," I say.

She pulls away and glares at me. "Is *that* what you think? Really? You think you're so easy to walk away from because we only just met?"

"Jesus, I hope not. I just think maybe the risk isn't as great since

I'm so new in your life. You were hurt by this other guy. Connor, right? Because you loved him and were with him for years. His accusation cut so deep because it was a betrayal. You trusted him with everything, and he used it against you. Maybe it was easier for you to tell me because my opinion has less riding on it."

She shakes her head and releases a long, frustrated sigh. "James, if you think that you're less of a risk because we've only known each other for a short while, then you really haven't been paying attention." She climbs off my lap.

"That's all I've been doing since the moment I laid eyes on you. Shit, I'm crazy about you." I grab her by the arm to keep her close.

"I'm crazy about you too. More than that, even. But you're implying that I don't value your opinion because we haven't known each other for long. When, in fact, it's quite the opposite. I value your opinion of me, of *anything,* implicitly. More so than anyone I've ever met. How could Dr. Watson not value the opinion of Sherlock Holmes? He'd be an idiot not to." She smiles at me and shoves my shoulder.

"I don't know what's happening here. Meeting someone and in a matter of hours falling this hard this fast. It's insane. I know it is. But..."

"But?" I ask, urging her to continue. I love where this is going.

"But you're unlike anyone I've ever met. I've been well on my way to trusting you all night. But for me, trust has to encompass all aspects of the word. And that's why I told you about what I saw that night. Because if I can't trust you to believe me, then I can't trust you at all. And I'd rather find that out now, before you take even more of my heart for yourself and leave me a complete mess."

My heart accelerates, compromising my ribcage. I run my fingers along her hairline, over and behind her ears, pressing my forehead to hers.

"You're giving it to me then?" I ask with a ragged breath.

"What?"

"Your heart," I breathe against her lips.

"You've been taking it from me all night," she coos as she traces her finger along my jawline. "And yours?"

"Sweet girl, you already have mine. You took it ages ago." I press my lips to hers and gorge myself on her strawberry taste. The passion, the *urgency*, of her kiss sends my heart rate skyrocketing.

She hops back onto my lap and straddles me, teasing my cock with her wetness. I grab her face and push it away, almost angrily, just how she likes it, and then I thrust my thumb into her mouth, just as I like it. She sucks it to the base, encircling it with her tongue, making my cock twitch with each bob of her head.

I yank it out with that loud *pop* I love so much. She throws her head back, opening her neck to me, and I nip at her throat as I caress her bare breasts. Reaching between us, she covers her fingers with her wetness, then rubs it over my erection.

"Do that again," I growl, watching her face as she massages my cock. "Touch yourself again."

She shoves a finger into her pussy, a low groan echoing in her chest, and then traces it up and around her clit, shuddering in ecstasy.

Fucking hell.

The sight of her pleasuring herself is about to unravel me.

I force her hand away from her pussy, and she jumps slightly, startled. Never taking my eyes off her, I bring her fingers to my mouth and suck. The way she tastes sends me into a topsy-turvy state of arousal. Her nipples, already hardened, grow warmer with each pinch I give them.

She yanks her hand away and kisses my lips.

She's too much in control.

That will never do.

You want me to be rough with you? That's what you like? Well, sweet girl, you've got another think coming.

I lift her from under her ass and push her down flat on the bed.

"I'm going to fuck you until you can't move. Until your pussy begs me to stop and even bleeds for me. I'm going to ravage every part of your body because it's *mine* now."

She cants her hips against my boner and arches her back, jutting her breasts toward me.

"You want me to suck on your tits, sweet girl?" I bring my mouth between them but don't make contact. My hand is on her throat when I lean close to her ear and whisper, "I will when I'm damn good and ready."

I climb up and straddle her face, my knees planted on either side of her head. Gripping the headboard, I look down at her and bark, "Open your mouth. Now." She does as I command, those luscious lips opening up and taking me in. I thrust into her, hard and deep, forcing her to gag against my cock as it hits the back of her throat.

"That's it, Wats. Let me in." The headboard shakes in my grip as I snake my other hand under her head and force my cock in deeper. She has such a perfect little mouth.

"My sweet, sweet girl," I moan.

I never take my eyes off her. The sight of her swallowing my cock is too incredible.

And then I wonder...

"Are you my sweet girl, Evie, or are you my little slut?"

She releases me, looks up with doe eyes, and asks, much to my surprise, "Would you rather fuck a good little girl in the ass or a dirty slut?" She blows a breath across the tip of my penis, rocking me to the fucking core.

"Both," I manage to choke out as she follows it with a kiss.

"Then you can have both," she replies. "Fuck my pussy, and I'll be your filthy little slut. Fuck me in the ass, and I'll be your good little virgin. You can ravage my body like no one else ever has and wreck me completely until I'm putty in your hands." She caresses my balls with a seductive grin. "If it pleases you, of course." Her sex-crazed eyes pierce straight through me as she takes me in her mouth again.

"Oh God, yes, it pleases me," I cry out, holding tighter to the headboard and resting my head against my arm. "Fuck, Evie."

She swirls her tongue around my cock and suctions around my tip.

I thrust faster—harder, harder, *harder*. But mere seconds before I explode in her mouth, I pull out. She regards me with wide eyes before reaching for my cock to finish the job. I let her take me into her mouth again, but after only two sucks of her pursed lips, I double over from the sensitivity and pleasure that's about to spill into her punishing mouth.

Holding back my orgasm is too much to bear, so I pull out and study her where she's trapped between my legs. Our eyes meet as she licks her lips, sending another twinge into my tortured cock. "Your dick tastes like strawberry now," she flirts. "Why'd you stop me?"

Her body writhes beneath me, perhaps aching for the seed I have yet to spill.

Such a dirty slut.

Ignoring her question, I climb off her and flip her onto her stomach in one swift, angry motion.

"On your knees," I growl.

She kneels before me, her elbows on the bed and that beautiful ass jutting upward, ready to be ravaged. The insides of her thighs glisten, and my balls retract at the sight.

I kneel behind her and tease her wet entrance with my cock. "Beg for me. Tell me how much you want it," I taunt, running one hand across her back.

"Please, James. I want you inside me," she begs against the bedding.

I slap her ass hard, and she gasps. "You can do better than that. A little slut like you? I'm sure you're used to begging to be fucked." I grip her hair.

"Oh God, fuck me, James." She pants against the sheets. "*Please*. Fuck me so hard I have to beg you to stop…"

She clenches the sheets in both hands, waiting to be penetrated. And I oblige.

I bury my rigid cock inside her with one hard, unforgiving thrust, shoving her forward on her knees and forcing a raw cry from her throat. Her pussy is so wet, and my cock revels in her tightness.

With a hand pressed against the back of her head, I pound into her. She reaches behind and rests her hand on the one I have pressed to her head. A loving gesture, sure, but I'm not making love to Evie. I'm *fucking* her. And those kinds of gestures simply won't do.

I pin both of her hands behind her back and use them as leverage as I pick up my speed. Her cries come out in staccato bursts that match my shunting rhythm.

Readjusting my grip so I've got her bound with one hand, I use the other to reach around her hips and play with her clit. It's swollen and begging for attention. She bucks her hips, panting into the bedsheets and screaming my name. "Oh God, James. *Yes*."

Her pussy pulsates around me, soaking my hand.

"That's my little slut," I moan, my neck craned in my own desire. I remove my hand and slap her ass. A red handprint emerges, and I grab it, squeezing hard.

"Do you want me to wreck you?" I sneer. She ignores me in spite of her own cries.

"Answer me," I bark, grabbing her hips and driving my cock in deeper.

"Yes," she whimpers.

I slap her ass again, harder than before, and she cries out, her loudest yet. Gripping her hair by the roots, I yank her upright, her back now flush against my chest. Her cries are suffocated by my firm grip on her throat, and her pussy contracts against my cock as she bounces hungrily upon it.

"Oh God, James, I'm gonna come," she chokes.

I pant against her ear and squeeze her neck tighter. She screams as her climax crescendos, so I cover her mouth to stifle them.

The more she loses control, the more my cock fills with blood and cum. The sensation builds upon itself until I can no longer contain it, and I explode deep inside her. "*Uh.* Oh *fuck.*" Her pussy tightens around me as I come, milking every last drop as I go rigid with pleasure.

Out of breath and reeling in bliss, we collapse alongside each other, and she nestles against my chest.

Things are different now. Better. More peaceful. She confided in me, and I love her even more for it.

"I love that you're a screamer, you know that?" I tell her.

"I love that you make me scream," she replies. "Sherlock Holmes making Dr. Watson scream with pleasure? What on earth would Mrs. Hudson think?"

We share in the laugh, our bodies shaking against each other, but we're interrupted by three rapid knocks on the bedroom door.

Startled, Evie pops her head up.

"Don't worry, I'll get it." I kiss the top of her head and hop off the bed.

She pulls the covers over her naked body and sinks onto her pillow.

I throw on my pajama pants and fling the door open. A woman stands in the hallway with a cart bearing two covered trays of food. "Ms. Jenna asked that we bring two plates up to your room. Shall I?" She motions toward the room behind me, and I step aside to let her in.

She places the trays on the table out on the balcony and promptly heads for the door. As she puts her hand on the knob, she turns back around and says, "Just a reminder that the ferry leaves the dock at one."

"Thank you, ma'am. We'll be ready by then."

After closing the door behind her, I reach a hand to Evie and pull her from the bed. "Come on, you've worked up quite an appetite," I laugh.

The morning light is blinding as it pierces through the crystal blue sky. Off in the distance, however, a bank of sinister clouds looms above the horizon. A storm is coming.

The food under the cloches smells divine. But I divert my attention to the assortment of fruit positioned on a coverless tray.

I go straight for a large strawberry and hold it up to her mouth, the perfect fruit for such lips. When she takes a slow, sensual bite from the fruit's tip, my cock flexes with avid interest. Before she can even swallow, my open mouth is on hers, that strawberry taste pulling me in and imprisoning me with its sweet perfection. We share the forbidden fruit between our tongues as I run my hands along her naked form.

With a tug on her hair, I expose her neck and run the remaining half of the bitten strawberry over its tender flesh. The red juice leaves streaks across her neck. One hard stroke of my tongue laps it up, and she shudders against me.

The bitten strawberry turns each of her nipples a bright red as I tease them with it. As she quivers in my arms, I bend low and take one peak into my mouth and suck as hard as I can. The thought of her bearing marks on her body, on her tits, makes me want to shove the plates aside and fuck her senseless right here on this glass balcony table.

Those seafoam eyes dance between mine as I tug and nip at her tender breast.

Those incredible eyes.

Screw the food.

With a wide sweep of my arm, I knock the plates of food to the floor. She giggles against my neck as I hoist her up and yank her to the edge of the table for easy access. I push on her chest until she lies flat, then sink between her knees.

With her legs thrown over my shoulders, her lips are wide open, impatient, wet, and hungry for another fucking.

I brush the bitten strawberry over her swollen clit in circles. She arches her back and releases carnal sighs into the morning sky.

"Holy shit, don't stop."

I keep the forbidden fruit pressed against her as I ram two fingers into that perfect paradise.

The forbidden fruit's juices coalesce with her own as she arches her back and screams through her climax, jerking and twisting as it tears through her. Once her body ceases to writhe, I remove the strawberry and suckle the juices from her clit with tight, pursed lips.

Her chest rises and falls as she revels in the languid release of her orgasm, shielding her eyes from the morning sun.

When I pull her to a seated position, her body is loose, pliable. She's exhausted in all the right ways. But those exquisite eyes of hers blaze with a passion reborn, and it takes everything in my power not to lose myself in them.

Except maybe I already have.

I give her a quick peck. "Come on, Wats, we need to pack. And there's one more thing I want to do with you before we leave."

She flicks an eyebrow at me and smirks.

I fling her over my shoulder so her bare ass moons the picturesque sky, and give it a good slap. I mean, how can I resist slapping a bare ass in such a ripe position? She squeals, playfully begging me to put her down as I carry her inside to get ready for one final game.

Chapter 18
Evie

The mist has dissipated with the rise of the morning sun. But the early light's gilded glow has since been concealed in an overcast of gray sky and shadows, forcing the balmy air to fade into less temperate conditions.

I stare into the dark woods from the edge of the tree line as a warm breeze sends a tremble through the branches. Despite the rain clouds on the horizon, the fluttering of leaves accompanies the musical notes of birds in a beautiful lullaby.

The approaching storm ignites me with excitement. A pluviophile through and through, my mind always finds peace during a good rainstorm. Droplets pounding pavement and rooftops, the smell of wet soil permeating my senses and filling me with an unparalleled sense of calm.

It reminds me of home. But not Providence.

My childhood home in Seattle. The one I shared with Papa.

"What are we doing here?" I ask, tearing my gaze away from the darkened woods to meet James's calculated expression.

"We're here for the final game. Except this time, it's just you and me. And we're not playing for points." His smirk is salacious.

My curiosity runs rampant. "What are we playing for? What's the game?"

"Before we leave this island, we'll play for something far better than points…we're going to play for each other."

I raise an eyebrow at him, and he laughs.

"On my go, you'll run into those woods as fast as you can, and you won't stop for anything. I'll give you a sixty-second head start before I come in after you. When I catch you, and I *will* catch you, I'll take you in every way I see fit."

My stomach swirls with excitement.

But the rules of the game are lost on me.

"Why would I run?" I ask. "Maybe I want you to take me in every way."

"You said it yourself. You love the idea of the chase, and I love the idea of chasing. But we're taking it even further this morning, Eves. You told me I could do whatever I deem necessary to claim you, to walk off this island knowing you're mine. *This* is it. Make me work for it. Run as far and as fast as you can. I'll catch you, and I'll take you. But don't make it easy on me. When I catch you, I want you to fight me. I want you to struggle, to claw away if you must."

My jaw drops to the ground. Is he asking me to pretend he's attacking me? I couldn't hit him even if I wanted to.

Could I?

I must admit, the idea does make my knees quiver, and that familiar yet torturous tingle is tugging at my core all over again. This is it. This is something I've craved for so long. What terrified me as a child, being locked away and hidden, hunted by something—or *someone*—on the other side of that wardrobe door, petrified by what awaited me, has morphed into a source of pleasure I can't deny. The violent attempt of an unknown figure who nearly broke down doors to find me as a tear-stricken child has been a source of nightmares for most of my life. But now, all I want is to run and hide, only to be tracked down, hunted, found, and ravaged by my handsome partner.

It has certainly been the most confusing weekend of my life. But one that has opened my eyes to an entirely new side of me. And opened my heart to a world of possibilities I never knew existed with a man I fell for in a matter of hours.

"And don't think that surprised look on your face is selling me on any sort of uncertainty or denial. I know you want this as much as I do. Your pussy was so incredibly wet after I found you in that maze last night. Almost as wet as when I broke into the broom closet and found you tied up. Your body never lies, my love. You like to be hunted, you love to be found, and you crave anything and everything that comes immediately after."

He's right. When I know it's him coming for me, the arousal is unmatched. The idea of anyone else—Ashton, let's say—elicits a fear in me I can't begin to describe.

It has to be James.

It *needs* to be James.

Every single time.

"I'm not denying anything, I promise. I'm just...I don't know what to say." My laugh this time is a nervous one. Now I know why he ditched his glasses.

"Say you'll do this with me," he pleads. "Say you'll let me claim you as my own before we leave this place. That you'll make me work for it. You're worth fighting for, Evelyn. And I'm going to fight for you. So run. Push and kick and pull...I want to subdue you and take you the way you desperately crave." He holds my face in his hands.

"And then we both win," I whisper.

He smiles, his smoldering gaze slicing through me like a frigid knife in warm butter.

"Like I said, we're playing for something far better than points."

His open lips meet mine, making my toes curl as my breath skips against his caressing tongue.

"But you need to know something." He regards me but doesn't go on.

I urge him to continue with merely a look.

"Once you're in there," he lifts his chin toward the muted pine, "you're surrendering yourself to me completely, and *anything* is fair game. Thanks to last night's festivities, I already know your safe word. Use it if you need to. I'm not playing around with any of that. Don't ever allow me to do anything you don't want me to, even if you're uncertain." He tucks an errant strand of hair behind my ears. "But once I've claimed you, you're mine from this point forward. We'll tell each other everything, we'll love each other unconditionally, and we'll leave this island as one. I don't care that we live in different states. I would travel to the stars and back for you. We'll figure it out, okay? But if any part of you has doubts; if any part of you is unsure about wanting to be with me, then don't you dare go into those woods. Because once you're in there, I will find you, and I *will* make you mine."

My heart pounds in my chest, echoing the low rumble of thunder off in the distance.

What he's asking of me feels more like a command, to accede to him like the good little girl I want to be. But despite our endeavors last night, I've only known him for a day. A *day*. Will it ever not sound insane? Maybe. But does it really matter? Like Jenna said this morning: call it love or don't, it doesn't change the way we feel.

For so long, I've wished for something that was just beyond my grasp. I yearned for someone who would hear me—*truly* hear me. I ached to belong, to live a life where I could leave my childhood behind and begin anew. My father, my only guardian and the only family I had ever known, was taken from me, leaving me to endure and navigate this world alone. My aunt wanted nothing to do with me, and once I started boarding school, my decisions were no longer mine. I was always at the mercy of someone else, hidden away where no one—not the monsters, not anyone—could ever find me. Until now, no one ever cared to seek me out for my own good, wanting me to be found, against all odds. But James wants me hidden only if *he* can be the one to find me.

And love me unconditionally.

He wants me locked away only so he can break down the walls and barriers to finally set me free.

No footsteps coming for me in the night, no fear of monsters tearing down walls. No stranger's heavy breathing or clicking shoes tormenting me from outside my coffin of darkness. It's only James and his undying need to protect me and claim me. A future free of being lost and unfound, desired but not believed, paralyzed come nightfall and feeling so unequivocally alone.

I will be his prey. I will run, and I will fight; I'll make him earn his place in my heart. Just as I've earned my place in his by trusting him.

His eyes never leave mine, the silence between us growing heavier as my thoughts cyclone around in my head. His nervousness is evident by the glint of concern in his beautiful eyes.

Running from him may be the hardest thing I ever have to do. But it's necessary. We need this.

I need this.

Which means only one thing...

"So the game is afoot, then?" I ask, curling my lips in a sly grin as I channel my inner Dr. Watson.

He exhales heavily and releases a hearty laugh. "Yes, I suppose it is."

"Just one question," I begin.

"Ask me anything."

"You want us to run in the woods without shoes on?" I peer down at my naked feet, comfortable on the landscaped grass that grows along the edge of the tree line.

"That's right, Wats. I can't have you running *too* deep. We have a ferry to catch in two hours."

I nod in acquiescence.

"Remember, you have a sixty-second head start. Now, are you ready?"

I grin and give him a saucy wink.

"Okay. On your mark…"

Facing the tree line, I take up a runner's stance.

"Get set…"

I bounce on my feet in anticipation.

"*Go.*"

I run full speed into the woods, sticking to as straight a line as I can manage to avoid getting lost. As soon as I breach the tree line, the trimmed garden grass gives way to a detritus of fallen leaves, sticks, bark, and uneven terrain of decaying vegetation and freshly grown moss. In only a few paces, I'm surrounded by darkness, made worse by the encroaching storm clouds that accumulate overhead.

The rumbling of thunder resonates in the distance, prompting a squirrel to scurry up the trunk of a nearby tree for shelter. Either that, or the sound of my feet crunching through the deceased foliage frightens it. I can't be sure.

My lungs heave as I run as fast as my legs can carry me. The singsong of birds sounds somewhere above me as I dodge left, then right around one tree after the other.

I catch mere flashes of the beauty of my surroundings as I navigate my tree-filled obstacle course: vines of ivy encircling tree trunks and covering the protruding roots at the base, the thin layer of moss that clings to one side of each trunk, the flitting of startled birds as they seek safety.

The smell of rain draws nearer, filling my senses with its musty scent. The impending storm's electricity only makes my legs carry me faster into the unknown.

Too fast, as I come to find out the hard way.

My lead ahead of James comes to a screeching halt when my

foot catches on a raised root buried beneath a layer of leaves and I fall face-first to the forest floor. A sharp gasp escapes my lips, nearly a scream. My foot is likely bleeding and cut to hell, but my adrenaline masks the pain beautifully.

I peer over my shoulder. James is nowhere to be seen. My labored breathing is all I can hear, but I force a held breath and listen for footsteps against the crunchy, lifeless foliage.

Nothing.

I climb back onto my feet and brush the leaves and dirt from the front of my sh—

Snap.

A twig snaps in the distance, catching my attention. A lump lodges in my chest, a blend of exertion and anxiety. My sixty-second lead is gone in a flash.

Did James already catch up to me? That can't be.

I turn toward the sound.

Snap.

Another twig, followed by the shuffling of leaves. Subtle but distinct. Without wasting another moment, I draw in a deep breath and run in the opposite direction of the noise. I leap over raised tree roots, dodge trees left and right, and catch myself from slipping more times than I care to keep track of.

The terrain suddenly slopes, steady at first, then steeper. I consider turning back to find another way. My only fear is that if I change course, I'll get completely turned around. Then I may truly end up lost. Sure, it's an island, so I can only go so far before reaching a shoreline and regaining my bearings. But with James searching for me, how long until we both end up lost in the thick of it? Plus, any second, it's bound to rain.

I follow the decline, falling to my butt and scooting my way down until I reach the trunk of a fallen tree. It gives me the brace I need to pause. I scramble over it and, using it for shelter, peek over the top to see if James is coming.

But there's no one.

Should I wait for him to catch up? What if he saw the decline and went another way? The idea here is to be hunted and to evade capture, but I do want to be caught eventually. How else is he supposed to use my body as he sees fit and claim me? But he asked me to make him work for it, and I intend to do so every step of the way.

I pivot around and survey the sloping ground, then fall to my butt and scoot along the terrain. Up ahead, the ground levels out a bit. I just have to get there.

The claps of thunder grow louder, and what daylight I have left is diminishing.

With a small leap, I traverse the last stretch of slope until finally finding even ground.

The leaves rustle above me as a warm gust of wind slices through the island. As they sing all around me, a drop of water pelts me on the cheek.

And then another in my hair.

And another.

The rain breaks through the dense canopy of trees, saturating my clothing and skin one drop at a time. The smell of wet soil consumes my senses, my mind swimming in its sweet, earthy splendor.

As a girl, I loved to twirl in the Seattle rain, spreading my fingertips and tipping my face to the heavens as the raindrops splashed across my skin and danced at my feet, my father twirling beside me.

The rainfall is heavier in a nearby clearing where the trees are sparse and the forest floor is covered with ankle-high grass. Drawn to the unobstructed cascade of water, I inch into the clearing as if waiting for an invitation. The rain washes over me in small droplets, my hair dampening and my clothing sticking to my skin.

There's nothing in the clearing except for me and the bursting clouds above. I listen for thunder, but the roars are silent. Only the pounding of raindrops and the shuddering of trees accompany my heavy breathing.

I angle my face toward the sky and close my eyes against the drops. Raising my arms away from my body, I reach out and spin. For a moment, all semblance of time and space fades away.

In their place, the world transmogrifies into another moment entirely. Another place, another time. Seagulls sing as they zip over the docks at the local marina. The smell of saltwater and fish hangs in the air as the boats settle into port, one after the other. Their low horns echo across the water, and the creaking of ropes that hold steady the docked boats resonate around me.

I'm perched on the grassy hill that overlooks the marina, the rain tickling my face. Papa sits beside me, his knees drawn up to his chest like mine. He smiles at me despite our soaked state, finding humor in being caught in the rain. We may be the only fools in Seattle without an umbrella. He always insists we never need one.

"Why would you when the rain on your face makes you feel so alive?" he says.

He's right. So many times, we found ourselves intentionally "caught" in the rain, like today, timing our outdoor excursions for exactly when the weatherman told us to avoid such things.

We were on our way to the marina to buy fresh local fish when the sky opened up above us. People scurried to seek shelter, but not Papa and me. He grabbed my hand and ushered me up the hill.

The seagulls sing despite the rain—heck, maybe they love it as much as we do—and the fishermen go about their business as usual, rain or shine.

"Come on," Papa says, bumping me with his shoulder before climbing to his feet. He holds his hand out for mine and pulls me up. With a laugh, he stretches his arms, tilts his face toward the sky, and spins. "Come on, baby bird," he urges.

I stretch my arms out to mimic him. Together, we spin in the falling rain, laughter filling our bellies and the earth spinning so fast we collapse onto the grass from dizziness.

I remember the stitch in my side from the laughter. The way my wet clothes hugged my skin and how fallen tendrils of hair adhered to my face. I remember my father raking his fingers through his black locks, brushing the wet pieces away from his face to reveal crimson cheeks full of laughter and love.

Snap.

I open my eyes against the pelting drops, and a shiver courses through me. I'm not at the docks with Papa. I'm in the woods, under a bleak and darkened sky. For a moment, I forget how I even got here. Or why I'm here in the first place.

Snap.

Another snap of a twig nearby.

Maybe it's James?

James.

A startled scream escapes me as a hand flies over my mouth from behind. Another plants itself firmly over my stomach. "You shouldn't have stopped running, sweet girl," he growls in my ear. "You made this way too easy for me." His chuckle is low and menacing as his violent grip brings me straight back to reality, all semblance of Papa long gone.

I squirm against his grasp and belt another scream against his hand, actual terror rippling through me at the shock of his arrival. He holds me firm as he slinks his hand over my stomach and rakes it toward the hem of my shirt. Reaching under, he runs his palm over my bare skin, skimming across my torso and wasting no time reaching my breasts. He grips one hard, squeezing it not for pleasure but for control. The more I squirm, the tighter he squeezes, pinching my nipple to force me into compliance.

But it doesn't work. Because I like it. Despite the sting that courses through my nipple, my vagina responds like the greedy little bitch she is, aching at the tease of being fucked into submission all over again. I won't let him capture me so easily, though. I want him to earn it as much as he does.

I reach behind me and grab his cock from the outside of his shorts, already hard as a rock. The shock of my hand forces him to loosen his grip on my mouth for only a second, but it's enough for me to open my own and bite down hard on his palm.

"*Gah*. Fuck."

He releases me with a sharp cry, and the taste of his blood lingers on my tongue as I take off running.

The ground is slicker than ever, the rain pouring as we sprint through the clearing and deeper into the woods. His rapid footsteps crunch behind me, closer than before, and my side stitches with each labored breath.

I maintain my lead. Is he allowing it for the benefit of the chase? A predator does enjoy playing with its food from time to time, after all.

But I'm exhausted, winded, and soaked. He may not have to catch me at all. He may be able to claim me simply because I can't push on any further. I glance over my shoulder to see how far behind me he is.

But he isn't there.

My mind reels, and I spin in all directions, looking for him.

He's nowhere to be found.

I turn back in the direction I was originally running and release a startled cry as my foot slips out from under me on wet leaves, and I fall straight onto my ass.

The pain is sharp, and my breath stings my throat. Scrambling to my knees, I stop when James appears from behind a nearby tree, sauntering toward me with his hands in his pockets. His lips upturn in a victorious smirk, and when his eyes lock on mine, I have to crane my neck to meet his gaze from down on my knees.

He lowers himself to his haunches, evening our gaze. Still with that malicious smirk on his face, he tsks. "Oh, Wats, when I told you

I'd find you, I meant it. You can bite…" he holds his wounded hand up to me. "You can kick, you can scream. But no one will hear you. No one will save you. You're mine to do with as I please. Now, be a good girl and take off your shirt."

His taunts are relentless, daring me to refuse, to fight.

My arousal burns at my insides, my sex throbbing with anticipation and, I must admit, fear.

I shake my head in defiance. "Fuck you," I huff, never taking my eyes off his.

His smirk devolves into a menacing glower before he grabs my arm and forces me onto my back. In a flash, he's on top of me, yanking at my shirt and tearing it from the neck down, exposing my bare breasts.

My nipples harden as they're bombarded by rainfall.

Screaming against the stormy sky, I shove him hard in the chest, but he doesn't let up. This is what he came here to do: to hunt me down and claim me. Before long, the shirt is completely torn from my body, and he's working on the button of my jean shorts as he straddles me into submission.

I flail beneath his weight, and as he cants his hips up to pin my arms above my head, I bring my knee to the inside of his thigh with a rapid jerk. The blow lands on the inside of his leg, just missing his balls. He bellows a harsh cry and releases my hands to check his family jewels. It gives me the perfect opportunity to shove him hard, my hands connecting square with his chest and knocking him backward until his balance is wavering at best. I manage to scoot out from under him and scramble to my feet while he fights to maintain his balance.

What's left of my tattered shirt falls to the ground, leaving me naked from the waist up. My breasts bounce with each frantic stride, and I resist the urge to scratch at the leaves that stick to my soaked skin.

His heavy footsteps and his taunting laugh trail not far behind.

A clap of thunder roars overhead, the first I've heard in ages. My strides stutter at the sudden boom, and I reach for a tree for balance.

James grabs me from behind and shoves me hard against the trunk, pressing my face against its wet bark. A wince escapes me as it scratches at my cheek and digs into my skin. He cages me in, his body hard against mine and his erection digging into my ass. I exhale a heavy groan and try to push myself away, but he pins one of my hands around my back with a cruel yank and presses his other arm against the back of my neck. His breath is hot on my ear as he chuckles against it, sending an erotic ripple down my spine and straight between my legs.

He frees my hand, and in seconds, he unfastens the clasp of my shorts and yanks the zipper down with a quick *purr* that's silenced by the lashing rain. My attempts to push myself off the trunk are thwarted by his unrelenting pressure against my neck, and the more I fight, the tighter he holds. He pulls my shorts down, and they fall around my ankles, revealing my panties underneath.

Another crash of thunder booms through the forest, closer this time.

He hooks his fingers into the lace fabric, tracing it down between my legs, which I squeeze together to bar his wandering hands. It's torturous, denying him access to my body for the sake of the game. But as much as I yearn to be fucked in the most primal conditions, the playing is almost as stimulating as the act itself.

He releases my neck and grabs me by my hair. I push against the trunk to alleviate the pressure on my face and breasts to no avail.

I told you not to wear these anymore, you disobedient girl." His voice is husky and raw. "Open your legs."

"No," I hiss through gritted teeth.

He grips my hair and shoves me harder against the tree.

"Open your legs *now.*"

"Go fuck yourself," I growl.

He grips my panties and tears them from my body, my bare ass now bearing the brunt of his engorged cock straining against his shorts.

A sharp cry escapes my throat when he shoves a finger deep into my ass, forcing my entire sex to clench.

"I don't need your legs apart for *this*, stubborn girl," he huffs in my ear, shoving his finger in and out with a purposeful, aggressive motion. The pressure borders on pain, but my vagina pulsates to a desperate beat, nonetheless, causing my legs to unknowingly fall open for him.

Oh God, don't stop.

As a moan of pleasure emerges from my parted lips, he stops. Tugging me by the hair, he tears me away from the tree and throws me onto the ground. My knees hit hard, and a twig snaps under my weight.

I'm free.

Run.

I clamber to my feet, seizing the small window of opportunity to escape despite my nakedness. My sex vibrates with pleasure, and my ass longs for the relief teased by his finger.

My feet slip, one step after the other, the soil now mud and the leaves so wet that it's like running on ice. I stumble and reach for something—*anything*—but find nothing to stop the crash to my knees.

On all fours, I scurry away, adrenaline coursing through my veins and fear preventing me from looking behind me again.

I don't make it back to my feet.

James is on me in a second, pushing me flat on the ground and flipping me onto my back. His weight bears down on me as he straddles my legs. He's naked, having removed his clothing in the mere seconds I was rushing to escape his clutches while on all fours.

And his erection is harder than ever.

I claw at his chest, buck my hips, and kick in hopes of throwing him off. He raises up off me to adjust his position, and I wriggle to sit upright in the sliver of space.

He grips my throat and leans in close, his eyes bouncing back and forth between mine, breaking character for only a moment.

What is he doing?

Waiting for me to use my safe word?

We exchange air as our pants intertwine, our lips nearly touching. He searches my face, and the electricity of an impending kiss makes my hair stand on end despite the pouring rain.

Yet our lips never find each other.

His grip on my throat tightens, his oaken eyes glistening against the rain that streaks across his face and matts his hair to his forehead.

My airflow reduces to a wheeze, and I ache for release. But the pleasure it brings is unparalleled. I've been captured once and for all, and now it's time to be marked and claimed by the man who was yesterday's stranger.

Closing my eyes in submission, I surrender my body to him.

He rakes his teeth against my jawline, dragging his tongue over my flesh and lapping up the wetness that trickles down my body toward my bare breasts. A quiver shoots through my spine as my clit electrifies with a thousand volts.

He eases his grip on my neck, clearly caught up in the moment.

I seize the opportunity it presents.

I shove hard against his chest, pushing him away and forcing him to face me. His eyes widen, but his shock is replaced by an evil gleam. He knows I'm not conceding to him. I would never make it so easy.

My hand connects with his cheek with a hard *slap*, and he recoils. It slows his reaction time long enough for me to connect the weight of my upper body with his chest and knock him off balance. He shifts on top of me, and I slide along the soaked leaves until I'm out from under him.

I spin onto my belly and crawl away with every ounce of

strength I can muster, trying to find my footing against the slick forest floor. Fear and adrenaline course through my veins like a drug, giving me the stamina I need.

He finds my ankles as I push myself onto my knees. With one quick tug, I fall face-first into the leaves and mud and pine needles with a hard *thud*. An intense scream bursts from my throat as he yanks with surprising ease. He pulls me along my belly toward him as I rake my fingers against the ground in a desperate attempt to find something to hold on to. The taste of mud is bitter on my tongue as forest debris sticks to my face and lips, my hair, my entire body...I'm filthy, a primitive shell of my former self, wrestling against my naked attacker in the downpour.

Another crash of thunder makes my heart skip a beat, and I gasp as the bombastic sound echoes around us.

He flips me onto my back, and I meet his narrowed gaze as he straddles me once more. I flail, slapping at his chest, his face, his arms; anywhere I can make contact. He tries but fails to capture my hands, and I land many blows before he finally grabs a wrist and wrenches it hard.

I lean in to bite his hand, but he jerks me back by my hair. His lips curl away from his teeth in a sneer, the cascading rain making him look like a rabid animal.

I twist back onto my belly in a desperate attempt to escape, to look away from that awful sneer. And he lets me.

He reaches under me and lifts my abdomen off the ground, forcing me to my knees. Gripping my hair, he presses my face to the dirt, ensuring I can't escape him again. I claw at the hand that forces me down, but it's no use. And my cries merely soak into the mud along with the deluge of rain.

He shoves two of his fingers deep into my pussy, and I scream against the dirt, this time from pleasure. The little pink bitch is pleased, but of course, never satiated. She clamps down around him as he thrusts his fingers in and out.

Leaning down, he presses his lips to my exposed ear. "*Mine,*" he roars, and my heart races with terror and arousal.

I slap the ground, trying to push myself up despite his weight bearing down on me, but my exhaustion is beginning to outweigh my desperation. He's too heavy, too strong, and my neck aches from the struggle.

My freedom slips further and further from my grasp with each passing moment.

His erection presses hard against my backside, my ass up and exposed in my forced position. It teases my other entrance, puckered and tight, an entrance never before breached by a man's cock.

Fuck.

My heart races beyond my control, the rhythm sending me into a tailspin of fear and anticipation. I expect pain. Lots of it. But the untapped nature of the particular act arouses me in a way I've never dreamed of, and I want it as much as I fear it.

For several seconds, he shifts behind me, and I'm desperate to know what he's doing. As my mind starts to go mad with curiosity, he presses his rabid cock into my ass. The scream I unleash into the mud and leaves is animalistic, driven by shock and pain. The sharpness of his cock, though controlled and less forceful than he's known to be, is beyond what I ever imagined.

The safe word rattles around in my head like a loose penny in a tin can.

But I'm not quite there yet.

For every bit of pain the act bestows upon me, my clit fills to the point of almost bursting and my ass tightens around his intrusive member. My nipples are rock hard against the wet earth, and the pleasure is slowly starting to outweigh the pain.

My clit yearns to be caressed. In fact, she's begging for it.

My cries escape in a staccato fashion that matches his angry thrusts, and his groans are so loud that even the pounding rain can't mask them. I move my hand to my clit and flick it, expecting punishment for doing so. It sings under my touch, and with each flick, a tingle takes hold deep in my bottom.

Oh God.

The more I stimulate my clit, the more the tingling sensation grows. And as he rams his cock into me, the tingling evolves into pulses of white heat and immeasurable desire.

His hands slip on my wet hips, losing their grip and bucking me forward. More than once, I have to release my clit to brace myself against the ground, our balance slipping as the thrusting intensifies.

Finally releasing my face from its imprisonment against the ground, he pulls me upward by my hair to meet him. I'm pressed against his chest, his cock piercing my ass like a sword in an unused leather sheath.

I open my mouth wide when he grabs my neck and squeezes it hard, pinching my breath from my lungs until I'm gasping for air. His other hand gropes and pinches at my breasts, twisting them until they scream from the sting and are red with anger. But I can't scream along with them.

With one hand, I grip on his hair. I'm no longer interested in fighting. He caught me fair and square, and this is his moment to prove to me that this has all been a ruse, a *facade*, to make me think that I could actually stop him from claiming me.

The ultimate power play.

And what better way to claim me than to take me in a way no one ever has?

Even though I've abandoned my clit, my climax draws nearer. The sensations that radiate through me set my body aflame, and I scream through pinched breaths as my orgasm unfurls itself across every square inch of my flesh.

The rain turns to white noise, its rapid downfall going unnoticed as my body vibrates and clenches against him.

As I surrender myself to the man who lays waste to my body, he comes undone inside me. Rather than release his cries of pleasure toward the angry sky, he cranes his neck forward and bites me hard on the back of my shoulder. I yell despite the piercing sensation it causes in my tightened throat, and the more I scream, the harder he bites. His own guttural roar penetrates my skin through his embedded teeth as he orgasms into the only virginal space I have left on my body.

Blood trickles down my shoulder from the deepest kiss I have ever received, coalescing with the raindrops that paint my skin.

I collapse against him, going limp with exhaustion and sheer pleasure.

He cradles me in his arms and lowers me to the ground beside him. Sheltering me with his body, he spoons me, wrapping an arm around my chest and bringing me into him so we're touching at every possible point. He nuzzles my neck and sopping hair with his nose, inhaling deeply. The scent of wet earth is the strongest I have ever experienced, and it stirs a primal urge inside me to lie in its cleansing downpour forever.

With James by my side.

Naked, we lie entwined in our own little slice of Eden, soaking wet and covered with mud and debris.

The rise and fall of his chest align their rhythm with mine as we bask in the afterglow of our intimate game.

Two bodies melded as one:

One flesh.

One heart.

One promise.

One night.

A night in which I surrendered myself in more ways than I ever dared.

What began as a simple surrender to my best friend for her one night of "uninhibited frivolity," ended with an unabashed surrender to *him*...

The man who ravaged my body and soul with merely a gaze.

The man who devoured my every weakness, every tear, and every kiss with a ripe, insatiable hunger.

And come morning light, I willingly fell prey to his urges and was overpowered in a rough, unapologetic manner.

I was marked. I was claimed.

But I was also found.

He found me.

And I'll never be lost again.

EPILOGUE
EVIE

A gentle hum fills the reception tent with low baritone notes as I glide the bow over the cello strings. My solo rendition of the song "Only You" by Yazoo emanates through the sea of silent faces, elevated by the finesse of the subtle vibrato of my wrist. Jenna's wedding gown billows as David sweeps her across the dance floor, the room watching the couple's first dance in wide-eyed splendor.

Almost trancelike, I drag the bow in a concise, rhythmic manner and fall into the vibrations of my most precious instrument. No sheet music. I don't need it. It's Jenna's wedding, after all.

As the audience stands silent—captivated—I am in complete control. Even if it's only for the duration of a single song.

And it makes me feel powerful.

I hold the final note, bringing the couple's dance to a sultry close as the bow comes to a dramatic rest at the end of the coda. After a brief silence that lasts about half a beat, the tent fills with thunderous applause.

Cradling my beloved cello by its neck, I stand and watch as the newlyweds absorb the crowd's love. David reaches for Jenna and cradles her face in his hands as they lean in for a quick yet passionate kiss. My heart could not be fuller. I've never seen Jenna look so happy or more beautiful. That smile may be permanently etched on her face, and it makes my heart sing with elation.

And closure.

She deserves every bit of happiness this world has to offer, and I think David may be the man to give it to her.

The couple turns and gestures toward me and the handful of band members behind me, clapping along with the guests. I dip in a slow curtsey, my face flushed and my heart overflowing. James catches my eye near the front of the crowd, his smile warm.

As the applause dies down, the live band revs things up on the stage and the dance floor fills with people. I step offstage and place my cello back in its case before returning to the table reserved for the wedding party. James is standing near his assigned seat.

"You were absolutely incredible," he gushes, scooping me up in an exaggerated spin. The uncontrollable laughter that escapes me is muted by the deafening music from the live band.

I run a hand over the placket of his shirt as I regain my footing.

"You have an amazing talent, you know that?" he says, his grin stretched to the max.

I respond with my own smile and scorched cheeks.

"And I knew it all along. See, that's why I never offered you this." He reaches into his pants pocket, fishing around, piquing my curiosity. Knowing James, it could be anything. My mind races with a million possibilities over the span of a single second.

He reveals a red plastic button about the size of a quarter. With holes in the shape of hearts.

"Wait, is that the same button? The one from the blindfold game?"

His adorable side smirk is all I need for an answer.

"Why do you have that?"

"For the same reason you held on to the guitar pick. Because it's good luck." He rubs it between his fingers, then flips it into the air and catches it like a coin.

"Touché. But how do you know it's lucky?"

"Because," he grabs my wrist and runs a tantalizing finger over the soft flesh, "that was the game where I felt your pulse for the first time. It was racing. And in that moment, I knew we shared a mutual desire to know each other better. It's lucky because it's such a simple, unremarkable object, but it brought us together in a remarkable way."

My heart reacts with a dizzying flip.

I take the button from him and rub it between my own fingers, tracing along the heart-shaped buttonholes. Maybe it is lucky.

"You do realize this was in my mouth," I tell him with a playful, disgusted look as I hand it back to him.

"Yeah. So was my cock." His full grin is infectious as he bounces the button on his palm. "Perhaps that's why it's lucky."

"Are you saying that your cock is also lucky because it was in my mouth?"

"Well, I have no doubt *he* thinks he is. Don't tell him otherwise."

My eyes bounce between his. "Shall I kiss it? You know, to keep its powers activated?"

He pauses, and his eyes widen. "The button...or my cock?"

Laughter erupts between us, and he pulls me against him.

"Both," I reply, wiping away a tear. "But I was referring to the button."

He holds it out, and I kiss its smooth surface before he returns it to his pocket. I close my eyes and inhale his luscious scent as I rest my cheek against his chest, his fingers in my hair and his arm secured around me. Our feet begin to shuffle, and before long, we are lost in reverie as we sway to the rhythm of the unfurling night.

ALL NIGHT LONG, WE DANCE. IN GROUPS, WITH partners, alone. We throw drunken arms around each other, sing along to every song with exaggerated fervor, and laugh until tears run down our cheeks. It's the perfect night, easy to get lost in, second only to the night in which James and I were assigned as partners for a tournament we didn't even win.

An absolute fairy tale.

The live band Jenna selected has long since retired for the evening. It has been replaced by a DJ who has been tasked with keeping the party going as long as possible. Thanks to said DJ, Queen's "Crazy Little Thing Called Love" tears through the reception tent at full volume. Jenna's undying love of eighties music is on full display tonight.

James reels me back toward him after the umpteenth spin on the dance floor. His eyes glimmer under the canopy of twinkle lights, an artificial night sky that dazzles overhead and illuminates everyone in a soft, romantic glow. The sweet scent of hundreds of white, powder blue, and lavender flowers that adorn the reception area permeates my senses, and James's boutonniere is no exception. He looks devilishly handsome tonight. His classic black tux paired with those glasses I adore so much make him look like a sexy, nerdy James Bond.

When I told him that earlier in the evening, he pulled me behind the sound stage, forced my legs apart, and slapped my pussy when no one was looking.

"Can you see the mark?" I ask as he spins me away from him.

He pauses, then turns me so he can inspect my shoulder.

"No, it's still pretty well covered."

I exhale a sigh of relief.

Between the bruises on my wrists and arms, the scrapes on my elbows, and the bite mark on my shoulder, getting ready for the wedding was an all-day affair. The downfall of being fair-skinned, I suppose. Jenna, unfortunately, saw the bite mark early this morning. In exchange for not being upset that I showed up on her wedding day looking like I had been chewed up and spit back out again—her words—she agreed to help me cover everything up only if I gave her all the details later.

And one day, maybe I will.

I haven't decided yet.

As the song fades to an end, James motions to the DJ up on the stage, who acknowledges him with a subtle nod.

"What's going on?" I ask.

He ignores my question as he slides his arm around my waist. The song that plays next is one I recognize instantly: "In Your Eyes" by Peter Gabriel. A warmth blossoms deep in my chest. It's such a simple gesture, yet it has me completely smitten as the opening notes fill the room.

"I put in a request," he whispers, pressing his body against mine. He intertwines our fingers as we dance to the song that, as far as I'm concerned, is cemented as *our* song from this moment forward.

His other hand lingers on my lower back, tracing small circles against the satin, powder blue material as we sway against each other, my cheek resting on his shoulder.

I'm lost in the music. Lost in the moment.

Lost in him.

Even through closed eyes, the canopy of lights is like a symphony of springtime embers etched into my vision. Peter Gabriel's dulcet voice rocks me like a lullaby in my lover's arms, my heart accelerating beneath his touch.

He leans in and places a soft kiss upon my lips, and I sink into it completely. Pressing harder with each passing melodious note, he devours me with insatiable hunger. It offers no reprieve from my champagne-induced euphoria. In no time, the line between arousal for James and the champagne lightness in my head has blurred beyond recognition.

It's a feeling I never want to escape.

Too late.

A light grip on my arm pulls me away from my passionate kiss.

It's Jenna. Still looking amazing after all these hours of drinking and dancing and mingling and being pulled every which way.

"Jenna. The woman of the hour," I exclaim, throwing my arms around her. "Or should I call you Mrs. Denardo?"

"Aww, I'm glad to see you love the champagne. I just love drunk Evie," she replies with a hearty laugh. "So sorry to tear you away from your date," she turns to James with a loving smile, "but David spilled champagne on my dress, and I need you."

"The night is nearly over, Jen. What's a little spilled champ—"

"Evelyn Foster, this is my *wedding dress* we're talking about. And you're my maid of honor, which means I *need* you."

"Oh—uh—right, of course, I'm sorry—"

She grasps my hand and yanks me away from James and the dance floor.

"I'll be back in a sec," I tell him as I crane my neck in his direction.

With his hands in his pockets, he watches me leave with a smile that makes a thrum of excitement echo in my belly.

Jenna and I weave through the clusters of people toward the country club beyond the gardens.

The restroom in the main building is empty except for Steph, who is at the sink washing her hands under the fluorescent lights. She perks up when she sees us enter, giving us a broad smile.

"Steph. The lucky girl who caught the bouquet," I gush, yanking paper towels one after another from the dispenser.

"Ha, you ladies didn't stand a chance." She chuckles as she also reaches for a paper towel. Yet her smile fades when she turns to face us and sees me working on Jenna's dress. "What's going on? Is everything all right?"

"Yeah, we had a spill on the back of her dress is all," I reply, soaking the paper towels in warm water.

"Let's soak up what we can first." Steph tears several more paper towels from the dispenser, then holds them against Jenna's dress. We take turns dabbing and wiping while Jenna leans into the mirror and admires her reflection. The worried look on her face dissipates the longer we go at it, and soon enough, the champagne spot is replaced with what I hope is a clean wet spot.

A heavy sigh escapes her lips. She's clearly exhausted and buzzing from champagne like the rest of us. "I should get back out there, guys. David will start to worry. Thank you. You're lifesavers." She throws her arms around each of us, kisses us on the cheek, then promptly exits the restroom, leaving Steph and me behind.

The warm water is soothing against my hands as I run them together beneath the faucet.

"Your maid of honor speech was really incredible," Steph says with a pensive look. Her tone is so sincere that it gives me pause as I watch her through the mirror.

"That means so much to me, Steph. Thank you for saying that."

She nods as I pull fresh towels from the dispenser.

"Can I ask you something completely unrelated?" She fidgets with her necklace and studies the floor.

"Of course."

"I couldn't help but notice that bite mark on your shoulder this morning when we were getting ready." She hesitates.

My stomach knots up. Shit. I didn't think anyone but Jenna saw it. But she notices everything, so I wasn't entirely surprised.

"Did James do that?"

I laugh, probably too loudly.

But fuck it, I'm drunk.

"Yeah, he did. He got a little carried away last weekend, I guess," I lie.

"Um, you don't say?" Her eyes are wide and playful. "It's like he tried to take a bite out of you. Like you're an apple or something." A drunken chuckle makes her quake, her styled curls bouncing as she tosses her head back.

"Well, we were on an island called Eden's Green." I giggle. "Maybe he got confused…"

She holds her hand up in jest. "Don't tell Keith, but I think it's kinda hot."

"Hmm, I don't know, maybe you should tell him. Maybe he'll take a bite out of you too."

"Ooh Evie, don't stop," she replies, fanning herself.

"I'm so happy for you," I gush. "Keith seems like such a nice guy. And it's obvious he adores you. Are you planning on seeing each other again?"

"Oh, definitely. We already have plans for tomorrow. And he agreed to join me on my prize trip to Barbados, courtesy of the newlyweds."

"Well, you two deserve it. And you'll have the best time."

She frees her necklace from her hand. "What about you and James? Seems serious…" She gives me a friendly smirk.

I laugh. "You could say that. I'm visiting him in New York next weekend. I know it's fast, but I'm crazy about him. More than I could ever explain."

"That's obvious. I can tell by the way you're blushing."

"Well, that's nothing new," I tease.

"It is. Because now you're blushing for a different reason."

I pause, her words washing over me like the rainstorm in which I was claimed. Without giving it a moment's thought, I move in and throw my arms around her in a warm embrace. I don't know Steph that well, and without the champagne influence, I probably wouldn't have made such a move. But I'm caught up in the moment, and her words are so genuine.

"I'm going to head back," she says when we pull apart. "You coming?"

"In a sec. The champagne is running right through me."

"All right, see you out there." The door closes softly behind her.

My heels click on the tile floor as I make my way to a nearby stall.

My dress is already a mess at this point, wrinkled from the dancing and from being hiked up by James's wandering hands more than once tonight.

It certainly makes it easier to not care so much come bathroom time.

I teeter on one foot as I lift the other and step on the flush bar, bracing myself with outstretched arms on either side of the stall.

That's when I hear it.

A muffled scream.

It's so faint, I can't be sure. With the flushing toilet, I certainly could have been mistaken. But it's distinct enough that it gives me pause, and I wait with bated breath as I turn an ear closer to the stall door.

Nothing.

In fact, I hear no sounds at all. No music. No din of the guests. No shuffling of staff in and out of the country club's rear garden doors.

Perhaps the reception is over and everyone is preparing to leave.

Maybe the restrooms are too far removed from the reception tent at the bottom of the hill.

Or the DJ is finally packing up, and James is waiting to take me back to his room at the Seaside Inn.

Perhaps the champagne really has fogged up my head—

Wait.

Another scream.

My pulse attacks my eardrums, and my throat tightens to a pinpoint, crushing my chest beneath the weight of my oncoming panic.

I have to get out of here.

I reach for the lock on the stall door.

The restroom door flies open with violent force, slamming into the wall behind it and shooting a deafening echo through the tiled room. I jump and cover my mouth to silence the scream that nearly gives me away.

With a shaky hand over my mouth, I peer through the crack of the stall door.

I can't see anyone.

But the sound of heavy breathing is unmistakable.

Tears well in my eyes, obscuring my vision and threatening to spill down my cheeks. Inching backward, I come to an abrupt halt as my back presses against the cold tile wall behind me.

I repeat a silent prayer that the person will turn and leave.

Click...

Click...

Click...

The distinct, resonating sound of footsteps on the tile floor as the stranger enters the restroom...

Followed by the *bang* of the main door slamming shut.

Click...

Click...

Click...

No, no, no, no, no, no, no, no...

My stomach lurches in horror as the stall walls warp and narrow, closing in on me.

Click...

Click...

Louder the footsteps grow. I squeeze my eyes shut, and the tears flow freely down my cheeks, burning my eyes and causing my lungs and throat to plead for relief.

Click...

Click...

Click...

The footsteps are slow—so *painfully* slow—as if taunting me, like a cat with a mouse caught in its vicious claws.

Trapped.

Just as I am.

A figure moves past the gap in the stall, and I catch only a glimpse of the unrecognizable mass. There's a shuffling sound between the footsteps, and then one final *click* on the floor as they come to rest right in front of my stall.

I pant against my hand, my scorching breath making my palm sweat against my lips. My body goes rigid, as it has countless times during my sleep paralysis.

Except this time, I'm awake.

And this isn't a dream.

When I look at the floor, I drop my hand from my mouth in shock, and a shaky cry escapes my lips as I realize that the stall door is the only thing between me...

And the pair of red reptile loafers that stand before me.

THE END

James's and Evelyn's story concludes
in the upcoming novel, *Come the First Snowfall*.

Please visit **www.charlottedae.com**
or follow the author at
www.instagram.com/charlottedaeauthor
for updates.

ABOUT THE AUTHOR

Charlotte Dae is an indie author who loves exploring the darker side of romance. Such taboo topics have a place in literature, and she is clamoring to bring them to light in her own way. When she is not spending her free time writing, she is working full-time as a Forensic Scientist and living her best life with her husband and two puppies.